WHAT READERS H

"*Kept* is such a beautifully written and involving novel. Yvonne Lyon's gentle, precise style admirably captures the Edwardian setting of this family story and the depths of emotion experienced by characters with who a reader becomes closely identified. A very enjoyable read." Annie Murray, author of *Sisters of Gold, Chocolate Girls* and *Black Country Orphan.*

"There is more than a nod to Hardy in this portrait of longing and limitation, and, like Hardy's characters, Sam and Jessie are both flawed and sympathetic at the same time. I thoroughly enjoyed reading." L. M. Nathan, author of *The Virtue Season.*

"I read 'Kept' over four evenings and whenever I had to leave it, I always looked forward to getting back to the immersive story of the lives of these Wigan families. A novel that sparkles with fascinating insights into life in the late Victorian era and a highly recommended read for anyone who enjoys social history combined with a good story." Helen Matthews, author of *The Sisters.*

This book is dedicated to my sister, Margaret, and in memory of our parents, Jack and May Lyon, and the women and men in our family who inspired this story.

THE FAMILIES IN 1889

The Gormans
    Patrick Gorman m. Mary, née Towneley
    Jessie, daughter
    James, son
    Kate, daughter

The Towneleys
    Edward Towneley m. Jane Chamberlain
    Mary, daughter. m. Patrick Gorman
    Margaret, daughter. m. Nicholas Worsley
    Agnes, daughter
    Rachel, daughter

The Dunbars
    John Dunbar m. Elizabeth Bedwell
    George, son
    Sam, son
    Frank, son
    Lizzy, daughter

Josiah, son
Polly, daughter
William, son

PROLOGUE

Dear Sam,

If there comes a time when I'm no longer able to would you keep an eye on Jessie and James for me every now and again? See they're well and happy. I ask this out of the regard you bear for me and the family.

A woman I worked with in the weaving shed wrote this for me.

Your friend,

Mary Gorman

PART I

SAM

Sam Dunbar, aged 20
Wigan Mechanics' Institute: January 1889

*S*he was a stunner, the girl in the row in front of me. Her dark red hair was piled wonderfully on top of her head giving me a clear view of her slim, white neck. She sat next to a man who resembled her enough in hair colour, with a similar narrow face, for me to think him her brother. The lecture wasn't due to start for another ten minutes so I watched them as they chatted together, like good companions. Even so, I noticed her turning around a good deal. Perhaps searching for someone special to arrive?

I strained my ears to fathom their conversation but under the noise of scraping chair legs, coughing and laughter, I heard nothing more than *yes* or *no*, with an emphatic shake of the head from her. The hall filled up with people taking their seats. Others, perhaps new to the Institute, paused in front of the large, framed posters that hung on the walls: illustrations of past and present inventions, mathematical instruments, parts of the microscope, engravings of the Ironbridge in Shropshire. I knew them so well I'd scarcely glanced at them on my way in. With the increase in numbers came the smell of damp wool as men removed heavy overcoats. I didn't own one and kept my jacket on. The brochure I was pretending to read lay on my knees, a useful cover for the threadbare state of my trousers. At home, I'd studied the titles of the lecture series and decided which ones I could afford to attend. Now, with my attention focussed elsewhere, I could hardly recall the name of any.

A minute after seven o'clock, a whippet-thin man with a neat beard walked onto the stage. Applause broke out and the girl in front turned around. Our eyes met for a second before she looked away. Had she sensed my gaze boring into the back of her head, and used the cover of clapping to find out? The speaker put a sheaf of paper on a stand and began.

Sometimes these talks went over my head though I liked to think I learned a little just by being there. A piecemeal education: reading by candlelight after a shift, saving the pennies for talks, night school at the Miners' Institute. The only way someone like me could pick up knowledge. But tonight my thoughts weren't on the speaker. The girl in front wore good quality clothes and I guessed there was money in the family. Likely she'd have gone to one of the private girls' schools in town.

The audience tittered at something the speaker said and I forced my attention back to the stage, but that night, Mr King, BA Hons, could have been talking about cheese-making… the natural history of Russia…rather than William Morris. There was a lot to take in: printer, political activist, wallpaper, Iceland. Beauty. I half-listened and allowed my eyes to trace the curve of her cheek, the slender neck; wondered what it might be like to unpin those dark, red curls. When thunderous clapping broke out, I realised the lecture was over. Had it been that good?

People stood in fits and starts, left their seats, and moved into the aisles. Bags and umbrellas were gathered.

I remained in my chair until the girl and her companion rose, too. I sidled out but could not prevent my boots from knocking against chair legs. I craned my neck towards the door for a last glimpse. No sign of them. Damn it! I'd left it too late; she'd be out of the building in a few minutes. I had no plan in mind, only an urge to see her again.

Out in the corridor I shuffled along with everyone else. Three fashionable women stood in front of me wearing hats like walking gardens: velvet flowers and leaves piled high on their heads. But no red-haired girl. I regretted not asking a mate to come with me; we could have gone for a beer which would have helped put her out of my mind. Ahead was the long staircase leading to the ground floor, then the main door to the street, and after that... the whole of Wigan to disappear into.

A gap opened and there she was under the large wall clock. Her red hair was startling against the white blouse and unbuttoned dark jacket. She held her hat, and it marked her out from all the other women. There was no sign of her companion. *Stay exactly where you are*, I prayed. *And don't let him turn up.* All I wanted was one last, good look. Only three or four people ahead of me now, but the length of the corridor seemed endless. I edged towards the clock, reached it, held my breath, and stopped.

She smiled. Excitement coursed through me. She held out her hand and I took a surprised step towards her. It was going to be alright.

'Good evening. Did you enjoy the lecture? I noticed you sitting behind us so I thought I'd introduce myself. I'm Lydia Holdsworth.'

Her voice was bright, bell-like, educated. The soft leather of her glove felt like butter in my palm. The way she looked at me

— I was sure she'd been as aware of me as I'd been of her. Something inside me melted. Did she have that effect on every man she met? For once I was tongue-tied. I tried to think of something clever to say about the talk then realised I hadn't introduced myself.

'I'm Sam Dunbar. Pleased to meet you. I like that jacket you're wearing.' She laughed and held my gaze, but before we could progress further her companion arrived. I felt a stab of disappointment and held myself straighter.

'Sorry, Lyddie,' he said, wiping his palms down his trouser legs. 'There was a queue.'

She turned to me. 'This is my brother, Daniel. Daniel, meet Mr Dunbar. He was sitting behind us. We were about to exchange views on the speaker.'

He had a pleasant, open, more serious face than his sister's. Taller than me, but narrower across the shoulders, I guessed he was a year or two older. He looked puzzled as well as he might: I was a working man. Even so, he thrust out his hand and I shook it. Was he being polite, or was his sister's unconventional behaviour nothing new?

How it happened I wasn't sure, but in no time we were chatting about the talk, the speaker, and whether we shouldn't carry on our conversation somewhere more comfortable.

A moment later the three of us were running down the Institute steps and crossing the road. I glanced at Miss Holdsworth and saw she was smiling, hat in one hand, the other curled into a pocket. Under a gas lamp frost gleamed and familiar roads grew strange. We walked along a dark stretch for a few yards before her brother halted outside a hotel and held the door open. I thought of my workmates sitting on stools, their feet scuffing up sawdust in a public house. If they could see me now, I'd be in for a ribbing. *The Feathers* wasn't the kind of place we ever went to.

After the darkness of the street, the electric lights dazzled my eyes and for a moment the corridor was a blur of red and gold. Daniel Holdsworth led the way and I felt my feet sink deep into the carpet. Without thinking, I trailed a hand along the wall and fingered a raised textured wallpaper. A William Morris design? An elderly man on his way out held a door open for us, and we stepped into a lounge area with tables, chairs, and a bar at one end of the room. The rich, warm smell of cooking, and alcohol hit me and I guessed the kitchens were close by. Men at tables looked up from their drinks and newspapers as we passed, all smartly dressed and barbered. I hoped their attention was directed at Miss Holdsworth rather than on me.

They glided over my awkward offer to buy the drinks for a sum my pocket couldn't stretch to, insisting I was their guest, and *Christian names only!* they cried when I thanked them. I glowed from the warmth of their informality like a child wrapped in a blanket on a cold night. All the same, when I looked down at my threadbare trousers, my clumsy work boots, I wanted to run. One smile from Miss Holdsworth changed my mind. Carefully, I lowered myself into an armchair and hoped my clothes wouldn't leave sooty marks behind. Yes, people were staring, amazed to see a working man in such a high-class establishment. My face grew hot. I gripped the chair arms and forced myself not to look for the way out. I was sure remarks were made but I didn't hear them. Probably had my fashionably dressed companions to thank for that.

While her brother went to queue at the bar I relaxed into the padded chair and my hesitancy vanished under her gentle probing; where she led I followed. We spoke of our families and I learned she was an art student in Manchester. Waiters, guests, customers, were as insubstantial as ghosts floating by. At last, Daniel appeared with a half pint of bitter for me, and wine for them and the conversation became more general. In between sips I studied Lydia's hands when she lifted her glass which gleamed under the wall light. I imagined her holding a brush, painting a portrait. Afraid of being caught staring I shifted my gaze to the far end of the lounge and realised she was the only woman in the room. She seemed unconcerned and her easy manner told anyone watching that she had as much right to be there as any man. This was her world, not mine.

I covered my ignorance about the night's talk as best I could, asking rather than answering, then for the next hour we shared stories from our lives with Lydia interrupting her brother with cries of, *no, it wasn't like that!* when she thought he'd given a false impression. They confessed they were on the fringes of politics, reading everything they could about Morris's socialist views. They knew more about the subject than I did. Easy to put that right. Weren't there newspapers and books aplenty to borrow?

'It's all about taking chances.' Lydia had moved on from radicalism. 'Seeing the world.' Her eyes grew bright and I wondered if she were thinking of Morris's visits to Iceland. 'I want to study art abroad when I've completed my course.'

I had a twinge of unease when she said Wigan was too small a place to stay in forever. They had money; they could travel. In twenty years I'd only been as far as Manchester but I agreed, not wanting to appear any different or look like someone with narrow horizons. Perhaps to prove a point I told them something I usually kept private.

'I won't be at the pit forever,' and I reeled off the list of correspondence courses I'd already taken. I hadn't had much to eat before coming out and even half a pint was loosening my tongue. 'I see myself in an office in the future. Book-keeping, clerking, or suchlike.' It was vanity to talk so but Daniel clapped me on the back as if I were a good fellow, someone like them, and Lydia smiled and put a hand on my arm.

'In that case, Sam, we will help you if you'll let us.'

· · ·

MY FAMILY WERE in bed when I reached home; it being well past ten o'clock. The fire had almost died down and the sitting room felt chilly. I lingered only to drink a glass of water before tiptoeing upstairs. I undressed with practised silence and slid between the cold sheets on my side of the bed without disturbing William and Frank. Already, I was seeing my home as if the Holdsworths had returned with me, looking at it with a bright gaze, their eyes falling upon shabby curtains, worn bed sheets and darned socks. Under my pillow I hid a torn piece of newspaper that Lydia had used to scrawl a date, time, and details of another lecture the three of us would attend. My mind was too active for sleep and in the dim light which filtered through the window from the streetlamp, I stared at the cracks running across the ceiling and calculated the hours until our next meeting. Three hundred and thirty-six.

'YOU WERE OUT LATE, LOVE,' my mother said the following evening, serving Pa first, judging how much stew to ladle onto his plate. George came next, followed by me, and the rest according to age. She waited for an answer.

'I met some people at the lecture, from Parbold way, and they stood me a drink at *The Feathers Hotel*. Don't worry Pa, it was only half a pint,' I said, trying for humour when he frowned; a Methodist to his core.

'That's a fancy place, isn't it? What sort of people were they?' Ma wanted to know. She'd reached Polly's plate when there was hardly any left in the pan for herself.

'The chap's called Daniel Holdsworth. He's twenty-two and works in his father's office as a trainee architect. His sister's an art student in Manchester. They go to all the lectures and said they're interested in Socialism. Next time, they want me to tell them about the mine and the conditions we work in.'

Father's fork clattered onto his half-full plate and he looked me up and down. 'More fool you, then.'

His words cut through me despite the musical brogue. I kept a grip on my temper, told myself he was dog-tired from his shift and was still hungry. As if the most boring and ordinary thing in the world had happened last night, I said, 'I don't think I've done anything foolish, or wrong. There's no harm in sitting in a hotel lounge for a quiet drink and talking to people.'

He picked up his knife, speared a piece of meat and spoke while he chewed. 'I know you won't go overboard on booze. But it's staring you in the face. Those types, they flirt with the working classes. I've seen it. Would-be politicians, college men, do-gooders. They hang around the pit head with notebooks, cameras, notions. They promise you the earth. Don't be taken in by them, son. They don't have the power to improve conditions, that's the union's job.'

'You're always down on people who want to change things, aren't you? I never said anything about improving conditions. Why take it that way?'

'Sam?' Ma shot me a warning glance across the table. She didn't like it when anyone crossed our father and hated ructions. Everything had to be light and easy as if we were the happiest family in the street, never mind our George's bullying and Father's mistrust of the world. I wanted to argue back but he'd have exploded, railed all evening, and I was damned if I was going to listen to his half-baked notions. I pushed back my chair.

'Don't yer want any more stew?' Josiah leaned forward. 'I'll have it if you don't.'

'No. I'm giving it to Ma. There's hardly any food on her plate,' and I slid mine over to her. 'You're already beefy enough Jos, fit for the army if they'll have you.' Our mother didn't like mention of Josiah's plans, but it would throw the attention off me for a while. I wasn't the only one who had an eye to the future. Jos was firmly of the intention that he'd be out of England one day, and Frank was talking the same way, too. We lads didn't think we were any better than our father, or George, it was just that we wanted different things.

I picked up my jacket, went outside and walked to the end of the street where I leant against a wall. Only twenty-four hours had passed and already I was changed.

2

JESSIE

Jessie Gorman, aged 8
Sarginson Street, Wigan: February 1889

'*A* wedding party! A party with a wedding. We're going to a...' I mouthed the words like a song no one could hear while I waited for Ma and Pa to come out of the kitchen. Behind the half-closed door the kettle whistled and Pa said a curse word. Steam must have fallen on his hand when he'd grabbed the handle. But he laughed, deep from the belly and Ma joined in so that was all right. One of them stirred the porridge with a wooden spoon, banging it against the side of the pan. Sounds of water gushed into the teapot. I strained my ears to hear what they were saying.

I'd woken early, come down specially to ask what time we were going out, but they were talking about something else. They giggled; words tripping over each other. Then I heard Ma say, 'Let's keep the baby a secret for now.'

My head jerked up and my eyes went wide. I remembered what Grandma Towneley always said: *eavesdroppers never hear anything good about themselves.* And though they hadn't

14

mentioned me, and were only concerned with each other, I knew I shouldn't have earwigged. I tiptoed away. My face felt hot and I went back upstairs. I'd wait in our bedroom 'til they called me and James down for breakfast. It was their secret; bigger than some old wedding party, but I knew about it.

After he'd eaten his porridge and played with his toy soldiers, James had rushed into the backyard. He was still there, banging a stick against a tin, pretending to be a drummer-boy. Ma and I had washed the pots and tidied up then she said I could read before we all went out. Now, upstairs, our parents' clogs clattered on the bedroom floorboards as they got ready. I was already washed and brushed and impatient to go but Pa said it didn't start till noon. I smoothed down my best, navy frock and pinafore and placed a new marble in my lap. To pass the time, I dropped it from palm to palm, admiring the swirl of colours; yellow to green, as it landed. But the thought of the secret I'd overheard earlier wouldn't go away. I jumped up, rucking the mat under my feet as I ran into the kitchen. I would tell James what I'd heard! How puzzled he'd be; asking me to explain. But by the time my fingers pressed down on the back door latch and I felt cold metal under my hand, I'd changed my mind. James would hear it soon enough, understand it better when our parents explained. But that was a fib. I didn't tell him because I wanted to keep the secret to myself.

At last, the landing door squeaked open and Pa peeped out, pulling a silly face. I batted my *Funny Folks* comic at him, pretending to be annoyed.

'When are we going?' I said, jumping up and hopping from one foot to the other. All the pies and cakes would be gone, the fiddle-playing and dancing over, before we got there. Pa had told us the groom was a work mate with a big family and everyone had chipped in money to pay for it.

'Very soon,' Ma said, hearing me, coming downstairs in her best blue dress. She went to the back door and called James in from the yard before going to the little cracked mirror where she put on her hat, then sat in her rocker. James rushed past me, pretending he was an eagle with his arms spread wide, then flung himself down on the rag rug, the one Ma made for us, to stop the stone floor from freezing our bums. He leant in against Pa sitting in his chair by the fire who bent forwards and pulled James's thumb out of his mouth.

'You're five now, not a baby. I'll find you a sweetie to eat, later.'

'Pa,' James said, climbing onto his knee. 'What's Lent for? Is it when you have to give away something?'

We'd had a lesson on it in Catholic Sunday School last week but my brother had forgotten. I sniggered and Pa wagged his finger.

'There's nothing wrong with asking questions, Jessie.' Pa turned James around to face him. 'It's a time in the calendar, son. For fasting and prayer, ending when we get to Easter and that's a day we look forward to.'

He answered in his sing-song voice and James sat bolt upright, his mouth as round as a plug hole. He thought he was going to be told a story.

'Why?'

'Because the mines and mills slumber for three days and the streets come alive. People can leave their stinking hovels for a few hours and enjoy themselves.'

I was wondering what a *hovel* was when Ma said, 'Patrick! We don't do as bad as some. At least we have a privy to ourselves.' Her voice sounded like she was climbing up a ladder. Pa laughed and tipped James off his lap.

'The only reason we are so fortunate, my love, is that the houses on either side of us aren't fit to be occupied.'

Ma pulled herself up from the rocking chair like Grandma Towneley did, but without the complaining. Her face smiled down at me and I thought she was the most beautiful person I'd ever seen.

'It's time we were off,' she said. 'Is everyone washed and tidy? We can't turn up at a party with dirty faces. Good thing the marriage is today and not on Wednesday otherwise there wouldn't be much to eat.'

Pa got up and pretended to straighten her hat. 'Being a Methodist, Mary darlin', you're ignorant that Father Gregory doesn't like marrying anyone on Ash Wednesday.' He plopped a kiss on her cheek. 'Now let's be having you.'

'A swing before we go?' James jumped up. There was soot from the coal bunker on his knickerbockers. I pulled a face. He was going to make us late, but Pa hadn't noticed and already had his jacket and muffler on. He clicked his tongue against his teeth.

'You're too big for that lad. I'd break a bone if I tried it.'

He wouldn't. He was taller and stronger than everyone in Pemberton. Pa could have carried us like coal sacks over his shoulders if he'd wanted.

'Let's turn our backs on the slag heaps, the winding gear and the pit heads,' Pa chanted, grabbing Ma's hand before spinning her around. Then we tumbled out of the house and followed a mass of people all heading for town. Pa shouted *good day* to his pit friends all down Sarginson Street. I was proud he knew so many folk and that they liked him. He grinned at Ma and I was prouder of that.

The sun was out and it wasn't wintery for once. I hated the cold and hearing who'd died. When we got to Market Street a noisy crowd bunched around us and we let go of each other's hands because it was difficult to walk straight. Two women came either side of me on the narrow pavement until I was squashed and pinched between them. The taller woman's clog clipped my ankle before they marched on. Ma turned round;

her face tight-lipped which meant she had a headache so I didn't say anything about the clog scrape.

She saw me looking at her and mee-mawed, 'Don't tell yer Pa.'

'I won't,' I mee-mawed back. It was good practice for when I got older and started work in the mill. She said I should go into the weaving shed because my fingers were nimble. Our parents linked arms and stepped out in front. James stuck to their side 'cos he was still a bit of a baby. Then I remembered, soon he wouldn't be.

I stopped to look at the crates of shiny apples outside the greengrocer's before moving on but a few yards later, I almost fell when a stout man's elbow dug into my back. I was near the kerb now, caught between grown men, laughing, paying no heed to me, inching me further away from Ma and Pa. It made me angry. Their arms and legs criss-crossed around me like a fence. I pushed against their backs but they were so tall and wide it made no difference. Suddenly, I was trapped.

'Ma, Pa!' I shouted but my cries were drowned by the noise above me, the laughter, the swearing, and the backchat. Black trousers and waistcoats were everywhere; sweaty and beery.

When I saw an arm swooping down towards me, I tried to duck out of its reach but wasn't quick enough. It caught the side of my head and shoulder. I stumbled and toppled into the road. Winded by the fall, I lay on my back trying to get my breath but my chest hurt when I tried to move. Above me, a grey cloud loomed and I felt a spatter of rain on my face. Then sounds came: grinding and clanging like a great machine. I saw metal wheels and I still couldn't move. A horse-bus was coming for me. My body froze and fear cut off thought. In a few seconds more...

'I've got yer!'

I was swung up into the air and when I opened my eyes it wasn't Pa, but a stranger who smelt of coal dust. His fingers gripped my legs, and his other hand supported my shoulder then he set me down on the pavement. The horse-bus lumbered past, its bell ringing for the next stop. Passengers stared at me from the windows and the top deck. They thought I'd be dead. Then they were gone. And another smell; horse dung in the road. The noise and stink overwhelmed me and I started to cry. The man who'd saved me crouched beside me and squeezed my shoulder.

'You're safe now. Are you hurt?' His voice was quiet and somehow familiar.

'No,' I whispered. I couldn't guess his age. He was young but a man not a boy. I saw my skirt and shawl were splashed with mud and I bent forwards to rub it off. 'I want my Ma,' I said.

'I'll find her for you and don't worry about that.' He pointed to my skirt. 'It'll brush off.'

'Jessie!' We were separated by legs and skirts, and I was still sitting on the pavement. 'Where are you, darlin'?' Ma called again.

'She's over here, missis,' the young man shouted. Then she was kneeling, pulling me to her. Her hair smelt of lavender soap.

'Thank God! Are you hurt, love? One minute you were with us and then you vanished!' Her soft mouth pressed against my cheeks and when she lifted her face away it was pale and worried-like.

'I'm all right, Ma. Don't fret.' I rubbed the tears away before she noticed. 'This man saved me from the horse-bus.' She clasped me again and despite being muffled by her coat I heard the clink of clogs and saw worn moleskin trousers. 'Pa!' The stranger stood up and I found I could move my legs. Father pulled me up, thanked God, and then shook the young man's hand, clapped him on the shoulder.

'An old chap I know saw what you did, lad. I ran the moment I realised it was our Jessie,' he paused, then smiled, as if he'd just had a good idea. 'We were on our way to a wedding party. Come along wi' us as a thank you. Have a bite and a drop to drink. We could all do with it.'

'Thanks, Mr Gorman.'

I wasn't surprised he knew Pa. It would be from the mine though neither were wearing their work clothes. Father's Sunday jacket and bowler were newer than the stranger's.

'We're that grateful,' Ma said, giving him the smile which made people stop and talk to her in the street. 'I'm Mary. Seems like you know my husband already, Mr...?'

'It's Sam. Samuel Dunbar. I work at Pemberton but on a different seam to your husband. I'm not wanted anywhere for an hour or two, so thank you. I'll come along if you think the hosts won't mind.'

PA PUSHED OPEN the swinging door of the public house and leapt up the stairs, two at a time. The wedding party was in a special room; so huge, I thought it might swallow me. Ma said we must greet the bride and groom first, but I shook my head and hung back. I smoothed down my skirt and hoped no one would see the mud.

'I'll look after Jessie for a bit,' Sam Dunbar said. 'I've got two younger sisters; she'll be all right with me.'

'Are you sure you don't mind?' Ma asked.

'I don't know the bride and groom, at all. I'd rather stay here. Out of the way.'

She put a hand on his arm and thanked him. 'We won't be long.'

She and Pa shrank in size the further they walked down the room. I could hear music: fiddles scratching and a piano tinkling. I think Ma turned to look at me, but I couldn't be sure because I'd leant into the backs of the coats hanging up. Fur brushed against my skin. I pressed my face in closer. They were soft and warm. I didn't want to leave them.

'What kind of fur is this?' I asked the young man.

'Probably rabbit.'

'I thought rabbits were just for eating.' He laughed and his blue eyes creased up. He had a nice face.

'Yes, but the skins are made into clothes for the rich to keep warm and they look good.'

I stroked the coats which were softer than cat fur. 'I'd never wear a coat made from a cat. Would you?'

'No, but I don't think us men wear fur apart from places like Russia and the North Pole where it's always cold.'

He sounded like a teacher and I wondered how he knew so much. I sniffed a sleeve. It smelt of damp and something sweet as if scent had been spilt on it.

'At first, I thought the fur was all black,' I told him, 'But it isn't.'

'What colours can you see?'

I sank my fingers in deeper. 'You know when you pull out the fire pan in the morning? It's like that. Grey ash, charcoal and dusty colours.' I separated the fur to show him. 'And there's some with silver tips.'

'You've a good eye, Jessie – about the fur I mean.'

I liked the sound of that, but it wasn't really true. 'Only when I'm close up. I can't see far away things so well.'

Sam Dunbar shook his head. 'Sometimes it's better not to. Then you can ignore the things you don't like.'

I puzzled it over. 'What do you mean?'

'Your father and I work right up against the coal face. It's dangerous, backbreaking. When I'm there, I need to find something worthwhile so as to carry on. Most days I'll stroke the ponies, give them a crust, or share a butty with a friend. Another good thing is when my face is close to the wall and I see the seam spark like black diamonds. If you were stood far off, you'd never see that.'

The black diamonds were easy to imagine because he talked like Pa did when he was spinning a tale. 'Are you Irish, too?'

'No, but my father was born there. I'd leave the work if I could —even if it meant never seeing that shiny blackness close to me again.' He fell silent, and I couldn't think of anything to say.

'Any road,' he started again, 'I've got friends who are helping me look for something else.'

Grandma said I asked too many questions but Sam Dunbar didn't seem to mind. 'Who are they? I know hundreds of people.'

'They're called Lydia and Daniel Holdsworth.'

I didn't recognise their names and imagined them as stout and wheezy. 'Are they an old married couple?' It was cheeky to ask, but he grinned.

'Hardly! They're brother and sister,' he laughed. 'She's twenty and he's a bit older. Their parents know people who work in business offices. I've told them I'll do anything rather than live my life down the pit.'

I pictured him below ground, the darkness lit by a flickering lamp. Then a thought entered my head that wasn't about coal: he was going to give me something. I left the fur coats and went to the food table and brought back two Chorley cakes. Food makes people happy. It does with us. At the bottom of the room, people were dancing and others eating and drinking but they seemed a long way off.

'Everyone likes sweet things,' I said, giving him one. He took a big bite and pastry flakes flew down his waistcoat which made us laugh. Then I felt a tap on my shoulder. It was my friend, Susan, who was the bride's little cousin.

'You're wanted for a game,' she said, staring at Sam with a

questioning face because he was a stranger. 'We're playing *The Big Ship Sails*.'

She slid an arm around my waist and in her other hand I saw a peg doll with a bright red mouth. I reached for it but she was too quick. She giggled, snatched it away then ran off. I wanted to see it properly but if I left, Sam would have no one to talk to. He didn't say anything about Susan or the game but fetched us two sandwiches and put one on my plate.

'Eat up.'

'But we've had our cake already! Savoury comes first,' I said, forgetting the doll.

'Not today. No rules on a Saturday.' When he'd finished, he thrust his hand into his waistcoat pocket and drew out a coin. 'Here's a penny for being a brave girl. Spend it on summat you fancy. I'll go find your parents. I'll have to be going soon but I'll call round some time and see you all.'

'You don't know where we live.'

I recited the address like it was a poem from school then followed him down the hall, weaving in and out of the dancers. When we found Ma and Pa they smiled and said *thank you*, over and over, and I knew he'd keep his promise to call.

'Forty-five Sarginson Steet, Pemberton,' he said, giving me a wink.

'What'll you spend yer penny on?' Susan asked me later when I showed it to her. Her eyes were so big they almost swallowed it up.

'I'm going to save up for a black kitten and call it Diamond,' I told her.

WE WERE CHILLED after the walk home and James flopped down on the rag rug in front of the fire, holding his knees up to his chin. He groaned and clutched his stomach. I thought he was play-acting. He'd been racing around the function room before we left.

'Get yourself to bed son if your belly's bad. Teach you to leave some food for others next time,' Pa chided.

'Not going to no weddings again.' My brother's lip stuck out half a mile.

'Drink some tea and you'll feel better,' Ma said, passing round the cups. 'Settle down because your father and I have some news.'

I sat up straighter, wanting to hear it properly this time.

'Are we going to move to a new house?' James asked. We'd heard them talking about having a house with a parlour when they thought we weren't listening.

'No, at least not yet. It's something else,' she said. 'At the end of summer, you're going to have another baby brother or sister.'

I put a hand over my mouth like I'd seen grownups do. I jumped up and ran over to her. I put my face against her warm cheek and thought about the secret I'd held close all day.

'A girl, please,' I whispered in her ear. It'd be summat to tell Susan, and Sam, when they called round.

I DIDN'T KNOW if it was the baby, the thought of a kitten, or the black diamonds which was the most important, but all of them crept into my dreams that Spring and I was glad, because they stopped me from having nightmares about the horse-bus.

3

SAM

The Whelley, Wigan: March 1889

*M*other, like the good soul she was, had already heated the water in the copper for me. I took over from her as soon as I came in and had half-filled the tub when George arrived. As usual he tried muscling me out of the way.

'Oldest always gets the first turn,' he scowled.

'No tussling tonight,' Mother begged, bustling in to see what the fuss was about. 'Sam won't be long because he's going out soon and then you can have it.'

Although he backed down with ill grace even George wouldn't go against our mother, and the last I saw of him that day was his brawny back disappearing upstairs. Alone, with my knees up to my chin in the scalding shock of clean, hot water, I did my best with the sliver of soap. I'd told Mary Gorman I would come to see her at four o'clock. I'd be retracing my steps back to Pemberton, but I couldn't have called on her without washing first.

Clean, and smelling of Jos's favourite, Vinola shaving soap, I walked into town taking a shortcut through the Market Hall. No time to exchange friendly insults with the stallholders today. Standishgate was crowded so I let a horse-bus roll by before I zigzagged away. Under an hour later I was in Pemberton's dingy streets. From the stink, and the cats prowling in the kerbs, I guessed the fish seller had been round. I took care where I stepped. Filthy alleys branched off the terraced rows which streamed with water. At the entrance to one ginnel, a sluttish woman in dirty finery stared boldly at me.

'Need a hand finding your way, son?' She leered.

Many doors lacked a number plate, but I knew the house I wanted well enough after two visits. I'd dealt with the woman's type before. Sweeping a low bow and in a voice copied from the music hall, I said, 'No, thank you, madam. Good day,' and she huffed and puffed at being surpassed in cheek.

Number forty-five was towards the end of the row, marked out from its neighbours by a polished brass plate. I rapped on it smartly and a moment later little Jessie peered up at me from behind the half-opened door. Beyond her, the gaslight cast a yellow oblong onto the facing wall.

'Let Sam in,' her mother called.

Mary was seated near the fireplace, wrapped in a shawl, and looking as if she might have just woken up. Napping in the day usually meant someone was ill in our house. There was no sign of James or Patrick which would account for the quietness. I stepped inside and suddenly wondered why I was there. Because she'd asked me of course! The last two times had been easy, but now I was worried. Would we have anything to talk about? Patrick's absence had silenced me as effectively as I'd stopped the mouth of the street-woman. The fire was unmade though a full coal scuttle stood on the hearth. I grasped the chance to be useful.

'Can I light the fire for you, Mrs Gorman…Mary? It'll only take a minute. Save you a job.'

'Please. It's kind of you to ask. I usually wait until Patrick gets home. And it's *Mary* amongst friends.'

I said I'd remember in future. Bringing in dry sticks from the outhouse, topping them with paper and a few lumps of coal eased my doubts about being there.

'Where's James?' I asked and she said he was at her parents' house, and they'd bring him back later.

'He begs them to play with him,' she laughed. 'Jessie's more of a one for books and likes her schoolwork. James not so much, but he's still young; there's time for all that.' She folded her arms. 'That's enough about us, how are you doing?'

Encouraged by her wide eyes, full of curiosity and warmth, I grinned at her. 'Gradely. Nothing that a day in the fresh air wouldn't cure.'

She said it was the same for Patrick. 'Any chance he gets he goes fishing. He loves the quiet and the water. Says it reminds him of Ireland.'

Jessie had sidled up to stand behind her mother's rocking chair. Her little face was red from sitting near the fire. Mary put a hand against her daughter's cheek then snatched it away pretending it had scorched her, making Jessie giggle.

'I'll fetch the tea in, shall I?' Mary said, getting up from her rocker. 'It's just made and there might be something to eat, too.'

She walked past me into the kitchen and when her shawl slipped off her shoulders I saw the curve of her belly. A baby was coming! She'd not mentioned it before but why should she? It wasn't the kind of thing a woman would reveal to a younger lad.

'Don't bother about cake on my account,' I called out in a rush. 'Mother'll have tea ready when I get back.' I didn't want to cause further expense if money was tight. I knew the room well by now: table, chairs, a dresser, and a few ornaments on the mantelpiece. Mary had made the room homely by hanging patterned red curtains and laying bright rag-rugs on the floor, stone-paved like ours; otherwise furnishings were scant. We'd moved recently into a better-built house. Could afford to with five adults bringing home a wage. Mother had it easier these days with more money to put food on the table. And I guessed Patrick liked his beer, judging from the amount he'd drunk at that wedding. Us lads liked a pint well enough on occasion, but we didn't make a habit of dropping into the pub after a shift. We were Methodists, after all.

Jessie had followed her mother into the kitchen and came out with a plate of biscuits. I took one and put it on my saucer but Mary refused, saying it would spoil her tea. I wasn't sure how old she was, about thirty I guessed. Her face seemed more drawn but she was as beautiful as the first time I'd seen her. My earlier unease dropped away. It was peaceful sitting with them by the fire.

'Is Patrick on a late shift?'

'No, he's on earlies. Visiting a friend right now.' She took a few sips, then put her cup down. 'I hear you're walking out, Sam. Is it anyone we know?'

I spluttered, almost spilling my tea. Was she a fortune-teller to ask such a thing? For a minute I couldn't think straight. As far as I remembered, Lydia and I had only walked out around Parbold. I certainly hadn't brought her to Pemberton.

Mary laughed. 'Don't look so worried. I'll say nowt if you don't want me to. I can tell you don't want it spreading. Patrick saw you with a lass a while back in Mesnes Park.'

'I wouldn't like it to get back to my parents. Her family live in the countryside. They've been helping me look for work other than the pit. But they don't know we're...,' Patrick must have seen us together after a lecture when she hadn't gone straight home.

'She's not a miner's daughter, I take it?' Mary was amused and not in the least bit critical.

I leant back in my chair and grinned. 'Sort of the opposite.

We...Lydia and I...we go for walks and her brother comes sometimes. Her father's an architect and she travels to Manchester, most days, to the Art School.'

'An artist? I bet you didn't meet her at a chapel social.'

I laughed. 'Hardly. It were at a lecture at the Mechanics' Institute. I was sitting behind them. Really friendly they were, no side to them, just like I talk to you...or a mate.'

'What's she like?'

'She and her brother don't care where I live or work, but I'm not sure about her parents. That's why we've said nowt.'

'You'll have to at some point.'

'I don't think too far ahead.'

On this subject I didn't. The present was too good to spoil by foreseeing its end. Lydia and Daniel flouted class differences for political reasons, and in her case, she'd told me, the personal. I'd heard Mr Holdsworth claim support for working men's entitlement but it would be a different story if he knew what his daughter was up to.

'Patrick said she were a bonny lass,' Mary added.

'She is that.'

'Does she talk about the future?'

'About her own: the galleries she wants to send paintings to. Trips to cities. What she'll paint in the studio her father's just built her.'

'And you?'

'She thinks I can have a future out of the pit, but I'm doubtful I'll manage it.'

Mary leant forwards and put a hand on my arm. 'She sounds like a rare girl, clever too, but rich families can look further than the likes of yours and mine. Am I right — painting's the most important thing to her, now? Does she talk about marriage?'

'Only that she wouldn't let it get in the way of being an artist.'

She twisted her hands in her lap and looked up. 'Jessie, bring in more firewood from the outhouse. We're getting a bit low.'

After the little girl had left the room, Mary told me that we reminded her of her own situation. 'There was difficulty for Patrick and me to be together. We didn't do it the right way around. We had Jessie first, then got married. People like *your* girl's parents would want to do it properly, as would most folk. My parents didn't want me marrying a Catholic you see, and I wouldn't give him up. We waited till we could afford a wedding and when Ma and Pa were softer towards him. Till they saw he was a good man who loved me. Was it the same with your parents?'

'No. They're sticklers for doing the right thing,' and I pulled a mock grimace which made her laugh.

Jessie came back with two handfuls of sticks, threw a couple of them on the fire then sat on the floor with a book. She seemed deep within it and I wondered if Mother had kept any old ones of ours I could give her.

'You will come again, won't you, Sam?' Mary said, 'I've enjoyed our chat. Come when Patrick's here and you'll have more conversation.'

'I will.' I thought the big Irish man was not as a good listener as his wife. The fire was crackling away now, and I wiped a hand behind my neck. When the doorknocker banged we broke our gaze.

Jessie jumped up to open it, 'Daddy!'

Patrick stooped under the lintel, saw me, and came in grinning. 'Good of you to call, lad, and keep my wife company. And how are ye, darlin'? Not malingering I hope?'

He opened his arms as if expecting her to run into them then, to my astonishment, he burst into song like a performer at the Royalty Theatre.

The lazy hours refuse to fly

As gaudy day goes creeping by
I count each moment with a sigh
Until the hour of shade steals nigh
When I shall meet my Mary – When I shall meet my Mary.

His rich baritone voice filled the small room and Jessie clapped as hard as her little hands would let her.

'More, Daddy!'

Patrick had done with singing and went to kiss his wife on the cheek. 'See how much I miss you when I'm underground? I sing that to remind me of you.'

'Get on with ye!' Mary said, looking embarrassed.

I felt a creeping envy at the closeness of the couple. I wouldn't stay much longer; they'd want time on their own.

'Another verse, please,' Jessie insisted, pulling on Patrick's jacket.

'You sing it lass; you've heard it often enough.'

'Start me on the right note and I will.'

Patrick whistled the first line for her and Jessie hummed along before singing the song in a tuneful lilt.

The flower is dear unto the lea,
The blossom to the parent tree;
Thou'rt more than flower of leaf to me,
And this fond heart, by love of thee,
Must bloom or wither, Mary.

We clapped her roundly and then Mary and Patrick began to recall other songs they knew. They were so close in their affection for each other that it made me long to be part of it. I stood, tied my muffler, and tucked it into the top of my jacket.

'Mother will have the tea ready and will be wondering where I am. Thanks for having me.'

Patrick and I shook hands and before he saw me off at the

front door he whispered his thanks, as he did every time I visited, for rescuing Jessie back in February.

As I walked along Sarginson Street I imagined them turning to another song: one warm, deep voice, the other soaring high above it. When a light rain began to fall I pulled my jacket collar up to my ears, taking care not to slip and take a tumble on the damp cobblestones.

Undressing for bed that night I tried to recall the tune to *The Lazy Hours*. The melody kept slipping away yet I could perfectly picture the way Mary had looked at Jessie on the hearth rug, and her smile for her husband. In contrast, Lydia's glances and smiles were mocking, seductive, and I was under their spell, but suddenly I knew I wanted something different as well. The look on Mary's face would stay with me for the rest of my life.

4

JESSIE

Sarginson Street: June 1889

*B*rown paper crackled as Ma pulled it apart and something small fell onto her knees. I was waiting for the kettle to boil and they didn't notice me watching from the kitchen door.

'Jessie! See what Sam's given me,' Ma called. I stepped into the front room and sidled up. She turned the little, black carved thing this way and that, smiling at it.

'It's a brooch made from cannel coal,' Sam said.

He looked happy. Like Pa did at Christmas when he made me a hobby horse. 'I came upon it by chance a few months ago. It was half hidden by leaves under a stretch of rail on the track leading up to Pemberton pit head. It caught my eye, the black amongst the green. After I polished it I saw its worth.'

'It's a flower,' I said, stroking it with my finger.

'A lily, I think,' Ma lifted it up again. 'Yes, look at the wide petals and the curling stem. Thank you, Sam, it's beautiful. I'll treasure it.'

He looked even more pleased and I was glad he'd seen it

before anyone else picked it up. The water was beginning to boil and Ma stood up. Sam followed her into the kitchen. I couldn't hear everything they said above the noise of the whistle. Something about a person called Lydia who already had lots of brooches and jewellery. I'd heard that name before. Cups clinked and water gushed out of the kettle into the pot.

'I suppose she will have,' Ma said, 'but all the same…?'

I poked my head around the door to ask about biscuits. Sam was smiling at Ma and shaking his head. He brought the tray in and then I remembered Lydia was the name of the girl he was walking out with. If she had lots of pretty jewellery it meant she was rich. I thought of the big doll that never got sold; standing in the toyshop window. It had staring blue eyes and a frilly dress. I always stopped to look at it. That's how this Lydia would dress. And she'd carry a parasol and sleep in a grand house. *I have no need for cannel coal brooches,* she'd say.

Ma was talking about the baby. She did that a lot, and one time she told Pa not to fuss so much, that they weren't beginners; whatever that meant. He'd told me to help mother as much as I could when he wasn't home.

'Course I will!' I said, and I shook my head until it nearly fell off. 'What about James? Has he promised too?'

Pa coughed and wiped his mouth as if he wanted to keep the words inside. 'I haven't asked him yet, but I will. Your brother could do a bit, now he's six.'

'Yes, he could,' I said, crossing my arms and frowning. Pa grabbed my hands and twirled me about in a dance.

'You should be on the stage, Jessie Elizabeth. You'd do any audience the power of good,' and he gave a great roar of laughter, though I didn't know what I'd said that was so funny.

The rattling of teacups stirred me. Ma and Sam had finished drinking. I gulped down the rest of my tea and moved my stool away from the fire. The heat was making my arms speckly. I had a feeling Sam would go soon and we'd not had a game. He played lots with us at first, but it was more boring when it was mainly chat.

'Do you want to play noughts and crosses?' I asked him, reaching for my school slate and chalk. Sam looked at Ma.

'If you have time,' she said.

He shook his head. 'Sorry, not really.' He stood and patted my shoulder. 'I'm going to a lecture this evening.'

'That sounds boring. Is Lydia whatsername going, too?'

'Jessie! That's very rude,' Ma pushed herself up from her chair. 'It's not the way to talk to a guest.'

'Sorry, Sam.' I started to put the cups back on the tray to take into the kitchen. 'Don't mind me; I've got my jobs to do'.

I'd heard Grandma Towneley say this when a visitor over-stayed their welcome. If Sam didn't want to join a game then he might as well go home. There was enough hot water in the kettle to scrub the cups without using the water pipe in the yard. I'd got rid of most of the brown stains when I heard the front door close. I knew I'd get a telling-off from Ma, but I didn't care. Perhaps Sam would stay longer next time and we could have a game, or I could read to him from one of the books he'd given me. Pa laughed at their funny goings-on but Ma never did and I didn't ask her to; not knowing her letters.

5

JESSIE

Sarginson Street: Two months later, August 1889

'How long does a baby take to be born?' I asked Aunt Margaret. She was putting our night things into a bag because someone had called round and said we could go home.

'Every baby's different. The birth can be very quick or last many hours.'

'Like Father Gregory's and Reverend Browning's prayers?'

'Something like that.'

I thought she'd smile because it was meant as a joke. But she didn't.

BACK HOME, we found it hadn't turned out like we thought it would. My stomach felt as if it had been punched and my cheeks ached. Me and James huddled up on the couch in the front room and did as we were told. Grandma and the aunts pressed handkerchiefs to their eyes and spoke in huddles. They said our mother was very ill, but we couldn't go upstairs to see her just yet. I was scared. The doctor had been and gone, but no one would tell us what was wrong. Pa came downstairs and his face was all caved in. I pressed my hands against my belly and closed my eyes.

Please, God, let everything be all right.

I repeated it over and over until the landing door creaked open and Father Gregory appeared. Pa stood up and they whispered together. I caught part of what the priest said... *last rites and the christening.*

'Why's he here?' I whispered to Aunt Margaret whose face was the colour of the ash can.

'He must have prayed over Mary,' she said dully.

I didn't understand. Ma never attended St Cuthbert's. Tears seeped down my cheeks. She wouldn't like having Catholic prayers said over her. They wouldn't make her better.

Father Gregory came over and stood in front of us like a black column.

'Prepare yourselves to say goodbye to your mother, children.'

His voice trailed off and he walked to the cupboard and lifted baby Kate out of a drawer. She was wrapped in a blanket and was mewling. The priest and Pa took her into the kitchen. As soon as they were gone, I grabbed James and pulled him upstairs. Grandma squawked and lurched towards us, but she was too slow.

I screwed my toes up while we waited on the landing then nodded at James, meaning it was time, and we pushed the door open into our parents' bedroom. When I saw our mother, I realised it was too late for prayers. She looked beautiful, but it wasn't really her, more like a statue with the same nose and mouth. I bent to kiss her cheek, hoping my breath might wake her like in a fairy tale. I thought I heard her voice in my head — *Aunt Margaret and Sam Dunbar will look out for you.* But maybe that was something she'd whispered to me a while ago. When I looked again she was still pale, and I wanted to shake her awake, but I knew it wouldn't work. Pain stabbed my belly. Noises came out of my throat. James was looking at me with eyes as wide as two moons, and then he let out a roar.

I pulled on his arm to force him out of the room and there was Pa on the landing. I wanted him to lift me up and hold me in his arms like he did when I was little. He lurched for the doorknob as if he was blind then closed it behind him, shutting us out.

WE CRIED in the darkened front room where no chink of light was allowed in. The grownups brought us sandwiches, water, cups of tea. Sometimes I took a sip and a bite to eat then pushed the rest away. People came and went — friends, neighbours — I hardly noticed who. The two of us went up to my room and lay in a huddle on the bed, arms around each other, not speaking. Tears ran down to my neck and wet my collar. I gave James another handkerchief and he buried his face in it. When I needed the privy, I tiptoed downstairs. Aunt Margaret was talking to Grandma about *arrangements*.

'The babby can come home with me. Patrick's got enough to contend with.'

In the backyard, the fresh air woke me up a bit. I crouched in the privy; glad Kate was going away. She was the reason Ma died. Back in the kitchen I tipped water from the can into the sink to wash my hands and closed my eyes. A picture of Ma and Pa dancing at that wedding in February entered my mind. It was a slow dance and they travelled all over the room before Ma sat down, out of breath. Then Pa asked the fiddle players to change the tune to something lively. I laughed and laughed when I saw him throwing himself about.

'An Irish frenzy,' Ma said when I put my arm around her.

I'd never feel that happy again.

From the kitchen, I looked through the open door. The room was a bit brighter because the gas lamps were lit. Grandma was leaning in towards Aunt Agnes, Ma's sister. She was a lot younger and still at home.

'I'll tell Patrick when he comes back that we'll help out. Have the kiddies live with us for a while.' She sighed, 'I only hope he's sober enough to understand.'

Aunt Agnes's face was blotchy and her eyes were red. 'Will Rachel and I share a bed with Jessie, Ma? It'll be a tight squeeze.'

Grandma's face turned sharp. 'I'm sure we can find a mattress for her. James can kip down in Margaret's old room. It's small, but there's nowhere else.'

My stomach felt punched again. I didn't want to live in their house or share a room with my aunts. But it was useless to protest.

ON THE DAY of the funeral, James and I stayed at a neighbour's house while everyone was at church until it was time for them to return for the wake. And that was another thing. Pa had arranged a Catholic service and Grandma and everyone was furious. We stumbled into the front room in our dyed black clothes and Grandad whispered we should sit on two low stools someone must have lent him 'cause I'd never seen them before. Sam stood across the room and I watched him from the corner of my eye. He couldn't speak when we arrived; when all the folk came up to say how sorry they were. I think he'd been crying.

The priest stood in front of us in a long robe with the hem covered in road dust. He tapped his fingers against his belly when he said his condolences.

Yesterday, I'd asked Grandma what the word meant.

'It's what people say when someone dies. They're sorry for your loss.'

'Why? It won't do any good.'

Grandma sighed and patted my back before turning away but I saw her tugging a handkerchief out of her pocket and drying her eyes.

Mr Mulrooney, a friend of Pa's, cleared his throat after the priest moved on.

'First through the door at a wake,' he muttered, 'To remind you where your duty lies.'

He turned his back on me, then I heard him hawk into a cup he'd picked up from the table. I felt nothing, though it was disgusting.

James's stool was empty. He'd slipped away without me noticing. I leant my back against the table where the sandwiches and things were laid out. I could see a plate of iced buns in the shape of frozen fingers, and sausage rolls which looked like pigs' noses. Same kind of food as at that wedding, but there was a borrowed black cloth on our table.

Sam was on his own, fiddling with his black armband. He went into the kitchen and when he didn't come out, I got up to see what he was doing. He was crouched on the floor talking to James who was hiding under the sink. I swallowed and felt bad. It should have been me who found my brother. James crawled out and stood up. I could tell he wanted to hold Sam's hand, but he didn't. I went back to my stool and took a biscuit off the table. It was in the shape of a star. I twiddled it between my fingers until Grandad frowned at me. He wanted me to stop but I couldn't. I scrunched it my hand and let the crumbs fall to the floor. It wasn't as bad as hawking into a cup. Grandad stared at me then looked away and I followed his eyes. Grandma was saying *hello* to Sam. She called my aunts over and they stood in a black huddle being introduced. Sam didn't look at them properly and after a minute he broke away. I thought he was going to leave, but he didn't.

He came up to me, squeezed my shoulder then pulled me against him. My face pressed into a button on his waistcoat which was rough and smelt of coal smoke. I felt both better and worse.

6

_____

SAM

At the wake: August 1889

At the wake: August 1889

*C*atholic service seemed foreign, fussy, wrong. But what could be right about Mary dying? I endured the funeral. Watched when everyone stood, and sat and prayed without a word passing my lips; more stone statue than living man. Outside, I took deep breaths and hung about the church rather than go off with everyone to the graveyard. One day, I might be able to visit her.

Patrick had pressed me to come to the house. I said I would, though I couldn't look more than once into his hollow, red eyes. I told myself, *I'm here for him and the children,* though I was mourning her, too.

Outside the church, I was introduced to the next oldest daughter, Margaret. She seemed a kind body. Despite her anguish, she welcomed me and asked how I was.

'Your sister was a rare woman,' I said. She nodded and clasped my hand before joining her family.

I saw her again in the house, handing out plates to new arrivals, and keeping an eye on the children who sat like lifeless

42

puppets. I found the small front room stifling and it was hard to breathe. Some of the men had gone outside to smoke but I wouldn't join them. I went into the kitchen for a glass of water and nearly stumbled over two chubby legs sticking out from under the sink curtain. Crouching down and drawing back the material, I saw James curled on the floor with his thumb in his mouth.

'Come on James, it's dirty under there.' Without protest he let me pull him out. 'Are you playing at *Tom Thumb*?' He shook his head and gave a weak smile. 'That's a good boy. Just try to get through this. For your Pa's sake?' He nodded and crossed his arms as if agreeing. Back in the front room, he clung to my side. I was a poor substitute for his mother but he seemed to derive some comfort from my presence.

It was clear that Mrs Towneley, even in her grief and after enduring a Catholic service, was in charge at the wake. She hadn't heard of me, but there was nothing strange in that, and I said I was a family friend. She introduced me to her two younger daughters. Rachel looked about fifteen and Agnes was perhaps a little older than me. I saw the ghost of Mary in their forms and faces but with blunter figures, flatter cheekbones, and narrower eyes.

'Any friend of Patrick and Mary is welcome at our house,' Mrs Towneley said, and invited me to call round. 'Sunday afternoons. Likely you'll see the children. They're going to live with us part of the time. Till Patrick sorts himself out.'

I could hardly take it in. No children. No wife. What would Patrick do? He'd loved her to distraction. When he came in from the back yard the room fell silent. I felt hot, and the greasy food smell was making me queasy. All over the house were reminders of Mary: the rag rug she'd been working on lying on the floor. Her green shawl still folded across the rocking chair. I remembered the last line of the *Lazy Hours*, having heard it several times during the months I'd known them, sung by one who'd loved her: *This fond heart must bloom or wither, Mary.* Patrick looked as if his heart was withering before our eyes.

Jessie was staring in my direction and the pain on her face unmanned me. I stumbled over and held her close. Not long after, folk started to dribble homewards, so I left, too.

BACK HOME, I took Mary's letter out of my bedroom drawer. I'd read it so often the edges were curling. Had she had a presentiment about her death… that the children would need a friend? I'd promised her I would keep an eye on them, and the invitation to take tea from Mrs Towneley provided an opportunity. But could I bear it? Too much talk about Mary, or lack of it, while the teacups clinked and the cake crumbs fell, would set me off. I had no right to think or feel that way about her.

7

SAM

3 The Whelley, Wigan: November 1889

I stripped, slid into the metal tub, dunked my head in the water and let the heat soak into my bones. It was eight months since I'd cleaned myself up for Mary Gorman and learned that she knew about Lydia. Since then, Lydia had become more than a friend: someone who made me forget myself and my sorrow.

From time to time I'd seen Patrick and was worried for him. But how could I, ten years younger, tell him drink wasn't the answer? I knew the children were well looked after by their grandparents, though I only saw them at Sarginson Street, seeing their father. During my visits, I tried to raise a smile with a joke or a story but it was hard work. The kiddies were often subdued.

I hopped barefoot on the freezing flag floor as I dried my hair and back — then nerves struck. Ahead lay the long-awaited dinner when I would meet Mr Holdsworth's invited business friends. Pa still thought my friendship with the Holdsworths a game: Daniel and Lydia flirting with the working classes, and that nothing would come of it. Naturally I'd disagreed, insisted we were real friends, that he'd got it all wrong. No one knew how close Lydia and I really were. Knew nothing of her end-of-year art show in Manchester and the night we'd spent together…

Yesterday evening, while waiting for potato pie to be dished out, I told the family where I was going. Pa shattered the silence.

'They're taking you for a fool, lad! There'll be no job at the end of it.'

'John!' Ma broke in. 'Give Sam a chance.'

He shook his head. 'I hope I don't have to say *told you so.*'

As usual, George followed where Pa led and insisted I'd make a damn fool of myself. Normally I could dismiss his nonsense but their combined doubt shook me. It was only later, alone with Frank and Josiah, that some of my former confidence returned.

'Take no notice. Go to the dinner,' they said, their eyes alight with possibilities; the only two in the family who looked beyond the pit head.

DRESSED in my Sunday suit and with a newish muffler around my neck, I thought about the dinner ahead. Daniel had been as encouraging as his sister, but it was her smile that made all the difference. The three of us had met in a teashop two weeks ago. By now I'd become used to sipping from a china teacup and ignored the many surprised looks that came my way. Lydia had inclined her head in a manner I was familiar with; a gesture both provocative and enquiring, so I told them about my latest unsuccessful attempts to find other work.

'We've hatched a plan,' she said, looking at Daniel who nodded in agreement. 'The family will arrange a dinner party for you, and invite father's colleagues. It's an experiment, but it's worth trying, don't you think?'

I gave them a dozen reasons why it wouldn't work, but Lydia batted them away.

'Borrowed evening clothes and an accent aren't obstacles to changing your life.'

For once she was serious. In between pots of tea, they explained they didn't yet know who would accept their father's invitation or what kind of work they might have to offer. I was left with the impression it would be clerking or shop work. Not as well paid as mining, but as long as I didn't have to spend my days underground I didn't care. Faith in God, faith in the Holdsworths. One or the other would change my life.

THE STATION FORECOURT WAS BUSY: people bustling to get home after shopping, or from work. I went through the swing doors onto the platform, bought my ticket for Parbold, and leant against a wall. The dinner party wouldn't start straightaway; they'd allowed time for me to learn how to use cutlery and change into Daniel's old evening jacket and trousers. I fingered the curly-edged invitation in my pocket, *Mr, and Mrs Richard Holdsworth of York House, Parbold, request the pleasure of the company of Mr Samuel Dunbar for dinner at 7 o'clock.* But was two hours enough? The Holdsworths had been brought up with cutlery. I'd held nothing more than a knife, fork, and spoon. It was stupid to be so worked up over a meal. I scrunched the thick card between my fingers and thought of questions I might ask the other guests, but nothing came to mind: only a ruddy, great table covered in silverware. I'd have to trust good judgement, common sense, and prayer, as mother would say. I brushed my hair out of my eyes and cursed myself for not having gone to a barber.

On edge and bored, waiting for the train, I watched the progress of a junior porter up the length of the platform as he lit one fish-tailed gas burner after another. I'd discounted the railway for myself knowing it took years before any sort of promotion from porter was considered, and at twenty-one, I'd be a late starter in the job.

As I leant against an alcove adjacent to the wall, a large man wearing a top hat, a long open coat and a paisley waistcoat which barely covered his vast corporation, came to stand a few yards in front of me. From his pocket he fished a small book and held it under his nose, oblivious of everyone around him. Then someone even more interesting came to stand beside him: a girl, no more than sixteen or seventeen whose black, wavy hair trailed down her back. She was tidily dressed in a loosely wrapped blue shawl, though I saw her skirt was patched in a couple of places. I decided she wasn't a mill girl on account of her footwear — shoes, not clogs, but besides being extremely pretty, there was something else that intrigued me. Her complexion was darker than most Wigan women's and I reckoned she was perhaps foreign born. She began to sway, toe to heel a few times, before inching a little closer to the man emersed in his book. Partly hidden by the alcove, and standing in shadow as I was, she didn't notice me, otherwise...

I scarcely understood what I saw...a flurry of darting fingers, a furtive movement with the shawl before pulling the garment tightly around her. In a flash, I realised what she was up to. She'd lifted something out of the gent's pocket and hidden it in her clothing like a stage magician. I scanned the platform, saw passengers searching for tickets in handbags, entering the buffet room, scanning chalked-up timetables. No one else knew anything was amiss. I wondered what was inside the wallet, apart from money. Tickets? An address card like the one in my pocket? Photographs? What if the gent was a stranger to Wigan with no means of getting home? Should I alert him or speak to a railway official? Any second now the girl could be off. But even as I dithered she remained where she was, nervously glancing from right to left as if looking for... Then I realised! She was eyeing up the other passengers, waiting for another rich mug to appear. Without further thought, I strode up and seized her by the arms.

'Give back what you stole from that gent!'

Wriggling and squirming under my grip, she protested loudly in a foreign language. I didn't understand a word, only that she was cursing me. Finally, the gent came to his senses and directed his anger... at *me*!

'Let her go you ruffian or I'll call the guard.'

'Not...' I gripped her arm tighter. '...until she gives you back what she stole. I saw her nick it from your pocket. It's somewhere in her shawl.' That would put the idiot right.

He gaped and then patted his pockets. 'She has! My wallet is gone.'

The girl wailed and made another attempt to escape. As the wallet fell to the ground, she burst into a torrent of speech and sobs.

'French.' The man said, stooping with difficulty to pick up his wallet. 'She says there is a younger brother and a sister, both less than ten years old. She claims she has no money to buy food until her aunt returns from France next week.' He clicked his tongue, more irritated than angry, and glanced at the station clock. 'Look, my train is due any minute. Here's something for your trouble,' and he took a half crown from the wallet and dropped it into my top pocket. 'I'll let you decide what to do with her,' and he toddled off towards the platform edge where the first-class carriages would halt.

I hadn't expected a reward. Wasn't sure I deserved or wanted one. I released the girl who rubbed her arms and threw me a contemptuous look before scampering towards the exit. I dug my hands into my pockets and wondered if what she'd said was true. If she did have children to support, then I was glad I hadn't reported her. Time in custody could have meant starvation for her family.

. . .

DURING THE SHORT train journey to Parbold, and on the walk to *York House* on dark, unpaved country roads, I forced myself to think only about the evening ahead. This was my chance and I would seize whatever lay before me. I would forget about what had just occurred.

I approached the house up a long drive and my rap on the shiny brass doorknocker brought Tilly, a girl my age, to the door. The maid knew me well by now but maintained a superior attitude. Though I was expected, she made me wait in the hall rather than in a sitting room while she went to inform her employers. I glanced at the gilt-framed paintings and shuffled my feet on the black and white tiled floor, exasperated by her nonsense. Then Daniel came running down the staircase followed by his parents who shook my hand and welcomed me warmly.

'Come into the parlour, Sam,' Mrs Holdsworth said.

As we walked down the hall, I complimented her on her dress which was a deep cherry colour. Since becoming friends with her children I'd received nothing but interest and kindness and had grown fond of her. On my second visit to the house, she'd told me that before her marriage she was a Quaker in Yorkshire, and that she still held to their practice of helping others whenever she could. I knew almost nothing about Quakers at that time and wondered if they were all as genuine and gracious as her.

There was no sign of Lydia until we'd been sitting in the parlour for several minutes. She entered the room looking lovely in a loose, flowing, green dress, but the tension I saw in her face and body alarmed me. She looked pointedly at her father sitting in the chair opposite. Then the bomb fell.

'I am sorry to inform you, Sam,' he said, looking at his wife rather than me, 'but it will be just the family dining here tonight. I'm sure there will be another occasion when you can meet my colleagues. Regrettably, none of those invited were able to come this evening. One man I had hopes for, Alfred Briggs, informed me was travelling South on business today.'

He stood suddenly and crossed the room to the fireplace where, to one side, a small table was set with glasses and a bottle. Mr Holdsworth was an impressive man. Tall and slim, with thick sandy-coloured hair, his face was all angles, but none of them too large. He was handsome for his age and looked at least fifteen years younger than my father. He gazed at me directly for the first time. 'You'll have a sherry, Sam?'

I shook my head, unable to speak. He knew I only drank beer.

'No? Will anyone else join me? Lydia, Daniel?'

He stared at his children until Daniel, probably unable to bear the silence, said, 'No, thank you Father, we won't. Who else made their excuses? I thought it was all set up.'

'Apparently not. Crossland rang to say his wife was ill and Theo Darke had last-minute theatre tickets.' He shook his head. 'So many telephone calls.'

I lost sight of who had said what and why. All I knew was that my chance to find another job had sunk like a rock chucked into a lake. After more apologies from all the Holdsworths, Daniel took me by the arm, as if I were an invalid, upstairs to the bathroom. Inside, he leant against the vast porcelain basin.

'I don't believe Father was telling us the whole truth. Lydia overheard something this afternoon when he was talking on the telephone. Perhaps some of his friends did have genuine reasons for not coming, but I rather suspect Father put the others off.'

'So, he doesn't believe in me after all!'

Daniel flinched at the bitterness in my voice. 'I don't know, Sam.' He put a consoling hand on my shoulder. 'He'll deny it and it will be hard to get the truth from him. Only Mother stands a chance of doing that.'

He left me in the large, tiled bathroom, and as I soaped my face and hands I told myself not to dwell on the disappointment; there would be plenty of time later for that. I dressed in my friend's dinner jacket and trousers, tried to loosen the shirt collar, which was a little tight, then looked in the mirror. I almost didn't recognise myself. There was some comfort in knowing I wouldn't look out of place at their table.

Lydia was waiting for me at the bottom of the wide staircase and quickly led me into the empty dining room where the table had been set for five. Her mouth still had a mutinous look.

'I'm sorry about Father. I'll speak to him when you're not here. Find out what really happened.' She leant against the table and waved her hand. 'We'll do away with the cutlery lesson 'til next time. All you need to know is start outwards and work in. 'Watch what I do and you'll be fine.'

I went up to her and wrapped my arms about her waist. 'You've just provided me with a good excuse to look at you without your parents becoming suspicious.'

She gave me a simpering smile and fluttered her eyelashes in imitation of a swooning actress then pushed me away.

'Shush, someone's coming.' And I heard the tap-tap of heels on the hall floor.

A moment later, Mrs Holdsworth opened the door and looked me up and down. 'Very handsome, Sam', she said.

I DIDN'T RECOGNISE half of what we ate and some of it I didn't like one bit. Daniel and Lydia put on a good show. They explained to me what capons and vol-au-vents were while their parents commented about art and plays they'd seen in Manchester, and everyone tried hard to forget why there were only five and not eight or ten around the table. By the time the dessert course was served, *Meringues à la Crème*, Tilly the maid announced with a flourish, I decided I wouldn't do this again. It was humiliating to sit next to Mr Holdsworth who probably despised me, and make chit-chat. Did he think my letters of introduction to his business colleagues weren't well written? That despite attending evening classes, my grammar and spelling were faulty? Was that what had put his business friends off meeting me? Or was it because I lived in The Whelley?

I made excuses to leave earlier than I'd intended and on the train back to Wigan, I had two overwhelming memories — not of equal importance, but wonderful in their different ways. I'd wandered around the black and white tiled bathroom, run my hands under the hot water tap and marvelled at the indoor plumbing, only ever having used their small downstairs privy before. And later, alone with Lydia in the porch, she'd daringly kissed me on the mouth knowing her parents were within calling reach.

Stepping out into the late-night bustle of Wallgate with its cabs filled with people seeking pleasure, I laughed out loud, startling a lad passing by. I would find my own way out of the pit.

8

SAM

Later that evening

The town hall clock was striking eleven when I dived into the back streets to make my way home, encountering scenes I could never have described to my mother. And a world away from the one I'd left just an hour ago. In his sermons, the Reverend Dootson sometimes likened this area to *Sodom and Gomorrah.* It disgusted and saddened me to see loiterers with tangled hair, their clothes askew, brawling outside pubs. And who were those men wearing knuckle-dusters, kneeling in the muck? Women leaned against lamp posts just to keep upright. And down the dingier alleys and ginnels, couples held each other in wild embraces. I hurried past. One snatched look was enough.

Closer to home, I turned into a broader road, free from rubbish, and saw a young woman standing against the end wall of a house. Orange light from a streetlamp spilt onto the pavement giving me a glimpse of a low-cut neckline and tattered frills. Street girls didn't usually stand on this corner.

She'd changed her dress, dabbed rouge on her cheeks and

stuck fancy combs in the long black hair. I took a deep breath. Was I to blame? Had I turned her from pickpocket to whore in a few hours because I'd stopped her from stealing? I felt sick, remembering how attractive I'd thought her at the station before becoming self-righteous. Lydia, and our times together in her art studio, flashed before my mind. Were we so very different from the French girl? I thrust my hand into my waist-coat pocket and pulled out the half crown from the toff on the platform. It seemed to glow on my palm. I strode over, stopped in front of her.

She recognised me. Her mouth hardened and she shook her head, the black hair tumbling around her shoulders. 'Non, Monsieur, not with you,' and she stepped sideways.

'Wait! I wanted to give you this,' I thrust the coin towards her. 'Nothing more. Do you understand? I'm sorry for what happened at the station. Please...?' I gestured into the distance. 'Go home to your family.' I pointed.

'No tricks, Monsieur?' Her eyes widened with disbelief.

'No! Course not. Go home. Buy food for your sister and brother.'

'Je comprends. I understand. Thank you, Monsieur,' and she snatched the coin out of my hand and gathered up her skirts to leave.

'Wait,' I called. 'What's your name?'

She turned her head and I saw her eyes glitter. 'Emilie Chambres, Monsieur,' then she hurried away without a back-ward glance.

I rested my head against the wall. I was done in. I looked down the road, but she was long gone. I hoped she wouldn't go back on the streets; that it was true she was waiting for her aunt to return. But how had a French family ended up in Wigan? Sympathy welled in me. What chance did she have of leading a decent life? She needed more help than I did to prosper. There was no Lydia Holdsworth at the end of her dream.

. . .

THE NEXT MORNING, I confessed to my parents that nothing had come of the evening at the Holdsworths. It was better to brave it out than wait for their questions.

'Waste of time like I told you,' Father scoffed, straightening his cap in front of the mirror, ready for work. His reaction was milder than I'd expected, though George reared in front of me pulling an ugly face, signalling I was a lunatic.

'Forget that idea and sign up for the army like I'm going to,' Josiah said. 'It'll be good. Brothers together.'

He was trying to cheer me up but I shook my head. 'Army life's not for me. I'd miss home too much.'

George sniggered, but I didn't see him pushing off to an uncomfortable billet either. He'd taken his usual chair, and with his arms spread across the table, he attacked his porridge as if he were wielding a pick. The Holdsworths held their spoons between their fingers and thumbs.

'You know those blokes,' George was saying, 'The agents who recruit for the mines in America? They were talking about you in the pub. They had a list of names of single men who they wanted to speak to, to see if they were interested in going out there.'

'Who do you mean?' asked Mother.

'Walter Dickenson, and his mate, Francis Love. Their parents still live in The Whelley.'

'What were they saying about me?' My mind was still on last night, but it would be wise to show some interest.

'They were going through the names and Walter said to strike *Sam Dunbar* off the list. Love wanted to know why.' George paused to give me a malicious smile. 'Because Sam's clever but in the wrong sort of way. That he'd be on the first boat going back to Liverpool.'

My brother shook with laughter, but he'd roused Ma's anger and she slapped his hand.

'That's not a nice thing to say about your brother!'

'Even if it's true?' George smirked.

I got up and left them to it. The younger ones, Frank, and William, were asking George about American mines, but what did he know? It was only pub gossip that he'd picked up. I went into the yard, out the back gate towards the little park at the end of the street.

Dickenson was a good deal older than me. Had been in Arizona four years already and was now an agent for the railroad company which owned the mines. Ma and the rest thought I'd been insulted. Clever, for miners and their families, meant digging coal more efficiently. For me it meant studying, exams, looking for opportunities. And if the Holdsworths couldn't help me surely there'd be others who would.

PART II

FIVE YEARS LATER

9

JESSIE

Aged 13
Sarginson Street: September 1894

$\mathcal{M}$onday, and for the first time in years, Mrs Gidlow, our washerwoman, was late. I poked my head around the front door and peered down the street: no sign of her. I'd be late for school myself if I didn't leave soon. It was a pity, because I'd wanted to tell her about our outing to Southport on Saturday.

I'd never seen a place that wasn't black with coal and factory smoke. The buildings looked as if they'd been scrubbed. Coming out of the station, I shaded my eyes because the light was so bright. After the short walk to the promenade, we saw the beach.

'Sand!' James screeched.

We looked at each other, flung off our boots and ran barefoot for what seemed like miles towards the sea where we splashed around; daft as three-year-olds. Even Pa rolled up his trousers for a paddle.

My news about Southport would probably have to wait until the following week. I wrote Mrs Gidlow a note about what clothes and sheets to wash and asked Pa to give it to her. With luck, she'd still be around after school finished. He was on a later shift, wouldn't be leaving until near midday. He told me not to worry about the washing, so I hurtled down the street, waved at neighbours standing in doorways, their arms folded, gossiping. It wasn't just the outing that made me want to skip. Pa wasn't shuffling about anymore and his eyes were brighter, like they'd used to be. I said the same to Aunt Margaret in case she hadn't noticed when I was at her house for my tea.

'I've noticed all right.' She put her knitting on her lap and looked at me. 'You're aware of it because you're growing up. Thirteen! A year's difference has given you older eyes. The truth is your father's been in a dark room for a long time, not just because of our Mary, but baby Kate dying too, and now he's coming out of it. I'm glad for all of you.'

I could never think about Ma without swallowing hard and making a blank space in my mind. I did it to stopper-up the sad feelings. I learned to do it as I'd got older, that, and forgiving my baby sister. When I was eight I'd hated her, thought she was to blame for Ma's death.

'Infants are innocent,' Pa had told me and James. 'They don't ask to come into this world. It's not their fault if someone dies.'

I thought about Kate differently after that though I still wondered why God hadn't let her live. Everyday life without Ma got easier over time, mostly, but I couldn't stop myself from welling up whenever she was mentioned.

I squeezed back the tears threatening to fall so my aunt wouldn't see them. 'You don't mean he's forgetting Ma?'

'Don't be a goose!' She said, stretching across and ruffling my hair. 'He'll never forget her, but he's finding it easier to live his life.'

She was right. He'd replaced a missing spindle on the rocking chair, broken years ago, and fixed the squeaking back door. And something he said around the time we moved back home from our grandparents' remained with me.

'Your other aunts don't have a thimbleful of the wisdom Margaret has. And she's a kind soul. Look how she nursed Kate when I couldn't. More like your Ma than Rachel is, and the only wise thing Agnes ever did was to marry Sam.'

Sam was part of our family now though I didn't think of him as an *uncle,* or call him that. He and Aunt Agnes lived with his parents though they'd be moving to their own home, soon. I supposed he wouldn't have much time to visit us when that happened.

RETURNING FROM SCHOOL, the house had its usual clean, damp Monday smell. So, Mrs Gidlow had been, but why had she left an apron with a sooty hem on the back of a chair? It was odd when she was so pernickety about cleanliness. James clattered downstairs in a hurry as usual. I blocked his way otherwise he'd be gone.

'Did you see Mrs Gidlow?'

'She didn't come,' he said. 'She's had an accident and a woman called Boyle was here an' did the washing in her place. Said she could take over the wash if we wanted. Pa thought it best. He gave her a penny for it.'

James dodged in front of me, shrugged off his clogs and put on a pair of soft leather boots. They were old but good quality. I'd nabbed them at the Cloth Market before anyone else seized them. He finished tying his laces.

'I'm off to play footie.'

'Don't go until you've told me a bit more. What's she like, this Boyle woman?'

'I don't know! Old, like Pa.'

I sighed at his uselessness. We went into the yard and I examined the sheets on the line for dirty marks but found none. I tried again. 'Did Pa think she was a hard worker and would do the job properly? She's left her apron in the front room and that's filthy.' With Mrs Gidlow's help, I'd kept house the last couple of years. A change of person made me anxious.

'How would I know?' James blew out his cheeks as if I was soft in the head. 'Pa said she sounded desperate for work because she was laid off from Sandbrook Mill. When she heard about the accident she went to see Mrs Gidlow's customers to offer her services.' James scurried past me towards the back gate. 'See you later.'

I unpegged the sheets, draped them over my arms with the vests and shirts and took everything inside. James only made time for me these days when he wanted something. But another thing bothered me. It was odd the way this Boyle woman had snapped up Mrs Gidlow's laundry work so quickly. I would pop around later. See how she was and seek her opinion.

The visit to Ada Gidlow unsettled me even more. Her daughter made us a cup of tea and after a concerned look at her mother, she left us to talk. I found Ada in low spirits and her bandaged hand was held up in a sling. It was obvious she was in pain though the doctor had prescribed something to take that away.

'I'm worried I won't be able to return to work,' she said softly. She held a hanky in her good hand and dabbed it to her forehead now and again. She mentioned the new woman. 'Clodagh Boyle isn't married, or courting, as far as I know. That's unusual for around here, her being well over thirty. But I'd advise you to keep her on. Good washerwomen are scarce.'

At home, Pa agreed. 'She seemed pleasant enough, willing to help out. What's the alternative; you doing the washing and missing school on Mondays?'

I shook my head making my plaits whip across my face. 'No, thanks! We'll keep her.'

All the same, I felt guilty, as if I were betraying Mrs Gidlow who'd lost her earnings. I did know how to manage the wash. Grandma Towneley taught me when we lived with them, but school was more important and I wanted to stay on for as long as I could.

A MONTH later I was still getting used to having a new person traipsing in and out of the house on a Monday. Mrs Gidlow had liked discussing things with me that she'd read about in the newspaper and listened to my opinions. Clodagh Boyle was the opposite. She could barely read and laughed when I picked up a book. Even water slopping on the outhouse floor was a joke and she snorted if shirt sleeves got tangled. But she didn't mind going outside in freezing weather either; though sneered when I said I couldn't stand the cold. I imagined her as a pioneer woman in the *Wild West*; the sort that was written about in the papers: shooting bears and chopping down wood. Cheeriness might have been a good thing for our house, but when there was no cause to laugh it irritated me. She did the wash well, I gave her that, and Pa said she was a good laugh, though I expect he kept out of her road if he was at home on a later shift. He always had with Ada Gidlow.

A few weeks later I was surprised to see Clodagh still working when I came downstairs; it being well after her usual leaving time. I stood in front of the little cracked mirror by the front door checking my hair. I was due at Aunt Margaret's for my tea. Clodagh sidled up and looked me up and down.

'Where you going all dressed up?'

'Only my aunt's.'

She edged closer and peered at my blouse. 'That's a nice little brooch for a young un. Who gave you that, a sweetheart?'

'Of course not!' I coloured and she laughed. I put my hand over the brooch to feel the smooth surface of the cannel. 'It was a present from Pa for my thirteenth birthday.'

'Was it now? It'd come in handy for a mourning brooch, too.'

Why did she have to say that? I never thought of Ma's brooch in that way. Clodagh chucked me under the chin as if I were three, leaving a fingernail scratch on my skin.

'I have to go now, I'm late,' I said, and pulled away. Close up, she smelt nice from the washing, but her expression unsettled me. Triumphant-like, as if she'd a won a fortune on a horse race; or got one over on a person.

The feeling accompanied me all the way to my aunt's house. I thought about the way she'd pried into my business. Thank God she hadn't wormed anything else out of me.

THERE'D BEEN talks just before I'd turned thirteen between Pa and Grandma about when I might leave school. They were thinking of the extra earnings I could bring to the household. But I didn't want to leave and had held out for staying on. Pa had seen reason and the subject was dropped.

On the afternoon of my birthday, he produced a cake and after he'd cut me a piece, he handed me a little velvet drawstring bag.

'I think a thirteenth birthday is the right time to give you this.'

I had an idea of what it contained and a flush of pleasure came over me when I drew out the lily-shaped brooch. I turned it this way and that as it gleamed against the lamplight.

'If you remember, Sam found it near the railway line and thought your mother would like it. Before she left us she told me she wanted you to have it.'

Pa swallowed and I thought he might jump out of his chair and scarper as he often did after he'd talked about Ma, but he pulled himself together and said jokingly, 'Don't lose it! You'd have Sam as well as me to contend with if you did.' I leant over, kissed, and hugged him. 'Get away with yerself,' he said gruffly, then sprang up to brew a pot of tea. When he returned, he handed me a cup, settled himself and didn't speak for some time. It was so comfortable, just the two of us in front of the fire. My worries about leaving school slipped away. Then he seemed to gather himself and his next words startled me.

'Sam could have given your brooch to his sweetheart, but he wanted your mother to have it.'

Was he speaking to me or musing to himself? I searched my memory for a sweetheart, but things were so jumbled up after Ma died that I couldn't recall anyone in relation to Sam, only my aunt. But they didn't start courting until a long time after. I remembered wanting to join him and Aunt Agnes on one of their Sunday walks, but she made it plain it should be just the two of them. Didn't want a little kid hanging around I suppose. High and mighty she was. Three of us shared a bedroom and I'd pretend to be asleep on my narrow mattress on the floor when she and Aunt Rachel came up to bed. Sometimes I heard them whispering about sweethearts and listened hard whenever Sam's name was mentioned. On his Sunday visits to the house, if he suggested a game with me or James, *Snap*, or *Blind Man's Buff*, Aunt Agnes wouldn't join in and whisked him away as soon as she could.

A thought struck me as I finished my tea. 'Should my brooch go to Aunt Agnes now they're married? Do you think Sam would want her to have it? I don't want to give it up, but...'

Pa sat upright and made his eyes bulge wide and mouth go slack. 'No, you eejit! Now how about we go for a stroll?'

My heart lifted as we left the house, arm in arm. Pa didn't mention my aunt again on that walk but I recall him being discomforted when their engagement was announced. And sometimes when his beer glass was empty, he'd drop the odd hint... 'I know she's Mary's sister and all, but...'

Now Sam was married, Pa, James and I hardly saw him. If I was in company with the newlyweds I secretly watched how they were together: my aunt did most of the talking and somehow seemed to have swollen up.

'Proud of landing a fine feller,' Pa said.

10

SAM

Windmill Street Mission Church: Four months earlier, May 1894

'*I*t was a long time getting here, but we've done it!'
Agnes laughed, holding up her hand to admire the
wedding ring I'd just slipped on her finger.

I kissed the top of her nose in full sight of everyone. 'It was
worth the wait. You look lovely.'

Her cheeks were pink with happiness and her eyes sparkled
as she twirled around, greeting every guest in sight. She was as
sprightly as the day itself. The Towneley women had worked as
a team on Agnes's outfit: Rachel embroidering the collar and
cuffs, Margaret covering the tiny buttons down the front of
Agnes's dress, in a blue material. I thought of our honeymoon,
two nights in St. Anne's, saved for over many months. How easy
would it be to undo those buttons when we were on our own?
Better to let Agnes undress herself, not rush her. She'd need
time to get used to that side of our life. She was no Lydia
Holdsworth; and I didn't want her to be. Over the years we'd
been courting, I'd come to value her down-to-earth attitude, her
cheerfulness and determination. I took my appreciation as a

sign I was growing up. The days when I could be infatuated by two different women were over, yet it was my visits to see Mary that had led to us standing on these steps.

I HADN'T TAKEN much notice of the other Towneley daughters when I was introduced to them at Mary's wake. Merely that they were the ghosts, not her. The only company I kept for a long time was with folk who had nothing to do with home or work. The Holdsworths, mainly, and specifically Lydia. That was until our affair was discovered and we parted. There hadn't been a repeat of the disastrous dinner party though Daniel, Lydia and I continued to attend talks and even concerts, when I could afford to. Our separation was inevitable even without Tilly the maid telling tales to her mistress. Lydia would have gone to study in Paris after she finished Art School and I didn't fit into that future. We had one last, loving tryst in a deserted farmhouse on the moors before she packed her art equipment and left. We didn't make any promises to write though I was sorely tempted to find out where she was living.

First came Mary's death, then the letter from Mrs Holdsworth saying she knew about me and Lydia, followed by my parting from her daughter: momentous events which kept me in a kind of corridor for nearly a year. During that time I'd sleepwalked from home to work and neglected my friends in favour of study. Then one Sunday in August when arguments between me and George had grown more heated, and sick of home life, I remembered the long-standing invitation to tea at the Towneleys. I didn't take a lot of trouble to spruce up: a flick of a hairbrush after a hurried wash, a change of shoes and I was off.

Mrs Towneley ushered me into the house with cries of delight and I found a cheerful household with plenty of hymn-singing around the piano. Margaret, who was now married, often joined us. It was a larger house than the Gormans', with cross-stitched devotional pictures on the wall and crocheted antimacassars the women had made. Mary had grown up here before living with Patrick, but I didn't sense her presence in any of the rooms which was probably for the best. When we sat down I was fussed over and fed. It seemed the livelier the family were the calmer and more like my old self I became.

I got into a routine, turning up every three to four weeks to drink their tea and listen to their news. The sameness of the visits and the care they heaped on me felt like nourishing broth after an illness. An added pleasure was finding Jessie and James sitting cross-legged on a rug, playing together then chattering to me about school, friends, and games. By keeping an eye on the children, something I'd neglected, feeling too sorry for myself while I mourned her, I felt I was half fulfilling my promise to Mary: a way of making things right; as if she was watching and thinking, *Sam let me down.*

Thoughts of this nature were interrupted by Mr Towneley who liked my company and frequently asked for my opinion on things he'd read in the newspaper. He was a kind, quiet man, the only adult male in a household of women. I sometimes caught glimpses of Mary in his manner and character. One day he spoke of James.

'The lad thinks he's a man now,' he laughed. 'Comes to the Sunday service with us on occasion, has his dinner then disappears.'

It seemed James was wavering between denominations, but Jessie had become a full-time Methodist since living with the Towneleys. It was a change I could have wished for the lad, too. He'd be less likely to follow his father in his drinking habits.

When Agnes, the third daughter, suggested a walk before the family took tea, I accepted, content to spend more time outdoors. On that first occasion, the weather was fine and Spring-like, for Wigan. She chatted pleasantly, showed an interest in my family and I enjoyed being with a woman again after the long absence of female company. These strolls became a regular part of my visits to the point where everyone, except me, thought we were walking out. One Sunday, Mr Towneley took me into the yard. I thought he wanted to show me the dove-tail joints of a table he'd been working on for Margaret, but it wasn't that at all.

'What's your intentions regarding Agnes, lad?' He asked, rubbing his hands on the sides of his trousers. He seemed as rattled as me. I honestly didn't have intentions, not with the sorrow of Mary's death and abandoning Lydia like I'd had to. I'd fumbled for an answer, but his question made me think about Agnes more seriously. It was only then that I realised the rest of her family generally made an excuse not to join our walks.

Practical and pretty, Agnes had a passing likeness to Mary and from her years in the mill was just as nimble-fingered at sewing as her sister had been. I liked her a lot. She was a planner and good with money, as I was, but not curious which was just as well. I saw she'd make a good wife for someone, but was that me?

STANDING on the steps to have our photograph taken, a surge of relief ran through me. The restlessness I'd felt over the last few years was about to end. I put it down to our long, prim courtship: holding hands, kissing when no one was around. Why had we taken so long to get to this point? It wasn't Agnes's wish; she'd been keen on an early marriage after we became engaged. I'd held back because once we were man and wife I knew my studying would fall away.

'I must get my qualifications first,' I'd told her on one of our sedate walks, sheltering from a shower under a beech tree as I smoothed her hair back from her brow.

She'd frowned a little. 'But they're not mining exams are they, so what good will they do you?'

These last years, besides economic theory, I'd learned patience. 'You know I don't want to spend my life down the pit 'til I'm Father's age and without money behind me, study is the only way of doing it. It will take time, but I'll get there.'

The day after I received news I'd passed my last exam in accounting and bookkeeping, I applied for a marriage licence.

OUR GUESTS WERE GATHERING around us, chatting and smiling. Agnes's mother was beaming and thanking God for the fine weather. Outside the Mission gates, I spied Patrick, a dark figure in the bright sunshine. He hadn't come inside for the service, though Jessie had been in the congregation. It had lifted my spirits even higher to see her. We hadn't invited the Gormans to the meal, wanting to keep it small and the costs down. Patrick swayed slightly, and his slack stare and hunched shoulders told me he was in a bad way.

'I'll be back in a minute,' I whispered to Agnes. 'The photographer's finished with us.' Another expense I couldn't afford. I looked for Jessie but didn't see her. Perhaps she was still inside the building. It would mean having a quiet word with Patrick on my own, to send him on his way. At the gates, I held out my hand and he shook it loosely: nothing like his former firm grip. His talk was rambling and at first, I couldn't make head nor tail of it until he mentioned Mary.

'Sam...you know I lost the finest woman ever...both of us make do with second best....'

My blood ran cold. Could he mean Mary? Surely not. He had to mean Lydia. Out of the corner of my eye, I saw Jessie watching us. How much had she heard? Nothing, I judged from her bright smile. And even if she had, surely she'd have no understanding of her father's meaning?

'Go with your Pa,' I urged her. 'Take him home.'

But before she reached him Patrick lurched away. I raised my brows as if to show surprise, and returned to Agnes, thanking God she'd been too far away to see or hear anything. I squeezed my wife's hand, as I must now think of her, and smiled. It took all my resources to do so then I put all thoughts of *second best* out of my head.

11

JESSIE

Sarginson Street: January 1895

O utside *The Griffin* I stopped to catch my breath. I'd run most of the way from Aunt Margaret's, thinking I'd be late to cook the family meal. The window had the kind of glass that bulged outwards so drinkers' faces loomed larger than they really were, like cartoon characters. A man with a bulging forehead sat at a window table cradling a pint, and I saw it was Pa. I stepped back in surprise, then grew annoyed. He should have been at home waiting for my return so we could eat our tea together. I wouldn't have left my aunt's so early if I'd known where he was and stayed singing around the piano with everyone else. I was on the point of going inside to ask how long he'd be when a woman appeared. She sat down at his table, a glass in her hand. The distorted window made her abundant, frizzy hair stick out in all the wrong places. I hurried away. Clodagh Boyle would say I was prying if she'd seen me.

. . .

A FEW EVENINGS later when James was upstairs, I asked Pa about it. He was blurry with drink but that wasn't unusual. I was puzzled; a respectable woman wouldn't enter a public house unless she was accompanied. Did that mean they'd gone in together? Pa drank with his work pals, not the washerwoman, or any woman, as far as I knew. He buried his face in his beer mug before speaking.

'We met by chance in the street and I asked if she'd like a pint along with me. I was needing a bit of company. That's all.'

He abandoned the empty glass and returned to his newspaper, keeping a finger under each line of print so he wouldn't lose his place. He'd once confessed his reading wasn't up to much. I knew better than to needle him when he closed himself off this way. I picked up a library book, *A Study in Scarlet*, which I was halfway through but only managed a page or two before flinging it down. I didn't think it would be allowed if I was still at school, with its Mormon characters and a forced marriage. Thinking about school always gave me a twinge in my stomach. Four months ago, I'd been sitting behind a desk for reading, writing, needlework and arithmetic lessons. Those days had gone forever, and I was too old for the part-time lessons the mill provided.

Aunt Margaret said it was *regret* when I'd described the feeling to her. 'You didn't want to leave, did you?'

I shook my head but said nothing because I'd have started crying. My chance to become a pupil teacher had been scuppered. I'd pleaded with Pa, but he said he needed another wage coming in. The following Monday I started my training in the weaving shed. I was glad the money helped and that sometimes there were a few pennies over for me, but it wasn't what I'd wanted for my life.

Without a good book to read, thoughts about Pa out drinking with Clodagh Boyle continued to flow. While he hid behind the newspaper, I dredged up what he'd said about her in the past. She was helpful, not just with the washing, but rustling up a sandwich for them both before he went to work. Did this mean they were friends? It wasn't something I'd thought about much until I mentioned it to Grandad after church. We'd almost reached my grandparents' house and were looking forward to our Sunday dinner. He paused, and his forehead creased as he pondered my question.

'Parents need people their age, not just their children to talk to.'

It wasn't what I was expecting. But he was right. I told him he was very clever but he shook his head.

'Not really. Just life lessons. I envy Sam for all the studying he's done.'

I knew how he felt. My chance at learning, like Granddad's all those years ago, was over.

ON SATURDAY AFTERNOON, I walked over to my grandparents' house to scrub the floors because Grandma's knees wouldn't let her bend. She'd made a Queen Cake and it stood proudly on the sideboard. I imagined the sweetness of it on my tongue and redoubled my efforts to finish early. But while I was on my knees in the kitchen, a neighbour arrived, Mrs Campbell, a big crony of Grandma's with a face like a hen. They forgot all about me so gossip flowed like the Douglas in full spate. Most of it washed over because I had my own thinking to do; how to avoid bumping into nasty-tongued Aggie from the spinning shed...

'You know he married our Agnes, last Spring...?' I paused my scrubbing. 'Well, they're expecting their first child...' Grandma's voice rose proudly up and down. I wondered if Pa knew about it. 'But we're not happy he wants to leave the pit. Anything else is a step down in my opinion.'

I dried my hands and turned my ear to the open door. Why

shouldn't Sam leave a place he hated? I squeezed out the cleaning cloths and spread them over the sink. His last visit to us was ages ago. I remembered it being a Monday because Clodagh Boyle was still in the house. Pa was greatly pleased to see him though less so when he knew Sam wanted to talk about an election, up in London.

'I'll hang those towels to dry. You get off home,' I'd said to Clodagh who hadn't the gumption to realise we wanted to be on our own with our visitor.

'You're awright. I'm in no rush. I'll stay for a gab with these two fine fellers,' and she plonked her broad beam in my chair and winked across the table at Pa and Sam.

I scowled and hung back. She was probably hoping a cup of tea would appear and when it didn't, she chatted about nothing in particular. It was Sam who rescued us. He looked at his pocket watch and cleared his throat.

'We wouldn't want to make you late for your next customer, Miss Boyle. Three o'clock already? Rather late to start a second wash isn't it?'

She pretended she couldn't find her shawl and hat, but as soon she'd gone I gave Sam a big smile.

'Make us a sandwich, lass,' Pa said, as if nothing had happened. 'I could do with some sustenance if we're going to talk politics.' He tapped Sam on the arm, jokily. 'The young feller's come to persuade me to get involved in campaigning for yon man Woods.'

I left them to talk and busied myself spreading margarine and cutting slices from the knuckle of ham meant for our tea whilst keeping an ear open. I didn't know the man who they said was a Lib-Lab Member of Parliament. I wanted to ask Sam what he meant by *Mr Woods might lose his seat in July,* but I didn't get the chance. Pa changed the subject: football or pit business.

I hadn't seen Sam since then. I supposed he was busy being

married and preparing to be a father. I hoped they'd bring the baby to see us, like they would do with the rest of the family.

12

SAM

Wigan town centre: March 1895

The French girl. Emilie Chambres. I hadn't seen her since that strange evening at the train station, and the awkward encounter afterwards, but I hadn't forgotten her. I suppose I thought our paths wouldn't cross, but that was stupid. Wigan wasn't a big place.

I was waiting for Agnes in a teashop behind Lowe's Department store. She was already ten minutes late and I presumed she'd bumped into a friend whilst shopping. I looked up from my newspaper when the door opened and saw a striking young woman searching for a table. When she saw me, she headed in my direction and sat down.

'Good day, *Monsieur*. You know who I am?'

'Of course!' However, I could not hide my surprise. So different was she from the furious thief at the station and the vulnerable girl of a few hours later. Her black hair was elaborately coiled. She was poised, fashionably dressed, and had obviously risen in the world, whereas I...well, I was exactly where I'd been six years ago.

It was surprisingly easy to fall into conversation. She asked my name and soon we were chatting like old friends who hadn't met in a while. We laughed, were flippant, serious, and relaxed at the same time. Perhaps our first unusual meeting broke the ground for something deeper.

'You have sad eyes, Sam,' she told me. 'What has happened to that indignant boy at the station?'

'Do I?' No one had ever said anything remotely like that to me before. I pulled a face but didn't contradict her. She was right, I'd grown up since those days. 'Well, I'm married and we're expecting our first child.'

'That shouldn't make you melancholy. What else is there?'

I shook my head, but not in dismissal, more in judgement of myself. I'd never spoken of this but something told me Emilie wasn't the sort to condemn. 'Perhaps it's because I found and lost two women I cared for within a short space of time.' I spaced the words out with precision. 'That evening at the station, I was waiting for a train to visit my friend Lydia and her family. We were not an equal match regarding class so we kept our relationship a secret. Some months later I was forced to give her up. The other person I lost was a married woman called Mary and she died in childbirth. I was, am, a family friend.'

'And your wife?'

'Is Mary's younger sister.'

Emilie stretched across and put her hand on my wrist. 'I see.' She didn't say what she saw but her expression told me she could imagine my past.

'Now your turn,' I smiled.

She pressed her lips together and shrugged. 'Very well. I didn't tell the whole truth that night but enough to make you release me. There were no younger brothers and sisters. But I *was* starving and without money. You see I left France to get away from what you would call a wicked uncle. I had no plan, only to come to England and stay with Great Aunt Adeline. I discovered she was not at home but on vacation, a neighbour said. I spent the little money I had left to find a room. I did not eat that day. So, I was young and stupid. At the station, I thought I could steal a wallet and it wouldn't matter. That I could go on the streets and fool a man into giving me a coin if I kissed him.' She shuddered. 'It was not so. I wasn't the same person after that. Your half crown saved me from further mistakes.' She spread out her hands, '*C'est tout.* My Great Aunt owns a draper's shop, and we live above it. This, and this,' she touched her hat and the lapels of her suit, 'Come from there. It is not easy living together; the difference in our age, you know, but I manage the shop for her. So, you see Sam, no shawls and patched skirts now. And...' She lowered her voice and glanced around the teashop which was almost empty. 'I am in love. But he is in France and married to a dragon and I am here.'

My eyes widened. I was a little shocked, but more amazed that she'd told me something so private. She cocked her head from side to side, smiled, and spoke of exhausting journeys to and fro to France.

Before we parted we exchanged addresses. I decided to go straight home thinking it too late for Agnes to turn up. I would tell her a little about Emilie with some details changed. She'd be interested in Madame Chambres's shop though it would do to scandalise her.

13

JESSIE

Sarginson Street: July 1895

The only sound around the table was the steady munching of food, apart from James leaning back in his chair, tipping it up and making the legs creak. At school we used to get a ruler across our knuckles for doing that but Pa seemed too jiggered to tell him off. His eyes and brows were gathered together like an uneven seam. I hoped he'd enjoyed his stew and dumplings which was a favourite. James pushed his plate away and looked around for seconds. His chair legs screeched on the flag floor making me wince.

'I hear Clodagh Boyle's started drinking in the same pub as you, Pa,' James said, emphasising her name.

Pa pronged a piece of meat with his fork and chewed hard on it but the meat wasn't gristly, I'd made sure of that when I bought it. James had a mood on him and the atmosphere was turning sour.

'How many times a week do you and Miss Boyle drink together, then? Just in *The Griffin* is it, or have you progressed to the Music Hall?'

YVONNE LYON

What was James doing? Hammering out questions like a policeman facing a wrong doer.

'Word on the street is that you're keeping her company. Paying for her beer too.' He pulled a pretend sad face at me. 'That's where your food money's going, Jessie.'

I flashed him a glance to shut up but couldn't stop my lip from trembling. I felt like sinking to the floor. If Pa was buying beer for two, no wonder we'd been short of money lately.

'It's only a penny here and there,' Pa mumbled into his plate. 'Nothing we can't afford, and it's none of your business, lad, who I see or drink with.'

James snorted, grabbed his jacket and shouted as he opened the front door that he was meeting his mates. I stared at my empty plate hoping Pa would talk but he remained silent. As I waited for the water to boil in the kitchen for the dirty plates, I thought back a few months. It must have been around the time Clodagh first started doing the laundry that Pa took the weekly budgeting away from me to do it himself. I'd learned how to manage money when James and I lived with our grandparents.

On Friday nights, I'd watch Grandma tot up a row of figures then she'd write a new list and ask me to do the additions. After four years, the sums were huge.

'Grandma! I'll never have that much money to buy food with,' I'd cried.

'No, neither furniture, nor oil paintings, but it's as well to have the knowledge, just in case.'

'So, some people do have thousands of pounds?' I could hardly believe my ears.

'Yes,' said Grandad, 'but they don't live in Sarginson Street,' which made us all chuckle.

Not many months later Pa arrived to talk to us. 'It's time to come home,' he'd said, and we whooped and hugged him.

But James's accusations weren't really about finances and suddenly I dreaded what might come next.

84

. . .

AFTER WORK ON FRIDAY EVENING, my friend Susan and I tumbled down the worn steps of the weaving shed and headed for her home. As was her custom, she patted one of the stone lions which decorated the entrance; her farewell to noise, dust and backache. And for the first time, I, too, touched the other lion's back. Two nights away from James's moods which swung like a pendulum and Pa's remoteness about Clodagh. On the pavement, I did a few jig steps.

'That's better! Time to stop worrying about your family, Jessie,' Susan said.

'Definitely! And tomorrow there's a party to look forward to.'

The weekend ahead felt like an escape and I thought I deserved it. We linked arms, and with my free hand, I swung a straw basket packed with my night things and a pretty blouse I'd bought at the Rag Market. This must be what having a sister was like. It was ages since Susan and I had done anything together and I'd missed it. Football games and dog racing occupied my brother, which, of course, I wasn't invited to.

'What's your Vince getting for his twenty-first?' I asked as we approached their street.

She laughed. 'It's a bit unusual. You know he's musical? Well, he wants a singing lesson. Mam and Dad didn't know where to find a teacher. They ended up asking the priest and he's recommended a lady in Standish. Did I tell you there'd be dancing tonight, too?'

I confessed I'd never learned to dance, apart from jigging around to Irish tunes at weddings. I was a bit worried I'd have to sit them out; like an old aunt against a wall. When we reached her house, she took out her key and opened the door and reassured me that her brother and his pals would teach me the steps.

'After they've shifted the furniture and moved the rugs,' she said.

On Saturday, my fears came to nothing and my efforts to glide like a lady made people smile so decided to play it up. Vincent and his friends, David Andrews and Walter Small, chatted with me and though I felt a bit shy, at the same time it was nice, and kind of them to teach me the movements for the country dances. Halfway through a waltz, David pressed me too close. I smelt a mix of sweat and soap. Earlier, Susan and I had agreed that he was nice-looking, but I didn't like being so… together. On impulse, I turned my foot on its side, slipped off my shoe and pretended to trip, then hopped to a chair. David leaned his arm on top of the mantelpiece, waiting until I was ready to begin again, but before I could think how to sit out the rest of the dance, I smelt burning. David jumped away and I saw that he'd knocked over candle. In front of us, flames shot up out of a vase filled with Mrs Greenhalgh's feathers.

'The paper chains on the walls!' Someone shrieked. 'They'll catch it!'

Vincent ran out of the room. He returned with a saucepan of water and threw it over the feathers. His friend must have nudged the candlestick towards them with his elbow. The smell was acrid but the fire was out and everyone cheered. An older man took over at the piano and sang a coalmining song in a tuneful voice.

'A Welsh tenor,' a Greenhalgh aunt told me. Some of the older relatives sang along.

For Death that levels all alike, whate'er the rank may be,
Amid the fire and damp may strike and flings his darts at me…

'Pack it in Uncle Joe,' Mrs Greenhalgh shouted. 'We've had enough excitement about fire for one night.'

But Joe was so engrossed he didn't hear her. Then came a line which spun me back in time.

Digging dusky diamonds all the seasons round...

I smelt beer, heard a fiddle playing Irish tunes and I was listening to a story about seeing diamonds... Sam talking about himself when I was eight.

'Jessie?' David loomed over me. 'Are you ready for another dance? Vincent's taking over from his uncle for a waltz.'

I shook my head. 'Sorry, I'm a bit tired. I think I'll sit down for a while.'

He went off to ask another girl, one who'd been looking in his direction, and I made my way into the kitchen. I opened the back door to stand in the yard and with my hands clasped around my elbows, I let the breeze cool my cheeks. My stomach was churning a bit, probably due to the sips of beer I'd taken, not being used to it. I touched the brooch at my throat and a wave of relief washed over me. It hadn't fallen off while I was dancing.

AFTER MRS GREENHALGH's beef and ale Sunday dinner and cries of *come again* from all the family, I headed for home. A hundred thoughts whirled around my mind. Who would have thought I'd end up loving to dance, or making people laugh? And why shouldn't *we* have visitors? Enjoy ourselves as the Greenhalghs did. I'd suggest it to Pa.

Twenty minutes later I was home, but as I walked up to the door I noticed it was ajar. Through the gap I heard Clodagh Boyle's voice coming from the front room. I frowned, hesitating before stepping over the threshold; my heart was beating like a mad thing.

'How was the party, love?' Pa asked.

He leaned against the landing door still wearing his Sunday coat, though Mass would have finished hours ago. He looked towards the window where James was hunched over at the table; his eyes roaming everywhere but on me.

'Anyone there I might know?' Clodagh butt in, patting her hair which was tidier than usual. She was wearing a smarter dress, too, and for once, I thought her quite attractive. There was no chance to ask Pa what she was doing here because both bombarded me with questions about the food, the music, the dancing, as if *I* was the visitor, not her.

'We're just off to the *Swan and Railway* for a Sunday dinner,' Pa said when they'd run of questions. 'See you later.'

I gave them time to close the door before turning on James. 'What's going on?'

He raised his head and gave me a sly look though I couldn't fathom its meaning.

'She arrived Friday and cooked our tea then went home. Saturday, she appeared without warning, did all the cleaning and cooking then she and Pa went out and came home drunk. Of course, she stayed the night. Today she's got her feet under the table and her head on his pillow. I kept my ears closed last night.' He finished by pulling a face.

'She's moved in! How…? Why didn't Pa talk to us first?'

'Do you need to ask? He let her. We've no say in the matter. He says it's his business and we should act like grownups.'

I was boiling mad, swinging from one idea to another. 'Do you think she waited until she knew I'd be out of the house?'

'Maybe,' James said. 'But the way I look at it there's naught to be done. Seems like Pa's ready to have another woman in his life.'

'But Clodagh Boyle!'

'She's passable in a low light.'

I stared at him, amazed. 'Maybe. But she's so…' The words I

wanted to say, *vulgar, loud,* sounded too snobbish. 'She drinks too much.'

'She'll help you around the house; you'll have less jobs to do. And less to complain about.'

I turned on him. 'You've changed your tune! A fortnight ago you were ranting about him spending beer money on her. And there's no call to be snide with me! I work nearly as many hours as you do then come home to keep house. How do you help apart from bringing in the coal?'

James shrugged. 'My advice is we keep out of their road as much as we can. Let them get on with it.'

I picked up the basket with my overnight things, went upstairs and flung myself on the bed. James said to keep out of the way but how did he expect that to happen in a house this small? He didn't have much imagination but he'd find out soon enough. I tried to picture our future. The most I'd seen of Clodagh was her broad back and strong arms hanging out the washing. We passed the time of day; she tossed me a few comments and now she was living in our house. How could Pa have done this without talking to us first?

I collared him the next day when he was alone. 'Isn't it a bit soon, Clodagh coming to live here? I wasn't even sure if you were walking out together. Why didn't you talk to us?'

He laughed, but it wasn't a merry sound. 'No need for walking out at our age. Her landlord was selling up and she didn't have a place to go to. She offered to take care of the house and there's nowhere else for her to sleep, is there? We'd had a good time on Saturday, she cheered me up and I didn't feel like sending her home.'

I protested that I was already doing all the housework, but he waved away my concerns.

'We get on and what's done is done. The two of us are old enough to know what we want so let's have an end to it.' Then his tone softened because he knew he'd been hard on me. 'I know she's nothing like your mother but try to be friends with her.'

'I will if she will,' I said in a low voice.

'That's my girl! You'll be fifteen soon, Jessie. It's time to stop thinking like a child.'

The conversation over, Pa went into the yard while I wrapped my shawl around my shoulders and left the front way. I walked the streets in a daze, scarcely taking in where I was going until I came to the park. Couples went arm in arm through the tall, iron gates. I followed them until I found an empty bench.

If it's what Pa wanted then I'd have to get used it, but I had no idea how. And what would my grandparents, Aunt Margaret, say about them living together, not married? Would they even speak to us? The gap that had grown between us and them would undoubtedly widen; perhaps too far for bridges.

14

SAM

273 Scholes: September 1895

I held no winning cards. All I could do was tell Agnes I was sorry, that we wouldn't starve because I was bound to find a job soon.

The truth was I was beginning to doubt my ability to persuade anyone to give me a chance. This would be my fourth day of tramping the streets. Over the last seventy-two hours I'd grown more despairing as each shop or office manager had shaken their head and turned me away. And there was no reprieve when I returned home empty-handed. For three days Agnes had plonked a plate of food in front of me, declared we could no longer afford puddings and must tighten our belts. Her sour face, her railing against my stupidity, continued every evening, even while she breastfed little Grace.

The sight of my daughter filled me with guilt and I determined I would rise even earlier to look for work. 'We won't go without food!' I retaliated. 'And we're not as badly off as some.' But in Agnes's eyes, we'd dropped several rungs down society's ladder in one afternoon.

. . .

I LEFT Pemberton Colliery a week ago for the last time. On the walk home, despite my indignation, and fearful at the enormity of what I'd done, a shiver of hope that this would be a turning point quickened my heart.

'I've handed in my cards,' I told Agnes as soon as I entered the house, seeing no point in delay. 'But I'm bound to find something else soon.' I'd expected shock, worry, but not the vast rage that poured down on me. At times I thought I might drown in it. She was utterly different from the woman I'd married last May.

'Which of us will go begging to our parents for the rent money?' She'd demanded.

I took a deep breath, and started to explain, but she wouldn't listen. She even put her hands over her ears and then continued to blast me. Hours later I found her sitting alone in the parlour, the fire unlit. I determined to get her to listen.

'Agnes, please don't block your ears to me. We'll get nowhere like that. Hear me out.' Her hands remained in her lap, but she refused to look up. 'Do you think I'd do something like this over a trivial affair? It was a matter of principle.'

'Go on then. Let's hear it.'

I ignored the scathing tone and began. 'Two brothers, Bill and Alf Flaxman, were the last into our cage. It wasn't until we were near the surface that I saw they hadn't secured the gate properly. Nine men could have plunged to their deaths through their carelessness so I took it up with the foreman, but the other men who'd come up with me wouldn't support me. The Flaxmans threatened them and they were scared. They're well-known as bare-knuckle fighters.'

Agnes lifted her head and stared out at the night sky. 'So you say, but that doesn't alter the fact that there's no wage coming in.'

I went to the window to draw the curtains; the brass rings jangled above my head. I turned to look at her. With a puff of breath, she'd blown away my explanation, and I'd always thought we shared the same values. I'd never felt so angry as I had when facing the foreman and hearing he was turning a blind eye. How could I have continued working for him, and alongside the Flaxmans, after that? Perhaps the deepest hurt was Agnes's lack of faith that I'd find other work. Countless times I'd told her I wouldn't always be a miner. Seems like she hadn't believed me.

Without another word, we went to bed and lay on the mattress like frozen logs. As I reached out for sleep, I wondered if our marriage would survive the week.

A FEW STREETS from a builder's yard where the owner had shaken his head at me, I spotted Emilie Chambres. It was a bustling shopping area, but she was easy to pick out amongst the more dowdily dressed women going about their business. Her red hat made a striking contrast against the black hair. We greeted each other warmly and she said that we must certainly take ourselves off to a teashop.

'What are you doing in this part of town?' I asked. The area we were in was about a half hour's walk from her great-aunt's shop.

'I will tell you when I have a mug of hot *chocolat* in front of me,' she smiled.

I knew of a decent place not far away and once we were seated she said she'd been visiting a warehouse as a favour for her aunt.

'The owner wanted to cheat me over the quality of his goods. He thought I knew nothing about fabrics, but I put him right. My aunt won't stand for second-best.' She sipped her drink and declared it wasn't *too bad*, then questioned me as to why I wasn't at work. I poured out my tale, hinting at the arguments at home.

'Sam! That is folly. Not to have work and you with a child.'

'I know, and Grace's not yet three months. Agnes wants a big family, but after this week...' I shook my head and let Emilie guess the rest.

She widened her eyes. 'Perhaps I can help; not with your marriage of course, but I might have some luck for you. My aunt is looking for an assistant for her Market Hall stall. It could be yours if you are quick. She wanted me to leave the shop and work there, selling pins and material, but I didn't agree. Aunt Adeline and me, we fell out about this move, though like today, I sometimes do errands for her,' and she gave the little twisted smile I remembered. 'I'm in a bakery now. I usually do an early shift so was able to visit the warehouse as well.'

The bakery had jumped at the chance of having her because she was French, with their sights set perhaps on fancy gateaux. I suspected she'd overstated her baking knowledge, as she had with other details of her life, but that wasn't my concern. The news about the stall was worth pursuing.

'I will introduce you to my Great Aunt if you want. It is better that way and will save time writing her a letter. You will find her manners very formal, Sam.'

I had all my certificates and letters of recommendation from my foreman and former teachers at the Miners' Institute with me, so we drank up and headed for the Market Hall. I was excited by the prospect ahead and ran through all the points I would put across in my favour.

'Great Aunt Adeline is working there today and as she dislikes it, preferring to be in the shop, I predict she will be interested in you.'

I knew the Market Hall well. Agnes had insisted we buy new crockery from there for our first home, but I'd never even glanced at Madame Chambres' stall. I had a moment's panic as we approached. Would her aunt want a *man* running it?

Emilie's relation was a tall thin woman with a white powdered face who gave me her gloved hand to shake. I was careful not to squeeze it too hard, imagining the hidden bony fingers. Her whole body looked as if it would snap apart in a strong breeze. She interviewed me with a mix of high-handed grandeur and sharp business sense. She studied my certificates in Accounting and Economics for several minutes, asked a few questions, but it was the long list of numbers to add up, percentages to deduct, that was the real test. I looked at her with no idea if I was suitable or not. By the end of the interview I realised her fragility was only physical.

'That all seems acceptable, Mr Dunbar,' she said, folding the paper I'd written on and putting it into her handbag. 'When would you be available to start your training? I can only offer you half a salary for that time. Do you accept?'

I looked at the pins and ribbons, the lengths of fabric I didn't know the names of lying on the counter. I thought of Father's reaction when he learned I'd left the pit and was working here as an alternative. Could I do it? The money was pitiful by comparison. I was about to shake my head and refuse when I saw Clodagh Boyle. She was weaving her way towards the haberdashery stall. When she recognised me behind the counter she pulled up slightly then proceeded on, a hard little smile on her face. A few weeks ago, I'd learned from Agnes's mother that she'd moved in with Patrick and the children. It had shocked me greatly, and so far, I hadn't been able to bring myself to call at the house.

'Good afternoon, Miss Boyle,' Madame Chambres said. 'Can I help you?'

For politeness' sake, I would have greeted her, but she got in first.

'Eh up, Sam. Didn't take you for a ladies' fashion sort of a man.' She picked up a piece of trimming, dandled it between her fingers then a few seconds later let it drop to the floor. 'No, thanks. I'll leave it for another day. I can see you're busy.' Her eyes gleamed with malice and with a flick of her head she swished her way towards a door leading to the street. Emilie muttered an oath, picked up the trimming and gave it to her aunt.

At a guess, Clodagh's gibe about me being *a ladies' fashion man* was an attempt to demean me because once, a while ago, I'd manoeuvred her into leaving the Gormans' house. I'd wanted to see Patrick on his own and hadn't understood why the washer-woman was hanging around. Now she was installed in Sarginson Street it was clear she'd set her sights on him early on: a good-looking man and a strong worker bringing home a top wage. His problem was that he was lonely, in need of company. It was easy to see how with a bit of flattery she might have wormed her way into his affections.

'*Rien*. It is nothing,' Madame Chambres said, speaking more to herself than to me. 'She never spends much and I don't care for the smell of gin on that one's breath.'

I agreed wholeheartedly though I kept that quiet. Madame Chambres then turned to me and her thin lips formed into a half smile. 'Now what do you say to my offer, Mr Dunbar?'

'I'll take it, thank you. And I can start tomorrow if that suits.'

Emilie, who had been hovering close by throughout the interview, looked pleased and said she'd be on her way. After a further few arrangements with Madame Chambres, I left too, determining to be a success. I would become a stallholder and learn all I could then... who knows? And I would not let the likes of Clodagh Boyle make my achievement seem trivial.

Despite my good news Agnes still fretted and questioned me about prospects. 'This wasn't what I'd hoped for when we married. I think you're being selfish.'

I stared at her, amazed. 'At least I won't lose my life selling

fancy goods! Is my safety nothing to you?' She had the decency
to look ashamed and so I relented and put an arm around her to
show she was forgiven. 'Buying and selling is what I want to do
now. I've waited years for this sort of chance.' I scooped up
Grace and cradled her in my arms. 'Daddy'll be able to find you
some pretty ribbons soon.'

'She's hardly got any hair to speak of,' Agnes scoffed. 'And
ribbons won't bring home the bacon.'

A stall was hardly better than working for the Rag Market in
her eyes.

In bed, a dark thought struck me. If I had died below ground
Agnes would have received some compensation. There was
nothing like that for a Market Hall trader. Less physical danger
of course, but risky financially.

Father said the same a day later when I told him about my
change of work — and several weeks on was still repeating the
foolishness of what I'd done. I managed Mother's sighs, my
brother George's and Pa's predictions of poverty during my
visits with as much humour and tolerance as I could muster.
The usual refrain was: *you have a child now. Shouldn't you have
thought about her first?* But in the heat of the moment, arguing
with the pit foreman about the Flaxman brothers, I'd thought
only of the wrongfulness of their attitude and the near disaster.
Of course, Grace was on my mind. She was the reason I'd
knocked on so many office and factory doors. Being a father
brought me more joy and satisfaction than I ever dreamed of,
but this wasn't something I could express. We didn't talk that
way in our family.

GOING to the Market Hall every day became something I looked
forward to: mainly because I could chat to both customers and
other stallholders without fear of reprimand. Conversations
with fellow colliers had often been pithy but frowned upon. We

were there to dig coal; discussion was kept for the pub. But since Agnes and the Towneleys disapproved of drinking, I'd given up having the occasional beer and become teetotal, like them. Then there was the stock. I relished learning about something so different. At the beginning, one blue cotton reel looked much like another so Madame Chambres told me to match the thread against lengths of material and that's when variations in shades became obvious. I learned too from customers who knew better than me which yarn was right for which material. An added enjoyment was picking up tips from other stallholders on how to sell.

The most mysterious aspect of the job, however, was fathoming how Madame Chambres's mind worked. That, and ways to keep her happy. Sometimes sales figures dropped: one week it rained without ceasing so fewer people were out of doors. And not long after I started, a colliery strike of several weeks kept the miners' wives away. I could do nothing about the weather, or strikes, but she still complained when she saw rows of descending figures. The hours were long, but thankfully new friends amongst the helpful stallholders kept me cheerful. I would have invited some of them to the house if I'd thought Agnes would have agreed.

A FEW MONTHS later I was able to carve out time to visit Sarginson Street. I should have gone sooner, but long days at work, and minding Grace, prevented it. If I was scrupulously honest, I was dreading seeing Clodagh Boyle installed in Mary's rocking chair. But with an evening free I'd run out of excuses. Besides, I hoped a positive reaction from Patrick about my new way of life would help counteract Agnes's negativity.

Jessie opened the door with a look of surprise that quickly turned into one of delight and her simple welcome confirmed that I'd done the right thing in coming. When I looked around the room and saw nothing had changed relief spread through me. Mary's rocker stood in the same spot near the fire; her red patterned curtains still hung at the window. Jessie saw me glancing around and I explained, 'I'm glad the room's no different.'

She raised her eyebrows a fraction as if querying me. 'Yes, same furniture but the arguments are new.'

'What do you mean?' It was unlike her to be obscure.

'Oh, Clodagh has different ways of doing things: the cleaning, cooking. What time to get up or go to bed.'

By the time she'd finished speaking, I was aware of subtle changes. Her face was still round and unformed, not yet that of an adult, but her air of resignation surpassed her years. How could this be? Only a few months had gone by since we'd last met. A wave of sadness ran through me as she described how Clodagh was always cross with her.

'I shouldn't complain or talk about her. Pa doesn't like it,' she finished. 'So no more of that. I want to know about Grace. When can I come and see her?'

I'd come to the Gormans with the intention of finding out how the family were faring. I'd learned a little, but with Jessie changing the subject I had to let it go. I said Grace was beginning to talk, told her how much weight she'd gained and her little funny habits. It was a joy to talk about my child to someone so interested and we arranged a day for her to spend time with her little cousin.

I asked how mill life was suiting her. It struck me that this was another big change in her life.

Jessie said she liked the friends she'd made at work but... 'One of the little piecers in the spinning shed got caught in the machinery last week. He was eleven years old and badly injured. Everyone's sad and bitter, even us in the weaving shed, though we didn't know him. Otherwise, it's the same day in, day out.' A shadow passed across her face that was gone in an instant. 'If I had more time, I'd take up studying, like you did. But I've not heard of such a thing, or place for girls to go to.' She blushed, embarrassed, I think, at revealing a secret longing, and slipped into the kitchen to make us a drink.

It was true that I'd saved my wages and grabbed what opportunities there were, but these had been for men, not girls Jessie's age. I racked my brains. I'd heard of craft courses for young women but that was about it.

'I'll lend you some books,' I said, 'and I'll keep my eyes open for studying properly. Things are changing all the time. Did you know, a woman qualified as a dentist this year?'

She shook her head then thanked me for the promised books. I didn't have a clue what a girl her age might read but decided she wouldn't go wrong with Mr Dickens. And she might like my Charles and Mary Lamb's *Tales from Shakespeare* which I'd read a good many times.

As I was preparing to leave, Patrick arrived in a mighty good humour. I stayed a while longer as he seemed pleased to see me, cracking jokes, wishing me well in my new venture, but changed the subject so rapidly I wondered if he'd absorbed everything I'd said. Jessie grew quiet and a pinched expression formed on her features, as if she were keeping something from both of us. Outwardly, my friend seemed in good spirits, but there was an air of desperation to him, a wildness that didn't bode well.

15

JESSIE

A YEAR LATER

Sarginson Street: September 1896

$\mathcal{O}$n a warm day in September, I took the longer route through the park over to Aunt Margaret's to benefit from the sun on my face. Time alone gave me the chance to think of all that had happened since her last birthday tea. I hadn't grown much in height but I felt quite different. We had someone outside the family living with us and because of it, my aunts' and grandparents' visits had dropped off. Despite this, when I was at their homes, they demanded to know what living with the washerwoman was like. I could have said she's a heartless stepmother and I'm her skivvy. But that would have been disrespectful and heap trouble upon me if Pa got to hear it secondhand. Just thinking about Clodagh angered me, and I stamped and crunched the innocent leaves under my feet.

'You can get away with doing that because you don't look sixteen,' Susan had joked last week whilst walking together. I was envious of the way she looked these days, so tall and slim, with her hair in a becoming style. She'd grown up a lot since starting work.

When I reached the house, Aunt Margaret ushered me into the sitting room. Aunts Rachel and Agnes, my grandparents, Uncle Nicholas with cousins Violet and Daisy at his feet, looked at me expectantly and the chatter I'd heard from the hallway quietened.

'What's this doing here?' Margaret smiled, pulling a crinkled leaf from my hair.

Flustered by the attention, I gave her my birthday card and watched as she tore open the envelope and stared at it in wonder. A surge of pride filled me. I'd saved my pennies for several weeks to buy the best card in the shop. She placed it in the middle of the mantelpiece where it made the others look paltry; though I shouldn't have thought that.

'It's beautiful, Jessie,' she said, giving me a swift kiss on my cheek.

'That looks expensive,' Aunt Agnes said, rising, picking it up and giving it a sniff.

The artist had painted a spray of violets in the left-hand corner. Three sides had lacey edging, and the main picture was of a river with swans. It was nobody's business how much it cost but it was the least I could do. Aunt Margaret had nursed me through influenza when I was eleven, sorted me out when my monthlies started and mopped up my tears when I quarrelled with Clodagh.

I was the last to arrive and soon the job of cutting up our grandmother's fruit cake got underway. I gathered with my cousins around the table, watching as the huge knife sliced into it. The little ones stood on tiptoe. Everyone, even the adults, hoped to find a tiny token in the slice we'd been given. Grandma Towneley had brought the tradition with her when she'd married. I kept my tokens from past birthdays in a special wooden box under the bed, sitting alongside Ma's cannel brooch and old birthday cards.

A lucky horseshoe, a coin for wealth and in my slice, a one-inch-high thimble which made a tinny noise as it fell onto my plate, were found right away.

'Ooh, Jessie,' Aunt Rachel said, 'maybe mother shouldn't have put that one in. It's unlucky for girls, isn't it? Means they won't get married. You know, spinster's thimble?'

'Nonsense,' Aunt Margaret said, coming up behind us. 'Tokens are just a bit of fun. I don't believe in superstition: thirteens, black cats, throwing salt.'

'Neither do I,' I agreed. All the same, I'd rather have found the coin, just in case.

'I'll swap you my horseshoe,' Aunt Rachel whispered in my ear so her older sister wouldn't hear her, 'because I'm walking out with someone.'

We younger ones peeled off and ate our slices together at the table. Everyone else congregated on chairs near the window. Aunt Agnes had the most comfortable seat because she was expecting another baby although I hadn't known about it until today. I half listened to the rise and fall of their voices, the more shocking the story the higher the pitch. When the last dreg of tea was poured, I offered to make some more. Ten minutes later, back in the sitting room, I found the gossip had switched to Pa.

...living together a year...no sign of wedding bells...our Mary...

The window group hadn't noticed my return. I felt like shouting...*Do you think me and James like being bossed around by that cow?* Mill language. Stuff I heard every day, and worse. I poured the tea with a shaky hand.

When Clodagh first moved in it was obvious she and Pa were having a good time. They shared jokes and chats at mealtimes, sometimes including me and James. But her two-faced nature soon appeared. Living with her was a daily round of complaints: *Don't sweep like that! Why've you got rid of the tea leaves I sprinkled over the doormat? Don't you know they soak up bits of dirt? The windows are filthy. Do them again!*

James fell under her scrutiny in different ways. When Pa was out of hearing she called him sly if he took a biscuit between meals. Said he was as thick as two short planks if he stuttered over a long word. A year on, she and Pa were rowing; mostly after they'd been to *The Griffin*. Once, I plucked up the courage to mention it but he brushed it aside.'All couples argue,' he'd said. But did they? I never saw it with Aunt Margaret and Uncle Nicholas.

Pa and Clodagh's bickering was a habit, like always buying fish and chips on Fridays. And when I thought about it, it was the way most folk in Pemberton lived.

I LEFT the birthday tea later than I normally would and judging by how much the sky had darkened, I guessed it was about eight o'clock. My mind was full of impressions from the visit: my little cousins wanting me to read to them, Aunt Agnes's piqued expression over my birthday card to her sister. The taste of fruit and spices in my mouth...

As I approached the house, I saw a woman on the doorstep, grey hair neatly pulled into a bun. From the slope of her shoulders and trim figure, I recognised her as Mrs Middleton. After a lifetime of nursing, she still treated people in the area for minor complaints. Perhaps Pa or James had come down with earache or stomach cramps. For anything serious, they'd send for a doctor. She turned when I called out a greeting, facing me squarely. Her face showed signs of exhaustion, and suddenly, I was worried.

'Jessie, as yer Pa's not here it'll be up to you to tell him,' she said, before I could ask what the trouble was.

'Tell him what?' I said, feeling more afraid.

'Clodagh Boyle's lost the baby, but she'll recover. It was only a few weeks old I reckon. I've had help clearing and washing the mess so there's nothing for you to do.'

I put a hand to my mouth almost choking in surprise. Agnes Middleton was here as a midwife, not a nurse.

'She was pregnant?'

'Aye, didn't they tell you? Well, I suppose it's their concern. It's a sad business so go easy on her. Though I don't know how you'd have managed with a babby in a house this small. You'd 'ave had to flit, I suppose.' Her stream of talk washed over me, but I needed the time to absorb the news.

In the front room, James was pretending to read a newspaper. I waited for him to speak but he didn't look up. Sighing, I made a cup of tea and took it upstairs. Clodagh lay in the bed wearing a clean nightgown, her face turned to the wall. I put the cup on a chair and waited. I tried to imagine what she might be feeling, but love, pregnancy... they were as alien to me as The Black Death.

'Mrs Middleton told me. I'm sorry...' Despite my innocence, I recognised suffering. Hadn't James and I lost our mother? 'Clodagh, can I bring you anything? Have you eaten? I can try to find Pa, if you like, bring him home.'

She didn't reply and her shoulders hunched together, drawing away from me.

Downstairs, I suggested to James that one of us go out to look for Pa. His eyes widened and I guessed he hadn't thought to make a search.

'Best not,' he said. 'He could be in any of two dozen public houses from here to Scholes. An' what if he comes home when we're still looking? There's naught we can do an' Mrs Middleton's fixed her up.'

James went to bed soon after but I waited up until tiredness overtook me and I went to my room. Only when I heard Pa opening the front door and come upstairs did I wake. From their room, across the landing, I heard low talk, sobbing, then silence.

Should I have persisted with Clodagh, stayed by her side?

She hadn't wanted my sympathy... or friendship when I'd offered it. All the same, I said a prayer for her.

IT WAS strange what people did to get over grief. After Ma died, Pa dug a hole and only climbed out for work, to visit us, or spend solitary nights at public houses. Grandma Towneley ate puddings and pies and got fat. James went mad for football, and I became chapel. Sometimes, memories from those days seemed like they'd happened last month, not years ago. Whenever I'd seen baby Kate at Aunt Margaret's, I'd wanted to yell while pretending to make a fuss of her. She was a sickly infant who didn't last long, and when she died, I couldn't sort out if I was glad or sorry. Not until Pa explained it wasn't Kate's fault Ma left us, did I begin to miss my baby sister.

AFTER THAT FIRST NIGHT, there was silence and no one mentioned the miscarriage. I was afraid to speak in case I upset anyone. About two weeks later, Clodagh disappeared and Pa said she'd gone to relatives in Yorkshire. The air in the house felt lighter and it encouraged me to tackle him. I chose a time when James was out. The fire crackled with occasional spits, as if arguing with itself. 'Will Clodagh be coming back?' I said in a small voice. My heart thumped like a mad thing as I waited for his reply.

'Not for a while,' was all Pa said.

'Perhaps that's good?' I left the question in the air, but when he didn't reply I pushed it. 'Pa, are you and she really getting on? Living with the two of you, well, it's like walking past those distorted mirrors at the fair which pull everyone's features out of shape so you don't know what's real and what isn't. And there are evenings when you're both too bright and loud, telling colourful stories, then the next day you're like a wet November. Me and James don't know how to act for the best.'

Pa looked at me with a tight face. 'You have your mother's way of expressing yourself, Jessie. It's a rare quality, but tonight I am not able to deal with such things.'

I picked up the skirt I was hemming and got up from the table. 'I'm sorry if I spoke out of turn, Pa, and sorry for... you know, about the baby. I just want things to go back to how they were before.'

He pushed his hair back off his face and ran his hands down his cheeks. 'You mean when your mother was alive?' His smile was twisted and not the broad grin I longed to see. 'They can't, love. It's not the way of the world. What's done is done. Clodagh's got a place here if she wants it. You're still too young to understand, and at my age, well, a baby...,'

He stood and briefly placed his arm around my shoulder before putting on his cap. He'd be off to the pub of course. But he was wrong. I did understand. He hadn't wanted a baby and Clodagh had.

WHEN SHE CAME BACK, she said nothing about her visit or the baby. It was as if there'd never been a pregnancy. She and Pa started going to the Music Hall and I was pleased, thinking they must be feeling a bit better. I waited to hear them laugh or recount the jokes they'd heard. But there was only the smell of beer, and a new tetchiness. To prove to Pa I could cope with the housework on my own if need be, I spent more time cleaning and cooking. After two weeks of slaving, I packed it in. It wouldn't make any difference. Pa wasn't going to tell Clodagh to leave.

JESSIE

Sarginson Street: December 1896

*P*ots from last night's tea and the morning's breakfast cluttered the table. I draped my work shawl over the back of a chair, kicked off my clogs, and stared at the mess. *Jessie'll clear those away,* said the voices in my head, and I listed the reasons why I shouldn't, and wouldn't.

It was winter now. Clodagh was recovered, had been back at work nearly three months. Today, she'd started her shift at noon so had been home all morning. There was no reason for her not to tidy up. I'd finished cleaning at Grandma Towneley's just before eight o'clock and now there was housework here. Despite the low level of light in the room, the congealed bacon fat gleamed on the plates. Out of habit I stacked the crockery then went into the kitchen. No sign of the water can. I wouldn't venture outside to search for it. Too dark to be floundering near the water pipe. In the front room I sat in Ma's rocker but it was hard to ignore the dirty plates on the table.

When the back door clicked open I sprang up with a sudden rush of energy and took a pile of plates into the kitchen.

Clodagh was pouring water from the tin into the sink to wash her hands after using the privy. I dumped the plates on the draining board in front of her.

'I've been at my grandparents' doing the cleaning there,' I said, using as mild a tone as I could muster. 'They rent a house with piped water. I wish we did but as we don't... you weren't on an early shift today. It would have been thoughtful if you'd done all this instead of leaving them for me.'

Her eyes become slits. I was used to that but the raised hand was unexpected. It slammed into the side of my head like a hammer blow.

'Take that, you little gob-shite,' she yelled. I clutched my stinging ear and cheek. It felt like I'd walked into a brick wall. 'I won't take lip from no one, especially not a sixteen-year-old.'

I ran into the yard clutching my burning face. I leant against the gate, shivering without the comfort of a shawl. Taking deep breaths, I closed my eyes. I should have known better than to cheek her.

Next day when Pa came home bleary-eyed, his shoulders sagging from being underground, he flicked off his braces and began the ritual of washing his face and neck. After he'd towelled himself dry I told him what she'd done. His face fell and he sighed.

'Did you say something to provoke her?'

'Sort of.'

'Jessie! Please... try not to for both our sakes. I'll have a word with her.'

He looked so miserable that my anger fluttered away and I crept upstairs. Later, I stoked the fire of my complaint as I stretched out on the bed. I hadn't been that rude, just blunt. Hardly a slapping offence. But telling tales got me nowhere. Nothing changed! I punched the pillow and let my head flop down. What was the alternative? Be more understanding? Was she still upset about the miscarriage? I didn't think so. Finally, I pondered on what our minister might advise. *Guard your tongue,* probably.

THE KNOCKER-UPPER HAD LONG GONE. Chair legs scraped on the floor downstairs; voices rumbled as the family got ready for work. I should have been making the porridge, but I wasn't because my legs, every part of my body and mind, wouldn't let me. When the bedroom door creaked ajar I felt a shadow fall over me and I squeezed my eyes tight. I heard her noisy breathing. I wanted to slip beneath the blanket but I didn't dare move. Then she left.

'What's up wi' her?' I heard her say from the landing. Pa grunted something before opening my door. After she clattered downstairs he entered my room. I turned over. His eyes bore into mine.

'I'm not well,' I whispered. 'Get Willie Gallagher to tell them in the weaving shed.'

He cleared his throat but it was still husky. 'Clodagh thinks you're malingering but I see you're not. Take yer time to get better. I'll deal with her if she complains. An' I'll call on Willie. See you this evening.'

After he left, tears dripped down my face. Sleep came and I only woke when I heard the factory hooter wailing at the start of the midday break, a dismal sound even when you felt cheerful. I looked at the purple bruise on my cheek in the cracked mirror when I went downstairs.

Next morning, I dragged myself into work and everyone thought I was recovered.

THE FOLLOWING WEEK, I attended a meeting at the manse where I chose a seat at the end of a row of four other people. It was a much larger house than any in Sarginson Street and every time

I went there I wondered why Reverend Schofield and his wife didn't make the most of their parlour. The talk and lantern slides seemed to go on forever. To pass the time I selected the ugliest items in the room to dispatch to an imaginary scrap heap. First of all the brown curtains and the carpet. Losing them would cheer everyone up. I imagined replacing them with something highly patterned, like a carpet I'd once seen illustrated in a newspaper. We'd come to the manse to learn about missionary work in British East Africa. The other people were older than me and involved in fundraising. I was only there because I wanted to speak to the minister in private.

At the end of the talk, I let everyone pile out of the room before I tackled him. With a barely concealed sigh, he asked me to sit down again. He'd probably had a long day too, but I'd steeled myself.

'There's something wrong with me,' I burst out. 'I'm scared of getting out of bed. Nothing seems normal. I hate my home and I've taken the pledge.'

He breathed in noisily and wiped his spectacles. 'You've kept this well hidden, Jessie. I hear you've had a change of circumstances this year. Your father has a... shall we say... a companion now?'

I nodded. 'They got on well until she lost an early baby, but it's all drink and argument nowadays. I can't stand it, an' I have to do most of the housework.' I didn't mention the slaps but perhaps he guessed from the fading bruise on my face.

'You must try to do your duties as God would wish, Jessie, and if the unpleasantness is too much to bear, then perhaps you could look for a position out of the home.'

I didn't follow his meaning and must have looked blank because he reached for a newspaper on the table and spread it open. 'Here, for instance, are openings for young people. Large houses on the outskirts of town advertise for girls to work in them.'

I saw columns of print. A word jumped out — *maidservant*. Reverend Schofield was suggesting I go into service somewhere in the country. A minute later I let him guide me out into the hall and he opened the door. There was no maid at the manse to do it for them.

'Thanks, I'll think about it.' And I did for the time it took to imagine being scolded by a cook, or a ladyship in a house where snooty footmen, stiff as brushes, stood outside doors, all for half the wage I got.

When I reached home I got out my Bible and read about suffering and how it built up character. I fell onto my knees: 'Give me strength, for Pa's sake. Show me ways to protect James, even though he's at Pemberton Pit and doing a man's job.'

I suppose God knew where James worked but I had to ask. Of the two of us, my little brother was the most like soft cheese without a rind.

PART III

THREE YEARS LATER

17

JESSIE

Central Methodist Church, Wigan: late October 1899

*B*eyond the heavy door the church smelt of old paper and disturbed dust. A red-faced groomsman tiptoed up and offered me a hymn book which I grasped with my left hand. The right one still ached from Clodagh's twist. I'd given up complaining to Pa about minor injuries because she always denied them. If I did say something, he would be faced with a dilemma: support me and all hell would break out. I hoped my injury would be less painful before I began work on Monday.

'Are you bride's side, Miss?' the groomsman asked.

'Yes, I am.'

He pointed me to the left side of the aisle. 'There's room at the front for a little-un.'

I gave him a snappy *thank you*, bridling at the mention of my height. I knew at least a dozen girls shorter than me. Five-foot-two wasn't so small in Wigan. In the back pews, a dozen or so guests were craning their necks towards the door, anticipating the arrival of Aunt Rachel in her finery. I felt I should apologize as I walked past: *sorry, it's only me; Jessie Gorman.*

For devilment, I looked for a space to sit amongst the groom's relations but all the pews on his side were full. Then I spotted a gap near the front, behind my grandparents, and slipped into it. Grandma Towneley was wearing a mauve, velvet hat which rose in folds to a small peak. A proper mother of the bride, she was. Must have saved for months for it. The organist struck up with *Love Divine All Loves Excelling* but the hymn could hardly be heard above the chatter of the congregation. I smoothed down my Sunday skirt, lowered my head and prayed that God would still my soul, and that no one would say anything nasty about Pa. When I opened my eyes Grandma was looking over her shoulder at me.

'Hello Jessie. On your own?' She cocked her head right then left, searching for Pa and James, knowing they'd accepted the invitation.

I leaned towards her. 'Pa couldn't make it… you know how he is. They'll be at the wedding meal though.' I smiled to ward off her misgivings. She smelt of mints and sweat; probably nerves on account of the day.

'Didn't I tell you, Edward?' She nudged my granddad's elbow. 'Their Patrick can't bring himself to come to a Methodist wedding after all.'

My face flushed. I wanted to say that wasn't exactly true but then the first chords of the *Wedding March* struck up.

OVER PORRIDGE THAT MORNING, Pa said his piece while I spooned my share into a bowl. I'd added a bit of sugar to the pan as that's how we all liked it and kept some back for Clodagh. There'd be trouble if I didn't, though it would be cold by the time she arose. He cleared his throat, usually a warning he was about to say something I didn't want to hear.

'I won't be at the wedding. Now don't look at me like that, Jessie. I'm not feeling up to it so leave it be.'

I pushed my bowl away though it was only half-finished. Why did nothing work out how I imagined it would? The three of us walking in harmony to the service and afterwards, catching up with Ma's family, pressing our little cousins against us to judge how much they'd grown. I turned to James who slouched over the table, spooning more porridge into his mouth before barely swallowing the previous mouthful. He didn't have Pa's tangled thoughts about entering the church where Ma used to worship. There was still a chance he might accompany me. I put on my best wheedling voice to lighten his sulky face.

'What about you, James? You'll come, surely?'

'He's told me he won't,' Pa interrupted. 'He'll be along later for the wedding meal, we both will. I'll make sure of it.' His smile was so wide and agreeable that you'd have thought there was nothing wrong with the world. But I knew better. Pa could never hide the haunted look in his eyes from me. My throat tightened with disappointment.

'Can't James speak for himself? Look at him! Sixteen years old and eating like a savage; scared someone will snatch the bowl from his hands.'

James flung back his chair. It made a horrible grating noise on the flag floor then he stalked into the yard. Never a big talker, his conversation could be fitted into his back pocket. I was sure I hadn't been like that. Only boys had time and chance to indulge in moods. Clattering the pots into the sink, I plunged my hands into the cooling water. At least the bowls didn't need a lot of scrubbing: there'd been little time for porridge crusts to form. It would be awkward going to the wedding on my own, not having seen any of Ma's relations for a while. And the longer I left it, the harder it became when we did meet. At least Aunt Margaret, who blew all kinds of nonsense out of a window, would be there. She understood, though no one else did, that Pa didn't want to sit beside me in the church where Ma had sung. And according to Grandma, I was the spit of my mother.

Clodagh had not been included in the invitation. She could barely read but knew enough to see that her name wasn't on the card. Talk about spit and fire! I didn't mention the forthcoming wedding at home though I wanted to talk about it; something to look forward to. But bravery wasn't cheap when you didn't know where the next slap would land. I was astonished that Clodagh even believed she'd be invited knowing the Towneleys' views: *Methodists get married first. They don't live in sin.* More like enduring in sin, these days.

WHEN THE WEDDING service was over, most of the congregation trooped outside. Remaining in my pew with my head bowed, I knew I wouldn't be interrupted. Methodists don't think twice about a girl wanting to pray. The harmonium gave a final wheeze and through the gap between my fingers, I saw the organist disappear. I straightened my back and breathed deeply. Chapel scent. The smell gave the place away: cold stone, flowers, and dust. Motes caught in a shaft of sunlight circled above my head. And silence fell like summer rain, reeling me in.

Drop Thy still dews of quietness till all our strivings cease. I whispered the lines of a favourite hymn I'd turned into a prayer. The sounds of the words reminded me of water. Not the deadness of the canal, but Spring showers, or the sea; the shush and feel of waves lapping my feet. When a full congregation sang it, my heart swelled until I thought it would burst: like having a present you ached for but never thought would come your way. *Take from our souls the strain and stress... O still small voice of calm.*

I thought of my aching wrist, the taunts, the clouts, and Pa's gloom. I wiped my eyes and walked down the aisle. I would put away sad thoughts, enter the church hall to find Pa and James and laugh and joke with Susan who was related to the groom.

Not least, my stomach was rumbling. I could almost smell the hot pies keeping warm in the church hall stove.

Close to the main door and hanging on a wall was a tapestry picture from a Bible story: *Suffer the little children to come unto me.* Yellow-haired kiddies sat on grass or clambered over Jesus. Before Ma died, when I was only a part-time Methodist, I'd asked her who had stitched it. I must have been six or seven and it would have been the chapel's turn to see us. The following week we'd be at St Cuthbert's where Pa worshipped. Neither the priest nor the minister liked our parents' arrangement, but nothing they said made any difference. Ma was a clever woman despite not knowing how to write.

'I don't know who stitched it,' she laughed, 'but it's obvious they've never been to Palestine. You won't see any fair-haired children there.'

When I stretched my memory to recall her features she was often a blur, but the sound of her voice and laughter still rang clear. That, and the smell of lavender on her clothes.

'But we aren't fair either,' I'd said, trying to work it out.

Pa joined in the conversation. 'No, we aren't and better still none of you are starving or have rickets.'

My next question, of course, was 'why?' Before Ma died, I had bags full, and Pa was always in fine humour.

'Pitmen like me, your uncles and your grandfathers, put food on the table, Jessie, so you can grow up healthy and strong. Coal mines are filthy, dangerous places to work in, but we're the highest-paid working men in the county.'

Conversations like those had become as rare as Wigan roses. Killed by drink, and Clodagh's demands to clean, cook, or get out of the road. When it came to my turn to be wed there'd only be a woman glad to be rid of me. I opened the chapel door with my good hand, stepped outside and was dazzled by the sunlight. It warmed my cheeks and I determined not to think of Clodagh.

I would enjoy the wedding party because *she* wasn't going to be there.

To one side of the chapel was a small border, empty now, but in Summer, yarrow and big yellow daisies grew in it. A man sat on the wall with his back to me. Being short-sighted, he was too far away to make out, but when he turned around there was no mistaking him.

'Pa! Have you come to fetch me?' I ran down the path. Closer up I saw he'd washed, shaved and taken care with his clothes. He dropped his cigarette stub and ground it on a paving slab with his foot.

'So this is where you're hiding! Prefer praying indoors to a party do ye? I'm glad to see you're wearing your mother's best brooch for the occasion.'

I touched the neck of my blouse where the black cannel was pinned. 'No, I just wanted a bit of peace and quiet before. It'll be bedlam in the hall. I'm sorry to drag you away from it.'

He looked down and brushed back a lock of hair. 'I haven't been over as a matter of fact. When I met your minister on the road he said you were still inside, so I decided to have a smoke out here and ended up thinking about your mother.'

I blinked but said nothing. The look in his eyes told me he was far from celebrating.

'How she loved to sing her little heart out over here while we were warbling away at St Cuthbert's.'

His talk came easy, like silk slipping through his hands. I dug my fingernails into my side. It wasn't always this way and I prayed the gloom wouldn't descend. When he visited Ma's grave he could be sunk in misery for hours.

'Let's be having ye away to the wedding feast,' I said, changing the subject and holding out my hands for him to take. I tried imitating his speech as a tease, wanting to see him smile. 'Though there'll be no beer o' course, but there is a pub next door.' Joking about his drinking habits was a risk but he seemed to be in a good temper. 'Pa?' I was close enough to breathe in the coal dust smell of him which lingered on his skin despite the weekly baths. For a moment his eyes creased in amusement then grew teary.

'Sorry, love. I just can't do it. You go over to the church hall and have a good time. There'll be too many memories, seeing all her relatives. Give my apologies will ye?'

He pulled his hand from under mine and shook his head before walking away. I stared after him. He looked so handsome in his best clothes, like a new-made shiny penny.

THE HALL WAS ALREADY sharp with the smell of bodies and egg sandwiches. I hung my coat up and glanced around. Babies, children running around; their cries pierced my ears. I wondered how anyone could stand it. A gas lamp cast a low, sickly light on those sitting beneath it. Chairs were placed around small tables, bagged by older folk. On a longer trestle at the far end my Aunt Rachel leant against her new husband; allowed to, now they were wed. Her bouquet was at least a foot long, jutting out over the teacups making a gaudy splash of pink and blue against the white tablecloth. The family spotted me on my own and soon nudges and whispers passed down the line; no doubt wondering where Pa was. I'd give his apologies, but later. Gossip flowed faster than the River Douglas about Patrick Gorman and I felt a prickle of sweat under my armpits just thinking of it. But I saw that nothing could dim my grandmother's pride; beaming like a lighthouse because her youngest daughter had married a grocer. And Graham could afford a honeymoon in a Llandudno boarding house.

The pies were brought out on a tray, all golden and crusty, and I took one to an empty table. It dripped with meat juice and for a long moment I thought of nothing except the pleasure of eating. Through a gap in the crowd, I saw Aunt Margaret aving and laughing and wondered if I had juice running down my chin. She often said that she and Ma were the closest of the sisters and it warmed me to think of it. I hoped she'd come over but a young man with a bristling moustache appeared, blocking my view. He handed me a glass of lemonade off his tray. No worry or embarrassment at refusing alcohol today.

'It doesn't mean you're going to be like *her* if you have a beer,' Susan said when I vowed never to touch a drop. That was three years ago. Since then we had moved up in the world and were now employed as trainers in the weaving shed, but drink still scared me. Pa and Clodagh liked the taste uncommonly well, but they weren't Methodists.

Pie finished, fidgeting and wanting distraction, I walked over to look at a picture hanging on a wall: a print of Queen Victoria painted about forty years ago. It threw me back to another wedding where the same image had hung in a different room. A room above a pub at a Catholic wedding for friends of Pa. Eight years old, too small to see the Queen properly, Pa had lifted me up for a better view. He'd have done anything for me on the day I nearly died. This picture hung at my eye level. Looking at it, a ridiculous notion popped into my head and I stifled a giggle; the small coronet perched on top of the Queen's smooth brown hair bore a strong resemblance to the bandstand in Mesnes Park. Don't people say laughter's infectious? Maybe I caught a whiff of it from the past: those long-ago whoops and cheers ringing out, fiddle music, the smell of beer, James and his friends running around like wild things.

And then I saw him; as if the thought had conjured him up. James, lounging against a wall halfway down the room, eyeing a couple of seated girls his age. I guessed he was too shy to approach them. My heart softened despite the morning's tiff. I would go to him, and encourage him to say *hello* to them. He wasn't a bad-looking lad. Handsomer than many. But then his face darkened and he looked down. Irritation, and then sadness filled me. Would he and I ever get it right?

A woman laughed; a harsh, suggestive cackle.

I spun on my heel. James wasn't frowning at me but at Clodagh who was clinging to the door frame. An elderly couple, groom's side, squeezed past and tutted. Could you blame them? Lord! With her stained skirt, hair untidy as a hay bale, she looked as if she'd slept under a hedge. Why she was so proud of that mop was beyond me. I touched my plait, wound around the back of my head. Was she going to block the doorway all afternoon? One of us would have to persuade her to move. I willed James to come over but he seemed intent on finding another way out. He strode to the back of the hall and spoke to a waiter who pointed to a door. James dashed through it like a rat down a hole. I sighed, but it was without blame. Clodagh was Pa's responsibility, not ours. All the same, I braced myself.

She was chatting to a scruffy sort of man as if he were her best chum. Perhaps he'd followed her from the public house. Then she opened her mouth and let out a belch which the nearest dozen people must have heard.

''Twasn't me, 'twas was my food,' she cracked, rubbing her belly.

'Beer, more like,' her companion laughed.

'I was stocking up against the famine I knew'd be 'ere.'

'Then you'll have plenty to spare for me, love, won't you?' And he gave her a leery grin.

'Aye, but you'd better get in there quick before my feller finds out. He's a taste for it his self.'

A stout, red-faced woman appeared behind them. 'Care to introduce me to your *friend*, husband? I wondered where you'd disappeared to.'

Under the open coat, her buttoned blouse strained against her chest. She grabbed her man's arm and yanked him outside.

'He'll be back,' Clodagh laughed.

She hadn't seen me and I wondered how I could get rid of her before the minister, or worse, my grandmother, heard her lewd chatter. Why were men drawn to her? According to mill gossip, she wasn't short of followers despite living with Pa. Was it this kind of talk which attracted them? It wasn't unfamiliar. During meal breaks, when chatter turned in that direction, I followed our minister's advice and closed my ears. He'd be scandalised by the swearing we heard every day. I was used to it, but it had shocked me at first, hearing only mild oaths at home.

Then I saw Susan in the doorway, bobbing up and down, wondering how to get past Clodagh. I stood on tiptoe and waved to encourage her to push through, but she shrugged and pulled a face. She knew about the slaps. With no alternative, I held myself as straight as I could and walked towards the door. In a pleasant voice, I asked Clodagh if she could let Susan through. She'd been too caught up in her bawdy conversation earlier to pay attention to anyone. Now, with her friend dragged away, she fixed her eyes on me, shook her fist and lurched from the doorway.

'Wassa bluddiell yerdoin inmeclobber?'

Leaving me no time to gather my wits, she grabbed my plait and pulled my head down. I tried prising her off, but she was what, five…six…inches taller than me? My wrist ached as I tried to battle against her. Amidst the tussle, I glimpsed Susan's distressed face. Suddenly, the fabric of a man's dark jacket pressed against my cheek. Whoever he was, he seized Clodagh's hands and wrenched them off me. Oh, the relief…I felt like I'd been scalped. I sank into a chair and held my head; my heart thumped like a mad thing. She'd done this at home, but never in public. Shame flooded through me because the world, at least the Methodist one, knew what went on in the Gorman household. And all because she thought I was wearing her clothes. My God! I'd rather die than wear one of her frights. I smoothed down my blouse with trembling hands before looking up to see who'd rescued me.

For a moment I didn't know where I was. Had Clodagh's grip on my head disturbed something in my brain? Past and present collided in a rush of memories – *I was eight years old sitting on a hard pavement – a man picked me up and I saw my mother's face over his shoulder.*

Susan, or someone, pushed a glass of cold water into my hand. I took and drank it without stopping. The room settled, and I came back to myself. I touched my blouse to make sure the cannel brooch hadn't fallen off and tried to pin up my hair.

Sam Dunbar. There were small changes: he was a little narrower in the face, and had a wrinkle or two. Not noticeably fatter. Still good-looking with those clever eyes. What was it? Two years since we'd last met? I'd lost my childish roundness, grown a couple of inches. What else? Pa said I looked more like my mother every day.

18

SAM

The Market Hall: November 1899

*U*nless they were the musing, wandering type, most people didn't notice or care about the Market Hall's more subtle qualities, only observing that it was airy, had a high glass roof and numerous iron pillars. But they missed a lot by not taking in its smells. The cheese, fruit, and meat stalls on the right-hand side of the market had a definite tang — of salt, damp earth, and animal. On the other side you inhaled glue, leather, wood, and cotton, evidence of the wares sold there. Mixed in with these smells, especially near the entrances when the wind was in the wrong direction, was the choke of coal smoke. Over the last four years, I'd watched shoppers hurry from crockery to grocery, end up at confectionary, and then leave the building without a twitch of a nostril.

It was a pity they did so, I once said to Agnes. But her look of amazed despair at my foolishness made me drop the subject, unable as she was to respond to such simple delights. It was a symptom of how much we'd changed: a failure to recapture the closeness of our early days. I think it was why we threw ourselves into being parents. My love for my girls went some way towards what I'd lost with Agnes.

I'd been on my feet since opening time, mainly selling ribbon, elastic, or thread; goods which only brought in coppers. Around ten o'clock a customer asked about material for a child's coat, which was more like it.

'You won't get this sort of quality at that price anywhere else,' I told her, shaking out a few yards of green gabardine. 'Go on, feel it.' I didn't know her name though she often bought from me. Young, but not the type to spill her woes to a market stall holder, like some I could mention. I fancied she was married to a clerk or an underling in a bank judging from the scarcity of her hat trimming. There wasn't much width to her coat sleeves either; should have been when leg o' mutton was all the rage. I looked across at Alf pottering about on his clog stall and willed him to look in my direction. If I asked nicely maybe he'd fetch me a mug of tea. He usually went about this time. The young wife picked up the brown and examined both fabrics, seeming perplexed over the choice. She caught me staring and blushed.

'I want to make my little boy a new coat for my sister's wedding,' she said. 'I'm hopeless with colours. What do you think?'

'What colour is your son's hair?'

'Reddish-brown.'

I heard a hint of pride in her voice. 'Then buy the green. It'll show him off to best advantage.' I told her the price, took her money, and wrapped the material. 'I hope you have good weather for the wedding,' I called after her.

The sun had come out for Rachel, to everyone's joy. We'd seen the newlyweds since then, of course, the Towneleys being keen on family gatherings. Their mother declared roundly that it had been an unforgettable day. And knowing her as well as I did, I was sure she had several reasons in mind. The ceremony

.s everything it should have been, but not that awful business .n the hall afterwards.

I tried to put it out of my mind, but the sight of Clodagh Boyle gripping Jessie's head was impossible to banish. I still had shivers of rage when I thought of the lass trying to fix her tousled hair, her fingers shaking as she pinned it up. I'd almost asked if I could help before I saw how inappropriate that would be. When she'd finished she looked pale but calm. I noticed she wore the cannel lily brooch. The sight threw me to the past and memories of the last weeks of Mary's life. Then Agnes appeared.

'Amy's with mother, asleep,' she said, her lips pursed in a way I knew well. 'And will you stop Grace and Helena from eating any more cake before they make themselves sick? Thank the Lord that woman's gone. I had to turn the girls' faces away so they wouldn't see anything.' She looked down at Jessie who was still sitting where I'd left her. 'It's a sorry state of affairs your father's got himself into with that woman. Wasn't he supposed to be here with you?'

Jessie looked up but I couldn't read her expression.

'Yes, Aunt, I wish he had been but he couldn't face it. He didn't know if he'd be welcome.'

I started to say, *of course, he would be*, but Agnes's flushed face contradicted me. Jessie had discomfited her. My mind raced: defending Patrick or Jessie now would only bring down Agnes's judgement on me at home. But I would try to make it up to the Gormans, somehow. My promise to Mary always hovered in my mind whenever I saw her children, especially Jessie.

A WHIFF of perfume on the air banished thoughts of my unfulfilled promise and I readied myself for the meeting. My employer was early today and her scent always arrived before she did, reminding me more of dead lilies than something expensive she said she'd bought in Paris.

'Good morning, Madame Chambres. Let me open the latch for you.'

'*Merci*. I hope you are prepared, Mr Dunbar. Here are my notes. I expect your takings to match my expenditure for this week.'

After all this time I still winced at her accent: a mix of refined Wigan and French. She wore a tailored jacket I hadn't seen before: a good quality maroon; a ready-made from her shop in Mesnes Street, no doubt. Agnes would have loved to select her own clothes that way. Madame Chambres still caked powder on her cheeks and was as gaunt as the day she interviewed me. What was it Emilie once said? 'My Great-Aunt only wears rouge when she goes out in the evenings.'

I couldn't imagine that red cheeks would improve her appearance, but how would I know? Meetings with me were always in the daytime and I'd never been inside her flat above the shop. I was allocated half an hour on Saturdays between eight and twelve. Four years we'd played this game.

I shook her hand; it was a business meeting after all. But why we had to do it in full view of the customers, I could only guess. It didn't take long because I'd made sure everything would be in order and when the last farthing was accounted for Madame Chambres prepared to take her leave and unfurled her umbrella.

'The stall is doing well this month, Mr Dunbar, so I want to introduce some new fabrics and various items for the ladies of Wigan. Expect a delivery very soon. *Au revoir*, luncheon is waiting. Give my regards to your wife.'

I watched her sail down the market aisles, nodding to some of the older, established stallholders, then out into the street. I remembered my *luncheons* as a pitman, sitting in the dark eating a jam butty, cheese, on a good day. If my employer weren't such a snob, I'm sure I'd have been a success working in her shop. I'd applied a year ago when there was a vacancy and was given the ise that I would do better to remain here. The thought of arning about business first-hand rather than reading about it .rom correspondence courses, had excited me. It would have been a step up. I would no longer have been the butt of my brothers' and father's jokes. *Selling pins and ribbons isn't men's work.*

Agnes didn't exactly share their view, but she couldn't help getting in a dig from time to time. 'We'd have been more prosperous if you hadn't left the mine,' she'd say.

Since making that initial decision, I'd learned my lesson. I didn't argue or contradict her on the subject. Something had died between us during that period, and it wasn't a time I cared to dwell on.

It had taken patience and a change in attitude to get used to Madame Chambres' high-handed ways. But sometimes, when Agnes asked how my day had gone, I did voice a complaint.

'Switch stalls,' she'd say, or 'move to another town.'

Of course, I made enquiries, more than once, and always received the same answer. To convince her, I passed on the information, word for word. 'They say there's no point going somewhere else when I don't have the capital. And Wigan Council will only let their current empty stalls to food sellers.' But that didn't stop Agnes from asking the same set of questions every year. It was clear that my wife chose not to listen to me for much of the time, but I suppose I was equally at fault.

During a slack period around four o'clock when I was drinking a mug of tea and flicking through the newspaper, a boy of about thirteen, a miniature fellow in a jaunty bowler and waistcoat, sauntered up to the stall and waggled an envelope under my nose.

'Are you Mr Samuel Dunbar?' he said in a fake important voice.

'Yes, what's it to you?'

'Nothing!' The office boy replied smartly and with a flick of his wrist he threw the envelope onto the counter where it slipped between two rolls of cambric. I slid my hand between them to extract it. When I looked up, the lad was strolling down the aisle peering at the stalls. No doubt the jumped-up little tyke was taking his time going back to work. I tore open the envelope and unfolded a sheet of heavy, cream paper. *Messrs Ratcliffe and Bibby, Solicitors, King Street*, was printed at the top. And there was a flimsier piece of paper still inside the envelope. When I pulled it out and saw the loops and curly writing of a banknote for fifty pounds, I almost fell flat on my face.

My hands shook as I picked up the solicitor's letter, never having dealt with such people before. Around me, the market hummed: soft chatter, clanking tins, the rustle of wrapping paper. The noise of my everyday life. The vibrancy of the morning trade had faded and I took advantage of the lull.

Dear Sir... Solicitors for the late Florence Holdsworth of York House, Parbold,... in her will of September 1895... I hereby enclose...

A *will?* My first thought was disbelief: Mrs Holdsworth couldn't be dead. Why, she was a similar age to my parents. I felt a sudden ache of sadness for the past. Holdsworth – a name once familiar and so dear it could have been tattooed on my chest. Images of Lydia and Daniel, their parents, flickered through my mind, none of them seeming quite real. So long ago and yet Lydia's mother had remembered me, hadn't forgotten what went before. My eyes jumped from one sentence to another... *a sudden heart attack...* until I reached the end... *a bequest of fifty pounds.* I slumped onto the stool I kept behind the counter. Hardly able to believe her generosity I reread it then turned the envelope over. *Number Three, The Whelley.* The only address the Holdsworths would have for me. Mother must have sent the office boy over here thinking it important. She wasn't wrong.

Thank you, Mrs Holdsworth! I breathed. *I'm sorry you're not here to know how much this means.*

,he sound of pottery crashing to the floor jolted me back to
ɟ surroundings. I ducked my head around the stall. At the end
ɔf the aisle, people were picking up broken china: a hazard you
didn't get with fabric or clothes. I returned to the letter, full of
questions. Perhaps Mrs Holdsworth had known my circumstances, made enquiries about me before making her will.
Running a market stall wasn't the kind of work she'd had in
mind for me when I used to visit *York House*.

I looked at the market clock fixed to a pillar. Another two
hours before I could close up and go home to tell Agnes. She
wouldn't be able to stop talking about it; would spread the news
amongst her family. Like me, she'd see it as a way of moving up
in the world. I looked around, worried someone might have
seen me with the banknote, but the aisles were empty. Was it a
good idea to tell her now or should I wait until I'd thought how
the money might best serve our family? Agnes would want to
rent a bigger, better house, but what good would that do us in
the long run?

I sat down again and pushed the envelope into my pocket,
picked up a cotton bobbin and rolled it back and forth. A stall of
my own was in my reach. I would be free to buy whatever stock
I chose. Arrange it to *my* liking. The bobbin rolled towards the
counter edge and I leant across to grab it. I'd have to find
another stall of course. This one wasn't up for lease and as there
were no more available it would mean travelling every day —
Leigh, Bolton, St Helens — they all had Market Halls. I slotted
the bobbin back in its box and frowned. Something about the
plan irked me. Was it the thought of going to a new town? I
didn't think so...then it dawned. There were other things I
could do with the money. All the reading and studying I'd done
over the years could be put to better use. But what?

19

SAM

273 Scholes: later that evening

𝓜 y high spirits wavered a little when I entered the house to find it empty and cold. No matter, I would make good use of the time while Agnes and the girls were out. I assumed they were eating with her parents. Patting my top pocket where the solicitor's letter lay, I went upstairs. From under the bed I pulled out a small suitcase, dusted it off and unlocked it with a tiny key I kept on my fob. I drew out a bundle of old letters on which I'd written the date *1889-1890*. The writing paper between my fingers had softened with age. I'd never examined my reasons for keeping them, but perhaps it was time I did.

York House
Parbold
February 13ʰ, 1890

Dear Mr Dunbar,

te in the expectation that a letter from me at this point in our
ʝuaintance will not surprise you. What I have to say cannot be said
ʝuring one of your regular visits as you are almost always in the
company of my son or daughter. Perhaps you have some inkling as to
the reason for my need for privacy?

Mr Holdsworth and I are concerned for Lydia's future. In the past we
have seen her many passions dwindle to ash with a new one appearing
as soon as the old one has been thrown on the fire. Unlike my husband,
I was rather hoping the same would happen to her art studies in
Manchester, but she seems fairly set on completing them. In the present
circumstances, we are happy enough to let her continue. What she
plans to do once they are completed we do not know. She has
mentioned Paris.

But it is the personal that I wish to address. Lydia has made no
pretence about her preference for you as a companion; a suitor even,
though she has evaded all my attempts to persuade her to speak plainly
on the matter. She is of age and by law can choose any husband she
wants but as her parents, and her only source of financial support, we
are concerned as to the kind of future for you both if you were to
marry. I trust to your intelligence that you know to what I refer. You
are a very good, able, kind of man and if your circumstances were
different I would have no objection, but they are not, and given Lydia's
impulsive temperament and history for short-lived enthusiasms, I
cannot see a marriage between you as being one that would be
conducive to the happiness and prosperity of either of you.

My dear Mr Dunbar, what I am proposing is unorthodox but perhaps
the circumstances require it, and I hope you will not think less of me,
as I will not of you, when I outline my proposition. You are an ambitious young man who finds himself trapped in his present employment
and I would like to help you escape from that prison. I hope you will
see your way to accepting a gift of fifty pounds which might set you up

in business or pay for further education. You will rightly guess on what terms this gift is offered. You both deserve the best that life has to offer, but in my opinion, that life is not one you and Lydia should share.

I remain, your sincere friend,

Florence Holdsworth

I'D BURNED with anger on reading it, though that emotion had died years ago as was right and natural. And tonight? Despite the lack of heating in the bedroom, I felt unaccountably warm. Memories of the hurt reviving?

At twenty-one, I'd thought the letter nothing more than a bribe to stay away from Lydia because I was from the wrong class. Without thought, I'd shoved it between the pages of the first novel I snatched from my bookshelf, which no one else in my family would open. But at the end of that week, wanting to give the letter more attention, I retrieved it from *Great Expectations*, grimacing at the irony of my unwitting choice.

A month later, my pride had recovered somewhat and common sense had replaced fury. In my heart, I knew Mrs Holdsworth was no snob. She wouldn't have invited me to tea so often if she had been. She didn't mind that I dropped my aitches and used dialect words. Nor thought the worse that I wasn't rich or middle class. And she was right about Lydia. I wouldn't have been enough for her, not for the long haul of marriage. It was a youthful affair; a dream lasting a year. I guessed it was Tilly, the maid, who'd informed Mrs Holdsworth. She'd seen us kissing behind the station yard once and standing too close for propriety on many occasions. As a youth, I'd taken risks. And the money Mrs Holdsworth had promised? I'd d it down, though I didn't deny I'd been tempted to .pt it.

I put the letter back into its envelope. Years on, there'd been .mes when I'd regretted that decision: coming home filthy and tired after a day's work underground. And newly married, I'd been helpless to improve our lot when Agnes moaned about the state of the house. But I'd let my conscience guide me and I felt clean because of it. How could I have taken Mrs Holdsworth's fifty pounds when I hadn't loved Lydia as a husband should? Even then I'd recognised my passion for what it was and knew she felt the same. It wouldn't have been right.

As for memories of the hours we'd spent together, there was no harm in daydreaming from time to time, was there?

I slipped the letter back to its original place, above another in a cheaper off-white envelope. This one, so different in style and meaning from the other, had arrived many months before the bribe. I could recite it by heart so wasn't going to open it, then I changed my mind. It still read as if the writer had spilt her guts out onto the page, *if I'm no longer able to, would you keep an eye on Jessie and James for me...* It was too painful, even now, and I put it away, locked the suitcase and pushed it back under the bed. In the days when I'd compared my feelings for Mary with those for Lydia, I'd thought of them as a purer kind of love, something God-given.

Downstairs, I built up the fire, made cheese and bacon on toast, took a bite then stared at the flames. When hunger took over, I wolfed down the rest. Sustained by food I resolved to revisit that place at the edge of memory, however difficult, for Jessie's sake. Deep down I knew I hadn't fully kept my promise to her mother. If I had, Clodagh Boyle might not have humiliated Jessie. Might not have been living in her house.

I shut my eyes and pictured Clodagh before she'd wheedled her way fully into the Gormans' lives. I'd thought her strong-minded, not unattractive if you liked that type. Not yet a drunkard, but rough, dismissive, open to argument. But the difference between then and now... She still had powerful forearms under her rolled-down sleeves.

I shook my head. How could Patrick have hitched his cart to someone like her after being married to Mary? If only I'd taken more notice, seen what was happening. Patrick seemed to enjoy my company and might have listened if I'd been around more often. It should have been he, or James, who'd frogmarched Clodagh out of the wedding meal, not me. In the street, I heard a comment as she'd stumbled away.

'She's like a rat, that one,' a man in a check cap had said to no one in particular. 'Steals your food, makes your house its home and spreads disease.'

I'd returned to the hall with a heavy heart, the memory of Mary's pale trusting face before me, and concern for Jessie. Then Agnes had come up and made things worse with her comments. At times like those, a thought I usually pushed to the back of my mind made its way to the surface: *marrying Agnes had been a mistake*. But what could I do? Nothing. I would get on with life for the sake of the children, especially as there was another one on the way.

The flames were smaller now, fading to a soft red. I fed the fire with kindling and lumps of coal before settling back into my chair.

I'd gone to the Gormans' house the day after Mary's letter came, a few weeks before she passed away. We'd sat hunched, looking at each other, the fire warming our faces.

'Why me?' I'd asked. 'I'm ten years younger than you and Patrick. And I hardly know you.'

'You're steady, trustworthy and why wouldn't I choose someone like you?'

Her voice had a melody of its own. By now she was talking to me like a fond, older sister, but we had a closeness I'd never achieved with my own flesh and blood.

'It's an honour, like. But there won't be the need, will there? I mean for me to keep an eye on the children. Everything'll be fine,' I said.

Her face brightened. 'I've a feeling the baby will be a girl. She'll be a companion for Jessie in years to come,' and she patted her stomach. She opened a drawer in the dresser and took out the cannel coal brooch I'd given her. 'I wear it at chapel and when I go visiting. It's a beautiful thing and thank you. I'll treasure it,' and she stroked its smooth surface.

I'd been slow at first to see it, but by April it dawned on me that my feelings for her were not exactly sisterly. How could they be when her smile melted me? But there'd been Lydia, too. Fire and storm compared to Mary's gentleness which made me think I was better than I realised. How had I got myself into a situation where I loved two women?

A noise at the door alerted me to the family returning: the girls' voices were high-pitched and over-excited. I put my memories behind me. What mattered now was working out what to do about the money and when to tell Agnes.

20

JESSIE

Mesnes Park, Wigan: November 1899

On Sunday I took a few turns around the park and tried not to think about the paltry dinner I'd just dished up. Potato pie wasn't something we normally had after a long church service. Finding a bench with a view of the pond, I sat down and watched a yellow and grey bird fly to and fro over the water. Its wings caught the surface, creating ripples to the far side. Then the mallards saw me. They swam to the pond edge, heaved themselves out and congregated around my feet. How velvety their green necks were. But I knew better than to put my hand out to touch them.

'I've nothing for you.' The nearest male quacked loudly, as if telling the others not to bother. After a few minutes, they slid back into the pond, giving me up as a bad job. Even the dry crusts I normally fed them with were in short supply. I'd saved those for our puddings then added a sparse sprinkling of sugar and raisins. Neither Pa, nor James, dared complain about the meals. No roast this Sunday, and perhaps not the next, but I'd have to be beyond desperate to buy the infected meat that was sometimes for sale. Pa would miss his favourite, marrow bone, but he agreed we should cut back for a while until we found the money to pay for Clodagh's fine.

I'd known that day would come, sooner not later. What did she expect when she continually rowed in the street with the neighbours? And shoved someone? The fight had brought her up before the Magistrate, but the rest of us were paying for it.

Pa had put in extra hours at the pit but by Friday he looked like death-warmed-up. I scraped together some food money to go towards the fine but neither James, nor even Clodagh, offered to do any overtime. We wouldn't starve, but the fine had scared Clodagh and was probably why she was lying low this week and keeping off the beer. Strangely, I heard her and Pa laughing when I was upstairs so perhaps some good had come out of it. There were no half-measures with them. One month they were all lovey-dovey and the next fighting like tom cats.

When the sun disappeared behind a surly, brown cloud of fog I decided to leave. The pond and distant trees looked dismal in the worsening light. Then I heard footsteps on the gravel path and a man appeared. He stopped and doffed his hat though I didn't recognise him. He leaned forwards and addressed me.

'Excuse me, Miss, aren't you at Pilkins, on the looms in the weaving shed?'

I tried to recall him from the hundreds of men who worked at the mill. He was wearing what you might call a Sunday suit but his bowler had seen better days. 'Yes, I am. Have we met before?'

'Sorry, I should've introduced meself. I'm Gerard Morris. How long 'ave ye worked at Pilkins? I've been a tackler there for three months.'

'About five years,' I told him. It didn't surprise me that I hadn't recognised him. He was new, and tacklers generally set up the looms before the weavers arrived. I guessed he spent his time with the other tacklers at Pilkins who kept to themselves;

in a cosy little room, until a weaver needed their help with maintenance.

He didn't walk on. Did he view me as the kind of girl who sat on park benches waiting for a man to stop and chat? Difficult to walk away while he was rattling on about work. Several more ducks were swimming towards us now, having seen Mr Morris as someone new. Someone perhaps with bread to throw. He'd stopped his flow of chat and was waiting for a reply.

'The ducks,' I blurted. 'They were all around my feet a while ago looking for food, but I had nothing to give them.'

'Were they? Do you mind if I sit awhile? I've been walking for ages.'

'Help yourself.' I hitched up a bit and he perched at the end of the bench.

'How do you find it? Workin' in the weaving shed, I mean.'

'It's all right. Pay's good.' What else could I say? I didn't have to tell him I thought it dusty, backbreaking, and deafening.

'Just all right? If there's anything I can help you with just give me the say so. I have the ear of Mr Holden, your overlooker.'

I stifled my surprise. Tacklers and overlookers weren't classed in the same bracket. I had a suspicion that Mr Morris thought well of himself. Curiosity got the better of me and I asked why that was.'

'Well, Miss Gorman, Arnold Holden is my uncle and fortunately, we get on. He listens when I tell him about day-to-day things. Not striking matters of course.'

That explained his interest but him knowing my name made me uneasy. He hitched further along the bench and gave an apologetic laugh. 'Sorry, I should have said at the start. It were my uncle who told me who you were.' He lit a cigarette and tapped the ash over the side of the bench.

It occurred to me that if he was so high up in Mr Holden's estimation then perhaps he could use his influence to get me the extra work I needed. 'There is something,' I said, and I told him how I'd been refused a second shift.

'Leave it with me, Jessie, I'll see what I can do.'

He moved a little closer and without speaking we stared at the ducks who'd swum back to our end. I pulled on the damp edges of my mittens and rubbed my thumb and forefinger together. It would be even more difficult to leave now that he'd agreed to do me a favour.

'Perhaps you'll have some bread for them the next time you come,' he said, pointing to the mallards.

'Maybe.' Had he guessed why I couldn't feed them? That we were short of money? He seemed a sharp sort, about twenty-five or six, with dark, curly hair and a wide brow. You wouldn't describe him as plain. If he'd read the paper he would have seen Clodagh's name up before the magistrate. But surely he couldn't know she was connected to me?

'Is this a favourite spot of yours?'

'Yes. It's quiet, after the mill and…the noise of the streets.'

'My uncle said you used to live in Sarginson Street. Are you still there?'

We'd moved because the landlord had turned us out. The neighbours had complained too often about Clodagh's arguments with them. I was uneasy about telling Mr Morris our address. He seemed to know a lot about me already. 'No, but we're not far away.'

'I live near Pemberton. Perhaps you'd let me call round and we could take a walk together one Sunday?'

AT THE END OF NOVEMBER, at the corner of Caroline Street, I waited for Gerard Morris. According to a man who gave me the time, he was five minutes late. I'd chosen an old plaid, rust skirt to wear; one I was fond of and the right weight for a mild winter day. The sun, though hazy, was thankfully out. A few minutes later he strode up, said how nice I looked, then linked my arm and steered me towards the canal. I thought longingly of the park where we'd met the previous week with its marigolds and begonias still in bloom. If the chance arose I'd tell him I preferred more open spaces.

The canal was oily, full of leaves and silt, dead-looking. On the towpath, we ducked our heads to avoid being clouted by low-hanging branches. In one of the tunnels, I kicked off layers of wet leaves which clung to my boot soles and put a hand against the brick wall to steady myself.

'Not tipsy are you?' Gerard joked.

'No, it's just the leaves make it slippery underfoot. Anyway, I couldn't be tipsy because I don't drink.' We were halfway through. It was very dark, lit only by narrow slashes of light on the floor from each entrance. I couldn't be sure, but I thought he frowned.

'Don't you? Well, it doesn't matter to me.'

I was relieved to hear him say that because some people at work made fun of me for being tee-total. Beyond the tunnel, the path was narrower and the stink from the water made me hold my breath. I said nothing to Gerard because it might seem rude to ask to go elsewhere. I didn't yet understand the rules for this walking-out lark. Books and stories about courting don't tell you the right time to let a man hold your hand or after how many meetings it was appropriate to kiss.

The first time we walked out, it was in the park and he supplied the bread for the ducks. We chatted later over a cup of tea in a café. He had a good deal to say about the mill, and workers' rights, which gave me something new to think about. I told him how James and I kept our heads down at home.

'One week it's all smiles and jokes, the next it's flaming rows.'

He was sympathetic and hoped the situation might improve. He had good news too, having arranged more overtime for me. I'd walked home with a lighter step. I liked his appearance and his energy, and as he'd kept his word about getting me more work, I said I'd meet him again. Perhaps this friendship would take off. I'd never stepped out with anyone before and had no idea how to judge these things. I decided to tell Susan on Monday during the dinner break. She'd been courting a lad at work for months. She'd probably say I was too cautious and Gerard would find someone else if I didn't give him more encouragement.

We passed a long line of barges piled high with hessian bags and *Wigan Coal and Iron Company* painted on their sides. 'Manure,' Gerard said, wrinkling his nose in disgust which made me smile. Other barges were full of loose coal, slack or stone.

'Where are the horses?' I'd hoped to see some, being fond of all animals.

Gerard jerked his head back. 'There's stables attached to that warehouse we just passed. Not many boats are moving, with it being a Sunday.'

Conversation was difficult on the towpath with him shouting over his shoulder, but when the path widened and we reached Fairlees Hall, an ancient brick and half-timbered house, I stopped to look and asked him if he knew anything about it. He probably didn't hear me, then realising I wasn't following, he turned around.

'Come on Jessie. What do you want to stare at a boring ruin for?'

It was disappointing not to view the Hall properly, though I was relieved when we reached a flight of steps leading up and away from the canal. On higher ground, we followed a wood-land path for a few yards before glimpsing a building with a red roof. A minute later, I found myself outside *The Boatman's Arms* and my spirits plummeted.

A dozen or so men ranging in age from twenty to sixty, simi-larly dressed in waistcoats and baggy trousers, leant against the outside wall, drinking from tankards. Every eye was fixed on us as we approached the door. A canal workers' pub was a strange place for Gerard to bring me to. A chap I thought was handsome until he gave us a gap-toothed grin, greeted Gerard with a cheery *good day* as we passed by. My insides squirmed at the thought of entering this rackety-looking building. Even *The Griffin* would be considered respectable compared to this drinking den.

I was right to be dubious. The interior was as gloomy and neglected as a cellar. Tall, straggly bushes grew up against the windows, almost hiding the overgrown garden. I thought of the muck I'd have to clean off my boots after treading on damp sawdust on the floor. A few seated couples stared at me curiously through plumes of tobacco smoke as we passed by. The straw boater I wore was completely out of place. I jumped at the scrape of chair legs on the floor and peered over my shoulder. A man and a woman were making a show of getting up. Under her powder and rouge, she looked to be about thirty, but it was hard to tell. She fussed with her skirt while her companion drained his glass. After she'd jerked her thumb at him, he followed her through a door behind the bar which I guessed led to the garden. I was glad when they'd gone.

'Can we sit in the saloon bar?' I asked Gerard. 'This place is a bit...'

'It's alright,' and he pulled out two chairs from behind an empty table, pointing to the other women with their men folk. 'There isn't a saloon, sorry.'

The publican came out from behind his wall of bottles and glasses and looked enquiringly at us. 'Mine's a pint of mild,' Gerard told him. 'What'll you have, Jessie?'

I shook my head, 'Thanks, but I'm not thirsty.' It was a lie, but if I didn't have a drink then the sooner we could leave. Rather than stare at the other customers I glanced through the window. Gerard was pulled into a conversation about an upcoming football match by one of the couples. He interrupted himself to put a hand on my arm and asked again what I would drink.

'Glass of port, stout?'

'Aye, go on girl, get something down yer rattle trap!' An unshaven man at a different table shouted across at us. His companion, a florid-faced woman smirked at me and patted her hair. Clodagh would look like her in a few years' time.

I gave her a hard stare. 'All right,' I told Gerard. 'I'll have a lemonade.' Perhaps a cold drink would help. Gerard went to the bar and chatted with the publican as he poured the drinks though I heard nothing of their conversation. At this end of the room, the talk was of horse races, bets, arguments for their favourite. Then the couple who I thought had left returned to take their seats. The woman's blouse was partly undone and the man's face was slack and red. I was sure now what kind of place this was. I picked at my fingernails until Gerard came back with my glass.

'Get that down you, Jessie, you'll feel better for it.'

I took a sip and then another because once finished, I'd insist we leave. The men at the other tables smiled at me in a leering kind of way. I swivelled round in my chair, gave them my back, and pretended an interest in the fireplace with its tarnished brasses and horseshoes. Then I saw something wrong with the display. Gerard finally asked if I was alright and what I was looking at.

'One of the horseshoes is the wrong way up.'

He put down his glass and peered at the fireplace, leaning in close enough for me to feel his breath on my neck. 'So what?'

'It shouldn't be upside down. It lets out all the luck. Not that I'm superstitious, mind.' I was talking for the sake of it, but it couldn't be worse than being left out of a conversation with strangers laughing and chatting about horse racing.

'That's nonsense!' Gerard said, pulling himself upright. 'We make our own luck is what I say.'

How I wished I'd kept my mouth shut. He had no truck with that kind of talk. I tried to smile as if to make light of it. 'Of course, you're right.' All the same, I itched to turn the horseshoe around. After a few more sips of my drink, I knew something wasn't right. There was a metallic taste to the lemonade. I glanced at the bar. The publican was still polishing glasses, one after the other. He stared as if waiting for some reaction from me. Gerard wasn't looking. He'd half turned away and was deep in conversation with his new friends, speculating about the big race at Haydock Park.

There hadn't been many times when I could thank Clodagh for something. At fourteen, curiosity got the better of me when she left an unfinished glass of gin on the table. No one was about so I drank the dregs. It was the same as the taste in my mouth now, disguised by the *Whites' Lemonade*. I tamped down my anger and took a deep breath. I'd come off worst if I made a scene with all these conspirators around. I nudged Gerard's elbow to get his attention, put a hand to my forehead and pulled a face.

'Sorry, but I need some fresh air. My head's buzzing as if it's being drilled. I'm going into the garden.'

He looked alarmed. He glanced at the barman and then back at me. 'Take some deep breaths and finish your drink. Have a little more, you'll feel better for it.'

I had a sense of what was hidden beneath his urging tone and when he squeezed my arm I was convinced he wanted me tipsy. A scene flashed through my head which sickened me. I could almost smell it on him. Once outside, he'd proposition me. Pin me up against a wall and ...

He turned away to continue bantering with the racing man and as soon as he was engrossed I raced out of the bar like a hare. Mr Morris was not as clever as he thought.

. . .

PA WAS ALONE; his head against the back of the chair, enjoying forty winks. He started in surprise when I entered the house as if blown in by a blizzard. I was out of breath and my hair was falling around my ears. His eyes were full of questions but he said nothing, sat me in his chair and brought me a cup of water. His gentleness was overwhelming and I told him what I'd vowed I wouldn't. He paced around the room for a minute then looked at me, his mouth curving into a smile. At once I felt better.

'You did the right thing, Jessie. The young man thought you wouldn't kiss him unless you were intoxicated. It was wicked of him to play a trick like that.'

'Then why are you smiling?'

'Because you saw through him and got away. It was the best thing to do if you didn't want to kiss him back.'

I felt my face burning, not having spoken to him about such things before. 'I don't know whether I did or didn't, Pa. But I wasn't going to wait to find out sitting in the public bar of the *The Boatman's Arms.*' I skipped over the part when the couple went into the garden and returned tousled. I couldn't be sure she was a prostitute though it seemed likely. The newspapers were full of reports about those sorts of goings-on in beer houses.

'It's a pity young Morris didn't take you to a respectable saloon bar. A man wants the woman he's with to have a good time and having a drink does that for ye, but you won't know that having taken the pledge.' He picked up the half-drunk glass of beer at his feet as if to prove his point. 'But the rest of it - it's part of growing up. You must learn to judge when a man is being friendly because that's his nature, or if he's after something else.'

'I suppose I'll find out the difference over time,' I said, unsure whether I ever would.

'Your mother would have sat you down to talk about these things, but you can always ask your Aunt Margaret. She's a decent soul who'll put you straight.'

I noticed he didn't advise me to ask Clodagh. 'Pa, I didn't intend to insult him but it didn't feel right with everyone staring at me, probably knowing he'd poured gin into my drink. I had to get away.'

He chuckled and put his hands on his hips. 'I thought you'd grown out of theatricals, Jessie. As I see it, you and young Morris were both out of luck with each other. He took a stupid risk and it didn't pay off, but the tide will turn, as will fortune, and one day it'll be the right man sitting on a park bench.'

In my room I took a comb to my hair whilst looking in the little mirror hanging on the wall. My eyes had a startled look and I wondered what Gerard Morris saw in me in the first place. And Pa talking about the *right man*. How could he be so sure there would be another park bench?

21

SAM

273 Scholes, Wigan: November 1899

I woke, bleary-eyed and thirsty after a turbulent night. In the bathroom, my reflection in the mirror told the same story. But not even lack of sleep could dim my happiness: Mrs Holdsworth's bequest would change our lives. I slathered shaving soap over my face and picked up my razor. 'Meringue!' I spluttered at my reflection, grasping at the memory which had eluded me during the night hours. With little thought to the safety of my throat, I shaved in double quick time, washed, dressed, and knew what I should do.

About two weeks ago, Agnes had said she had a craving for macaroons: something new for this pregnancy. I decided to buy them at the bakery where Emilie worked. The shop was a little out of my way, but I hadn't minded; it would be good to see her again. After making my purchase she came outside to join me and let slip something she shouldn't have.

'*En toute confiance,*' she said, pressing a finger to her lips, 'Great-Aunt Adeline is giving up the lease on the shop soon. She wants to take life more easily.'

A large plate of meringues featured as a centrepiece in the window. I glanced at them as we talked, wondering in a haphazard way how they were made.

At the time I'd put Emilie's news aside because it had nothing to do with me. The shop wasn't my concern. But now it could be...Why bother with another market stall when I could lease a shop and take on the business myself? I ate breakfast and readied myself for work with an energy I hadn't felt for months. Poor Agnes, resting on the couch exhausted by her fourth pregnancy, was pale and hadn't brushed her hair. I kissed her forehead before leaving but said nothing of my revelation. There would be opportunity to celebrate when she knew everything.

Towards the end of the working day, I gathered up rolls of cloth lying on the counter, stacked them and went through the motions of closing the stall. *Pull down the shutters, don't forget to lock them.* I wouldn't wait for the Saturday meeting to see my employer; instead I'd leave early and walk over to Mesnes Street. As I pulled on my jacket I imagined asking my question, *what would you do, Madame Chambres, with the money?* Without doubt her twittering voice would reply, *start my own business, Mr Dunbar.*

In my hurry to leave work, I tripped over a block of wood left on the floor. Alf the cobbler saw me and shouted something about part-timers. I waved at him, laughing out loud.

Evening. Gaslight illumined the street. I halted before crossing the road causing a woman to bump into me and give me a filthy look. 'Sorry, my mind was elsewhere,' I apologised, and she went off, huffing.

I hadn't been inside *Chambres' Drapery* for a while and noticed immediately the new counters and cupboards. Made from a lighter wood than the previous ones, they were highly polished. Very smart. Madame Chambres hadn't said anything about having the place refurbished. However much it pleased me, I couldn't think about that now. I jigged from one foot to the other while I waited behind the solid backs of Wigan matrons queuing for lace collars and gloves. No sign of Adeline, though the young lady assistant showing rolls of muslin and taffeta was run off her feet. Eventually, it was my turn and I asked if I could see our employer.

The noise of my boots on the stairs up to the flat brought someone to the door. I was thankful I hadn't worn my clogs that day which I sometimes did.

Emilie peered down at me. 'Good day, Sam. I do not think this has happened before, a visit from you out of the blue. Very mysterious.'

I mumbled a greeting and wiped my sweating palms on my trouser legs when her back was turned. I was relieved to see her and my confidence rose, sure she'd be on my side. She ushered me into a parlour that was different in almost every respect from any room I'd ever seen. Even on a November evening the effect was feminine and light filled. Had Madame Chambres brought all these possessions over from France? I glanced at the wallpaper which had a pleasing, pale, flowery design. I wouldn't tear that down if ever I were lucky enough to live here. There were fewer pieces of furniture than you normally saw in a parlour and instead of the dark, bulky sideboards and tables most people had, there was a white painted writing desk and a low table. In my experience, painted furniture was for cottages, but these looked far too elegant for a country dwelling. I was full of curiosity but tore my gaze from the paintings and photographs in ornate gilt frames to attend to my employer.

'Sit down, please, Mr Dunbar,' she said. 'May I offer you a cup of tea? I've grown very partial to *Twinnings* over the years.'

It wasn't a brand I recognised but I accepted a cup. I avoided sitting on a spindly looking chair, afraid it might tip over, and chose instead a plush green armchair which I immediately sank into. The room was brightly lit by four electric light sconces on each wall; a shock and a pleasant surprise. I hardly dared let the idea of living in a flat with electricity cross my mind. In pride of place on the mantelpiece stood a dark pink, marble clock. If this didn't announce a French room then nothing did.

Madame Chambres sat stiff as a dummy in a high-backed chair pouring tea into cups you could see your hand through, and handed me one. She was dressed in a flowing blue afternoon garment, not her usual Saturday morning visiting-me costume. I doubted Agnes and I would have the time, or money, for such niceties. Although my armchair was the height of comfort, it was lower than the two women's chairs; a disadvantage when begging a favour. I was reminded of Queen Victoria receiving General Tom Thumb and felt as tall as that performer. I apologised again for closing the stall early.

'It is something of an emergency. I had to see you as soon as I could. Your niece mentioned your plan to give up the lease here...' I glanced at Emilie whose face expressed surprise. 'I have recently come into some money...' and I poured out my ideas.

By the time I'd stumbled to the end of my speech, Madame Chambres' expression of calm disinterest hadn't changed a jot. She flicked a crumb off her dress, left by one of the fancy pink works of art on the cake stand. Nowhere in Wigan sold pastries like that, not even Emilie's shop. My employer must have sent for them from Manchester. Emilie smiled in encouragement but she didn't have the power to turn my life around, did she? She turned to her Great-Aunt and there was warmth in her voice.

'I mentioned to Sam that you wanted to retire; perhaps I was wrong to do so, but he is an old friend, is he not? And as your employee, we have known him for many years. I think it is a very good thing he wants to do.'

Madame Chambres nodded then continued to nibble on a pastry and sip her tea. Eventually she put her cup down, went to her desk, took out a sheet of paper and wrote something on it.

'Chapman is the land agent's name. It is up to him now whether he takes you on or not,' and she handed it over.

It could have been any of our Saturday meetings. As brief and as cold as they. No offer of help for the likes of me. I read the name and address and thanked her. She expected me to leave, but I wasn't going home without trying for more. It was overstepping our usual way of conversing but I said it anyway.

'You have much influence Madame Chambres. I'm sure if you spoke up, put in a good word, the agent would think kindly about me.'

She blenched under the face powder and her reply was as guarded as ever. 'I will have to think about that, Mr Dunbar. It is a big step from stallholder to shopkeeper.'

I kept a smile pasted to my face but my spirits sank. It was no use. She didn't think I was good enough to take over her empire. I sat up straighter. I must convince her she wouldn't lose out by recommending me. Desperate, I tried again. 'I'd be very grateful if you would. This is the area of work I know best. I couldn't go in for ironmongery… or bicycles, or…cobbling,' I said, grasping at the oddest things that came to mind and thinking of Alf's stall. 'I know nothing of those trades, but I do know fabric and the drapery business and now I have the money to fulfil my ambition. You wouldn't lose anything by a recommendation.'

I mentally crossed my fingers. Talking about personal finance was a risk, not being a polite topic for conversation. I hoped she realised I meant there was enough money to pay for the lease and buy her stock.

'It is true Aunt, everything Mr Dunbar says. There are no other drapery shops for rent presently, are there?' Emilie flashed me a glance. 'He would have to wait years for another, perhaps.' There was a new formality in her speech addressing me as *Mr Dunbar* and I prayed it would work upon her aunt who disapproved of the slapdash way people talked in her adopted town. 'And we would not want someone we could not trust, someone dishonest, to take over from you, would we?'

She'd lowered her voice but my hearing was good. I blinked. Had Madame Chambres dismissed a deceitful assistant recently? All I knew was that Emilie was pulling out the stops for me. Her aunt looked startled, afraid even, and I thought it best to take my leave. I stood, gave a slight bow, and expressed my thanks for the tea. She rose stiffly and shook out her skirt, which had bunched around her ankles. I glimpsed a black shoe with a round diamante buckle. Good quality at first sight. Her handshake was light and loose and for the first time, I saw vulnerability in her eyes.

'Because my niece has reminded me of all your good qualities, I will support you in your application and you can convey this to the land agent when you apply. Tell Mr Chapman he can contact me directly for a reference.' Her lips twitched and I guessed she was trying to smile.

Thank you didn't seem strong enough but I could hardly kiss her. Instead, I grasped her hand and only remembered I'd already shaken it when she pulled it away. Speech almost deserted me though I'm sure my dazed expression managed to convey my gratitude. I left them to their fancy tea, and even after the parlour door had closed behind me I could still smell her peculiar fading lilies scent.

Downstairs, the doorbell tinkled my departure and released me into the sharp nip of the evening as I strode along Mesnes Street; my sights set on Scholes. It felt like seven days had passed rather than one. Was it possible that the next time I entered the shop I might be the leaseholder? I quickened my steps, eager to leave behind the noise of the streets: the clang of the new electric new electric trams, the clop of horses' hooves on cobbles loud in my ears. I ached for quiet, to think and to plan my letter to Mr Chapman. As I drew nearer to home it occurred to me that I should wait a couple of more days before saying anything to Agnes. Not until I'd heard back from the land agent. A delay would also give me time to think how best to explain the bequest to my wife, to keep my good news secret.

TWO DAYS later I was bunching my fists in joy and kissing the top of the letter that had just arrived in the last post. *Subject to an interview at our office...see no reason why not ... Madame Chambres highly recommends you...*

Adeline Chambres had made it possible! I'd done it, well almost. I would call in at Chapman's on my way to work tomorrow to make the appointment. With no one in the house to disturb me, I took up my pen, the Towneley family's wedding present to me. I wrote our name on a piece of paper in copper-plate handwriting, imagining it as a letter heading. It led to thoughts about the shop frontage. I pictured a sign writer on his ladder with a tin of paint obliterating *Chambres* and replacing it with *Dunbar,* in black and gold. Finally, I tried out a few versions of the tale I would tell: *Daniel Holdsworth had once been a good friend. His mother had been fond of me. The family had tried to help me leave the pit but it hadn't worked out. It was unfortunate that we'd lost touch a long time ago. Sad that she'd died at an early age.*

Overall, this was an accurate version of events; my friendship with Daniel was only a little embellished and Lydia's name need not be mentioned because Agnes had never heard of it. Impatient for my family's return, I went to the window to see if they were walking up the street but only a lamplighter was abroad; a ladder hoisted over his shoulder. I took out one fish supper from the range and set a single place for myself.

Always, a mix of heat and shame filled me when I thought about my youthful love for two very different women. Lydia, whose mother had made this dream possible. Why hadn't I given the cannel brooch to her? We were lovers after all. But she'd had wealth and Mary hadn't. Not a difficult choice. And in the end, I'd made my bed with a third woman.

Over the years, I'd found that daily life, being married to Agnes, was like walking up a steep hill at the top of which was a pretty, but almost empty house. But wasn't it possible to view life differently? To believe and hope that things would improve between us? Perhaps now, with a business and going up in the world, they would.

22

JESSIE

Teck Street: January 1900

'Thanks for your help with the cleaning love, that brass pot's come up a treat. You get off now.'

'If you're sure, Grandma.'

She was looking at me as if she had more to say. I recognised the tight-lipped expression and hoped she wouldn't speak again of Gerard Morris. Ages ago, James had let slip that I'd walked out with someone and at the time, the family had seized on it. I'd protested it had been nothing but Grandma still hinted she hoped the friendship might be revived. Like those who thought we still had a year to go until a new century started, she preferred to live in the past.

'Patrick coping alright?' She asked finally in a strangled tone.

How disappointing I must be. So evasive where Pa and Clodagh were involved, but he was too proud a man to be gossiped about. Was that uncharitable? Grandma did look concerned. I relented a little. 'Clodagh's back. Went over to Yorkshire for a few weeks to stay with her brothers.'

'Well, that's something,' she said, drawing out the words. 'Gives you a break, love. How often does she go there?'

It was no secret we had disputes but it was Pa I wanted to protect. 'Around three times a year. Doesn't care what type of work she does when she comes back, cleaning, washing, spinning, if she feels like it.' I didn't add that I looked forward to those times. The freedom of having her out of the house was...

'And Patrick doesn't mind?'

Whether she meant Clodagh leaving or coming back I wasn't sure, but the answer was the same for both. 'No, he doesn't mind.' It was hugs and kisses all round when she showed up this week and the inevitable drink to celebrate their reunion.

'You take care lass and I'll see you soon.' She patted my arm which amounted to a lot, not being one for over familiarity even with the little ones.

Hurrying along the streets brought on a stitch. I rested for a minute though the evening was chilly and I didn't like lingering in this area. The house we now rented was larger, and had piped water, but Pa and I said it was less friendly than Sarginson Street. People were suspicious of each other and less willing to help out so I wasn't surprised to hear raised voices at the far end of Teck Street, near the water pump. Two women were arguing though I was too far away to recognise them. I set off more slowly, hoping the quarrel would be over by the time I reached them. Rowing was common around here though not women fighting together. An old fellow stood near them, waiting for the clamour to stop, I supposed.

Suddenly, they were at each other, pulling clothes, unsteady on their feet with the taller woman grabbing the other's hair. A chill ran through me. I knew exactly how that felt and I knew who was fighting who. The smaller figure was Bessie Gough, a neighbour who regularly feuded with Clodagh. But this was more serious than a spat. Bessie's short height and stooped back made her an easy target. Clodagh broke away, her mass of fair hair all over the place. I saw her pick up a large can by the side of the water pump, and though the man shook his fist at her, it was to no avail. Clodagh tipped whatever liquid it held right over Bessie's head. The old woman shrieked as the water descended and wiped her cheeks with her apron. But it wasn't over. To my horror, Clodagh whipped off a clog and struck Bessie's face with it. A moment later she was haring down the street.

I ran to the Goughs as fast as I could. Bessie was wailing and bent over with a hand clasped to her face. A trickle of blood crept down her cheek. I scrabbled for a handkerchief, seized the pump handle and held my handkerchief under it and prayed that the iron had missed her eye.

'Let me dab your face Bessie,' I pleaded, holding the soaked cotton square out to her. She grunted *no* and turned away. 'Fetch Mrs Middleton,' I yelled at her husband. 'Now!' He looked uncertain but shambled off. Bessie peered at me from her good eye.

'You live with that whore, don't you?' She walked unsteadily after her husband, a hand still clamped to her face. I stared at their retreating backs knowing that within the hour they'd be straight down to the magistrate.

Clodagh was waiting for me when I opened the front door. She paced the room, rubbing her hands together and flashed me a look. 'Did you see how I got one over on that cow? Bessie Gough was calling me names, so I showed her what for.'

'By nearly taking her eye out?'

Clodagh was het up and dangerous. The pacing stopped and she considered me. 'You'll swear this never happened, right? If you do there'll be trouble.'

Pa surprised us both by coming in from the kitchen. He put his newspaper down and sized up the situation. 'What's going on?'

I sank into a chair and squeezed my hands. I would tell him

the truth. Bessie Gough might be blind after this. 'There was a fight in the street...' but I was too hollowed out to continue. Clodagh's face was a picture of malice and fear. She never expected me to tell tales. Courage rose from somewhere. 'I came upon them and saw...'

We jumped at the sound of banging on the front door. Pa opened it and dodged out of the way as Mr Gough pushed roughly into the front room.

'Mr Gorman, come outside and see my wife. She says she won't come indoors after what your Missis did to her.'

Pa was outside for under a minute and when he returned he told Clodagh, 'Get upstairs. I don't want to see your face 'til tomorrow. I'll be sleeping down here.'

THE SUMMONS from the magistrate arrived three days later. When Clodagh came home from work and read it she waved her arms around and ordered me to be her witness. 'You'll tell them I never struck her.'

Not on God's earth would I lie for her to the police or the magistrate. Even so, I was afraid of what might happen; that she might hit *me* with her clog. What she didn't know was that Pa was in the kitchen, listening. He came in, stood behind me and put his hands on my shoulders.

'You will not involve Jessie in your lies, or you'll be out of here by the evening. Is that understood?' She nodded and stormed out of the house without her shawl.

DURING THE DAYS she was away an uneasy silence filled the house. Neither James nor I dared broach the subject with Pa. On Monday evening, Mr Gough tapped on the window, wanting us to come outside. We crowded in the doorway and hoped no one would pass by to hear what was said. He stood near the edge of the pavement though he was in no danger from us.

'I know she's not here,' he said, 'but she owned up, got a fine, then cleared off.'

'And what about your missis?' Pa asked. 'How is she?'

'She's recovering. She'll show you the scar if you ask nicely.'

And though that was the end of the matter, an uneasy truce and atmosphere existed within the house for many months. I felt I was continually holding my breath.

23

JESSIE

Hope Street Methodist Chapel: March 1900

I recognised Sam even though I was seated several rows behind him. Thick dark hair and the broad shoulders of a former miner. Was he here to listen to the visiting speaker? No sign of Aunt Agnes or the children. But she wouldn't want to oversee three kiddies in an unfamiliar chapel. I ran through all the reasons why Sam could be at the service. Was there news which couldn't wait? Were my grandparents ill? Had my aunts or cousins been in an accident? Searching for reasons put me on edge though I prayed, sang and stood with everyone else. After the final hymn, I waited for him to break free from people he knew who kept him chatting. He waved, smiled, and said he wouldn't be long.

Outside, he put his hat back on and tipped it towards me. 'Good day, Jessie, are you well? I'm sorry if I startled you, turning up without warning, but I thought it better to speak when you were on your own. Do you have time for a walk?'

We headed for Mesnes Park, a good place to stroll, but

clouded by the memory of my inexperience with Gerard Morris which still embarrassed me.

'So you've not brought me bad news?'

'No, not at all. The opposite in fact.'

It was still early for afternoon strollers and we were the only people entering by the wrought-iron gates. I stopped a few yards in front of the bandstand.

'What are you smiling at?' He asked.

Perhaps it was relief after being anxious during the service, or the weather being fine. I looked up at the scudding clouds before turning to him. 'You'll think I'm daft.' Then I told him about the painting of Queen Victoria, her little coronet, and its likeness to the building we were standing in front of. 'It was hanging in the church hall at Rachel and Graham's wedding.'

Sam cocked his head to one side as if considering its structure. 'Yes, the similarity's obvious. The artist must have made a special visit to Wigan to paint it before presenting it to her Majesty.' We laughed, and he took my elbow to find a bench. In the distance, treetops swayed in the wind like a troupe of dancers.

'Not this one,' I said, walking past the bench I'd sat on when Gerard Morris first spoke to me. 'The next one's a bit cleaner.'

We took our seats and Sam twisted around to face me. 'You've probably heard that I've had an inheritance from a friend's mother who died last year. It's a lot of money. It was a shock because we hadn't been in touch for years.'

His words tumbled out and I had a job keeping up with him. Of course, I'd heard it from Grandma. Guessed it would change his life and wondered who the rich family were. None of the Towneleys had ever mentioned them.

'I'm very pleased for you.' I still didn't know why he was telling me. 'What are your plans?'

'You don't know?'

'Grandma said something about a shop.'

He looked as if he didn't believe it himself but stood up and pointed at the park walls.

'This is my last week on the market stall. With the inheritance money, I'll take on the lease of the draper's in Mesnes Street. It's the one my employer, Madame Chambres, currently has. She approved my plan and the land agent's accepted me. We aim to open for business soon.' He paused for breath. 'Jessie, I would like you to be my assistant in the shop. What do you say?'

'I... don't know what to say,' I stuttered. What he was suggesting was unbelievable. 'Why me? I've no knowledge of customers or sales.' Of course, I'd stood outside the shop and looked admiringly at the clothes displayed because Hope Street Chapel stood almost opposite. I'd never ventured inside. It was too high class for my purse. 'I get most of the things we need from the Rag Market,' I told him. Surely he could do better. I was nothing but a mill girl with nimble fingers. I shook my head to clear my thoughts and perhaps he took that for a *no*.

'You don't want to come and work for me?'

He sounded disappointed. I didn't want to let him down. 'No... I don't know. I'll think about it.'

'Good. I asked you because I wanted to help, you know, after Rachel's wedding. Give you a chance elsewhere. Thought you might like working in a shop better than the mill. We'd be selling all kinds of materials. I remember you had a good eye for colour when you were a child. It would come in useful.'

I felt my cheeks redden. When we met, which wasn't often, we never talked about the time he rescued me, though Pa used to. He'd turn it into a story to tell people who hadn't heard about it. I think Sam felt shy being the centre of attention, though as a child I'd lapped it up, that is until Clodagh moved in. It struck me that Sam and I had swapped places in that respect. I covered my feelings with an attempt at flippancy.

'I was probably showing off and gabbing too much that day — at the wedding — I mean. Something about a cat, wasn't it?

Or a fur? Anyway, nonsense talk.' I never did get the cat I was going to call Diamond. During the years when we mainly lived with our grandparents, it was out of the question.

But Sam wouldn't accept it. 'You were remarkably aware for an eight-year-old. You saw I was the stranger and you made me welcome. I shouldn't have been there really, but your father insisted. That was him all over, big-hearted. Wanted to share everything.'

During that afternoon in the room above the pub, I'd tried my best to keep the sound and sight of the bus wheels and the horses coming for me at bay. Chattering to Sam about anything I could think of had worked: the colours in a fur coat that had caught my eye. But what use was that sort of talk now I was grown up? Why should colours matter if your everyday world was made up of black and grey: buildings, pavements, clothes for the Monday wash? No, not quite true. We had one splash of cheerfulness in our house: the red curtains in the front room which Mother had made. We'd brought them with us to Teck Street.

It was enough to change my mind. 'I do still like colours but I don't know if I'll be any good at the job.' I wanted to be honest and there were other considerations, practical ones. 'Father will want to know if I'll earn the same as I do now. He and James might object if there's less money in my pay packet.'

A look of annoyance crossed Sam's face, but I was so used to putting my family first.

'Your wages would rise in time to equal what you get now. But tell your family it's a chance for you to work in a safer, healthier place.' He frowned, seeing he hadn't convinced me. 'You stayed on at school, didn't you? I bet you can read, write, and do sums quicker than most. And I'll teach you all about shop work.'

My heart thudded. He'd found my weak spot: pride in my learning. 'I left school at thirteen and a half.' It was longer than most girls from my background and meant I'd got a half-decent education. Only a few people knew I had ambitions. 'I wanted to be a pupil teacher, but things were difficult. Pa needed another wage coming in.' Sam would fill in the gaps. Pa wasn't always reliable, and James had still been at school.

'I understand, but think it over. It's your future, Jessie, no one else's.'

We said no more apart from a kind farewell from him and a promise from me to do as he asked. I watched Sam until he turned a corner then I set off for home, full of a fizzing spirit... I could be the first in the family to leave mill employment, despite every unmarried female relative working there until they had children. And marriage? That wouldn't be to someone who knew my family. No decent lad from chapel would walk out with Miss Gorman. Chapel mothers would tan their sons' hides if they approached me.

I was beginning to see how Sam's offer could change my life. By working in the shop, I'd meet people who knew nothing about my background. Besides, the thought of Sam as my boss was reassuring: he believed I could do better in life, and above all, he was a friend. Being his assistant would be something to be proud of. Tonight, when Pa came back from fishing I'd talk to him. Cook whatever he'd caught for our tea. A tasty meal might help my cause.

PA ARRIVED with a bream and a roach and I ran out to the shop to buy chips to go with them. But despite their praise of the meal, Pa and James were against me leaving the mill far more strongly than I'd imagined. James, as usual, spoke before he thought.

'You were born to work in a mill,' he told me as if it were Biblical truth, 'and you'll still be in one 'til yer marry or they carry you out in a casket.'

I flared up at him. 'Like you? Because you don't look further than the end of your nose? Are you jealous because Sam's giving me a chance to do something else?' I regretted the words as soon as they were out of my mouth because Pa looked like a wounded dog. I'd always thought he was happy enough as a pitman but now I wasn't sure. Maybe like Sam, he'd wished for other chances. No one said anything until Pa cleared his throat.

'I can't encourage you lass because you know we need the high wage you bring in now. But when all's said and done, 'tis your decision.'

I supposed he was hoping family loyalty would swing it in his favour. Clodagh hadn't spoken but now she leant back in her chair, eyes gleaming, arms folded.

'I reckon Miss Jessie'll be givin' herself more airs as a shop-girl than she does already.'

I buttoned my lip and stalked off into the kitchen with my cutlery and plate and left them in the sink for someone else to wash up. Alone in my room, it struck me that if Clodagh had spent as much time saying *nice* things as she had nasty ones, she would have been rich in friends. She had a way with words though she never used them to spread harmony or to be poetical. In bed, I tucked the blankets around my shoulders and back, as if needing a protective layer. Why couldn't they see my plan as something positive? They were all so sunk in their own concerns it frightened me. I swore that in the future I would not be like them.

AFTER I WROTE to Sam to accept his offer, I invented a life for myself where it was just Father and me living in a bright, little cottage with a garden. I saw him grow happier as he tended a vegetable plot. I waited to hear his jokes when I gave him news about my day in the shop and recounted stories about the fine people I'd spoken to. I imagined visits from neighbours, cousins and aunts who called and stayed for tea. I imagined a day when a young man who perhaps worked in the Town Hall, or in a large furniture store, would come knocking on our door and ask me to walk out with him. Was that too much to ask?

While I waited to start work in Sam's shop, I added to the story: children appeared, the schools they attended, and their pet rabbits. It was a daft pastime, but it kept me sturdy when Clodagh was aggravating, when James gave me the cold shoulder and Pa's sighs accompanied the rustle of his newspaper.

24

SAM

Mesnes Street: March 1900

'Are you worried about all this?' I asked Agnes, waving my hand as if conjuring up a picture of our future. Although she hadn't mentioned it, I noticed she'd taken more care with her outfit this morning. She was right to do so. The day the shop became ours warranted new gloves and a freshly trimmed hat and I was gratified she thought it an important occasion.

'Why should I be worried? We've gone through all the details with the land agent and the solicitor. And you've worked alongside Madame Chambres this last month.'

I wasn't referring to the paperwork though the legal language had baffled me at times. 'I mean keeping customers, attracting new ones. Adeline Chambres built up a loyal following and they may not welcome the change. You know how people are about all things French.'

'If that's the case then you'll have to tell them your suppliers are the same as hers!'

I laughed, 'I will, until I find others who'll give us better rates than she was getting.'

Agnes's dogged practicality, at my side on all matters to do with the shop, had been a relief. Astounded beyond measure when I'd told her the good news, she was too excited to delve closely into my past friendship with the Holdsworths. Despite there being other competition for the lease, Madame Chambres had proposed me to the land agent as *eminently suitable*. At the end of my training, before she and Emilie moved out of the flat, I'd thanked her for explaining the intricacies of business, the kind not needed on a market stall.

'Despite your earlier background Mr Dunbar, the size of your ambition has overcome that deficiency. I did not see the same determination in your competitors who also asked for my recommendation.'

No change in her views about class then, and I smothered the retort on the tip of my tongue. As usual, beneath the compliment was the put-down. I'd shared it with Agnes, who didn't see Madame Chambres' comment as a slur.

'It's time to bury the miner's part of your life,' she'd said, 'now we're moving up in the world. You look after business affairs and I'll stick to what I know best — fashion. Choosing new lines for the shop will be my contribution.'

Although Madame Chambres implied that she alone had changed my fortunes, I discovered that Emilie had played almost as large a part. To celebrate the end of my training, she and I ate our mid-day meal at one of the town's chophouses. I mentioned the puzzling exchange I'd witnessed in the flat between aunt and niece on the day I'd pleaded my cause.

'What is it you haven't told me?' I'd said, thinking it something trivial.

She pulled an amused face. 'You have noticed the shop fittings are new?'

'Of course. What about them?'

'Nine months ago, Aunt Adeline found a great deal of furniture and fittings abandoned outside a shop and paid a carrier to bring them to Mesnes Street. But before they were installed I saw the name of the shop stamped on them and asked my aunt if she had the owner's permission to take them away. She hadn't, thinking them unwanted. I told her that under the law what she'd done was theft. She ordered me to say nothing, so when she seemed reluctant to recommend you to Chapman's, I thought I would remind her of it.'

I frowned, taking this in. 'So even if someone discards something, they still own it?'

'*Exactement*. I learned about this in a newspaper article in my English class. The teacher explained it. Aunt Adeline took the furniture without establishing whether the owner intended to abandon it. My reminder scared her.'

'For that, Emilie, I will give you as many hours' work in the shop as you desire.' I ordered a glass of wine for her and a lemonade for me and we toasted to success, the future and friendship.

AGNES and I reached the corner turning into Mesnes Street and slowed our pace. Both of us, I think, wanted to savour the next few moments, taking possession of our own business.

'Here we are. You have got the keys?' She asked.

I stifled my irritation at her question and pulled them out with a flourish and inserted the largest into the lock. The windows looked drab with the shutters down and needed a wash but we'd soon sort that out. I was looking forward to rolling up my sleeves, making lists, rummaging through boxes and rearranging shelves as I saw fit. The children were taken care of, installed at my parents' for the week.

'It's very dusty,' Agnes said, once we were inside, taking off her hat and gloves before opening the cupboards. 'I didn't think it would be so bad. What time are Jessie and Emilie arriving? They can scrub and mop while I unpack our boxes in the flat.'

With their agreement, I'd arranged it so the two girls could become acquainted whilst helping us sort things out. After all, they would sometimes be working together.

Agnes enjoyed taking charge and giving instructions about the cleaning and though Emilie might have thought this demeaning, having lived and worked here before us, she ignored my wife's tone and tackled each job with enthusiasm. She had her way of doing things, even with spit and polish: singing and swabbing the floors like a sailor and climbing onto chairs to wash the windows, inside and out. The four of us worked hard all morning and when we stopped at mid-day, I brought in some pies from a baker's down the road. We sat upon slatted crates in the flat and ate them with our fingers. Not the high society way Agnes would have liked, but beggars, and all that. The two girls tucked in with relish and didn't mind a bit of gravy on their chins.

Madame Chambres hadn't revealed her plans to me whilst I'd worked alongside her but Emilie had no qualms about telling tales.

'Great Aunt Adeline has moved to Lytham St Anne's and has bought a house on the seafront. She says she is going to take up golf.'

'Well, I never!' Agnes exclaimed. 'That will have cost a pretty penny.'

'And what about you?' Jessie asked, 'Don't you want to live by the seaside?'

'I will go there for visits, of course, but there is more work here in Wigan and St. Anne's is far away from many places. I have found two comfortable rooms near the Grammar School.'

Agnes raised her eyebrows, impressed by this respectable address, but remained silent, and she hadn't joined in the chatter while we'd eaten. From things said in the past, I realised she had a predicament when it came to placing Emilie. Madame Chambres was a prosperous businesswoman, yet her great-niece worked in a bakery and came and went as she pleased. And her manners were too free for Agnes's taste, who put that down to being French, a mysterious nation. It was as well she knew nothing of Emilie's past. There'd be no sitting on boxes together, never mind accepting her offer of help in the shop. I had little fear she'd ever find out and put it to the back of my mind.

And there was another thing I'd decided not to tell Agnes: Emilie's love for a man called Jean-Luc living in Northern France. And the reason she worked as hard as she did was to pay for train and boat tickets to see him.

'He's separated from his wife but as they are Catholics, divorce is nearly impossible,' she'd told me.

Another secret to keep.

After we'd wiped our mouths and washed the plates, we went downstairs. Agnes was happy to get on with arranging her new kitchen while we inspected the storeroom. This had previously been a cellar but was now fitted with rows of tall shelves. Emilie told us how to reorganise the rolls of material already lying there that I'd paid for as part of the deal.

'Have categories like *Cottons, Delicates, Wools, Hard Wearing*, and in each section put the shelves in alphabetical order. I think it is best. Great-Aunt Adeline, she did it all wrong. It was very hard to find anything.'

She went back upstairs while Jessie wrote out labels, copying them from an order book, then pasted them to the shelves while I hoisted rolls of material onto my shoulder and moved them around. She was easy company and we worked well together both in silence and in companionable chat, though we didn't rattle on unnecessarily. Knowing her as I had for so long, I knew I wouldn't regret my offer.

The last task of the day was undertaken by a sign writer and his work pleased me almost more than anything else. Slowly, our name took shape over the window in black and gold. And in a drawer, I placed a stack of writing paper with our name and business printed at the top. This Thursday and Saturday, an advertisement would appear in the newspaper for *Dunbar's Drapery, 35 Mesnes St. Grand Opening under New Management.*

PART IV

TEN MONTHS LATER

JESSIE

Dunbar's Drapery Shop: January 1901

'Y ou're looking cheerful, Jessie. Have you had good news?'

Aunt Agnes had unlocked the shop to let me in. Her youngest, Victoria, was grizzling across her shoulder, leaving her with only one free hand.

'No, Aunt, nothing special. Just happy to be out of the house.'

She sucked in her cheeks; a small frown creasing her forehead and immediately I regretted my honesty.

'Still drinking are they? It won't do yours and James's prospects much good. At least *you'll* meet a different kind of person, working here. You've your uncle to thank for that. Wanted to give you a chance even without any experience, and I must say, you've made great strides.'

'Thank you, Aunt.' I lowered my head, accepting the compliment, but she'd sunk my good mood before I'd even taken off my jacket. 'How are you today?' I asked, attempting to turn the conversation. It was unusual for her to be downstairs then I remembered Sam saying he'd be out first thing.

'Did I tell you Helena's having tantrums? And this one—' she nodded at Victoria who was wriggling on her shoulder, '—isn't sleeping well. Grace won't stop asking questions and Amy's turned into a fussy eater.'

I hadn't seen her for a few days so was regaled with all the complaints of the week. Despite the moans, she was a good mother. It was just her nature to tell everyone about it in great detail. Did all women change when they had their own little ones? I supposed so, because Aunt Agnes had never taken much interest in me and James when we'd all lived together. Once, back then, I overheard her complaining to Grandma that there was less food to go around now we were installed. She must have been a few years older than I was now. I felt guilty for a long time and when we sat down for a meal, I never asked for seconds. She couldn't hide her delight when we returned to live with Pa. Probably that experience had made her less friendly towards me.

'Where's your uncle this morning?'

She lingered near the window looking flustered, her face red. What you might call a *sight* if you were being unkind. With so little help in the flat no wonder she looked drained though there'd been talk of hiring a nurse-maid. She looked at me sharply and I realised I hadn't answered her question. It surprised me that Sam hadn't told her but maybe it slipped his mind. I tied a clean apron around my waist and started to attach sale prices to items he and I had agreed upon. I had half an hour to do this before we opened.

'He's seeing Mrs Marriott up in Shevington,' I said. 'She owes twenty pounds for black satin and chiffon and a whole lot of other stuff she bought six months ago. He thought it better to talk to her privately. Doesn't want to have to take the matter to court.'

I wished, as I'd often done, that my aunt wouldn't refer to Sam as *your uncle*. Why would I call him that when I'd known him years before they were married? In front of customers, we used *Mr Dunbar* and *Miss Gorman*. During my first week behind the counter, Aunt Agnes had bustled through from the back room to correct me when I'd called out, *Sam*.

'Shop assistants must be professional at all times.'

I was ashamed to get something so important wrong.

'Do not worry,' Emilie reassured me when I told her. 'Mrs Agnes Dunbar only knows such things because she reads about them in *The Drapers' Record*. She was not brought up in the business, as I was.'

I was cheered by her support and plied her with a hundred more questions. Never once did she make me feel I was ignorant or foolish, though she must have despaired of me at times.

My aunt put a hand through her tousled hair, jolting Victoria who began to wail. 'I'll get back upstairs. Can't leave the other girls for too long.'

'Aunt...?' I knew I wasn't a favourite of hers but she seemed out of sorts. 'If you like, I can mind the children this evening if you've jobs to do.' I had often put them to bed, although she usually asked me first. She was a restless body, frequently at her parents' or church meetings. I was useful to her... and I didn't mind not going home straight away. She weighed up my offer, and perhaps the thought of an hour to herself tipped the balance.

'Thank you, Jessie. It'll be a help. You'll take your tea with us of course? You're not going out this evening? No young man on the horizon?'

Her coy humour made me want to grind my teeth. 'No Aunt.'

My family's attempts to winkle information out of me on that subject were wasted. Although Gerard Morris was in the distant past, I still got comments. *It's odd, a pretty girl like you not having have a fellow.* I laughed them off. Told them I wasn't ready to settle down. And I never mentioned the awkward moments when I'd run into Gerard before I left the mill, or his persistent invitations. Sam knew most of it: the gin in the lemonade and escaping from the beer house, though I hadn't described the prostitute bit. It came out when we were talking about the mill. He called Gerard Morris an idiot, which bucked me up.

After Aunt Agnes disappeared upstairs I rearranged some of the displays and removed the veiled tulle hat that someone had placed on Penny's plaster head. It looked more like a giant cream puff than headwear. I was sure it wouldn't sell. A neat boater would be far more suitable for Wigan streets when Spring arrived.

When the shop first opened, I heard Emilie calling the model head *Jeanne*. 'After a girl I knew at school who had a very stiff face. But why did you choose *Penny*?'

'Because she's short of the full shilling.'

Emilie raised her eyebrows and I explained the saying.

'That is good. It is how do you say, *witty*.'

I thanked her for the compliment then she took me through a list of fabrics: *Longcloth, Nainsook, Pique* and *Silesia*. Names I couldn't then pronounce.

'Don't put yourself down, Jessie,' Sam had said in the early days when I mentioned that I found it difficult to remember all the terms. 'I always knew you were capable. I wouldn't have asked you to work for us, otherwise. You're the quickest at finding everything, even bringing material up from the storeroom.'

I was grateful for his trust but knew the main reason he'd given me the position was because he was sorry for me. He often asked if Clodagh was behaving herself at home. Sometimes I told him the truth.

AT ABOUT HALF PAST TEN, Sam appeared and with one customer lingering he simply tipped his hat at me and nodded. Once we were alone, he described the conversation with Mrs Marriot. It had gone well. There would be no need to take the non-payment any further. Like me, he'd had a lot to learn. He never spoke to the husbands about their wives' debts.

'They're not liable for the cost,' he'd once said, 'and generally they refuse to pay their wives' clothing bills. No point going to court as the law always supports the husband.'

Everything I learned in the early days was a revelation. I'd never bought from shops like *Dunbar's* and found that I loved learning about the business and what we sold; admiring the shine on satins, marvelling at the delicate embroidery on chemises. Right from the start I put aside a few pence from my wages every week so I could buy new undergarments for myself and sale linen for Teck Street.

THAT EVENING AT HOME, tired from playing with my little cousins, I faced my family's grumbles at returning late again, and not being around to cook their evening meal. I quickly peeled some potatoes, set them to boil and fried up some ham and onions.

'Any one of you can put a meal together,' I told them, setting the plates onto the bare table. Someday, I'd fling a white table-cloth over it. 'You can't expect me to do it every night.' I clattered around, too irritated to care.

'The Dunbars use you as a nurse-maid,' James was at pains to point out.

'I suppose you'd rather I was here, skivvying for you!'

Pa stepped in before it went any further. 'Don't take it that way, Jessie. I appreciate what you do, but now Agnes is a shop-keeper's wife she has a high opinion of herself. Thinks she can order you around after hours.'

'Not always, Pa,' I said. 'I offered tonight. I won't make a habit of it.'

I hated being at odds with him and had avoided it for most

of my life. I went into the kitchen where the linoleum looked more worn and cracked each day. I took the kettle from a rusting wall shelf and waited for the tea to brew. An hour earlier, in Agnes's bright green kitchen, I'd poured cocoa for the girls into spotless china cups.

I took the tea back into the front room. Now wasn't the right moment to mention that Sam and Agnes wanted me to train to use the stocking machine they'd bought and would send me for lessons to learn how it worked. I couldn't wait to start but I knew what my family's reaction would be, *not another evening away from home!*

As I slipped my nightdress over my head I remembered what my aunt had said to a church friend who'd come into the shop.

'Miss Gorman is going to be stocking knitter for us.'

A small amount would be added onto my wage for any work I did out of hours. But it annoyed me, the way I was introduced, despite standing behind the counter in my best black skirt and white blouse.

'I also work full time in the shop,' I'd told the friend. The woman's eyes widened in what I hoped was respect. It was a small thing but another example to add to what I'd learned that year. That what you do and where you live makes all the difference to how people treat you. People like the Dunbars, and even the Towneleys, spent their lives climbing invisible ladders. As a Gorman, I was judged to be on a lower rung but in my mind, I'd joined them. It was as important to me, as it was for my aunt and Sam, that I made something of myself. Hopefully, I'd be fixed in the shop for good and there wouldn't be any cause to return to the mill where I'd probably be deaf by the time I was forty.

26

SAM

Dunbar's Drapery Shop: late January 1901

Though the mornings were often too busy to exchange much news, during a lull around ten o'clock I took advantage of the empty shop to tell Jessie about my brother Frank's plans to emigrate to America, to become a Wyoming coalminer.

'I'll miss him, being closer to him than to the others. His sense of adventure is stronger than the rest of ours put together.'

Jessie laughed at that, but interrupted by the tinkle of the doorbell we assumed our usual formality. It was easy to switch back and forth, a bit like actors in a play.

A YOUNG WOMAN entered around noon and before I returned to the back room to work on the accounts, I sneaked a look at her. To my amusement, with much sighing and fuss, she rooted around in her handbag eventually pulling out a piece of paper and began telling Jessie her woes. With the back room door left partially open, I leaned against my chair to listen.

'A leaking water pipe in the linen cupboard. Four weekend visitors arriving on Friday and no sheets for the guest bedrooms,' she complained.

Jessie attempted to extract more information but the young woman wasn't listening.

'Lady Egerton is beside herself! Mr France, the butler, telephoned the family's usual linen supplier, but they are still closed as a mark of respect to the Queen. Everywhere has pulled down the blinds. It's a catastrophe! You're my last resort.'

Now I understood. The Queen's death had upset the Egertons' plans, hence the unexpected visit. Yesterday, after learning the news via the newspaper offices, I'd closed the shop from eleven o'clock until five. It was a sad occasion for many, and walking through town, I saw several lowered flags on public buildings. Further away, the dull strike of muffled bells could be heard in St Michael's belfry. According to today's paper, dances, theatres and sports events had all been cancelled. As this was the case, it seemed strange that the Egertons hadn't postponed the weekend visit. Pushing the account book to one side, I continued to listen. It was the first time Lady Egerton's personal maid had called for our services. I knew of the residence. Dunscar House was about five miles out of town. Peeking around the door, I watched as the maid clasped her head in her hands, sighing in a performance worthy of a farce at *The Grand*. And I was curious to see how Jessie would handle the situation.

I needn't have worried.

'There's no cause for concern, Miss,' Jessie's manner was warm and reassuring. 'We can supply everything on your list.'

'Are you sure?'

She spoke sharply but perhaps that was from anxiety rather than high-handedness. You never knew with staff who worked for titled gentry. Sometimes they assumed more airs than their employers did. After the maid left, out of courtesy to me, Jessie came through and presented me with the list of items needed: not just sheets but towels, pillowcases, two bed jackets, several napkins, and a tablecloth.

She looked at me with an amused expression, probably thinking of the maid's dramatic request.

'We can supply practically everything,' she said, not at all cowed by the large order. 'We have most things but you'll need to find some finer pillowcases than those in the stock room. They're only cheap calico and won't suit Lady Egerton.'

I thought quickly. The best linen shops in town would be closed but perhaps there was a way around it. 'Alright, I'll ring Lowe's. The manager there owes me several favours. I'm sure I can persuade him to open up and find me some good quality pillowcases.' Jessie was moving towards the door. 'Thank you for reassuring the maid so well. I don't like asking this but do you think you could stay on a bit longer tonight? I'll need help wrapping the goods after we've closed.'

'Of course. I'll begin while you're preparing the invoice.'

'Thank you. And you're better at parcelling than I am.'

She laughed. 'I learned to be quick-fingered when I worked four looms and it's helped me be accurate with the knitting machine.'

'We'll order a cab to take us to the Egertons' house,' I told her, 'Then it can drive you home when we've finished.' There was nothing I needed her to do after the parcelling was completed, but I thought she'd enjoy the excursion.

Her eyes widened. 'A cab?'

'Why not?' It struck me that she might not have ridden inside one before, never mind seeing Dunscar House. My life had changed so much this last year that I didn't think twice about using them. Once you had money and experienced the benefits it brought, it was as easy to shed former thrifty ways as if it was a threadbare jacket.

It seemed that Jessie agreed. 'I'd love to. It'll give the neighbours a surprise, a horse and cab in Teck Street. The only nag who comes around our way is a poor broken-down thing attached to the rag-and-bone cart.'

AT MIDDAY, I told Agnes my plans for the evening and she flushed with delight.

'It would be a fine thing if we could get Lady Egerton's business, Sam. Make sure you speak to her.'

I promised to do my best but thought it unlikely that her Ladyship would concern herself with a town draper. We closed at five o'clock, earlier than usual, and while I fetched the goods up from the storeroom, Jessie started the parcelling, including tissue-wrapping the exquisite lace-edged pillowcases I'd secured from Lowe's. It didn't take too long and when we'd carried the linens out we put them in the cab. They took up the whole of one seat so we sat side by side. Despite her tiredness, Jessie spent the journey looking out of the window, though little could be seen, but commented whenever something caught her eye: warm lights illuminating the front of a cottage, ornate iron gates securing an estate. What pleased her most was the round white face and staring eyes of an owl perched on a fence only a yard or two away. I couldn't help but share her enjoyment. She'd changed a lot from the sad, fearful girl she'd been at Rachel and Graham's wedding. At last, I'd fulfilled my promise to Mary and I was proud of the way her daughter was blossoming into a confident young woman. I was only surprised no young men were vying for her attention.

· · ·

AN HOUR later the cabby drove us through a pair of tall, formal gates, then up a tree-lined drive until we reached the house. When we stepped out of the carriage, we almost forgot our reason for being there. Even at night, the house was enchanting, combining airiness with grandeur. Standing on the gravel drive, looking up, I observed that almost every room, on every floor, was lit by electric light. The many slate roofs, the array of tall windows half-covered by trailing plants, had a delicacy you seldom saw in these sorts of houses.

'It's like something out of a fairy tale,' Jessie said, pointing at the turret-like towers.

The butler, a bald, middle-aged man in a black suit with tails and a stiff white shirt supervised a group of garden lads who took all the parcels from us. After I handed the bill to the butler I climbed back into the carriage. Jessie lingered a moment longer, surveying the gardens.

'Your aunt will be disappointed in me,' I said as we set off again. 'I think she hoped I'd be invited in to drink tea with the family.'

'Was that Lord Egerton we saw?'

'No, it was Mr France, the butler,' I said, laughing.

The carriage light showed her blushing and a moment later she giggled. 'I should have known, after all the stories I've read about big houses!'

IT WAS ONLY when we reached the outskirts of town and saw the giant pit head wheels, their shadows darker than even the night sky, that we returned to a more serious mood. Trading ideas about possible goings-on at Dunscar House this weekend had made us giddy.

A few minutes later the cab stopped and the driver let his horse drink from one of the stone water-troughs set deep in the pavement. I poked my head out of the window to see how long it might take. On the pavement, a fellow got into conversation with the cabbie and the few words I heard turned my stomach.

'What is it?' Jessie asked, when I'd settled back in my seat.

'I don't want to worry you, but there's been an accident at Pemberton Pit.'

Suddenly, the driver's face appeared at the window. Jessie leaned forward to hear him.

'That chap says a fire's broke out in the engine house in Pemberton Four Foot Mine. Thought you'd like to know, Mr Dunbar.'

He'd driven me many times, and knew I'd once been a collier. He gripped the window frame, and from the gas light shining down on him, I saw nails ingrained with dirt, like mine had been. Jessie gasped and we looked at each other. Pemberton Four was where Patrick and James worked. Sitting beside me, her face was a copy of my mother's, of the wives and daughters of all my old work mates' when rumour of a fire broke out. Fear like that never died. I had to keep calm for her sake.

'Do you know which shift Patrick and James are on?' I asked, leaning out of the window again. Streams of people were running towards the pit. I turned to her. She was on the edge of tears.

'I'm not sure. They changed shifts this week, but what to...I can't remember,' and she thumped the seat in her distress.

I took her hand and squeezed it. 'We'll go to your house first. See if they're at home.' I gave the driver the address in Teck Street and told him to be as quick as he could. As we trundled on our way I tried to reassure her. 'They may be sitting in front of the fire with their boots off for all we know.'

'Now I think of it, I don't believe they're on the same shift.' Her voice choked with fear and I patted her hand as I did Grace's or Helena's when they were distressed.

'Try not to worry.'

'I'm glad I won't have to go into the house alone.'

The driver had barely stopped the horse before Jessie slipped out of the cab. I followed and took the key out of her shaking hand. Already faces were at windows gawping at the waiting cab. By tomorrow, the whole street would know how Jessie had come home. Inside, the table was unlaid and the rooms silent.

'That wasn't here this morning,' she said, snatching up a piece of paper on the table. 'It's from James. He says, *there's been a fire and I've gone back to see where Pa is. Wait in for us.*' She turned it over but there was nothing else. Her eyes were huge, her face white and pinched. 'Can we go over to Pemberton? Find out what's going on?'

I steered her to a chair. 'You're done in. It's best if you stay here as James suggests. Your father might return of his own accord and will need you. I'll go and look for him, then bring back what news I can.'

She thanked me, but I saw she was eager for me to leave. Neither of us mentioned Clodagh. Wherever she was, I guessed there'd be a glass of ale in her hand.

27

JESSIE

Later the same day

The clip-clopping of hooves coming down the street startled me awake. I hadn't intended to fall asleep and didn't know how much time had passed. Still thinking about my dream where all kinds of oddities had occurred, I rushed to open the door. Pa came in first, his face a ghastly white and I smothered my questions for later. Sam sat him down and James fetched him a glass of water. His chest rose and fell in painful breaths as he sipped.

In a low voice, James briefly recounted what he'd learned.

'When I arrived at the pit the rescuers said a doctor was called as soon as the fire was known about. He tended the injured who came out of the explosion and sent the worst cases to the hospital. They think about fifteen men lost their lives. There were lots of us hanging about, waiting for news.'

A picture formed in my mind of the dead being brought to their homes throughout the night. It was too dreadful to dwell on and all I could do was pray and dash away my tears. Sam saw me weeping and said I needn't come into work the next day, that he'd manage.

'Keep an eye on your father.' His voice was too low for Pa to hear and I pressed his hand to show I was grateful.

'Thank you, lad,' my father said hoarsely.

Sam got back into the cab and the clatter and grind of wheels faded as it took him out of Teck Street. Together, James and I helped Pa upstairs and when he lay on his bed in his filthy trousers and shirt, I pulled off his boots and left James to undress him. A few minutes later he joined me downstairs and I asked for more details.

'A fire started in the engine house; it's also where the south tunnel starts. Once it got going the air blew smoke and fumes down the tunnel into the workings. Pa was lucky. He and some of the others weren't too close but smelt the smoke and escaped through one of the other doors out of the intake and ran along the return airway to the pit eye.'

'He must have been trapped in the smoke awhile,' I said. 'He still can't get his breath. What about the others? You said there were bodies.'

'Fifteen, I don't know, maybe more. Those lads tried to get out the way they'd come in, being closer to that door than Pa and his mates were, but the brow to the south tunnel had too much smoke in it an' they were suffocated. Young uns mostly.'

I put my hand to my face and let the tears run over my fingers. Lads of thirteen worked that seam, Pa once said. Their poor, poor mothers. In silence we ate some bread and cheese, being all we could face, then went to our rooms.

ABOUT AN HOUR LATER, I heard Clodagh stamp in and go upstairs. There was some harsh talk between her and Pa before the door latch clicked, and she headed back down again.

In the morning I got up to prepare the porridge and found

her asleep on the couch. It was easy enough to creep around. Even stoking the range and clanging pans didn't disturb her. I imagined she was sleeping off a hangover. As Pa wasn't too badly affected, I went in to work as usual. Far better to be busy than get in Clodagh's way at home.

THE TOWN WAS USED to pit disasters, but they never got easier to bear. Three or four of the bereaved came in for black armbands and it was hard to look into the eyes of those bleak faces. There was no call for mourning clothes; Sunday best dresses and suits would suffice. Only the rich who died in their beds could afford that kind of fashion. As always with a pit disaster, an inquest was held and people were held up for reproof. Or not.

'The Mine Inspector's Report's in the paper,' Pa told me six weeks later. He'd fully recovered. 'Constitution of an ox,' he'd always said, and jabbed at it in disgust. 'The bosses, they should never let lads of thirteen anywhere near paraffin.'

'Is that what set the fire off?' I asked.

'It is. No sign of the under-manager in the Engine House to supervise him. The boy used a torch to thaw the outlet of the exhaust on the engine. They freeze up in cold weather, you know. This wasn't enough so he poured paraffin on frozen parts of the engine, setting it alight. Listen, I'll read it to you.' He took his time, pausing at a difficult spelling.

'*The mine officials denied knowledge of a fire being lighted on the engine in this way, but the boy, name of Crowley, who attended the engine and others working in the vicinity, bore out the facts.*' Pa looked up. 'Mother of God, thirteen, and only worked underground a few months. '*Efforts were made to extinguish the fire but to no avail,*' Pa lay the paper down. 'The bosses come up with all kinds of excuses as to why such a young un was left without supervision, but this takes the biscuit. '*When Crowley was asked if he'd ever handled paraffin lamps before, he said no. He was then asked if he'd ever lit a lamp at home. 'No, Mother won't let me mess with it.''*

I thanked God, as I'd done many times these last two months, that Pa had survived. My blood ran cold when I thought, what if...? I spoke of it to Sam, who knew the dangers first-hand, and we spent a moment in quiet reflection. If he hadn't left his job at Pemberton years ago, he could have been caught in that fire, too.

As was the way of things, good luck fell on some folk and not on others. I took part in the general rejoicing when Sam and Agnes received some news.

'Lady Egerton is transferring her patronage to us,' he told me, sweeping a mock bow as if being presented at court. 'Thanks to you and the way you dealt with her *crisis*.'

After this, Lady Egerton's maid appeared regularly with lists for the family and asked to see lace and collars for herself. She thawed, turned friendly, and we heard that her employer was pleased by our quick response to the *catastrophe* on the night of the fire. I could have said something to her about real disasters but didn't. Better to keep my trap shut than lose my job. But I often thought of those poor women who'd bought their mourning bands from us and the way their eyes never lifted any higher than the shop counter.

2 8

SAM

*H*elena and Amy wouldn't put their coats on and Grace, who'd already dressed herself, thought she was helping. 'Bending your sisters' arms backwards only hurts them.' I raised my voice to hear myself above the noise of their squeals, and begged for peace.

Finally, I shepherded them downstairs then found I didn't have my keys and ran back up to the parlour. A minute later, three pairs of eyes stared up at me accusingly when I jangled the bunch above their heads. Victoria in her perambulator, blessedly, slept on.

'Where's Mama?' Amy asked.

Grace sighed and said in her eldest sister voice, 'I told you at porridge time. She's staying in bed. I 'spect she's got a temperature. Stand still,' and she fiddled with her sister's hair bow which was coming loose. Then Helena wanted to know what *a tempy thing* was.

It was like this all the time, questions and answers. Sometimes I felt Grace knew more about our day-to-day life than I did.

'It's when you're hot and bothered,' she explained. 'Daddy, why are we all dressed up if Mama isn't coming? Aren't we going to the photography place after all?'

'Of course we are. I made a promise, didn't I? I've asked your cousin Jessie to help you push Amy and Victoria in the perambulator. But don't step off the pavement until I tell you to.'

I'd dithered about whether to close the shop or not after Agnes suddenly decided she was too tired to come to the photographers. She'd got up once during the night with Victoria who had been sick, but was now well again. Keeping the appointment meant losing the morning trade, which was a pity, especially on a Saturday, but I couldn't let the girls down. They'd talked for days about sitting for Mr Wragg. Even Amy, nearly three years old, could point to a photograph if someone said the word. Luckily, we already had photocards of ourselves with the two older ones.

'Are you sure?' Jessie had asked when I'd broken the news. 'Is it all right with my aunt?'

'She's asleep and I think a short break away from me and the children will do her good.' And the sooner the nurse-maid we'd hired could start, the calmer life would be. Before Victoria's birth, Emilie had suggested we hire the same cleaning woman her Great Aunt had used and Molly, a cheerful lass from Ince, came in two or three times a week which was something.

Outside, I gave Jessie the keys and clung to the girls' hands while she locked the shop door. When she turned around, her face was glowing. She was looking forward to the outing far more than I was. And there was something else I could do for her.

'Have you ever had your image taken, Jessie? We can get one done if you like.'

'Really? It was never thought of in the family and I doubt Pa
had the money. I wish...'

'What?'

'Sometimes I wish I had one of mother to look at.'

I swallowed and stooped to lift Amy into the perambulator,
opposite Vicky. I'd often wished the same myself, or that I'd had
the ability to sketch Mary's face from memory. All I carried was
a picture my head, the same as Jessie did, I supposed. 'Let's go,' I
called. This was not the time to start remembering Mary
Gorman.

I'D CHOSEN *Wragg's* over the other half dozen photographers in
the town because my brother Frank, and his soon-to-be wife
Henrietta, had used them before he left for Wyoming. Now,
their images took pride of place on my parents' mantelpiece.
Also, I was intrigued by the nameplate over the shop: *Wragg and
Daughter*. It was a fine thing to have a child work alongside you.
Seeing the sign sparked ideas: I imagined a future where one or
more of my girls learned the business. Grace, at six, was already
taking an interest and loved sorting coloured buttons into piles
and putting them away in drawers.

'You're too soft with them by half!' Agnes once said as Grace
emptied a packet of buttons onto the parlour carpet. 'A shop is
no place for children.' But I didn't agree.

At the sound of the shop door opening, Miss Wragg came
out to greet us. She was a tall woman in her mid to late twen-
ties with a confident, pleasant face and a good figure. She
showed us into the back of the shop where there was a large
studio with chairs ranged against two walls, and a small table
piled with books and dolls. A chemical smell hung about the
room which I guessed came from the developing workshop.
On one wall hung a painted canvas depicting a view of hills
and streams; a typical background for posing against. Jessie

lifted Amy out of the pram whereupon she ran to the table and snatched up a book while I guided the others safely around a camera fixed to a wooden tripod in the middle of the room.

'How would you like the children posed, Mrs Dunbar?' Miss Wragg said to Jessie.

'Jessie's not our mama,' Grace piped up before I could explain.

I could have kicked myself. Jessie was blushing furiously and of course, Grace was staring at her.

'I'm sorry, Miss Wragg. I should have made the introductions as soon as we arrived. Miss Gorman here is my children's cousin. Jessie's helping out because my wife is unwell today.'

'Mama's got a temperature,' Grace told her.'

'It's a pity your mother can't be here, but she'll love seeing the photographs of you when they're ready,' Miss Wragg said.

To head off further talk about Agnes, I pointed to a display of *Carte de Visite* photographs of the Pit Brow Lassies. 'I used to know some of the girls when I worked as a collier,' I told the children. Grace ran over to see them and I lifted her up for a better view.

'Those were taken by the previous owner about thirteen years ago,' Miss Wragg said. 'Did you know there was a protest march to Westminster in London to try to save their jobs at the mines?'

Helena was the first to ask, this time. 'Why?'

'Because their jobs were at risk. Some people thought they shouldn't be doing that kind of work, but they were overruled, and the women were allowed to continue earning. The Pit Brow lassies were asked to come here and pose for photographs because there was a lot of interest in them after their march on Westminster.'

'What do they do at the pit?' Grace wanted to know.

'They sort out the coal and wear trousers like the men do.

They find them easier to work in and it keeps their skirts clean,' Miss Wragg said.

I liked how she spoke to the children.

'Speaking of working women, your father is lucky to have you in the business and keep the family name going. I'm hoping one or more of my girls will join me. It's a new century. Life is changing, and we mustn't stay stuck in the past.'

'I very much agree with you there, Mr Dunbar.'

I took her to mean suffrage. What man in his right mind wouldn't want his daughters to have as full a life, even a political one, as any man: though my father wouldn't have agreed. But this wasn't the time or place for discussion. Miss Wragg was an interesting woman, educated and talented. Someone my daughters could grow up to be like.

'I want to run the shop, Pa,' Grace declared, as if reading my thoughts.

'Come over here, girls,' Miss Wragg said. She led them to a chaise longue where they sat straight as soldiers and looked in awe at the equipment. Grace held Victoria carefully and Helena and Amy clutched the doll between them.

'Look up when Miss Wragg tells you to,' I told them. She was fiddling with camera settings and positions but thought to include Jessie who had rather been left out.

'Do you work in the shop as well, Miss Gorman?'

'Yes. Sam rescued me from mill work. I was very grateful for the chance.'

'Now, girls, look at me!' Miss Wragg called from under the black blanket which covered her head and shoulders. And when she emerged from it, in one perfect moment they lifted their heads before the flash went off. I'd prepared them for it but Helena had forgotten and let out a wail. Grace nudged her to shut up then complained that Victoria was too heavy on her lap.

'I'll hold her for a while,' Jessie said, lifting her up, and jigged her about in her arms. Once Victoria was resettled and a few more pictures were taken, I told Jessie it was her turn.

'Are you sure? This dress isn't very smart.'

'Please, Cousin,' Grace wheedled, pulling on her hand. 'You must have one on your own. Your daddy will like it and you can give another to Cousin James.'

'It's true Pa would like one, but James isn't living with us now. He's renting a room with one of his work friends.'

Jessie had told me about this move a fortnight ago and like her, I regretted it. James was too immature to break out on his own, tending to moodiness when things didn't go his way. They'd miss his wage, but Jessie said they were looking for a lodger to help with the rent.

While the children were busy with the toys and books, Miss Wragg positioned Jessie on the chaise longue for a studio portrait. I thought she might be self-conscious but her expression was composed. She seemed to be in a private world as she turned her head slightly away from her body, a position I'd seen in portrait paintings. It reminded me of the one time I'd visited Lydia Holdsworth's art school in Manchester. She'd given me a tour of the studio where three or four of her classmates were posing for friends. Jessie's face and figure had the same stillness. Her dress may have been plain, but she certainly wasn't. What I used to think of as her *prettiness*, had turned into real beauty. I decided I'd ask Miss Wragg for a few more copies when they were developed. One for herself, another for Patrick, and the third for me. Her faraway intensity made the resemblance to her mother even more pronounced.

29

JESSIE

Teck Street: May 1901

$\mathcal{T}$he strong afternoon wind bowled me along the street and tore at my shawl. I stopped to rearrange it while hoisting my grocery bag against my chest. The handles had made red dents in my palms. Thankfully, Teck Street lay just around the corner.

By the time I reached the house the wind had dropped and a welcome shaft of sunlight warmed my face. Above me, slate roofs shone and the grubby houses took on a glitter. Outside our door, I put down the grocery bag and slid my hand into my skirt pocket for the key. The smeary front window needed a good clean but screwed up newspaper and vinegar would shift the dirt.

While I was deciding when to tackle that task, a sudden movement within caught my eye. Two figures came into view, dark shapes against the reflected light. The sight was so strange that for a second I thought I was outside the wrong house. The pair saw me, broke apart, and moved back into the darkness.

I'd had suspicions for a while about Clodagh and the lodger,

202

Brendan O'Donnell. She'd known him before he moved in with us. Now here was proof: they were carrying on right under my father's nose. I took my time unlocking the door but I needn't have worried. They'd disappeared through the backyard gate, which was still swinging in the wind.

Pa couldn't know what was going on or he'd have kicked the lodger out already. I'd seen them flirting and hoped that Clodagh would stop it of her own accord. Unlikely now. That's what came of choosing someone young and good-looking for James's room.

Potatoes and ham would have to do for the evening meal but my mind wasn't on food. It was hard to believe what I'd seen; kissing him in the front room without bothering to close the curtains. Didn't she care who might be looking in? The first chance I got to be on my own with Pa, I'd tell him. Perhaps he'd throw them both out. I drank the tea I'd made earlier and felt more cheerful. Once she and the lodger were gone, we could return to the people we'd been before she'd blighted our lives. Maybe James would return and Pa become his old self again.

With the ham cooking in the range, I rested in Ma's rocking chair and thought about the conversation which lay ahead. The idea unsettled me. How would Pa take it? Would he be hurt or angry? I started at every noise within and without. Eventually, I lit the gas lamp and took up my knitting, hoping the repetitive click of the needles would calm me. When the food was ready I ate my meal alone and left the rest in the range.

The hours passed. The moon rose and I fell into bed knowing I'd be woken later when the public houses closed.

Clogs banging on the stone floor woke me in an instant. Pa? No, it was Clodagh cackling and a man snorting with laughter. I lay rigid. Two, three minutes passed. I heard gasps, then a bang as if something had knocked against the table. I sat upright, wrapped my shawl around my shoulders and crept onto the landing taking care not to make the stairs creak. When I reached the bottom step I opened the door an inch.

Clodagh was leaning against the back of the couch with her arms wrapped loosely around the lodger's waist. He pressed against her, his hands all over her body, kissing her mouth and throat. Then one hand went down and pulled up her skirt. At the same instant, the front door opened.

Brendan O'Donnell was quick, I gave him that. He let go of Clodagh who floundered like a carp while he scampered into the kitchen. It was only after I heard the backdoor slam behind him that I realised his shirt had been unbuttoned and his braces were dangling around his thighs. Pa stood in the doorway until Clodagh righted herself, perched on the edge of the couch, and smoothed her hair. Before I could draw breath, Pa whipped across the room and whacked her once across the shoulder. Befuddled with beer, she fell into a heap on the couch. I gripped the edge of the landing door so hard it dug into my hand. I must have gasped, or perhaps the door creaked, I don't know, but they both looked up.

Clodagh was upright in a second despite the blow. 'What's that spying little rat doin' up at this hour?' She snarled. 'Aren't Methodies supposed to be in bed by nine o'clock?' Her mouth twisted in disgust at being found out. Fury surged through me and I wanted to hit her pudgy, smug face.

Pa must have guessed from the look of me how I felt. He came over, turned me around and gave me a gentle push upstairs. 'Not now. Wait 'til morning.'

I DOUBT there was much sleep for any of us and when I rose to make breakfast, I saw that O'Donnell's few belongings, taken out of James's old room, were bundled together by the front door. No doubt we'd be looking for another miner to take his place. Please God the next one was too old or ugly to tempt her.

'Where is she?' I asked Pa when I placed a bowl before him.

'In James's room,' he muttered.

We were still eating our porridge when she sailed downstairs like the Lady Mayoress herself. She stood in front of us with her hands on her hips.

'Save me some of that, won't you?' She pointed at our dishes. 'I'm not stopping to eat as I'm goin' round to the Magistrate to complain about that thump you gave me, Patrick Gorman.' She pulled down her blouse at the shoulder where we saw a blossoming bruise.

'Do your worst,' said Pa. 'As if I care.'

'And I'll give him Jessie's name as witness for me'.

Pa's face crumpled. Satisfied, Clodagh slammed the door with no apparent difficulty.

I bit my lip, ruing last night's impulsiveness. If only I'd stayed in bed and seen nothing.

'Superficial bruising,' said Pa when he'd recovered from the shock. 'She'll put in a day's work, no problem. Only hope the magistrate works it out.'

'But what if you're fined or sent to prison? You'd lose your job.' I twisted my hands together, despairing at the plight we were in.

'I know it's a bit late for *sorry*, and I am.' He looked at me ruefully, and his face hardened. 'But I couldn't help meself when I saw that lout pawing at her. I'd have clobbered *him* if he hadn't made himself scarce.'

'If I tell the Magistrate what happened before you arrived he'll understand you were riled. You must back me up. It'll be better for you in the long run.'

He said I could be right. Even so, I set off for work depressed by dark thoughts of what lay ahead.

30

JESSIE

The Police Court: May 1901

*J*essie. Are you ailing? You don't seem yourself today.'

I'd run up from the storeroom for the umpteenth time and though I was a little weary that wasn't why Sam was asking. I shook my head, unsure how to answer, but was saved from replying when the doorbell tinkled. He gave me a sharp look before stretching up to replace a box on a high shelf.

I turned to the customer and pasted a smile on my face and engaged in conversation with Mrs Birch, a regular. I wrapped the five yards of muslin she'd chosen and bid her good day. As soon as the door closed I flopped onto the stool behind the counter. Sam hadn't been the only person to ask after my health and I suppose he'd heard those enquiries, too. It was easy to fob off customers but he knew me better. He went into the back room, and a few minutes later, brought me a cup of tea.

'Drink this while it's quiet and tell me what's going on.'

I mentioned a sore throat then decided to be honest. It

would be a comfort to confide in him rather than keep this to myself. He'd have to know the truth when I needed time off to go to court. But I didn't want to involve Sam in our affairs any more than was necessary; it was obvious my aunt wanted to forget Pa was ever her brother-in-law. She thought the Dunbars were *refined* folk now. Clodagh's carrying-on would isolate us even more than we already were. With some hesitation, I recounted what had occurred the other night and that I'd been called as a witness against Pa.

Sam hissed through his teeth, said I could have time off and would pay me anyway, even though I offered to make up the hours.

'No, Jessie. If I need help, I'll ask Emilie or cancel my appointments.'

Surely there was no other employer as kind as Sam. For the rest of the day, I gritted my teeth and refused to think about the Magistrate, but at home there was news.

'The case is coming up a week today, at the Police Court,' Pa told me.

FRIDAY MORNING. The Courthouse reared up, gabled and turreted, blackened by smoke. Hundreds of windows looked down on us like accusing eyes. Pa and I squeezed each other's hand, put on encouraging smiles and stepped inside. We were directed to an upstairs room. On the landing were a dozen other people standing or sitting: waiting to tell their own tale, lay blame or avoid fines.

The air was dusty, but the landing was bright from the bare electric light bulb hanging from the ceiling. Pa nudged me to look at it, though I was used to electricity by now. Clodagh leaned against a wall, unsmiling, and for once silent. We hadn't seen her for a week. She'd made herself scarce from his bed and my board. She could have slept on a park bench for all I cared.

.   .   .

WHEN OUR NAMES WERE CALLED, we entered a large, dark room with wood panelling on the walls. Three men sat at separate desks. Immediately, I broke into a sweat, thinking about how I must put the truth across. The Magistrate, Mr Sheffield, introduced himself but not the other two. He was a big man with a dark, jowly face who shot us a look of contempt. We were told to sit on the narrow bench in front of his desk. He asked Clodagh first, as the complainant, to tell him what happened. She stood quickly.

'I was just sharing a bit of a joke with the lodger, Sir, and he,' she pointed at Pa, 'Got hold of the wrong end of the stick and whacked me hard.' She snorted, then put a hand over her mouth.

'Is that all?'

'Yes, your honour. Nothing more to it,' she simpered.

Mr Sheffield frowned and I saw that her play-acting wouldn't wash with him. They'd know she'd been hauled into court before. It lifted my spirits, but Pa had to play his part, too, except his expression was shuttered. He hadn't looked at the Magistrate, or Clodagh, once. His gaze was fixed upon a clock sitting on a bookshelf and I wondered if he was reflecting on all the wasted hours we'd spent in strife. Clodagh, on the other side of me, was stroking the fringes on her shawl. I suppose she thought she'd told a convincing story. It didn't seem real, this room with its plaster ceiling mouldings, and paintings of stern-looking men. Or sitting in front of a stranger who was about to lay before us the shabbiness of our lives.

'I'd like to hear your version of the events now, Mr Gorman.'

Pa stood up and blinked as if surprised to be there. 'Sir, I came home after a few pints in the public house but was not exceedingly drunk and found her with another man, namely our lodger. I slapped her across the shoulder, once. She was only bruised. I saw the mark in the morning. She did not need to see a nurse.'

He told it plainly. No ranting. No anger. It was unexpected. Mr Sheffield looked across at Clodagh. 'And this is the witness to the assault? Mr Gorman's daughter, Jessie, aged nineteen?'

I rose to answer. 'Yes, Sir.'

'I understand that you work in a draper's shop.'

'That's right, Sir.'

'Tell me in your own words what you saw.'

'Well, my father hit her across the shoulder, once, but he had cause to. She and the lodger, Brendan O' Donnell, were...' I should have thought exactly how I would describe this part because I didn't know what term to use. Kissing wasn't strong enough. It didn't tell Mr Sheffield what would have happened next if Pa hadn't arrived. If I was going to save him from a sentence, I had to use language that had never crossed my lips. 'They were kissing and about to have intercourse on the couch. She let him put his hand up her skirts. Father came home, saw them, and then Mr O'Donnell ran away. We haven't seen him since.'

'Mr Gorman, is this what happened?'

'It is, Sir, and I'm sorry I saw red. This woman has lived with me as a wife for the past six years, on and off. It's not what you expect of someone you share a bed with and provide for.'

The Magistrate looked down his nose at us. Clodagh said nothing, but bit her lip and leaned forwards. 'I've decided to drop the charges, yer honour. It's all a bit of a misunderstanding. We'd had a drop to drink, me and Brendan, before coming home and he were just being friendly like and he went a bit too far. I don't want no harm to come of it so I'll say nothing more.'

Mr Sheffield glanced up at the ceiling and put his hands around his neck as if his head needed support. One of the other men broke the silence. I recognised his uniform. He was a high-up policeman.

'It seems to me that your behaviour, *Mrs Gorman*, isn't as upright as you made out when you brought this charge to the Police Office over a week ago, so I conclude you've made the right decision.' He turned to Mr Sheffield. 'I recommend The Bench overlook it this time. It is his first offence.'

The Magistrate wrote something in a ledger and fixed us with a stern eye. 'Mr Gorman, although you were provoked, I hope I won't see you before me again and that you'll keep your fists under better control. Case dismissed, but you will incur a fine of five shillings and costs.'

In the waiting room, people looked up as we came out, hoping to gauge from our expressions whether it was a thumbs up or down. We left them unsatisfied. The case would be written up in the newspaper so everyone here, and our relatives, would read about it whether we liked it or not.

ON THE ROAD, Pa didn't speak but I could tell he was relieved. He nodded at me, then at Clodagh and set off for the pit. Relief flooded through me because, in a few minutes, I'd be at the shop where I could slip into another life. In that world, people talked decently to each other. I'd have Sam at my side, a friend who encouraged me when things appeared bleak. I walked away from the Court House without acknowledging Clodagh. It would be awkward when we all met this evening, but I hoped she'd learned her lesson.

I WAS ALMOST at Mesnes Street when a hand grasped my shoulder and twisted it around. Clodagh's rough, insistent voice hissed, 'If you ever pull a trick like that again, I swear I'll find a dog and set it on you.'

I jerked away but she pushed me against a shop window and I couldn't escape her fingers digging into the side of my head.

Suddenly, she let go and swung away, confident after her threat. My legs refused to move. My eyes watered from the pain in my temples and all I could see was a mastiff with slobbering jaws: the kind tied to lamp-posts outside drinking dens. I didn't doubt she had a pal who owned one. *Do us a favour, mate. Let it loose. I'll tell you when and where.*

Terror propelled me away and I dodged through the streets, desperate to close the door on everything my world had become.

I almost fell inside *Dunbar's*. Sam paused his greeting mid-sentence. 'What's happened? You're as white as linen.'

We went into the back room while there were no customers and I stumbled through the session with the Magistrate. When I reached the point where Clodagh grabbed me, the shop door tinkled open.

'Stay here awhile. Get something to eat and drink and tell me later,' he insisted.

AT CLOSE OF DAY, he asked if I'd stay on and mind the girls because Agnes was sleeping at her mother's, *for a bit of peace.* He'd be at a supplier, but not for long, and the nurse-maid would give the girls their tea and put them to bed before she left. 'Help yourself to anything in the larder,' he finished.

I was grateful not to have to go home and face whatever was in store. After I'd eaten and read a story to the older ones, I curled up in front of the fire. I'd tamped down my feelings all day but now alone, the horror of Clodagh's threat overwhelmed me. My tears started just before I heard Sam's step on the stairs. I mopped my face and tried to pull myself together. He was back earlier than expected and I didn't want him to see me like this.

He bombarded me with questions. 'Are you warm enough? Can I bring you a drink or more food?' When I shook my head he took a seat on the other side of the fire, opposite me. 'If you're up to it Jessie, can you finish your story from this morning?'

There was something about the quietness of his voice, the low crackle of the flames, that allowed the tears to fall and I told him, in incoherent phrases, that I wasn't safe.

'She threatened me. Says she'll set a dog on me. I can't live with them anymore.' I found I was shaking and clasped my hands to keep them still. The thought of the pain inflicted by a mastiff made me feel faint. I stared at the flowery, yellow wallpaper as if I'd never seen it before and jumped up. 'I'll leave Wigan. Get as far away from her as possible. I'll be sorry to give up my job, but what else can I do?'

Sam came over and pushed me gently back in the chair. Exhausted from crying, I watched him walk around the room. He picked up a stool, brought it over and placed it next to me. He lowered himself on it and took my hand. 'Jessie, please don't give up your work here. I can't lose you. I'll think of something and I won't let that bitch hurt you.'

I'd never heard him use a word like that and suddenly he was both a stranger and familiar.

'You're precious to me... to all of us.'

I felt as if someone had sawn me in half and both halves were still breathing. One part urged me to jump up and rush out of the room, and the other part said, *this is what I wanted to know.* I pulled my hand away. 'You're very kind,' I managed. From somewhere I found the strength to stand and throw my shawl about my shoulders. 'I ought to go now.'

'I'll get a cab for you, it's late, and if Clodagh tries anything send a note round and I'll be over. Doesn't matter what time of night.'

· · ·

To our relief, Clodagh decided to make herself scarce and went off to visit her brothers in Yorkshire. The house was blessedly peaceful even if my mind jumped around like a firecracker. In the shop, I smiled, dropped coins into the cash register, and made up parcels of cotton gloves, silk stockings and lace collars. I forced myself to concentrate on the customers and I did.

I put everything into my work so it was only at night, in bed, that my mind felt as if it was a scrapbook; full of ruined pictures and inky scribbles. In the end, I told myself a story. *He felt sorry for my situation. A sympathetic friend who saw me crying.* Would he really have come out in the middle of the night if I'd been threatened at home? Of course not. It was probably one of those things people say when a crisis happens and don't really mean it.

31

SAM

The night streets of Wigan: May 1901

$\mathcal{A}$t the end of the Stewards' meeting I broke away from the small knot of men stacking chairs and tidying up, giving the excuse I was needed at home. Setting my sights on the outside door, my escape was blocked by a thin, grey-haired man making a bee-line towards me. I knew Herbert Gaskell well and it would have been rude to have dashed away without speaking. I stifled a sigh and let him talk. The evening had already been a stream of trivia, and on tonight's topic, blocked drains between the chapel and the meeting room, I hadn't contributed. Without a full understanding of what Gaskell wanted, I promised I'd look into it then flew down the stone steps and into the street.

All week, shop and home life had been hectic, providing little opportunity for reflection. I decided to take a longer, less direct route to Mesnes Street.

It led me past a public house of an inferior kind where a thick-set man was unchaining a dog from a railing. Bill Sykes came to mind and I told myself not to be fanciful. It wasn't such an unusual sight... I grasped the same railing and watched the man and dog lumber out of sight. It was only then that the real danger of Jessie's situation struck me, and the dilemma of her living with someone as vicious as Clodagh Boyle.

One by one, as the streetlamps were lit, I walked in and out of dark circles on the pavements, with my thoughts skittering back and forth, unable to land on any sort of conclusion; very unlike my usual methodical way of sorting out a problem. When I stopped suddenly, the fellow behind me uttered an oath and swerved away.

I carried on walking. Was there even a solution to this mess? Had I been too hasty in promising Jessie I'd keep her safe from that woman? Things said with the best of intentions aren't always rational, or possible. Of course, she was scared by the thought someone might strike at her. Who wouldn't be? But could I keep my word? More familiar streets were now in view, and I hurried on, knowing I had to do something.

Sitting beside her at the fireplace as she told her tale, the image of a mastiff attacking her had overwhelmed me. I'd been impetuous by holding her hand but at the time my only thought had been to comfort and protect her. After she'd left the flat I'd paced the room feeling useless. Mary's letter played on my mind. I'd not fully kept my promise when Jessie was young: a few visits to the house, handing out pennies, a toy on her birthday, didn't really count. And now, when she really needed me, I might fail her again. The obvious thing would be for her to leave Wigan and the shop, but...

I REACHED HOME HOLDING a seed of memory. Upstairs, Agnes was already asleep, so without disturbing her, I went into the parlour. Resting my head against the back of the couch I allowed my thoughts to flow, towards someone I'd once met at a church meeting. His name was hidden from me, but I remembered he'd talked about looking for a lodger. I tried to conjure his features and a red, cheerful, nameless face swam into view. Nothing for it but to make a search. I gathered my files: agendas, minutes, letters, and lay them on the desk and began. I must have scanned and set aside fifty different documents before the name *Mr F.Urmston* leapt out. It was then I remembered our conversation: nothing to do with church matters.

'My late wife was a customer at Madame Chambres's shop,' he'd told me on learning I was the new proprietor. 'She wrote down the titles of some French songs when she knew I was a singer. Interesting woman, if a little mad.'

I had the address. I quickly wrote my letter, convinced he'd remember me. I delivered it by hand early the next morning. Haste seemed paramount. Even an hour's delay might prove disastrous.

32

JESSIE

The following week: Wisley Road, May 1901

*D*uring Clodagh's absence from Wigan, I told Pa about her threat with the dog. On her return, he pushed a Bible into her hand and made her swear on it not to touch me.

Whenever I recalled that evening, I always thought the scene must have resembled something from a lurid half penny newspaper. Her promise did little to calm me and I was full of jitters whenever she opened the front door. What had we come to when I couldn't trust a member of our household not to harm me? From that time on, there was a frozen silence whenever Pa, she, or I, passed each in the house, or in the street.

I took my worries to chapel. I repeated *Amen* when the minister prayed for the safety of all who laboured underground and for the health of the new King. Then I offered up my own prayers. *'Please God, keep us in this state for as long as possible and thank you for Pa getting off so lightly at court.'* The service over, I slipped away without speaking to anyone. Yes, I had friends there, people I liked, but everyone enjoyed a good gossip.

· · ·

THE SHORT REPORT in the newspaper about Clodagh, Pa and the lodger, brought my grandmother into the shop with raised eyebrows and questions on her lips. I managed to fob most of them off before she went up to the flat. Most customers didn't know me well enough to connect me to Teck Street and the goings-on there. Their interests lay upstairs with the family, not with the assistant behind the counter. With Sam in and out for much of the week, we didn't get the chance to speak again about Clodagh's threat. But that didn't stop me from pondering on his promise — *I won't let her harm you.*

During his absences, Emilie worked alongside me and I appreciated having her there. Her humour and way of looking at things almost made me forget about home and the questions wheeling around my mind.

ON FRIDAY, an hour before we closed for the day when I was hoping for a quiet finish, Sam came down from the flat and handed me a piece of paper with an address on it.

'This could be your new lodgings. That's if you still want to move out of Teck Street.'

His mouth was tight and I couldn't read his expression. I'm sure my eyes bulged like a *Comic Cuts* character. 'Do you mean it?'

He gave a slight smile. 'You can move in this evening and I'll introduce you to the owner. Mr Urmston is a respectable widower, a solicitor nearing retirement age. I know him through joint church meetings.' He led me to the door and opened it. 'Go home before Clodagh returns and leave your father a letter. Don't tell him where you are but say he can contact you at the shop.' His words tripped over each other as if speed were vital. 'Tell the cabbie to wait for you. Pack everything you need and come back. Here's the fare.'

He shouted after me as I walked down Mesnes Street. 'We'll go to Wisley Road together.'

FIFTEEN MINUTES LATER, fingers shaking, I pushed the key into the lock and opened the front door to an empty house. I followed Sam's instructions: packed, left the letter for Pa and slipped away like a ghost. I bundled everything I had into the cab. One case and two bags weren't a lot for twenty years on this earth.

On my return, Aunt Agnes came down with some linen goods for me: pillowcases, sheets, towels. 'I expect you'll want to get settled in as soon as you can Jessie.'

I thanked her for the goods, but despite her show of support I was uneasy. The impression she gave was one of disapproval. Was that for the move, or for me? Girls my age lived with their families, didn't branch out on their own. But how would she have felt if she'd been threatened with having a dog set upon her? She whisked away, and I stared at her retreating back, feeling muddled. Perhaps I'd misunderstood her, or was she simply weary from being with the children?

I climbed into the cab after Sam and decided that the time for tears was over.

WHEN WE REACHED Wisley Road I almost fell off my seat in surprise. It was a part of town I'd hardly ever been to. Doctors, bankers, headmasters, and such like chose to live in this area. We stopped in front of a large house with a small front garden. It was hard to grasp the building as a whole: three storeys, numerous windows and more chimney pots than I could count in one glance. On both sides of the street were young trees enclosed by tall metal railings keeping them straight. I turned to Sam who was collecting my bags.

'Are you sure this is the right place? I can hardly believe you've found me somewhere so grand.'

'When I thought of Mr Urmston, I didn't know what the house was like but I remembered he was looking for a lodger and got in touch. I hope it meets with your approval?'

'Sam! How can you doubt it? But what about the rent? I shan't...'

'Wait a moment till we're outside.' He climbed out of the cab and helped me down. 'Mr Urmston will discuss that with you, but your rise in wages will cover it. You were due one anyway,' he smiled.

'Really?' I wanted to ask more, but there was no time because we were walking up the front path. Sam rapped the brass knocker and Mr Urmston who must have been looking out for us, immediately let us in. He was a stout, jolly man in his late fifties who told me to leave my bags and parcels in the hall and took us into his kitchen where he brewed a pot of tea himself.

'I have a housekeeper, Mrs Green, who comes in daily, but I'm perfectly capable of fending for myself.'

When we were seated he asked me a few questions and I briefly explained my home situation, knowing that Sam had already filled him in on most of the details. I breathed in relief when he pronounced himself satisfied. Then we were taken down a corridor to my quarters. I could hardly believe it; two rooms at the back of the house on the ground floor: a bedroom and a small sitting room, as well as a tiny back kitchen and a bathroom off it. Best of all the water was plumbed in. Upstairs were other empty rooms, but Mr Urmston said he wasn't inclined to advertise them. I was glad I'd be the only lodger. It was going to take a while for me to feel safe.

In between explaining how the range and boiler worked in the kitchen, he told us his passion was singing. 'I'm a member of a number of choral societies and smaller ensembles so I'm not at home awfully much.'

'Jessie is a good singer too,' Sam told him, embarrassing me.

'Oh, I don't do much now except in chapel.'

'Then we must practise some duets!' Mr Urmston cried. He gave me a key to my door which I found opened into a side passage leading to the garden and out into an unpaved lane. It meant I didn't have to enter by the front door. In some ways this made my new lodgings feel more secure. I wouldn't be seen on the main road.

'This place was built as a flat onto the side of the house when our children were young. Originally it was the governess's quarters,' Mr Urmston told us. 'Once Freddie and Martha were at school a series of maids lived here but since my wife died Mrs Green comes in. You'll probably only see her at the weekend if you're at work all day. Nevertheless, it will be nice to have some young company. Now, I'll let you settle in and do call me if you need anything. I'll be in the drawing room on the second floor.'

He was such a straightforward, cheerful man, I didn't have any misgivings. Wisley Road, I decided, would be my new home. It was almost overwhelming what Sam had managed to find: a landlord who looked as if he would enjoy a joke and tell me funny stories, and lodgings with a bathroom. We brought the linen packages and my bags in from the hall and Sam examined the furniture and suggested ways to make the rooms brighter and offered to lend me a hand.

'No, you've done enough for me already in finding this place,' I protested, shaking my head. 'And you're busy with the business and the family. I'll manage from now on.'

'You're very independent, but if you do ever need...'

His eyes were full of concern and I looked away. 'I know. But I'm sure I'll be fine. It's years since I've been able to depend upon anyone at home.'

'Patrick will miss you.'

'Maybe. I just wish... Anyway, once I'm settled I'll meet him and we can go for walks but not till I know there's no risk from Clodagh finding me.'

Sam went into the kitchen and examined the lock on the back door and pronounced it could be a little sturdier. 'Do you think you might be lonely here if you can't tell anyone where you're living?'

I shrugged. 'Better that than worrying about having a dog set on me. I can trust Emilie and my friend Susan not to blab about where I am.'

I thanked him for all he'd done and when he'd gone I went into my own sitting room and sat in my own armchair, looked at the empty walls and thought about what pictures I might hang upon them, to make my first real home since Ma's passing.

When I eventually climbed into bed, I was filled with a swirl of feelings which kept sleep at bay. I still couldn't believe it had happened: that everything I was worried about, leaving Wigan, my job, and being attacked, had been resolved, and I had Sam to thank for it. He asked if we could meet next Monday when the shop was closed for the Bank Holiday.

'There are some pleasant walks not far from here. It'll give us more time to discuss what further precautions you could take. A new bolt on that door for one thing. I could fit it in no time.'

I nodded. But something besides the faulty bolt troubled me.

33

SAM

Wisley: Bank Holiday Monday, 4ᵗʰ June 1901

y father's axe was heavier to lift than I'd foreseen and my first attempt at splicing the log missed its aim. I cursed my clumsiness and hefted the blade out of the soil and lay it on the path. Earthworms and a beetle wriggled up through the black soil. I rubbed my underused shoulder muscles. Years of being a soft trade man had done that for me.

Serviettes, lace and fancy bits for women on a market stall, is it? My father had said all those years ago because I was no longer a pit man. He sounded more Irish when he was irritable, and had delivered the jeer over his brawny shoulder in the middle of washing himself at the sink after a shift. Hanging in the air was the belief that my new path wasn't suitable for a working man and would come to naught.

While I rested my muscles I glimpsed my mother passing to and fro in front of the window, fetching something for father, no doubt. The old man was off work again with one of those illnesses none of us could spell. Second bout this year and worse than the first. Pa didn't want my pity so when the wheezing overtook him I left the room. But I often glimpsed him covering his face with a handkerchief, capturing the phlegm that erupted from his throat.

There'd been no jeering about my work for a long time, and as for scorning my first market stall earnings, he'd dumped those views in the privy. Nowadays, it was an awkward *thank you* when I slipped him a weekly half-crown. It paid for his doctor's visits and medicine, and we kept my brothers ignorant about the arrangement. With Frank living in America, George lodging on his own in town and Josiah stationed in India, my parents missed their contributions, though Jos's photograph wearing a large cocked hat and a bristling moustache, was proudly displayed on the mantelpiece; every inch the military man.

Picking up the axe again I steadied my aim and this time spliced the wood cleanly. I worked steadily until there was nothing left of the tree trunk and there was a stack of kindling in the outhouse. Next week I'd return on Sunday after church. Mother wanted me to fix the outhouse's leaky roof after failing to get George or William involved.

'If I get Whittle's to deliver a few planks on Saturday, can you come round about this time again, after church?' She'd asked. I said I would, that it was no trouble. It would suit me to be out of the house for a few hours on a Sunday.

BANK HOLIDAY MONDAY and the lanes beyond Wisley were almost deserted on my walk to the meeting place. There was the occasional farm worker to nod to, but no one who might wonder what I was doing in that neck of the woods. My mouth was dry and I regretted not staying for a cup of tea at my parents' after dinner. Blossom hung from many of the trees and I breathed in the fresh smells on the air. Ahead was the finger post where I'd said we'd meet and beyond it, the gravel pits. At the sound of light footsteps, I swung round.

'Well, I'm here,' she said, looking everywhere but at me.

'Yes, good,' I said stupidly. Then it occurred to me she might not have walked out this far before. 'Is this new for you?' Her eyes grew wide and I realised she could have misconstrued my meaning. 'I mean up here, beyond Wisley?'

She half-covered her mouth with her hand and laughed. 'No, I walked here one evening to explore the area, to make sure I knew where we'd be meeting.'

All week I'd swung from believing she wouldn't come to having her stand before me. She was astonishing. 'Let's look at the quarries,' I cut in, desperate to be doing something. I offered her my arm and she took it but her slight body barely touched mine as we walked up the lane.

At the first quarry I felt a stab of disappointment, trying to see it through her eyes. Not much of a view: white stone dazzled my eyes in the sunshine, mining equipment standing at the far end of the quarry. It was a barren sort of place, but Jessie wasn't looking ahead, her face was turned upwards. She'd seen a large bird of prey circling us and was staring at it as a child might, with her mouth slightly open. Tiny blue veins patterned her throat and the tips of her ears were pinker than her cheeks.

'What kind is it — do you know?'

'I'm not so good on birds,' I admitted, hoping she wouldn't be disappointed. 'I've heard there's buzzards and sparrowhawks up here.'

'You could look it up if you had right kind of book, with pictures,' she said in a rush. 'If I had one of those I'd know what the bird was if I saw it again.'

Again? Was she thinking of another walk with me, or was the rumour Agnes mentioned a few months ago that Jessie had a follower, true? My mother-in-law, who kept a sharp eye on her grandchildren's private lives, thought that a man had asked Jessie to walk out with him. Where she'd got that from I didn't know. Perhaps it was wishful thinking, wanting to see her grand-daughter settled. But I doubted there'd been anyone since Gerard Morris. As her employer, I'd no business asking her about private matters - but a friend might. She kept her gaze on the bird until it wheeled away to become a dark speck in the sky. When it had vanished, she turned to me. Her grey eyes seemed larger than usual.

'You wanted to talk about keeping safe?' She looked down then and fingered the braid on her Sunday jacket.

'You'll work that loose if you keep fiddling with it,' I laughed, and took hold of her fingers. 'I hope moving to Mr Urmston's has banished your fears. But I think you should discuss the kitchen lock with him. See if he'd like me to reinforce it, and the back gate too. It's best to be careful.'

She pulled her hand from mine but didn't move away. 'I feel less scared now I've moved out of Teck Street. And I did as you said, wrote to father again and told him why I'd left.'

'And are you settling into your new home? How much have you seen of Mr Urmston?'

She told me the rooms were fine and that she and Mr Urmston had drunk tea together after she finished work. She didn't see a lot of him as he was out at rehearsals nearly every evening. 'I'll be all right so long as *she* doesn't find out where I am otherwise I'll have to flit. Warrington, somewhere like that. She's given her word, but I don't trust her to keep it.'

I took a deep breath. What I wanted to say might change things between us, but I felt compelled. 'I hope that never happens, Jessie. I wouldn't like you to leave.'

She clasped her hands and dropped her head. 'It frightens me a bit when you say that.' Her voice was very quiet.

'That wasn't my intention. It's just that I wanted to tell you how I felt.' I moved closer to her, bent my head, and brushed the space between her forehead and hair with my lips. To feel her skin beneath my mouth was astonishing. Then it happened, the moment I'd only dreamt of. She raised her face and our mouths met briefly. Instinctively I took a step back, not wanting to press her for more. She was, too, like a wild creature at that moment, fragile, unknowable. She was not a Lydia Holdsworth and I wasn't twenty. Neither was she Agnes who rarely kissed me these days. This was illicit, dangerous. I wasn't sure what I was doing here with her.

We walked quickly back, as far as Spencer Road, but before we parted I asked the only question on my mind. 'Next week?' She blushed, nodded, and hurried away.

34

JESSIE

Dunbar's Drapery shop: June 1901

That evening after our walk, I opened the window in my sitting room, sat in a chair and let the night scents drift in. But not for long. I was restless. Though the clock in the hallway showed the hour to be well after ten, even so, I unlocked the back door and stepped out into Mr Urmston's garden where a single tree grew, laden with pink and white blossom. I pulled a thin branch towards me to smell the flowers better and closed my eyes. I walked barefoot on the grass feeling taller and older, and let the night scents surround me like the lightest of shawls.

When I eventually retired to bed I was unable to sleep. I could think of nothing but our walk, and how it ended. I had no right to linger on that moment but failed to stop myself from doing so. Since it was almost nothing, a kiss so light it was hardly there, like a feather brushing against my lips, I almost convinced myself it didn't happen. That it was no more than a token of friendship. The difference was in the way I felt.

.   .   .

I WOKE LATER than usual the next morning and had to hurry to dress, eat my porridge and ready myself for work. On the walk over to Mesnes Street, despite the restless night my feet felt light on the pavement which was already busy with people. I knew them by sight now: office workers, shop girls like me. We murmured *good morning* to each other and I arrived a little out of breath. The door was locked but I had my own key.

Inside, the counter was bare except for an envelope with my name written on it in Sam's handwriting. I tore half the letter in my haste to extract it.

> *Dear Jessie,*
>
> *Emilie will be coming in this morning and has agreed to help you in the shop all week. We are having a family holiday in Southport and will be home on Saturday evening. No need to wait until our return so close the shop at the usual time. If there are any problems that you need my advice about, do not hesitate to tele-phone me. We are staying at The Royal Hotel, The Promenade. In the back room is the parcel you prepared for Lady Egerton which will be collected today.*
>
> *Yours,*
> *Sam.*

MY THROAT THICKENED. I felt I might choke. I shoved the torn note into my apron pocket and ran to the back room for a glass of water. There were jobs to do before I opened. For now, I wouldn't even think why... I scurried around, raising the window blinds then dusted the customers' chairs.

When everywhere looked presentable I opened the cash register. Silver sixpences, half crowns and three-penny bits gleamed in their trays. There was a stack of one-pound notes stuffed behind them. Sam must have practically emptied the safe to fill the drawers. I caught a glimpse of a dark figure at the door, Emilie. Maybe she could explain what was going on.

I turned the *Closed* sign around and let her in. She greeted me in the French way with a kiss on each cheek which I'd grown to like. Her black dress was similar to mine; the shop uniform Aunt Agnes preferred us to wear.

'Cherie, you look *distrait*,' she said, as I swept a hand across my hair. I'd learned a few of her expressions and put on a smile.

'I'm all right, just puzzled.'

'You are not worried about being left in charge?'

'No, I'm sure I'll manage but here, read Sam's note,' and I took it from my pocket. 'It was so unexpected; he never said a word to me on… Saturday. What do you make of it?'

'Have they already left?'

'Yes. No sounds from upstairs.'

She put the note down on the counter. 'He says very little here which makes me want to fill in the spaces. I will tell you what I know. Sam came to my lodgings late afternoon. He knew already I was working part-time this week at the bakery so he asked if I would agree to help you out and I said yes.'

'But what about your job? Weren't they angry with you?' It seemed a queer affair to me, very unlike him to act this way.

'Sam said he would telephone Mr Sullivan, the owner, and he would pay them my wage, and more for the inconvenience of bringing in someone else. I called at the bakery before I came here and found that my employer was quite satisfied with the financial arrangement. Now is there anything you want me to do? I see there is a lady on the other side of the road who is looking at the shop. We should be ready for her.'

I gave her a quick hug. 'We'll talk later. There's nothing special I can think of but I'm very happy you're here.'

. . .

ABOUT FOUR O'CLOCK, Emilie finished with a customer who wanted help with quilting fabric and while there was a lull we sat in the back room and enjoyed a pot of tea. My curiosity was not yet satisfied about Sam's peculiar arrangements.

'Did he say anything to you about why they decided to go so suddenly? He usually plans things well in advance. None of them are ill, are they?'

'Not *ill*, though perhaps Sam is a little, how do you say, over-working his brain. He is not sleeping well, he said. Also, your aunt has complained of tiredness and talked about a holiday all year. He decided this week would be a good one because it will be quiet. No sales or promotions until the Summer.'

'He does study a lot, reads books on Economics, he's told me.' I wondered if my aunt had badgered him into it. But would he do something he didn't want to? Emilie drank her tea but she had a brooding look which worried me. Did she know more? 'Is that all he said?' I spoke in an off-hand manner, tamping down my interest although it was like a fire that wanted to blaze.

'Yes, *cherie*. But I wonder if there's something *you* are not saying to me?'

'No! Of course not. It's just very odd. And I don't mind being in charge.'

She continued to drink and then put her cup down. 'It will be a break for you from your aunt, won't it? I have noticed there is a coolness between you. I don't share her thinking about society, where people are placed in it. She has only followed on Sam's coattails if that is the right expression. Remember that.'

'I'll try. So you've seen that she looks down on my family?'

She twisted her mouth. 'It is obvious, Jessie.'

After we closed up and went our separate ways, I walked home thinking of all that had passed. Emilie seemed to be on the point of asking me something very personal then changed her mind. Was I glad? I didn't know. Perhaps if I'd confided in her about what had happened on Monday then she might have helped me put it in perspective.

35

SAM

Southport: June 1901

The walk with Jessie left me in state of chaos. So much so that on my return I shut myself in the parlour for half an hour. Away from the family's chatter, I attempted to read a newspaper, write a letter. And failed to complete both.

When Agnes opened the door to announce the meal was ready, I was relieved to see the children were already seated, with Victoria squirming in her highchair. Usually I helped out at mealtimes but tonight I hadn't heard Agnes shouting for me. The smells coming from the kitchen were tempting, but after the first taste of the ham, potatoes and cabbage, my appetite fled. No one else thought the food too salty, but I left most of it uneaten.

'What's wrong?' Agnes asked. I didn't usually spurn her meals for she was a good cook.

'Nothing, but my appetite seems to have disappeared.' What would be gained by speaking the truth? I tried laughing it off.

'Lack of appetite, tiredness. I keep saying we should take a holiday and nothing's been arranged. It would do you good to get away,' Agnes said, scraping the plates.

A holiday? An opportunity not to be here tomorrow? I lifted Victoria out of her highchair to crawl on the carpet then sat down; my thoughts jumping about like a flea circus. *Book a hotel. Luggage. Take the nurse-maid. Employ Emilie.* Everything could be accomplished, but only if I put the wheels in motion now.

I went into the kitchen where Agnes was clearing up. 'All right. Let's go to Southport in the morning. I'll telephone a hotel, reserve two rooms, then call on Emilie to ask her to take my place.'

Agnes's eyes widened in disbelief. 'I didn't mean straight away!'

'Yes, yes! A holiday, please!' Grace and Helena cried. They had left the table before asking permission to get down and were standing in the doorway.

'No time like the present,' I said, encouraged by the children's support, knowing Agnes would find it hard to disappoint them. 'Start packing things for you and the children. I shouldn't be very long.' I went back to the parlour where a telephone had been installed earlier in the year and asked the exchange to put me through to *The Grand* in Southport.

With the hotel rooms booked for the week, I threw on my coat and stepped out into the night air. For the first time in hours, the tightness in my chest diminished. I set off at a good pace towards Emilie's part of town and hoped that our friendship, and the chance to earn more money than usual, would persuade her. I wasn't usually this impulsive, hadn't done anything like it since taking on the shop, but it was in my nature. It would be good to spend time by the sea and stop whatever had happened this afternoon from going any further.

I called at our nurse-maid's house and told her to pack a bag for the week. We would pick her up in a cab at eight o'clock the next morning.

. . .

SOUTHPORT WAS a town which embodied many of the traits I usually sought in a place to stay – gentility, sedateness, fine architecture, good manners. So why was I thinking about Blackpool further up the coast which I'd visited a few years ago?

When we shopped in elegant Lord Street I longed for the jangling noise of Blackpool's funfair. I imagined passing the time of day with tousled men and women strolling along the promenade. Saw myself throwing balls at coconut shies, winning a prize, and wandering unknown through a crowd of raucous, unrestrained people. And at the exit to the fair, I imagined a slim person with dark hair waiting for me. Only when I was alone could I give myself up to such imaginings. Of course, nothing would happen when I returned home.

Agnes would never have agreed to Blackpool: not even for The Illuminations, or the North Shore, which was said to have a better class of hotel. Southport suited everyone and the girls loved the boating lakes, the little fun fair, even the Punch and Judy show whose violence I found disquieting. Yes, I agreed, it was good to get away from blackened Wigan for a while, but I struggled to banish all thoughts of Jessie.

In the busy streets, walking behind any young woman of a similar height and the same colour of hair, my thoughts ran unchecked. Sitting on a deckchair, I trailed sand through my fingers and thought about time running out and lost opportunities. I grabbed Amy's spade, thinking to build a sandcastle. There would be no opportunities. I wouldn't let it happen.

'Daddy? Can we have a donkey ride?' Grace and Helena stared hopefully at me. I had no objection and we held hands on the walk over to the Donkey Man. At the end of the ride, a quarter of a mile up the beach, I stretched my neck and shoulders to free myself from obsessive thoughts. Perhaps a spell of sea bathing would help.

. . .

BEFORE BREAKFAST THE NEXT DAY, I donned my bathing suit in our hotel room, then my outer clothes, and headed for the men's swimming area of the beach. Shunning the expense of a bathing machine, I plunged into the waves. It did me good and for about half an hour, I was myself again.

THAT EVENING, when the children were settled in the adjacent room, I found Agnes less brittle than usual and more ready to talk to me about the week's events, and what the children had done. The girls, though exhausting, brought joy to both our lives and the holiday only reinforced that. I'd been right to be impulsive if it meant Agnes and I grew closer.

36

JESSIE

Dunbar's Drapery shop: June 1901

'*M*rs Hough,' Emilie said in a confiding tone, 'only bought that pattern because your aunt has a dress made from it.'

I looked up from counting, and twisting rubber bands around a pile of bank notes whenever I reached a hundred pounds. 'How do you know that?' It was late afternoon and Mrs Hough, the last customer, had just closed the door.

'While you were in the storeroom she said she saw Mrs Dunbar wearing it at one of the dinner parties she and Sam go to. All the wives at these dinners come in here for material or buy hats and ready-mades if they have seen Agnes Dunbar wearing them.'

'So the dinners are really business meetings?' This hadn't occurred to me.

'In a way. And your aunt is as ambitious as Sam in that respect. While the gentlemen drink port and smoke cigars, the ladies discuss fashion and are tempted into the shop. Great Aunt Adeline did the same thing until she became too old and weary to bother going to them. She invited me one time but never again.' Emilie shook her head and pulled a face. 'But Agnes Dunbar, she is clever about business though perhaps not in other ways. Now I must put these away,' and she gathered up several rolls of material and took them back to the storeroom.

I was dying to ask what she meant. Emilie came out with the most surprising remarks at times. But perhaps it was best I didn't. To do so would be like taking sides against my aunt.

During the late afternoon a rather shabby, stout young man opened the door and I readied myself to greet him. He wasn't our usual type of customer. He asked if the proprietor was about and I replied, *no*. Nevertheless, he said he was a rep with new lines to offer. Something about him seemed off, like three-day-old beef, and I was on the alert. I knew reps never made appointments at that time on Fridays; they wanted to travel back to wherever they lived for the weekend.

'Mr Dunbar will be back at work on Monday,' I told him. 'If you want to leave them with me...?'

'No, no, I can't do that...' He mumbled. And reps didn't stutter. They oiled their tongues before delivering their patter and were far better dressed. But I didn't want to judge him if he'd just started out in the trade. He hung around, picking up gloves on display and putting them down, gabbing on about the town then the postponement of the coronation, still insisting he couldn't leave anything with me. We both heard the storeroom door creak open at the same time and he stared at Emilie coming through the doorway. Suddenly, the rep backed away, turned the shop door handle and fled.

'Who was that?' She asked, coming up to the counter. 'I don't usually have that effect on the male customer.'

I smiled and repeated what he'd said. 'And not even a thank you for taking up my time.'

We peered out of the window and saw him loping down the street. Emilie flashed a scathing look.

'It is my guess he is not a salesman. Perhaps he recognised me from serving here, or on the Market Stall. I suspect he was hoping you'd disappear for a moment so he could snatch as much stock as he could carry from the shop.'

'A thief! My goodness. I didn't suspect that, though I thought him very odd and rude. Do you think he'll come back when I'm on my own?'

'It is unlikely now he knows there may be two of us here at any time.'

Sam was home tomorrow, but I wondered if I shouldn't telephone him and describe what had happened. Perhaps he'd want me to report it at the police station.

I dithered about what to do until closing time but didn't mention my indecisiveness to Emilie. Finally, I decided to write him a note which he'd read tomorrow. It would have been nice to speak to him, but... I pushed the thought aside. He and my aunt needed to forget their cares and relax. This was the reason why they'd left so suddenly, and what this strange week had been about.

37

SAM

The Towneleys' house: June 1901

*D*espite the busyness of arriving home in the evening: unpacking beach paraphernalia, tipping sand-filled shoes into the backyard, and finding homes for the girls' sea-shells, I made time to read Jessie's note, which she'd left on the counter. With each reading, I hoped to discover more in it than there was, but there were few details and no hidden message. She wrote of a con man, or thief, that I might want to report to the police. There were no wishes that we might have had a good time. No *looking forward to seeing you soon*. I put the note in my top pocket and tried to forget it.

We were still tired when we rose on Sunday and as Agnes insisted we attend chapel, I stifled my yawns during an uninspiring service. Only when it was over and we were mingling with friends and family did my restlessness ease a little.

'I want to hear all about your unexpected holiday, Agnes,' Her mother said as we made our way to the door. 'I'll expect you for a cup of tea at four o'clock. Not a meal, there'll be too many of us for that.'

I tried to persuade Agnes against this unnecessary visit, listing all the things to be done around the flat, but it was a thankless task. Predictably, at four o'clock, we presented ourselves; the girls rushing into the parlour eager to see what varieties of cake were laid out on the table. They loved visiting their grandparents who tended to spoil them. Victoria wriggled in my arms and waved her fat little hands in the air, enraptured by her reflection in the mirror and tried to grab Mrs Towneley's earthenware dog from the mantelpiece. She was too young to know what was going on, but I believed time would reveal her to be a clever child, as her older sisters were.

Apart from Victoria, who sat on my knee, all the youngsters perched on small stools around a low table and whispered over their cake plates. I was proud of their behaviour though that wasn't always the case. Agnes and I took a less strict approach with regard to discipline than either of our parents had with us, and I saw we were closer for it. The children respected but did not fear us. I had read several current books on child rearing and infant education and with Agnes's assistance, was putting it into practice. While we were chatting, the door opened and Margaret with her brood came in, followed by Jessie. I swallowed and tried to smile having no notion she'd been invited. I looked away so as not to be caught staring; but how young and beautiful she was in her fine striped blouse and navy skirt.

'More tea, Sam? I see your cup's empty.' My mother-in-law hovered over me though the newcomers had not yet been greeted. Under her gaze, I became flustered and looked for someone to blame. If I'd known Jessie would be here...

'No, thank you. I've had plenty.' It was said too sharply. I saw her surprise and was about to apologise when she sailed off. Across the room, the children were clustering about their cousin, giving her their news. She still had a place in the Towneley clan, though often seemed distanced from it. My mother-in-law was questioning Margaret and though she lowered her voice, I was close enough to hear them.

'What's the explanation for Jessie's rosy cheeks and bright eyes? Has she got a young man to walk out with?'

Her eyes sparkled as much as her granddaughter's in her hunger for news.

'She hasn't mentioned one to me,' Margaret replied. She shifted her position in her chair to include me in the conversation, and said with a smile, 'Do you know Sam? You and Agnes see her nearly every day.'

I don't know why I didn't tell the truth, that there was no one.

'She hasn't said as much but she does seem more cheerful these days. Getting away from Teck Street has helped.'

My in-laws congratulated me on finding her somewhere so suitable, and when the conversation about Jessie stalled, they moved on to James who was a disappointment, not making anything of himself, according to his grandmother. Inevitably her drift led to *poor Patrick*.

Unwilling to listen further, or intervene, I rose and went to the window. Perhaps Jessie would come over for a chat after she'd spoken to the children. But I failed to catch her eye and our visit ended without us speaking one word together. In one way I was relieved. I had no idea what I would have said to her in front of the family, and my burning face might have given rise to questions.

Climbing into bed that night, I resolved I would show her no partiality when we were at work the next day.

38

JESSIE

Wisley: June 1901

I walked to Mesnes Street the next morning in a state of anxiety. Not since Clodagh's threat had I felt this way.

During my short time living in Mr Urmston's house, life had fallen into a steady, happy rhythm at work, and at the end of the day, I came home knowing there'd be nothing to fear when I opened my door. I had no cause to be nervous: no one shouted, slapped, or despised me, and yet that morning I found my heart pounding, wondering how Sam would act towards me and unsure of how I should respond.

Face to face with the shop door, I decided to take my cue from him.

As the first hour progressed, he looked through the list I'd made of what we'd sold and how much we'd taken, but there was no smile, only a very polite *thank you* for all I'd done. I asked him about his time away, hoping for a lively account, a return to normality.

'Yes, the family enjoyed their holiday,' he said. 'If you'll excuse me, I'm due at a meeting at half past nine.' And he put on his jacket and went out without telling me where he was going.

That morning set a pattern which lasted all week. I endured his business-like ways, the lack of banter, smiles and shared stories. I tidied the storeroom and put away the haberdashery like an automaton. At home, I spent my evenings reliving the empty days, wondering if we'd ever recover our former friendliness. But if that was buried under the Southport sands, what did the future hold?

ON SATURDAY I fumbled with the *Closed* sign and turned it around for the last time that week, relieved to be leaving. Sam came out of the back room. I expected him to say, *see you on Monday,* or some other farewell, but he didn't. My heart sank seeing his stern expression.

'Are you free to meet tomorrow? I wanted to talk to you more about the con man. I haven't decided yet whether to report it to the police.'

His voice was quiet, unemotional. I hid my surprise, unsure what this meant and whether to be happy or disturbed. Nevertheless, I didn't refuse his request.

FROM THE MOMENT I woke on Sunday until I set out to meet him, I veered from one thought to another but found no answer. I almost convinced myself that this second time would be nothing like the first, and the reason for doing it was different: two people related by marriage had a work situation to discuss. But what had led to the stilted atmosphere? Why the surprising holiday? Either Sam really did need a break, or he regretted what had taken place at the Gravel Pits. I longed to know his mind, yet what I might hear scared me.

. . .

THE POST'S crooked outline was in view but no one was in sight. Standing in a lane was not like being in a town centre where you can seem to be busy. I breathed with relief when I saw a figure at the bottom of the hill. A few minutes later Sam arrived and after a stiff greeting we set off. It was unbearable walking two feet apart, talking about nothing more interesting than our chapels and the weather.

'So what do you need to know about the *con man?*' I asked eventually, determined to end the distance between us. We weren't at work and at that moment I didn't feel like an employee. 'Emilie's met his sort before, people pretending to be someone they're not. I just thought his behaviour was odd. Would you like me to describe him?'

'Yes, do, I might recognise him.'

He sounded uncertain and for the first time since his return from holiday, I guided the conversation. 'You wouldn't *recognise* him if he were a thief, would you? Unless you're mixing with all sorts these days.'

My joke provoked a small smile and I continued in the same vein. 'Let me see, he was about your height... but much stouter. With a thatch of fair hair. Aged around twenty-six or so.'

'A youngster, then?' Sam said, picking up my light-hearted tone.

'An old-looking youngster,' I corrected. 'And there was something shifty about him. I'd know him again if I saw him in the street.'

It was as if a spell had been broken and our old habits returned. Even the hill seemed less steep and we swung along, inventing a story about the false rep, taking it in turn to add new bits of information. I said the man was walking around town in a waistcoat and a cravat and had come from a circus while Sam imagined him drinking sherry in the *Prince of Wales*.

By the time we reached the gravel pits, we'd moved onto Mr Urmston and were laughing about some of his comical sayings.

'By the way, he's given me two tickets to a concert he's singing in. I'll ask Susan if she'd like to join me. I've only ever sat through chapel ones and they're not always very good.'

Sam frowned and I wondered if he knew something about the concert that I didn't. Did he think it too highbrow for me?

'I'd like to have gone too, but we've been invited out to dinner that night. They're sometimes tedious but it's what's expected when you're in business. I hadn't reckoned on that side of it when I took on the lease.'

'Does Agnes dislike these dinners?' I saw my aunt in a new light after Emilie described the parties, that she influenced the business even when it was closed. But I wanted to hear it from him.

'Not nearly as much as me. It's a chance for her to dress up and show what we sell in the shop. The ladies invited always ask about what she's wearing and come in to buy the same thing.'

My curiosity was satisfied, but I didn't feel good about tricking him into telling me; we'd always been open with each other. But then he hadn't explained Southport and I didn't dare bring it up and spoil the mood. We walked away from the road and took a farm track, bordered on one side with hedges and tall trees and open fields on the other. There was a breeze and the trees shifted and sighed as we walked alongside them. I paused for a moment, held by their spell.

'Why have you stopped?' Sam asked. 'Are you tired?'

'Not at all! I'm just listening to the sounds the trees make. If you shut your eyes. you'd think you were at the sea.' I turned to look at him. 'Try it.'

He gave me a lop-sided smile but closed his eyes and I did the same.

'I could listen to them for hours,' I declared after a few minutes, 'but I suppose we'd better make our way back. Do you know, I'd never really looked at a tree properly before, or a hedge, or birds, 'til I started walking up here. Even my feet feel different walking on grass and earth.'

Sam took my arm and squeezed it. 'I'm glad you're enjoying yourself. You haven't deserved to be treated like you have.'

WE REACHED the back gate leading into the garden and Sam said he was dying for a cup of tea so I invited him into the flat. I apologised for the room not being tidy but I hadn't expected him to come inside: the table was strewn with the stockings I was currently knitting on the new machine. I gathered them in my arms and hastily shoved them in a drawer. When the pot was brewed, I set it down on the table and we sat across from each other. The fresh air and peace of the countryside had soothed me and without thinking I mentioned something I'd meant to keep to myself.

'I ran into Clodagh in the street yesterday.'

Sam frowned over his teacup. 'What did she say?'

'She told me a lie about Pa being unwell and not being able to work, that he needs any money I can give him. I think she expected me to hand some over.'

'So, she still doesn't know you and he meet in the town?'

'No. We've all managed to keep it from her and there's nothing wrong with Pa.'

'Was that all she said?' He stretched out his hand, placed it over mine and squeezed it.

I shivered, feeling the pressure of his fingers. 'She mentioned her friend again, as if in passing.' I mimicked Clodagh's voice, *I saw Albert Clegg last week, you know, the one with dog?* 'I don't think she'll try anything since Pa made her swear on the Bible. It was said just to frighten me. I tell myself not to dwell on it.'

'I hope not! You must call for a policeman if she tries anything, but I doubt she would in daylight.' Sam's voice and eyes were hard and cold like glass.

'I will, don't worry.' I said, hoping the peace and easiness between us would return. I'd been a fool to mention Clodagh.

'I can't help worrying.'

He leant further across the table and ran his hand up and down the sleeve of my blouse. The only man who'd come close to touching me in this way was Gerard Morris, and I'd never felt the least bit tingly or breathless whenever he'd taken my hand. I couldn't look Sam in the eye, but when he stood, I rose too, and we met each other halfway around the table.

'I won't let anything bad happen to you Jessie, ever. I promised your mother I would look out for you.' He kissed me lightly on the mouth and I couldn't stop myself from returning it and leant against him. How long the kiss lasted I don't know, but it was too soon when he released me. He looked at his pocket watch and caught his breath.

'Sorry, but I have to leave. They, Agnes…'

Everything in me begged him to stay, yet I had no right to stop him.

ALONE, I sat for what seemed like hours in my chair looking out into the garden wondering what we'd done. I longed for him to return, yet Aunt Agnes and my little cousins couldn't be wished out of existence. Eventually, I got up and started to make my tea. Bacon and eggs, usually so appetising, tasted like cardboard. Later, I tried again with the stocking machine but gave up when I made too many mistakes. Pa would have said I was as mixed up and as jumpy as a box of frogs.

Before he'd left, Sam apologised for his coldness at work and dashing off to Southport. Discussing what to do about the con man had been an excuse to see me, which I'd already guessed. We were on the edge of a different world and if we entered it fully, no one must suspect a thing.

He left me with tangled thoughts about my aunt. She wasn't a monster. She was a good mother, but I wondered what she was like as a wife. Were they happy, or did they put up with each other? They weren't like Pa and Clodagh, of course, but I knew they argued a lot; I'd heard them. Then again there were four children. They couldn't be indifferent to each other. And when it came to business it was obvious they were of one mind. I thought of the wedding photograph in the parlour. He, younger, standing to attention, uncomfortable before the camera. Agnes with a broad smile. And why wouldn't she be smiling on her wedding day?

A memory stirred. After the marriage service, I'd felt awkward standing amongst the guests because I wasn't invited to the meal. Then I'd seen Pa standing outside the gate, the worse for wear. If he'd stayed any longer, he might have spoiled Sam and Agnes's day. It was only when I was about sixteen that I gathered Pa thought Sam could have been wiser in his choice of a wife. I thanked the Lord he'd kept his views to himself.

I put the stocking machine back in the cupboard, hoping I'd do better on another night. What would Pa say if he knew what had happened earlier? How shocked and disappointed he'd be with both of us. The front door banged open, and I heard the *click click* of Mr Urmston's shoes on the tiled hall floor.

'Are you still up, Jessie?' He called. 'I see you have your light on. Join me for an *Ovaltine* if you're not sleepy.'

Relief flooded through me. Suddenly I didn't want to be on my own. I pulled my shawl around me and followed him upstairs to his parlour where for an hour, I forgot my concerns and behaviour and indulged in frivolous chat with my kind landlord.

39

SAM

St Paul's Independent Chapel: June 1901

How dull the services were: every Sunday an exact copy of the one the week before. Today, a stranger was preaching, younger than many, but offering no new ideas or ways of interpreting the gospels: intoning the same set phrases about redemption and goodness. It made me wonder if I'd hear a higher order of sermon in the Parish Church. No doubt the standard of music would be better too. The organ-playing during the first hymn was so discordant I'd raised my hands to my ears to cover them, forgetting where I was. Agnes noticed and twitched her eyebrows. I mouthed back, *earache*.

Leaving the building and coming out into daylight felt like a whole day had passed, not just two hours. During the prayers, I asked God for forgiveness. I'd tried my best to control my feelings for Jessie, but they'd proved to be too strong.

Agnes and the children made their way home and I went on to my parents to continue with the outdoor jobs they had ready for me.

Mother was disappointed I only had time to mend the gate but I placated her with a promise to return next week. Once she was back in the house, I fixed new struts to the frame, banged in nails whilst probing and questioning everything I'd made happen. Yes, I felt guilty about deceiving Agnes, but no, I couldn't stop what was happening. With every contact the hammer made to the wood, I repeated the words, *be careful*. I needed to keep some part of my brain focussed in the here and now so it wouldn't be consumed by heated, roiling thoughts.

THE WEEK HAD BEEN a mix of pain and pleasure, but not in equal measure. Yesterday, it struck me like a force of nature that I was an outcast in my own life. Reading, studying, totting up the accounts, letter writing, tasks I usually relished, felt like eating dust. All I could think about was my need for Jessie. I'd dragged the family to Southport at the last minute without telling Jessie why, but after that first brief kiss in the lane, I'd panicked. I'd been morally weak and in Southport, I'd tried to convince myself my resolve would be strong. But as soon as I saw her enter the Towneley's parlour, I was lost.

After we'd kissed in her flat, I knew she returned my feelings. The following days were bliss and torture. I tried but failed to resist her. I caught myself humming, wanting to capture and hold each sweet, secret glance we gave each other. And there were perilous moments when we brushed against each other in the storeroom and I smelt the freshness of her hair and skin. Only once did we kiss downstairs. The smell of the stone walls somehow intensified the moment. But customers were waiting in the shop. It took all my self-control to run upstairs and carry on as normal. On Thursday, the delivery boy, Bert, dumped a pile of boxes on the floor.

'Care to share the joke?' He enquired, looking at me and then at Jessie.

Lying seemed to come easily to me or was I just a quick thinker? 'I was telling Miss Gorman about a funny cartoon I saw in the newspaper.'

For the rest of the week, I put on a sober face and stood further away from her. When Agnes commented that the holiday seemed to have done me good I reinforced her opinion with a hearty, *yes*, and said that she looked well on it too, though that wasn't strictly true. It wasn't the first time I'd hidden the truth about my feelings for a woman, but this seemed much more dangerous than when I was twenty.

40

JESSIE

Wisley Road: end of June to July 1901

hen I was alone in my room, I longed to be with him, but in chapel, I asked for forgiveness. Nowhere was free from the torment of questions. They came like driving rain, but was I strong enough to stop what might happen next? Should I go away to another town? Did I want to?

The evenings were quiet but I was too occupied by my thoughts to be lonely. Mr Urmston was usually out, singing in a hall somewhere. Susan and Emilie had visited me but my old mill friend was now engaged, and Emilie told me that after her shift in the bakery, she studied at the new Technical College, for Maths and English. She encouraged me to join her but I was afraid to be out after dark. There was more chance of bumping into Clodagh if I was in town at night.

To find a distraction, I read or slipped into the garden. The smell of the night flowers was powerful. I breathed in the scent of the stocks and wondered what it would be like to stand there with another person. I tilted my head back and peered up at the sky. With poor eyesight, smoke and smog from the mills and mines, there was no chance of seeing any stars, but I could imagine them.

Indoors, I went about my tasks with a new awareness. I filled a yellow vase with wildflowers. I rearranged my food tins on the kitchen shelf according to the colour of the labels. I smoothed out an Indian paisley shawl I found in a cupboard across my bed. All was done with the knowledge that *he* would see these things, too. I wondered if the shawl belonged to the Urmston children's governess or perhaps their mother. It didn't bother me if it had been a dead woman's because the way Mr Urmston talked about his wife I knew she was still dear to him. It would make you feel so safe and secure to be loved like that and know that when you returned home, his was the face you would see every night.

Sam whispered to me in the storeroom, that he loved the way I touched him, with caresses and words. Like a tormenting itch I had to scratch, I mulled over how he and Agnes were with each other. Before I'd worked in the shop I hadn't seen them often, only at one relative's or another's house. He was usually the one who kept the children amused while my aunt gossiped with her mother or sisters. He'd give me a wink or a smile if I crossed the room or brought him a drink. He was different before he got the shop. Less sure of himself, more subdued. I thought about Pa's dropped hints and Sam's loving words. Did he regret his marriage? But then lots of couples, even chapel ones, and, of course, Pa and Clodagh, had worse relationships than the Dunbars.

I didn't often see my aunt, for which I was grateful. She was busy with the children or talking to the nurse-maid. But when I was in the back room where there was a sink, tea things and the ledgers, and the flat doors were open, I couldn't help hearing conversations on the landing. Yesterday, she and Sam were arguing and I think it was about me. She seemed to think he spent too much money on equipment, on newspaper adverts, travelling to other towns and on wages. I froze and listened harder, but there was no more.

Wages? There was only mine and the nurse-maid's. But of course the part-time cleaner and occasionally, Emilie added to the outgoings. It made me feel queasy thinking about it.

I hadn't seen much of Sam until the end of the day when I was folding a length of material and he came up behind me. 'Tomorrow? Same time?' I gripped the fabric but didn't turn around. I nodded, slid the material into a drawer and got ready to go home.

AT THE END of our Sunday walk, we turned into what I now thought of as *my street*, slipped down the ginnel and into the garden. We'd kept some distance between us while walking along the roads and pathways, there being more people abroad due to the fine weather. But there'd been no constraint; our conversation had been full of laughter. Once indoors a reserve fell upon me and I made no move to boil water for the tea. There was something I needed to ask him which I hadn't yet summoned the nerve for.

'I heard you and Agnes talking on the landing, yesterday. I think it was about money. It worries me that I'm costing you. My rent is…' It was difficult to say it. 'You could get another girl for the shop without the additional expense.'

'I could, but I won't.' His face reddened.

'But my wage… this?' I waved and turned to indicate my lounge and all it meant to me. 'Am I worth so much expense and the disagreement with Agnes?'

'We can afford it. Agnes… worries over business matters. I'll show her the figures. They're rising every week so her concerns are needless.' He put a hand on my arm. 'Do you believe me?' He leant in closer. His eyes were an intense blue.

For a second I thought about pulling away, stopping whatever was going to happen, but I didn't. He raised his fingers and stroked my cheeks and hair. 'Do you think I could manage without you? You know I can't.' And he pulled me to him.

The kisses were longer, more passionate than we'd given each other before. I believed him when he said he'd missed talking and being with me in the week. We went into the bedroom where I touched my lips and felt the imprint of his kiss still there. I had hoped for love but never thought it would come this way. For years I'd been deprived of the light, repressing something I didn't know I felt for him. I put my arms around Sam and kissed him slowly. His breathing was rapid. That day I crossed a river in one jump and became someone else, leaving my old life behind.

41

JESSIE

Wisley Road: July 1901

*I*t didn't seem possible that only a week had passed. I was changed, more conscious of my body than I'd ever been. Details that had previously passed me by were now remarkable: the intricate patterns of the fur on a neighbour's ginger tom as he let me stroke him. Mr Urmston's habit of tapping his spoon against his cup after he'd stirred his tea. The way he lovingly polished the clock in the hall. And something else I hadn't noticed: an engraved message at its base. *For my dear husband on his fortieth birthday.*

On Sundays, when Sam and I lay in bed holding hands and I thought back to all the stories I'd heard when I worked in the mill. As a youngster, I'd gathered with my friends around two newly-wed girls. The older ones egged them on to tell us what being married was like. They'd looked sharply about to see if the coast was clear of men then regaled us with horror stories, of what *it* was like. I never forgot their scowls and spat-out words. The *bed* part of marriage, I understood from then on, was something to be endured. I'd gone home with a dry throat and panic

257

in my chest. But Sam wasn't like the men those girls married. He was considerate, gentle.

And another memory: after Clodagh moved in with us there were groans at night from the room they shared. I shut my ears against them, not wanting to think about the *whats* and *hows*. All the same, her daytime smirking remarks banished my ignorance.

It sickened me to think that she and I had something in common, but there it was. If she'd ever described the early days in Sarginson Street, I was sure she wouldn't have thought the bed part of living with Pa an endurance.

SAM VISITED me after finishing his outdoor jobs at his parents' house. Each Sunday we slipped under my cotton sheets which now felt like silk. I told him I was sorry for those married girls at the mill and hoped they'd found the joy to be had. I knew I'd be changed by being with a man but never imagined how my soul would be turned inside out. My bed was wider than the one I had at Pa's so we lay facing each other. Sam wasn't over tall but he was still broad in the shoulders, thanks to his coal-hauling days. His skin was pale and warm to the touch.

We never had very long together, and after he'd left to return to Mesnes Street, I relived the past hours: the joy of being together and the pain of parting. But it was an encounter a few weeks later that brought me face-to-face with reality. Pausing in the street to let a stream of mill girls surge past after finishing work, seeing their tired faces, hearing their ringing voices as they called out to each other, the truth of my alliance with Sam struck me. The road I'd chosen would require qualities and reserves of strength that few mill girls would ever need.

42

SAM

Dunbar's Drapery Shop: July 1901

I was downstairs before Jessie arrived for work, eager to greet her. We rushed towards each other then stopped and shook our heads. She glanced at the door which opened onto the staircase up to the flat. I'd made sure it was firmly closed. Her shoulders relaxed and I allowed myself to take her hands and unpeel her gloves. That was all. We'd agreed that working together meant no smiling, no touching, and no visits together to the storeroom.

That evening she came upstairs having been asked in the morning to mind the children. Later, while Jessie was carrying out an errand, my wife changed her plans, deciding she'd take the girls to see my parents. I didn't object. It provided us with an opportunity to be alone in the flat for the first time.

I watched Jessie as she walked around my sitting room as if in a trance. She put a hand out and stroked Madame Chambres's flowered wallpaper.

'What are you thinking?' I asked.

'Isn't this beautiful?' She turned around. 'I was thinking

something both silly and impossible. What it might be like to live here with you when I'm not… your wife. I'd feel more guilty than I already do.' She paused. 'Have I stolen her from you?'

I hesitated. We hadn't yet had a serious conversation about what we were doing, too taken up by the joy and fun of being together. Society did not permit me to love Jessie, and though Agnes and I had made vows in the chapel to love one another, we both knew love had fled for good.

I was going against everything our world considered to be respectable behaviour. But who was to say that Jessie and I should follow everyone else? Both of us were becoming the people we were meant to be, changing from shadows into our true selves. I'd once thought something similar about my feelings for Mary: known myself to be a better person because of her.

Now, we came together, held hands, and leant against the door. 'No. As far as my heart is concerned, I was not hers to steal from.'

'But weren't you happy with her in the beginning?'

'It was contentment rather than happiness, I think. We were youngish, she was pretty and lively. Both our families approved and it was fun setting up a home, becoming parents.'

I didn't tell Jessie this but almost from the start, deep down, there'd been a fear I'd never allowed to rise — that Agnes and I were wrong for each other. 'What real love there was didn't last long: in fact, not since Grace was a baby. We share only ties of familiarity, parenthood and the business.'

I rested my chin on the top of her head. 'I'm sorry, love. But we'll do our best to be together, always.' I kissed her, and of course, desire replaced caution. 'Do you want to…?' I pointed to the closed door of the bedroom.

'It's too risky.' She stroked my hair, then said she must leave. 'Agnes may come back at any moment. It would be difficult to explain why I was still here.'

After she left, I went to my desk and wrote frantically for ten minutes then stuffed what I'd written into the small suitcase I kept locked under the bed.

Our love is new and precious and I hardly dare believe it has happened. It's like finding it's Summer after living only through cold, dank Winter years. Don't the preachers tell us that God is love? Of course, they mean spiritual love, but I won't let theology keep us apart.

The next day I wrote her a note and slipped it into her jacket pocket. I thought of her reading it when she was at home, knowing it would please her.

I will make amends for the distance we've kept between us in the shop.

IT SEEMED an age until our next Sunday walk but at last it came. On our return, she checked that Mr Urmston wasn't at home then signalled for me to come in through the back gate. We didn't have long, a couple of hours before I had to leave and put on a different face. But the joy and sweetness of it was worth the deception at which I was becoming an expert. I was told I had a quick mind when I was a youth attending lectures at the Miners' Institute. I never thought it would be put to this kind of use.

I might have felt worse about deceiving Agnes if I thought she was interested in anything I told her, or asked questions about the so-called meetings I said I'd been to. But she wasn't. Being married had turned us into people older than our true ages — a state that had crept up on me. Even before Jessie, I realised what I'd become and why, imagining it would always be that way. That was how my life would roll on. Love renewed me, and I didn't want to lose something so valuable.

Of course, I had a business to run and couldn't let things slip, but occasionally, on work visits to other towns, I allowed myself to daydream. I often had to take a train to meet suppliers in Warrington. Usually, once business was concluded, I came straight home. One day, after shaking hands with my linen supplier, I walked back to the station thinking of Jessie.

It had struck me suddenly one night at home that she was simply and wonderfully a revelation, and with this insight came an overwhelming need to do more for her than she allowed me. On our last country walk we'd taken refuge from the hot sun behind a row of tall trees and with no one in sight we'd kissed. Full of love and extravagance, I said I would shower her with presents. She laughed but took hold of my hands. Then her expression grew serious.

'I'm more than grateful you found me lodgings and provided the kitchen equipment I needed. But don't spend more money on me,' she pleaded. She cupped my face. 'I don't want you to buy things for me. I have your love and that is enough.'

I said I wouldn't spend money unless it were necessary, but it hadn't stopped me from looking inside shops at vases or figurines I thought she might like.

A few yards from Warrington station was a shop that had often caught my eye. It sold amongst other things, paintings and prints. It was cramped inside with framed pictures rising up the walls on all sides. It sold books too, displayed in open cases. I would look at those another time. I said good day to the owner and silently looked up and down the rows.

Hanging high up were landscapes of Scottish and Lake District mountains and rivers, lovely, but far too large for what I wanted. I wasn't an expert, but spending that year with Lydia, and frequenting the Holdsworths' house where there'd been drawings, prints and original paintings a-plenty, had taught me something. At the back of the shop, I saw a smaller, medium-sized oil painting of a milkmaid with a white calf in a wood. I couldn't resist picking it up for a closer inspection. The bright greens, light browns and yellows of springtime had a freshness which reminded me of Jessie, and when the owner came up and said it was painted by a Parbold man, I got out my wallet. 'I'll have it,' I told him, unable to resist the connection between my past and present lives.

At home, I smuggled the wrapped painting into the store room where I didn't think Agnes would find it. I knew my logic was flawed, but I told myself it wasn't right to keep a gift for Jessie in the place where Agnes lived. Having hidden the painting in the store room, I took off my shoes before going up to the flat to save muddying the stairs.

A few minutes earlier, on the walk home from Wigan Station, I'd made a vow. I wouldn't stop caring about Agnes's welfare, nor be less attentive at home. I would help her as I'd always done and mind the children when she wanted to go out. But it was a double-edged sword. It would prevent Agnes from becoming suspicious, but the time I spent with Jessie, who I was greedy to be with, would be curtailed. I knew myself to be a pragmatist: I couldn't have everything.

Another rule: though I often failed to keep it; neither would I daydream about Jessie at home. It was vital that I created a separation of time and place, the only way I could manage the two halves of my life. However, when walking down the street, or travelling by train or in cabs, I let my thoughts run wild. What would life be like without Agnes? Could I make it happen? Wretchedly, I thought it impossible. Almost certainly, it would mean leaving the children behind. In a case like mine, wouldn't the law be on the mother's side? The thought of not seeing my girls distressed me more than I could describe. Then there was the shop to consider. Businesses went under when the taint of scandal fell on them. How could separation or divorce be possible when so many people's livelihoods were at stake?

. . .

ONE EVENING, I managed to slip around to Wisley Road to see Jessie, giving the pretence of visiting a chapel friend. It was always difficult speaking to her about my home situation. She was quiet and sad but accepted the reality of what we were doing. She knew that for our love to continue, my two lives must never touch.

'Where do you write those letters you give me, if not at home?' She asked.

I told her I sometimes took myself off to the library. 'It's an inspiring place to write in.' I always chose a shadowy corner where tall shelves reared up on either side of my table.

How has it come about - this luck, my happiness? I see it like a photo-graphic series: images of us apart and together; first friendship, then desire, then love. And always laughter. It strikes me that only when Agnes and I are with the children do we laugh. They, and the business, form our sole topics of conversation. Other couples I know acquire a dog or take up a hobby, something to occupy them down the long years of marriage. I wanted more and now, perhaps selfishly, I have it. You have the ability to give and receive love and I indulge that as often as I can. But there are always risks. That first time we were together we were awkward, shy with each other. I could hardly breathe, you were (are) so beautiful. I covered you with kisses. You returned them as passionately as I could have wished.

'I've kept every single letter,' she said, and showed me a wooden box her father had given her. Patrick had carved her initials on the lid. 'In your last letter, you mention...' She blushed then said in a rush, 'I'm scared I'll start a baby.'

I explained something that Lydia Holdsworth and I had done — the oldest technique in the world.

'I heard about it when I was down the mine. A method pit

men use to avoid getting their sweethearts pregnant. They call it getting off at Meols Cop.'

'You mean the station before Southport, the next but last one on the line? You stop it with me when you get to Meols Cop. But why sweethearts, not wives? Husbands don't bother then?'

'No, not often.' I was embarrassed and said no more. It would be obvious to her that I hadn't practised it with Agnes.

She smiled. 'Anyway, I like train journeys.'

She'd got used to the fact I was more worldly-wise. She asked questions and I told her the truth about Lydia. She was shocked at first but curiosity got the better of her. She gave a cry of surprise when I told her where and when.

'Lydia's art studio with the curtains drawn.' Jessie knew we hadn't been deeply in love. That I wasn't old enough at the time for anything lasting. 'And she was too wayward, too different from me,' I said.

A couple of weeks later she told me that she remembered Lydia's name from when she was little.

'You talked about her to Ma, a bit, and I recall being annoyed. I couldn't put a name to the feeling, being so young, but now I think it was jealousy; I didn't want you to leave us to visit her.'

I'd never mentioned my fondness for her mother, and I wouldn't, but I think it made us even closer. It struck me that Jessie, in one person, combined the purity of Mary and the sensuousness of Lydia. That day I stayed with her longer than was sensible and got some sharp looks from Agnes for coming home late.

4 3

SAM

Parbold: July 1901

The weather on Wednesday evening was the right kind of warm, neither sultry nor baking. I waited at the bottom of the Manse steps while the Minister's wife informed me, stuttering a little, that the meeting I'd come for was cancelled.

'My husband isn't feeling well. I'm sorry you didn't get one of the notes I sent round.'

She retreated indoors, flushed and flustered which made me think I was being told a white lie. Seemingly the Manse had secrets, too. I strolled away remarkably happy; a free evening, and there could only be one way of spending it. Luck, fortune, or providence was on my side.

I hesitated at Mr Urmston's front gate. The lights in the first floor rooms were ablaze which meant he was probably at home. It would be unwise to sneak around the back tonight. The solicitor answered my knock after a few moments. He looked debonair in a smoking jacket and a pair of quilted house shoes of the same shade of maroon. It wasn't an outfit *Dunbar's* sold, but I saw no reason why I shouldn't add it to our stock. It seemed the men of Wigan, at least the better off ones, weren't averse to changes in fashion.

My solicitor, Mr Bailey, was pleasant enough, correct in speech and manner, but Jessie's landlord was a bird of a different feather, more like an actor than a legal fellow. His face could show gaiety, disapproval, and astonishment in a matter of seconds. If he was surprised to see me on his doorstep perhaps I missed it in the dim light under the porch. But I'd prepared my speech.

'I wonder if Jessie could sit with the children for an hour or two while my wife and I visit my parents?'

'Very good to see you, Dunbar,' He shook my hand and showed me into a downstairs sitting room. After summoning Jessie and while waiting for her to get ready, he offered me a cigar, which I declined.

'Are you still in touch with Madame Chambres?' He asked, throwing himself back into an armchair.

'No, but her great-niece works for me from time to time so we do hear about her. She's in good health as far as I know.'

The door opened, Jessie declared she was ready and we bid Mr Urmston farewell. I could not stop smiling as we hurried away.

'I'm glad I saw the lights on. I thought your landlord would have been out this evening.'

'He was meant to be but decided not to go to his choir. I think he was under the weather though he disguised it from you.' She pulled on my sleeve. 'Where are we going, Sam? I don't suppose you really want me to look after the girls.'

'No. My meeting was cancelled, so I thought we'd take the train to Parbold for a walk. It'll be quicker than the tram.' I took out my pocket watch and looked at it under a streetlamp. 'We have plenty of time.'

· · ·

DUSK WAS STILL a long way off as we walked up the lane away from the station, the sky just beginning to crimson. We pressed ourselves into a hedge as a woman driving a governess cart bowled by. I felt like a conspirator while we refrained from holding hands until the cottagers, gossiping outside their homes, were behind us. Soon, we came upon the turning leading up to York House, the Holdsworth home, but a mix of guilt and sorrow stopped me from pointing it out to Jessie: that was all in the past. When streetlamps ran out we trusted our feet to the ground beneath them. I was acutely aware of Jessie beside me and her attentiveness to the stilling of wings in trees, the openness of the wide sky and the early evening moon. When the lane petered out and turned into a dirt track we held hands and moved in step. Almost silently, a large bird flapped above us and glided away.

'A heron?' Jessie said. 'There's water not far away.'

'You've been looking them up in a book,' I teased.

'And what's wrong with that?' There was an answering smile in her voice, and I squeezed her hand.

'I have a surprise for you.' My voice was husky. 'We're nearly there.'

'If you've brought me to see the new King's drinking fountain, then I'll be disappointed. There won't be any water from it until the coronation.'

'No royalty has ever been where we're going. Just commoners and cows,' and I pulled her towards me.

44

JESSIE

Parbold: the same night

$\mathcal{I}$ let him lead me along a path and across a field. At the far end was a bulky-looking building silhouetted against the sky. A barn. An unlit, deserted-looking farmhouse stood behind it. I knew what was going to happen and a rush of feeling flooded me. Another person was here but I wanted to become her.

We stopped outside the barn and looked up at its height. 'Are you sure?' he asked.

I nodded, unable to speak. I knew about Lydia Holdsworth but I wasn't jealous, just curious. She took Sam to a barn, or a farm, once. It had nothing to do with who he was now. He said goodbye to her and now he'd chosen me. The only things I envied were her appearance, as he'd described it, and that she was an artist. Stocking-knitting seemed commonplace compared to painting in oils.

Inside the barn the hay was still warm from the sunny day and though empty, it smelt of animals, of grass, and rustled as we moved through it. When we sat he stroked my hand.

'I'm glad you're here because you want to be, not just because I've asked you.'

'This barn.' I looked up at rafters far above our heads where there was another level and a long ladder to climb up. 'It's like a secret world where anything might happen, as if we're in a story we've made for ourselves.' I blushed, but in the low light he probably didn't notice. This was more waking dream than anything I'd experienced.

'Do you mind it's here?' Sam said. 'Your room is fine but I wanted to take you somewhere special, different.'

'How did you know it would be empty?'

'I saw the farm and land advertised for sale in the newspaper. I came up here a few days ago to look around. Found the barn wasn't locked and the house unoccupied.'

I almost laughed. Sam was such a planner. Clever too. 'It's just right,' and I wrapped my arms around him.

The bed we made was softer than any I'd slept in. Despite my lack of experience I didn't feel at a disadvantage or like the wooden doll I was that first time. 'You've got straw in your hair,' I told him, and he pulled out a strand and stuck it in his mouth,'

'Now you're a farmer,' I laughed.

'I don't think I'd make a good countryman. Not like father when he was lad before he left Ireland.'

'We have that in common,' I said and I was about to mention Pa when he stopped me with kisses. Then he rested his head on my shoulder. He smelt of hay. Our closeness made me gasp. I was falling ever deeper in love and yet it set me free, though the world was still outside and would be against us.

'I can hear you thinking,' he said, moving his hand across my hair.

'I was imagining what it must be like to be old.' I stroked his neck.

'We're not old yet. At least you aren't.' Sam lifted his head and looked at me, 'And we don't have to worry about being old because we'll be together.'

'We will?' With deep joy and thankfulness, I closed my eyes.

HE DIDN'T GET off at Meols Cop that evening. In the dim light, I saw panic, and shame on his face.

'I'm sorry Jessie. Sorry...I couldn't... ' He passed a hand across his eyes.

'Nothing may happen,' I whispered, and rubbed his back but I was scared all the same. We lay in a sweaty tangle before rearranging our clothes and opening the huge doors. Outside, night had fallen and a breeze stirred the grass; nothing more than a settled peace.

Walking across the field, twigs cracked beneath our feet. I heard stirrings in the hedgerows and saw strange shapes of twisted tree roots. It put me in mind of Pa's Irish tales of a fairy kingdom under a hill. But wasn't there always a bargain to be made in those stories? Feasting and dancing with the fairies, eternal life in exchange for losing your home, loved ones and freedom?

The lights of the village were ahead of us. Then as we reached the station a shadow crossed my mind about what I was doing. Sam was a man strongly attached to his family. I'd always known it, and loved him for it, but where did that leave me? As he looked down, searching his pockets for our tickets, I touched my belly. What if I started a baby? Would it tear apart this dream we were living in? Would he still want me as much as he did now?

'I've found the returns,' he said. 'Not lost in the hay after all.'

The train was pulling in as we proceeded to the platform and I put my worries aside until a later time. We stepped into a second-class carriage and easily found an empty compartment. Daringly, we kissed almost all the way back to Wigan. He told me it was something Agnes would never have done, even when they were engaged. I was embarrassed, but also pleased, and wrapped the secret around me.

The wheels screeched. The train jolted to a stop and while Sam pulled down the window I smoothed my hair. He leant out and undid the leather door strap. On the platform, I rubbed smoke out of my eyes. Figures rushed back and forth and we almost bumped into a woman leaving the carriage next to ours. In the gloom, it took me a moment to recognise Miss Wragg, the photographer. Her eyes widened when she saw us. We greeted each other and though her look was warm and friendly she seemed guarded.

'How are your girls?' she asked Sam.

'They're all well thank you. But Jessie and I have been visiting a sick cousin in Parbold. My wife wasn't able to come with us this time. Too much to do in the home.'

The words slipped off his tongue like he'd practised them, but it was just his quick thinking. At the forecourt, we bid her goodbye and went in different directions.

'Do you think she believed you?' I asked.

'Possibly not, but I don't think she's the type to tittle-tattle and there's no reason for her to speak to Agnes.'

'All the same, if we go to Parbold again perhaps we should travel separately?' I surprised myself with the remark, for such scheming had once been beyond me.

45

JESSIE

Wisley Road: August 1901

I lay on my side and listened to the night noises of the house: the glugging of the pipes, the wooden floors settling after feet had long since trodden them. Comforting sounds that kept me company as I failed to reach for sleep. I clung to them as I surveyed the last few days: waking to feelings of nausea, the late arrival of my monthly and the compulsion for cheese. I needed nothing more to tell me the truth. It was happening.

A mistake? Yes. Not deliberately done.

At times throughout the day, I'd shouldered the blame onto Sam. But what was the point? I hadn't refused to lie with him. Still, my worries ranged wide. How long would I be able to hide my condition? Could anything be done at an early stage? I pictured the bottles on the shelves of Slaters, the Herbalist's in King Street, the ones labelled *Female Mixture*. The owners knew me from buying their cough medicine and other innocent remedies. The wrong establishment to make enquiries of that sort. So where else?

I slipped out of bed, put on a cardigan and turned on the light. I reached for the newspaper. The hall clock struck twelve as I scoured the advertisement columns. I tore out the description for *Holloways' Pills*. The cure was neither temporary nor superficial but permanent, it said. If they did *remove every consti-tutional disturbance*, I might get away with it. I thought of Pa. My father was not what you'd call a good Catholic, but he would be shocked if he ever found out what I planned to send off for.

THEY ARRIVED a few days later and I swallowed them with water and a prayer. Then I waited and kept silent. Sam had outside appointments with suppliers, which kept him away for most of the week, so he remained ignorant. I would tell him, but I needed a few days before I did. How to describe my swinging feelings, the terror of my situation? I wasn't yet ready to do so.

THE BLOOD WOULDN'T COME and the ritual of clinging to the bathroom sink continued as I willed the nausea to lessen. I'd wasted money I would need for the future. Sam still didn't know. It would be Sunday before I could tell him.

ON FRIDAY NIGHT, common sense deserted me and I considered ways I'd heard of to end my trouble: all were dangerous and costly. When sleep came, I dreamed I was walking the streets, a hungry beggar holding a sickly baby wrapped in newspaper sheets. I woke drenched in sweat and hurried to wash myself down with shaking hands before I dressed for the day.

I was quiet at work. Maybe he noticed; I don't know. We were used to hiding our feelings and acting professionally. Before we closed on Saturday he passed me a note and a tender look. He would be free the next afternoon. At home, I paced up and down thinking what I would say in the snatched time we'd have. I worried that I hadn't been to a doctor. Sam would want me to be certain; not to have made a mistake. Gossips say some women used pregnancy as a ploy to get a man to marry them. That wouldn't happen with me.

ON SUNDAY he came through the backyard and stepped into my living room with a warm smile which I quickly dashed.

'I think I've started a baby,' I said, not giving him time to take off his coat. His hand reached for his hat and his face stiffened. It was only what I'd expected. How could he be happy about such news? It wasn't the same as it had been with Agnes: every one of their daughters was welcomed. Worry flitted across his face before he smiled and reached for me. Wrapped in his arms I rushed my words and told him about the pills.

'The ones you see advertised — but nothing happened. It was the only thing I could think of. I won't go to some woman in a back street. I'd rather live with the shame than end up dead.' We'd both read the horrible accounts in the newspaper from the coroner's court. Women dying after miscarriages, and no one admitting knowledge of an intervention.

He kissed my forehead. 'Don't ever think like that again.'

I tried to keep the tears back, but the words came out as if I'd been coughing all night. 'I panicked. I thought the pills would work... I don't know what to do.'

'Jessie! I'd never ask you to get rid of it. Did you think I would?'

'No. But it would have been my decision if I thought it would work.' He led me to the couch and we sat down.

'Do you think Mr Urmston will let you live here once the baby's born?' He looked around the room, at the few ornaments I possessed, the chair covers and my small row of books on a shelf.

I shook my head. 'There'd be talk... with him being a widower. Some might think he'd taken advantage of me. I'll stay until I start to show.'

'About three months then before you give him notice. Sorry if I seemed... I was taken aback. I suppose it happened when we were in the barn.'

'I think so. But I don't regret going there.'

He didn't reply. Distracted, he walked over to the window and stared at the garden before turning around. I could almost see his brain whirring with ideas.

'Would Margaret take you in when you leave here?' He asked at last.

'I think she would, for a time.'

'We'll have to think up a story to tell everyone. What if I drop some hints before you start showing, say that you're courting?'

'A pretend sweetheart?' I hadn't thought of that and couldn't imagine how it would work. 'The family will want to know why he won't marry me and why he doesn't visit if I'm staying at Aunt Margaret's.' I tried to catch hold of the shirt-tails of Sam's mind, as I'd done in the describing game we'd played about the false rep only a few weeks ago. 'I'll have to say I'm engaged. It's bad enough without them thinking I'm a tart.'

'People from our background do what they have to. Not everyone can get married at the drop of a hat. Tell them he can't marry you because... tell them he's a mill worker who enlisted before you knew a baby was on the way. Say he's in South Africa. We'll make the story watertight.'

Sam's mind worked as fast as a shuttle on a loom. 'They'll believe *you*,' I said, knowing he was the golden apple of my grandparents' eyes. Lucky Agnes to have plucked him.

He took my hand. 'It will work. Plenty of unemployed men and workers are joining up. Look at our Josiah.'

His younger brother had joined the army when he was

recently married, spending more time abroad than at home. Surely I'd see a lot more of Sam than Jos did of his wife?

In the middle of the following week, we had a snatched hour together when Mr Urmston was out. Sam had told Agnes there was a chapel committee meeting he should attend. I saw that being on a committee had its benefits though they often bored him. While the pot of tea brewed, he talked about how the baby would feel when I held it in my arms.

'I like the names *Mary, Frances and Jennifer.*' He spoke as if musing over a tribe of daughters. 'What do you think of those?'

No boys' names. Of course, he'd never had to think of any.

'Can you only come up with girls' names?' I blurted out. He said nothing but a hurt look shadowed his face. I tried to make amends. 'Sorry, I only meant you've had no practice with boys.'

He stood and went to pour the tea. 'Whatever sex *our* child is I will love it as I do my girls, I promise you.'

I tried, but failed to join in with his talk about the baby. My thoughts spun like a pit head wheel — if anyone found out the truth it would be all over for us.

'I suppose I'd get letters from South Africa, wouldn't I?' I said, thinking of my made-up fiancé. 'I'll have to write them myself so I can regale everyone with his exploits.' Was that a cruel thing to say? Unnecessary? Perhaps not, but Sam looked uncomfortable and we were quiet as we drank our tea and soon it was time for him to leave.

The next day, a simple action brought home to me the consequences of being pregnant. I was serving in the shop, and without thinking, I covered my stomach with both hands. Sam frowned, tipped his head and looked up at the ceiling where Agnes was in the flat above. I understood at once. He didn't want me doing something she'd done for most of her married life. If she'd come downstairs and recognised the action...

. . .

THE FOLLOWING evening we met at the fingerpost when he was supposedly at the library. It hadn't rained for two weeks and dust rose under our feet leaving a layer of grey grit on my shoes. On the road up the hill I plied him with questions because despite being a man, he knew far more about pregnancies and birth than I did. Before he could answer, a horse and cart piled high with stacked hay rolled past, forcing us to press our backs into a hedge. Strands of hay floated down and got caught in my hair. Sam stood so close I felt his breath on my cheek as he plucked them out.

We walked on and he mentioned that I'd get tired and would have swollen ankles. Suddenly, I didn't want to know. I broke away and set off leaving him behind. The baby was all we seemed to talk about. I was only twenty. I should be... what? Dancing? Going to the Music Hall? Why those pursuits sprang to mind, I didn't know. I'd never done them even when I could have.

Having a baby was making me feel old. Sam caught up with me and I turned to face him. 'If I miscarried, it wouldn't be my fault, would it?'

He snatched my hand and held it though we were still on the main road.

'Let's get off here,' he said and we unlatched a gate into a field. Under a tree, he put his arms around me and we leant into each other. He thought I was worried about losing the baby and talked about keeping in good health. But it was the condemnation that was about to fall on my head that scared me. I'd be an outcast to the family, lose my place in the shop. Then I remembered Ma. There was danger in giving birth.

'What if the same thing happens to me as it did to my mother?'

He didn't speak for a long time. 'It won't! You're younger

than she was and stronger. You must see a doctor soon to reassure us that all is well.'

I lay my head on his shoulder and apologised for running off. 'I know I have to be strong but sometimes...'

'We have each other,' he murmured in my ear, 'Don't ever forget that.'

Soon, the ever-present pocket watch was brought out and we stood up to leave. We said goodbye before we reached Wisley Road and I marvelled again that no one we knew had seen us.

ON SUNDAY I got up early for chapel, but as I was putting my hat on in front of the mirror, I snatched it off and stowed it away. I decided I wouldn't show my face there again. It wasn't a question of faith, just that I couldn't face God in a place of worship. My praying would be done here, without minister and congregation.

46

JESSIE

Wisley Road: September 1901

*E*milie followed me into the bedroom when I went in to lay her coat on the bed. She leant across it to view my new picture hanging on the wall.

'I haven't seen this before. Where did you buy it?'

I couldn't give her the shop name because Sam bought it for me in Warrington. 'Do you like it?'

'It is all right, but I prefer something more modern. Why did you choose this one?'

'I like woods and spring colours and I was told it was painted by a local artist. A man living in Parbold.'

'But a milkmaid, Jessie! Such a funny choice of subject for a town girl.'

'I suppose it is a bit old fashioned but... don't you think it suits the room?'

'Perhaps. Now let us have that cup of tea. I am sorry I have never persuaded you to enjoy coffee. Maybe one day?'

. . .

AT FOUR O'CLOCK, Emilie rose and said she must leave as she had studying to do before her class that night. We had laughed and gossiped for over an hour. She hadn't been needed in *Dunbar's* for a while so I related the latest goings-on which she was always interested to hear. She lay a hand on my arm when we were standing at the door and gave me a mysterious smile.

'You must not worry about that missing packet of buttons you mentioned. Your precious Sam won't notice. His eyes are elsewhere, aren't they?'

I stared at her and was sure I turned red. 'What do you mean?'

'He's sweet on you, isn't he? *Amour interdit*. He has a wandering eye for a Methodist.'

'I don't understand.' She couldn't know, could she?

'Forbidden love. Uncle and niece.' She smiled again. 'I am saying no more.'

'We're not related! He married my mother's sister. I don't think of him as an uncle, never have.'

'That's why he can think of you in that way.'

I clutched at her arm. 'You won't tell anyone, will you?' No use protesting I didn't know what she was talking about. My heart thudded. I let go of her sleeve.

'Don't worry, *cherie*, I don't judge anyone. My own life is not so, how do I say, open to an inspection? It is hard on us women if we don't want to walk the same path as everyone else.'

'You have… someone you care for? You've never mentioned it.'

'Jean-Luc and I live together, unmarried, here and in France, because he has still a wife living though they are separated. It is harder for him to get a divorce in France than it would be here. He visits me about every three months. Fortunately, he lives in the North, near Calais, close to the boat harbour, but it is a long train journey afterwards. It is not easy for us.'

I was shocked at the difficulties they faced. 'Will he ever come here to live permanently?'

'I do not think so. I will go back to France eventually because he does not speak your language as well as I do.' She shrugged. 'I earn more money here so we work hard when we are apart, save, and when we are together it is as if our holidays, *Noël* and birthdays all arrive together. But what of you? How long…?'

I wanted to tell her but didn't know if I should. 'I'm nearly three months gone.'

Her mouth fell open and she put a hand to my cheek. 'Ah! I did not realise. I meant, how long have you been together?'

She took my arm and led me back to a chair and crouched beside me. Tears spilled from my eyes and she passed me a handkerchief. The sound of the front door opening made us jump.

'It'll be Mrs Green, the housekeeper,' my voice cracked. 'She won't come in here.'

'I will stay longer,' Emilie decided. 'Eat with you then go to my class. You should not be on your own just now.'

I thanked her for staying and for telling me about her own situation. 'It makes me feel a bit better that I'm not the only one to break the rules.'

'But you are taking a risk enormous,' she said, her eyes serious for once. 'He will not leave her or the children.'

'I know. But he won't desert me and we are very careful. How did you guess?'

'It was the way you were together when the shop was empty. Love cannot hide itself. His family see him with her, not with you. As do his friends and church people. Just take care not to be seen together because your faces will betray you.'

Emilie made omelettes which I'd never had before, and after we'd eaten she bid me goodnight. 'Try to sleep well, *cherie*. You face another day of hungry customers.'

After she'd gone I thought about her last remark. Were

Dunbar's clients greedy? Emilie suggested as much. She was clever, even in a language not her own, though she once said she hadn't had much schooling. But did that matter when she saw things that lay hidden, like the envious wives at the dinner parties? When I served those women I noticed they coveted things they couldn't afford. They ended up buying something cheaper, not so perfect, and I wondered if it would satisfy them once they were unwrapped. Probably not.

But life was like that much of the time until you discovered something precious. I knew what I valued more than anything: my *Pearl of Great Price*. It was an apt description for how I felt about Sam and the child I was carrying, but was I wrong to use a parable? It wasn't something you could ask a minister.

47

SAM

Wigan town centre: September 1901

group of miners lounged against the bar; indulging in quiet talk. And as I looked at them, a great need arose in me for a friend. Hadn't I once been part of that kind of brotherhood? Problems made known, friendships cemented because underground we trusted each other with our lives. Years on, there was no one at chapel I could share this with. If Frank or Josiah were still in Wigan, then... perhaps. Of course, there was William, and we were close, but I quickly dismissed the idea. He was too young and too righteous for this business. I was still friends with Emilie and she knew of our situation now, but... no! That would not do. Very inappropriate when she still helped in the shop and had Jessie's confidence. Only despair drove me to think of it.

Beer stains on tables, the sweet smell of pipe smoke and bursts of laughter were the background to my confession to her father. Jessie and I had concluded, independently, that her family but no one else must be told the truth. She met Patrick and James regularly in teashops, the park, and even in Teck

Street when she knew Clodagh wouldn't be there. To not tell them would have been a lie too far, we agreed.

I joined Patrick at his table in a corner. It was the hardest thing I'd ever done and his face was more than I could bear. I looked away in shame. He knuckled his fingers like a boxer and for a moment I thought he might hit me.

I was two years closer to his age than I was to Jessie's. What would I say in fifteen, twenty years, if a relative came up to me and said he was the father of Grace or Helena's unborn child?

Patrick was silent for a long time. 'What do you propose to do? I take it you're going to stand by her. You wouldn't have asked to see me otherwise.'

I took a sip of water and cleared my throat. 'We love each other. It's as simple, or as complicated as that. We've talked it over endlessly and have come up with a story. She wants to keep the child but will put it about that she has a sweetheart who is in the army, overseas. It's a common enough reason why a couple can't wed straightaway. I know this lets me off the hook but it's the best we can do.'

Patrick took a swig of his beer. 'I don't doubt it'll convince most of them. But what about a home, rent and food money? You'll take care of that, will you? We have little enough coming in by the end of the week.' He frowned. 'Did you know the doctor has told James he has a heart complaint and must cut down his work? I'll have to help him out a bit. He's too fatigued to do more.'

'Yes. Jessie told me he's officially a dataller now.' These men usually worked up to half a week for half pay.

'I can't see the lass wanting to move in with us again,' Patrick said. 'And she'll have to leave her job with you, won't she?'

'You don't need to worry about money. I'll take care of her and the baby. And we've decided it's best if she leaves Wigan after the baby's born, so there'll be less gossip. I'll find her a house to rent in Warrington as I'm often there on business.

Make up reasons to stay overnight. She says she's going to call herself Mrs Towneley when she moves.'

Patrick gripped the edge of the table. 'Not Gorman then?' His face fell and he drank deep from his pint. Perhaps he found Jessie throwing off her name harder to bear than bringing an illegitimate child into the world.

'We thought *Mrs Gorman* didn't fit the story and Jessie insisted on *Towneley*. She said it made her feel closer to her mother.'

Patrick wiped his brow with a handkerchief and I saw he was sweating. 'I don't know what Mary would have thought about this, Sam. I mean, she was fond of you and if you'd been single there'd be no problem.'

Hearing him say this was like a knife in my heart. 'I can't abandon my other children, but I promise you I will never desert Jessie.' From now on I'd have two families and I'd be torn between them.

'If I'd been a better father...' He stood suddenly. 'I need another pint. Will you have one?' He towered over me and most of the other men in the pub. He was still a fine figure in many ways.

'This'll do me,' I told him, pushing forward my half-empty glass. He returned a minute later, sat down and cradled the beer before raising it to his lips.

'It's a right odd way to celebrate becoming a grandfather but I'll do it all the same. Here's blessings upon you both and the babby. Have no fear, I'll keep your secret and Clodagh won't hear a word about it from me. But if you tell James the truth you must make him swear on The Bible never to breathe a word of this.'

I left soon after. Walking away from Patrick and the miners' pub, changing one cobbled street for another felt like I was leaving behind a known and simpler world.

48

JESSIE

Wisley Road: October 1901

M r Urmston was quiet with me. Whenever we coincided in the kitchen he made some excuse to leave: a letter that needed posting, a window he'd forgotten to close. There was no more gossiping over tea and buns. I was so at home in his house that it had made me careless of my appearance. I hadn't always worn my shawl to cover my growing stomach. He would have seen how tight my skirt was around my waist. His sideways looks convinced me I had to say something, but he got in first.

'Sit down, Jessie.' I pulled his kitchen chair out awkwardly and the way I sat made my condition obvious. 'You've put on weight since you came here, I think.'

'Do you want me to leave Mr Urmston?' I said what I had to quickly. He shook his head and a rush of joy filled me. But that was desperation on my part.

'Jessie, there'll be talk soon. If my wife were still alive, well, the gossips couldn't say anything and I'd be happy for you and the baby to stay, but a young, single girl living with a widower…

you know how these things look. If the head of my firm heard about it he'd make life very difficult for me. The man comes down hard on any kind of personal irregularity.' He fell silent. Then, 'I hope no one's taken advantage of you and that this baby will be loved.'

Tears filled my eyes, astonished by his sympathy. 'I wasn't forced, Mr Urmston. I had a young man but he's in the army. South Africa now, fighting the Boers. The baby will be born before he can come home to marry me, but it will be loved.'

The lie tripped off my tongue. I'd practised it in my head a hundred times since Sam and I thought it up, but I wasn't sure Mr Urmston believed me. Sam was the only man he knew who visited me here, but he was too kind and too much of a gent to press me for the truth. I saw disappointment on his face. It was almost worse than the thought of leaving.

'Don't go until you've found somewhere else, will you? And I shan't say anything about what we've just discussed.'

'Thank you, Mr Urmston. I'll ask my Aunt Margaret if I can bed down with them. She's always been very good to me.'

'I'm pleased to hear it. You'll need your family around you in the next few months.'

I rose and pressed his hands in thanks then went to my room. Family? What choice did I have but to keep the lie going if my child was to be born safely? Nothing else mattered. No one must find out about me and Sam.

That night, I saw it plainly: hide the truth in a box and bury it under the earth. But it would be surrounded by snares: ones I could blunder into at any time. Fear for the future pressed down on me like an iron bar on my chest and didn't shift when daylight seeped through the curtains.

SOMEHOW, apart from Mr Urmston, I successfully managed to hide my condition from everyone by clever dressing. Loosely tucked in blouses, larger-sized skirts, artfully draped shawls, which Emilie helped with. It worked because they weren't expecting something like that to happen to me. I was always the good Methodist youngster who didn't have sweethearts. It was why Agnes and my grandparents didn't guess.

When I went to see my Aunt Margaret, I didn't hide my condition. The look on her face would be imprinted on my mind for a long time.

AFTER I PACKED MY CLOTHES, I left the devotional calendar on the wall for the next person who came to live here. It was marked up to 1ˢᵗ November, the date agreed for my move to Lorne Street. There was no place to hang it in the bedroom I'd be sharing with cousins Violet and Daisy, and why would I want to be thought a hypocrite?

I arrived at their house by cab and Aunt Margaret asked her girls to carry my bags upstairs to the cramped bedroom. They huffed and puffed as if it was an inconvenience and I remembered what it was like to be their age and have an unwanted person in the house. I told myself it was only a stopgap and once the baby was born, I'd be moving on. Sam said it was too early to put a deposit down on a rented property.

'I can't thank you enough,' I told my aunt. 'I didn't know who else to turn to.'

She continued to slice bread for sandwiches, and then looked behind her. Though Violet and Daisy were still upstairs, she lowered her voice, 'I couldn't let you move back in with your father and Clodagh, now could I?'

I pressed her hand. James had told me that Clodagh gloated when she learned about the baby — called me all sorts of names and had pried for information about my soldier sweetheart.

'I wouldn't feel safe living there. But you can tell me everything I need to know about the birth, feeding it and...' My mind went blank at the enormity of my ignorance.

She passed me a plate and a cup of tea. 'Get this down you, you're looking peaky. Don't worry. We've all gone through it and you're no worse off for not having a husband. Some of them are a right waste of time and money though I'd never say that about my Nicholas.' She smiled, and I felt encouraged about lodging with them.

After I finished my sandwich she patted my left hand. 'I see you're wearing a ring. Probably for the best. When do you expect to see your young man next? Will you look for a place to live together?'

'Probably won't see him till next May. He'll still be serving abroad when the baby's born, but he wrote to his parents to tell them and they're helping me out. They've been very kind, giving me a small allowance.'

'Do I know them?' Her face was lined with curiosity.

'Doubt it. They live in... Parbold.' I plucked the name from the top of my head. I hadn't thought the lie through enough. 'Top of the Hill. Not well off but better than some.' As I said it, I imagined a kindly couple living in one of those cottages Sam and I saw on our outing there. It seemed to satisfy my aunt.

'I'm pleased for you, love. You need a bit of luck after all you've been through. What's his name, by the way, I don't think you've said?'

'Peter,' I told her, grabbing at something at bit uncommon.

She left me and I went upstairs to unpack my clothes. Sam had put the rest of my things in the storeroom at the shop, including my milkmaid picture. I'd miss having it hanging over my bed. I began to unfold my blouses and as I did, I realised the name I'd chosen for my absent fiancé was also that of a liar. Peter was Jesus's disciple and he told the Pharisees that he didn't know his master. I felt dreadful lying to Margaret who'd nursed me when I was ill and was now prepared to teach me how to be a mother, but it's what Sam and I had agreed.

I trod carefully down the rickety stairs and found her in the kitchen preparing the tea and wrapped my arms around her. 'If it's a girl, I'm going to call her after you.'

TELLING her sister was a different matter and discussing when to do it with Sam was almost as hard as speaking to my aunt. He was embarrassed, and ashamed that he was the cause of me leaving a job I loved. We both knew nothing would be the same after this step.

I chose a time when the shop was closed and he was away from home. I sat on the edge of my chair in their light and airy parlour. I always thought of Emilie and her aunt when I was in that room. Laughter and chatter came from the girls' bedrooms. Grace, I guessed, was bossing the younger ones. After today, I would no longer have their friendship or respect. I guessed Agnes would keep them away from me. She looked tired and I enquired after her health. She said she wasn't eating well and then abruptly asked why I wanted to see her.

I said my piece rapidly, desperate to be released: *the sweetheart, the engagement and planned wedding*. She listened with narrowed eyes, shrugged then tilted her head upwards as if despairing of the mess I'd made of my life.

'I'm sorry it's turned out this way, Jessie. It's your Ma and Pa all over again. You might have to wait a couple of years like they did before you're wed, but I trust you'll do the right thing in the end. Have you told Mother and Father?'

'No, not yet. I... haven't had time...' I hadn't been able to face my grandparents.

'I'm seeing them tomorrow. I'll pass on your news about the engagement if you like.'

I thanked her, relieved that that trial had been taken from

me, though I could imagine the tut, tutting once they knew. Grandma would urge me to marry as soon as possible. That's all everyone wanted, and I couldn't blame them. Sitting in Sam's parlour, I smothered the thought that it wasn't going to happen. Agnes passed her hands across her stomach and stood up, signalling the visit was at an end.

When I closed the shop door — she'd stayed upstairs, hadn't seen me out — I gulped in air like an asthmatic and walked back through the park to Lorne Street.

49

JESSIE

Lorne Street: November 1901

*D*espite having the stocking knitting machine with me, and payment for the work I did on it, sometimes the hours dragged and the weeks fell heavily. I helped my aunt with the shopping, cooking and serving meals, and on fine days I was encouraged to walk outside.

'It's good for you,' she told me, though I felt guilty I found so much pleasure in the short escapes.

Nicholas, her husband, didn't say much, but I knew he'd be glad when I was gone. He thought of me as an unwelcome shadow hanging over his family. An overseer at Pemberton Pit, he was tall and broad-shouldered, taciturn with me though not with visitors when it was all jokes and cups of tea. I became envious of how he looked with open fondness upon my aunt. Sam's visits to Lorne Street centred on both families' lives. He showed me no special interest and pretended, like my grandparents, to be disappointed at the position I'd got myself into. If we were ever alone, it was the first thing he apologised for.

On a windy day around Guy Fawkes Night, I dragged myself

to the shops conscious of the dark circles under my eyes and my lank hair. I slept badly and there was little opportunity for hair-washing in a house with one sink and five people wanting to use it. At the bottom of Wallgate, waiting for a line of cabs to flick the whip and trundle away, I heard my name called and I turned around. A flutter of excitement surged through me when I saw Susan. Her beaming smile lasted as long as it took to see my swelling stomach. She put a hand to her mouth.

'You didn't know?' I got in first, giving her time to recover. 'I suppose not. I haven't been attending chapel or going out much.'

She shook her head, unable to speak. I filled the silence with our list of lies. *He's gone to be a soldier. We have plans to marry...* Susan nodded but the shocked expression didn't fade.

'I'm living at my Aunt Margaret's for another few months, in Lorne Street,' I told her.

'Yes, I know it. End house at the bottom of a steep brew. Overlooks a colliery.'

I had the impression that unrelated facts were all she could deal with. I invited her to visit me but she shilly-shallied, and wouldn't commit to a day, or a month.

'I will, sometime. Sorry, Jessie, but I'm on my way to meet our Vincent's sweetheart. She's a smashing lass. It looks like wedding bells are on the horizon.' She gave a tentative wave. 'Be seeing you.'

Suddenly the noise of cab wheels, and drivers shouting to each other, became deafening. Without thinking, I clambered onto a horse tram going back up the hill, paid the fare for two stops and got off at Mesnes Park. I passed through the gates and hurried to a spot under the trees where the only sounds were birdsong and children shouting in the distance. I sat on a convenient bench and grasped the wooden struts of the seat until my thudding heart was under control.

I shouldn't have been surprised by Susan's shocked face. I was never one for the boys and until recently, a regular chapelgoer. It puzzled me why she'd mentioned Vincent and his girl. Then it struck me: perhaps her brother had liked me in the past but I'd never noticed. Was it Susan's way of saying he'd had a lucky escape? Despite the cold wind, my face felt hot. No! That was unkind. My old friend wouldn't think so badly of me: more like guilt on my part coming face to face with her; I'd become too self-critical.

I got up and walked on a little further, drawn by the laughter of playing children. I watched how the toddlers fell to the ground like soft cushions before their mothers hoisted them up. Groups of nursemaids with their charges sauntered past. The grander ones wore cloaks over white pinafores like a kind of uniform. They gathered in groups to gossip, the perambulators forming a sturdy circle around them; the world of privileged babies. And where did I fit in this realm?

Two other nurse-maids were pushing their charges along the path towards me. I recognised the taller girl, Dora, Agnes's nurse-maid. The infant under the blankets would be my youngest cousin, Victoria. I rose and slipped behind a tree until she'd gone. She may not have been told why I'd left my job and my size would reveal everything. I left the park, glad of the exercise, but was unable to dispel the downcast feeling that had fallen on me. Sam had said to expect these shifts in mood. He'd gone through them with Agnes.

'They're not unusual and your craving for peppermints is to be expected.'

I was glad to be well-informed, that I wasn't abnormal in any way. But I didn't want *my* body, *my* state of mind to be compared to Agnes's all the time.

EVERY DAY I felt the child stir in my belly. Sometimes I panicked, thinking something was wrong, then at other times I was elated, longing to hold my baby in my arms. Whilst my moods swung like a pendulum, I didn't neglect to pray that the child would be born alive and healthy. I had a sense it would be a boy, although Sam never said he wanted one.

One afternoon, Aunt Agnes visited Lorne Street to see her sister and of course, the children of both families were the focus of the conversation — how they were faring, followed by shop business. I didn't join in as I would have done in previous times. Sitting quietly with my head lowered seemed to be required when company came. Margaret offered us scones, spreading mine thickly with jam. I scoffed it quickly, being hungry all the time. Aunt Agnes proved to be less greedy and abandoned hers after one bite. I looked at it longingly but it was taken away. Margaret didn't waste food. It could be mine later if I secured it before Violet or Daisy came home. I pleaded tiredness and went upstairs. Half an hour in Agnes's company was all I could endure. It had been torture to sit and listen to stories about her life with Sam. They never visited together which must be how he planned it. He called into Lorne Street on his own when he had baby clothes for me.

'From the sale,' he told Margaret, though this wasn't true as I recognised them as best quality. I'd never dressed an infant but I'd sold many an outfit. He said I should have twelve shirts, six for day and six for bedtime, twenty-four napkins and four pilches which went over the binder. Aunt Margaret demonstrated on a doll how everything should be worn.

Before he left, Sam put the money I earned from the stocking knitting into an envelope and with it a letter. I read these when I was alone, my heart leaping at his loving words and the details of where and when we'd next meet. There was extra money too. He told me to pretend it had come from *Peter's* parents who I had met by arrangement. It was the best we could do in the absence of letters from imaginary people.

After Sam's departures, I would pass some shillings to my aunt. 'For my bed and board'. Though she said it wasn't necessary, I insisted she take it, having an inkling it would appease Nicholas, somewhat. But no amount of money could cancel out my deception of her, or how wicked I felt.

PA ARRIVED at the park before me, sitting on what we'd started to call *our bench*. He'd sent a note to Lorne Street that he was free before his late shift. Sometimes we sat in a teashop when it rained though he never seemed as comfortable indoors as out. He said he was too tall for their chairs.

'How's James?' My brother dropped into Teck Street now and then though he rarely visited me. I think it embarrassed him to see me pregnant. He hadn't mentioned Sam once though Pa had told him about us and that he must keep it secret.

'James isn't as tired now he's a dataller and he sees the doctor regularly though how he pays for his medicine I don't know.' Pa spread his fingers out as if grasping for answers.

I didn't tell him that Sam handed James a shilling from time to time. Pa would feel inadequate if he knew someone else was supporting his son. When it was time for him to leave we promised to meet again soon. Our meetings were both better and worse than when I'd lived with him. There was no conflict, which was good, only a sad sort of regret that things had turned out this way.

A few minutes after he'd gone, I decided to head back to Lorne Street where there were always household tasks to do, though guilt, rather than enthusiasm for cleaning, compelled me. At the park gates, a tall, fair-haired woman lifted her chin and stared at me. Clodagh! Somehow, it wasn't a surprise but I took an inward breath, and prepared myself to be both brave and pleasant.

'Hello Clodagh, are you waiting for someone? I was just on my way home.'

She tossed her head perhaps unnerved that I'd spoken first. 'I wanted a word so I followed yer Pa here.'

'Really? You could have come along with him. I'm prepared to meet you as long you're civil.' I couldn't believe how calm I sounded.

She looked me up and down, her gaze lingering on my belly. 'I could hardly believe my ears when Patrick told me. Who's this sweetheart in the army, then?'

'If you've heard so much you'll know he's called Peter and his parents live in Parbold. What are you really here for?' I suspected it was money.

Her laugh was throaty and scornful. 'Despite your Methody ways, Jessie, you've managed something I haven't,' and she jabbed her finger towards my face. 'That story you're telling everyone is as fishy as a gutting shed. I saw you grow up from fourteen. You were never a good liar then and you aren't now. Yer Pa refuses to discuss it and when he's set his mind against something... But there's other ways of finding out. I'll be seein' you.'

She swung around and took her time going down the road, enough for me to cling to the iron gate to recover. Was her bluster a defence because she'd never fallen pregnant again, or a real threat? I'd tell Sam. We would have to be more watchful; change our meeting places more frequently, just in case.

When I reached Lorne Street for once the house was empty. I moved aimlessly from parlour to front room, not knowing where to settle, and ended up staring out of a window lacking the energy to pick up a scrubbing brush or duster. All I could think about was seeing Clodagh. Perhaps it wasn't so strange that our lies had convinced our families — decent, upright people — but hadn't convinced *her*. Determined to put the encounter behind me, I glanced at the mantel clock. Time enough to put in a good hour on the knitting machine before I started preparing the family's tea. I braced myself and lifted the heavy machine off the shelf.

50

SAM

Leigh: December 1901

I'd searched my diary for a time I could legitimately be out of the shop on business and combine it with seeing Jessie. With everything arranged, I caught a tram to Leigh a couple of hours before I was due to meet her. A brisk walk under a bank of yellow-green low-lying fog brought me to my first appointment: Isaac Rylance's warehouse. A long-standing business acquaintance, Rylance was a big man, ten or so years older than me. Besides warehouse affairs, he'd agreed to a discussion about a vacancy for James, who was now finding datalling as a collier more strenuous than he could manage.

We greeted each other warmly, shook hands then assumed our usual roles: he the knowledgeable older man, and I the apprentice. Framed honours and commendations hung from the walls of his office, badges of his success. I tolerated his patronising because there were worse attitudes to take, and over the years I'd learned a lot from him. Orders and delivery dates for a new line in ladies' undergarments exchanged, smiles and handshakes concluded, he gave me the news I was hoping for.

James could start on Monday as a checker-in of goods coming in and out of his warehouse. Best of all, he wouldn't be required to do any heavy lifting.

Satisfied with my morning's work, I walked the half mile to the little park where I'd arranged to meet Jessie. Leigh was seven or so miles from our usual haunts and a town where no one knew us. Our geography was widening as the weeks progressed.

She was sitting on a bench arching her back as if it was aching and greeted me with a smile that split her face. I saw she wanted me to take her hand, or kiss her, but I couldn't in such a public place and the meeting with Rylance still lingered in my mind.

'Let's go,' I said and set off at a brisk pace. Despite the chilly weather, I was warm in my heavy overcoat and Jessie beside me, though not so thickly dressed, walked with a lively step despite her swelling belly. But when she rubbed her gloved hands together I wondered if we shouldn't have met indoors. On the path, I kept some distance between us, which was not our usual way. I know it was ridiculous, but a picture of upright Isaac deciding to come out for a stroll filled my head. He'd met Agnes once and would know Jessie wasn't my wife.

By the time we reached another bench, I saw my caution had sunk her good mood. Even the news about James's job failed to raise her spirits. Unable to think how to improve things, I fell back on practical arrangements.

'I've been working on how you can improve on the story.' Distasteful though it was, we should get it out of the way. 'If anyone asks if you've heard from *Peter,* say his parents have been in touch and he's been offered a job. There are lots of large metalworking places in Warrington: ironworks, aluminium, and wire factories, one of those will do for when he leaves the army. If I call round this week to drop off your pay packet, ask me for help in finding lodgings. I'll say I know people in

Warrington who can make enquiries, but we must sound convincing.'

Jessie said she wanted a drink from the tea stand opposite us and before I could get up, she was on her feet and walking towards it. I thanked her for the mug she brought back, and while I waited for mine to cool, she cupped her hands around hers, taking several sips in quick succession though the liquid must have burnt her tongue. She seemed unwilling to talk and blinked rapidly, then...

'You put it all so coldly, Sam. Like a theatre manager giving directions to an actress.'

Her tone was flat. Had I been that officious? I tried to explain. 'I'm sorry it came out like that. I thought we needed to put these things in place.'

She turned to look at me; her eyes on the brink of tears. 'I know it has to be done but it's hard! You seem changed and I'm not. It makes me doubt.'

'Doubt what?' I looked around. Still no one in sight. Suddenly I longed to be indoors by a warm fire; not talking like this.

'That you still love me. That we'll be together.'

It felt as if we were on the edge of a precipice, in danger of losing our footing. And I hadn't told her my latest news. 'Please don't say that! I'm trying my best. I wouldn't be making arrangements about Warrington if I didn't mean to go through with it.'

Jessie's face crumpled. 'You think I'm silly; that I don't trust you. You wish you'd never started anything with me, don't you?'

Her words cut me like glass. I grasped her hand and put an arm around her, not caring if anyone saw me. This wasn't the right time to talk about Agnes. I'd have to find another way, but opportunities were scant. 'Not for the world! I care about you more than ever but we can't act like we did in your flat. You do believe me?'

In my mind, I listed all the things she'd lost: her job, the independence of Wisley Road, our loving embraces. I'd taken it for granted that relations would be strained as her pregnancy progressed, but she hadn't. She was inexperienced. A weight of guilt descended on me for what I'd put her through and what lay ahead. I'd been married ten years and Jessie's baby would be my fifth child. I closed my eyes, wearied by the stream of questions for which there were no answers.

She straightened. The unshed tears were still there but she brushed her hand against my cheek. 'Yes! I believe you. I only doubted because my thoughts are all over the place. But I can't vouch for how well I'll put this next bit of the story across. I didn't pull the wool over Mr Urmston's eyes, did I? But he knew things the family don't. And there's something else.'

'What?' I dreaded what she might say. Had anyone in Margaret's household guessed our secret?

'Clodagh followed Pa when I met him in Mesnes Park last week. She doesn't believe the story she's heard.'

I breathed my relief and said in a rational tone, 'But how would she find out the truth? No one at Lorne Street knows the real story or would let her into the house. And James never visits your father when she's there. He won't blab. You should impress upon Margaret and Nicholas again the need for silence where Clodagh's concerned.' I continued in the same manner as best I could. 'And we can be more careful, vary the places we go to. My belief is it was an empty threat. She tried to scare you because she can.'

Mr Urmston probably knew far more than Clodagh Boyle. He may have guessed why I visited his house at odd times in the evenings and weekends. The difference was that he was fond of Jessie. And as for our families, Jessie once said I was *whiter than white* in their eyes, and so they'd never guess my secret. Being frank with each other loosened the tightness in my chest and Jessie too, seemed to rally.

'A house where it will just be me, the baby, and you when you visit. A little family! I thought it would never happen. You know, I had nightmares of being on the street...'

I let her run on and agreed that it would be a fine thing for all of us. 'It shouldn't be difficult to find somewhere suitable.'

Before we parted, I gave her hand a squeeze and a kiss on the cheek. I held her arm again as I helped her board the first tram back to Wigan. It was all the physical contact we could manage until after the child was born. I ached to be with her, to lie side by side. *Soon, soon,* I told myself. And the thing I hadn't spoken of that would have devastated her — Agnes was pregnant with our fifth child.

AT THE START OF AUTUMN, she told me that she wanted to try for a boy, seemingly obsessed by the idea, sometimes raising it daily. I tried to dissuade her. It wasn't practical. Weren't our four girls enough? There wasn't room for another baby, especially if it were a boy. By November I knew she wouldn't let the topic drop. We hadn't had relations for over a year and I'd developed the habit of turning over in bed as soon as the lights were out. There was no mistaking my intentions. In the middle of October, she entered the bedroom later than me and caught me reading. I was trapped. She asked me to put my book down.

'About the baby. The upstairs flat next door is being leased again. Why don't we apply for it? It would provide us with several more rooms though we'd have to knock through the dividing wall, of course.'

I hadn't known about the lease ending. Before being partitioned, the two buildings had once been one big residence. Our ground floor became a shop and next door an insurance agent's office. I struggled to speak and saw a small triumphant smile form on Agnes's lips. How to get out of this predicament? Yes, we needed extra space; had been cramped for a while now the girls were growing. In other circumstances, I'd have agreed immediately. But Agnes's reason for taking on the lease to get pregnant? Was abhorrent. And if I said no? I switched off the light. I needed darkness. Time to think. I had a dry mouth but remained lying down. If I got up to find a glass of water, she might start up again. I said *good night* and that I'd think about it. I hadn't slept with Agnes for over a year and she hadn't asked why. At the start of our marriage, though eager for children, she didn't enjoy the means of getting them.

One evening, a week later, she pressed me on the subject again. Told me she'd enquired in the insurance office about the next door flat and learned there'd be no obstruction to us having it.

'Now you should do your duty to me as my husband.'

I had no good reason not to and because of my relationship with Jessie, wasn't I in her debt? And so it happened. Another new life started.

51

JESSIE

Lorne Street: April 1902

$\mathcal{M}$y boy was born in a blur of pain, heat, cries of *push, don't push, come on now,* and a pale thin face full of anxiety peering down at me. At some point during the night, I understood she was the mid-wife's assistant. A fifteen-year-old girl called Gertie who I wished would vanish. She scared me and made me imagine all was not well. I tried not to look at her and kept my eyes, when they were open, on Mrs Judd who went about her business with a calmness I couldn't believe in. I longed for my mother's presence as I hadn't done in years. I was drained, half-fainting by the time Mrs Judd put a baby into my arms.

Dawn. Streaks of red light against a grey sky. I was sore, tired, but desperate to cradle my child. I lifted him up and pressed my face against his head. He had a lot of dark hair, both a Gorman and a Dunbar. It struck me that I'd never even imagined what pretend *Peter* looked like. He'd better be dark, too, if anyone asked. My baby smelt of milk and biscuits.

As the hours passed, he proved to be a quiet infant, for

which I was relieved. I would have felt guilty if he'd kept everyone in the house awake when he needed a feed. Aunt Margaret's girls stayed at our grandparents for the week, and I was reminded of the time my brother and I were sent away the week Ma died. How I wished she was here to meet her grandson. When I was ready to go downstairs despite my aunt's reassurances to the contrary, I saw that Nicholas wished me to be gone. I couldn't blame him. The house was cramped: elbows caught on doors, we turned sideways to pass one another entering rooms, though because of my size, they'd let me go first.

Our son was two days old when Sam appeared. Violet and Daisy were back for a brief visit and were ushered outside to play in the yard.

'The grown-ups have things to discuss,' their mother told them, and I realised it would be all about me.

'Sit down, Sam. You'll take a cup of tea?' He nodded and sneaked a glance at me when her back was turned. 'How is Agnes?' Margaret asked. 'She said she wasn't feeling well the day I visited. Stomach ache, wasn't it?'

'She said it was nothing and that I was making a fuss. Probably indigestion. I want my doctor to examine her. It would reassure me about the baby. The new man is more progressive than old Thornton but she refuses to see anyone else.'

I listened hard and a pain, nothing to do with just giving birth, seized my chest. In January, Sam had told me about Agnes's pregnancy, stumbling over his words. I understood why he'd complied. Yes, my aunt was clever as Emilie had once pointed out. Using the notion of leasing more space from next door to get what she wanted was cunning. But for me, it was one more thing to be endured.

I didn't join in, unwilling to draw attention to myself. Sam spoke in his shop voice, measured and unemotional. He cleared his throat. 'On the other matter, my contacts have found a little house for Jessie and Peter, low rent, and a short walk from the station. I'm in Warrington tomorrow on business so I'll arrange with the landlord to view it. I'll make a list of what she might need. I'm told the area is decent enough.'

Our baby was in his cot across the room and gave a small cry but stopped before it became a wail. Sam broke off from what he was saying. I noticed, even if no one else did, that he was finding it hard to remain poker-faced. He hadn't yet confronted the child in the cot. It was only when Aunt Margaret went out of the room to make a pot of tea that he leant over the cot and kissed him.

'I want to call him Michael, it's Pa's middle name,' I said quickly. Sam nodded a *yes* and managed to kiss me a minute before Nicholas came in with my aunt and the tea cups. Because we were busy pouring, talking about the move, I prayed no one else would notice his emotion. There'd been no chance to talk on our own and only a fraction of time for him to slip me a note and some money. He presented the facts about my move in front of everyone as if he were simply the organiser. We seemed to have got away with it.

Over the next couple of weeks, in between visits from Pa who arrived sober and charming, I learned to be a mother. Margaret showed me how to latch Michael onto the breast, wash him, put on a napkin and all the other baby clothes. I couldn't have had a better teacher. She mentioned my mother which made us both teary. My baby sister died at twelve weeks. It was a precarious time for infants and because I hadn't been to chapel, I said special prayers for Michael's health.

THE NEXT DAY I would leave Wigan for my new home, but there was one errand I wanted to carry out alone and I made sure I was there on time. At ten o'clock, I pushed the photography shop door open and stepped into a well-remembered room.

Sam said it was in this studio that he began to think differently about me.

Miss Wragg was as pleasant and kind as before, and if she was surprised to see me with a baby, she didn't show it. I noticed she was wearing what looked like a diamond engagement ring on her left hand, but it seemed too forward to congratulate her. I sat with Michael on my knee, jigging him about a bit, as I once had with Victoria. And unlike his half-sister, he was as good as gold. The session took about an hour but when I opened my purse to pay, I was dismayed to find only a few coins. How stupid not to have checked it beforehand!

'I'm so sorry, Miss Wragg. Can I bring the money round later?' I was flustered that I couldn't pay immediately, but Sam was coming to Lorne Street that afternoon.

'Of course, Jessie. Please don't worry about it.'

I thanked her and wished her well. Outside, I shifted Michael onto my other arm and set off for Lorne Street. I could tell he'd put on a few pounds already. Miss Wragg had called me *Jessie* and it struck me that though I wore a wedding ring she had no idea who I was supposed to be married to. Should I have told her it was *Towneley* now and not *Gorman*? I would have to get used to being someone else. And the practicalities of relying on Sam for money were like a thicket.

At three o'clock, the time expected for his visit, I opened the front door to find Agnes outside. I stuttered a greeting, which she barely acknowledged. She went ahead of me into the parlour, and I saw that this time, her pregnancy barely showed. I asked her if she was feeling better, remembering Sam mentioning Dr Thornton.

'What do you know about that?' She asked sharply. 'It was only stomach ache. Gone now.' Her sister, hearing voices, came in from the kitchen.

'Margaret, Sam asked me to bring these,' Agnes said, handing her a pile of documents in brown folders meant for me. 'He couldn't get away from the shop. They're from the landlord. Things Jessie must sign. Perhaps you can read them together so nothing gets missed? I won't stop now but I'll call next week.' She took a swift look at Michael in his cot but said nothing then departed.

Her visit shook me and I rushed upstairs to be on my own. Sitting on the bed, I worried away at a handkerchief, pulling it back and forth. Why hadn't Sam come as arranged? Was Agnes keeping information from me? And how would I pay Miss Wragg?

I wrote a hasty note, stuffed it into an envelope, added his name and address and asked Violet, the older of my two cousins, to walk over to Mesnes Street with it. I promised that she could help me bathe Michael when she got back. Though my cousins resented me taking up space in their bedroom, they were devoted to my son and thought of themselves as aunties.

It would be crystal clear to Miss Wragg who Michael's father was on the day Sam paid for and collected the photographs.

PART V

5 2

JESSIE

Dickensen Street, Warrington: April 1902

'That's it, Mrs Towneley,' the carter said, tipping his hat when all my furniture was inside the house. I understood this was a signal for more money but I thanked him and wished him *good day*. Sam had paid for the furniture and the delivery when here at the beginning of the week. The carter wouldn't get any more from me. I needed to keep a close eye on my purse from now on.

The rooms were under-furnished compared to my flat at Mr Urmston's, but they were fine as a start. I had a kettle, teapot and cutlery and Aunt Margaret would be over tomorrow with Michael who was having bottled milk overnight. She'd been pleased at the thought of an outing and I'd pushed her to accept the train fare from me.

'There's a chance I can get hold of a third- or fourth-hand perambulator to bring him in and leave it with you.'

'I'll pay you back. I've got some savings from my job,' I'd told her, though, of course, it was Sam's money.

In the larger bedroom, I found the suitcase he'd left when he was here on Monday. In it were his flat cap and a jacket. Always one for planning, he'd told me that a cap on a peg in the hall would convince callers that a man lived there. If it helped pass me off as a married woman, I didn't mind, but it was a stark fact that while Michael and I were permanent, Sam was the visitor.

The little house looked more homely the next day when Margaret and Michael arrived. She said the journey had passed without incident and handed my son to me. I pressed him to my face and then showered him with kisses; it was the first time we had been separated. It had been an excruciating and lonely night without him. After I'd secured him between two cushions on the settee, we brought the perambulator, still outside, in through the house. Its paintwork was already scratched and battered, and the sides gained further dents as we jostled it through the front door, into the kitchen, and left it in the lean-to beside the mangle and bathtub. Margaret walked to the end of the yard where the stone-built privy was housed and, beyond that, the back gate.

She saw a solution at once. 'Wheel it in and out that way,' she said, pointing to the gate.'

I hadn't thought to do so, not yet being a practical mother. When we were seated in the sitting room she glanced around, as if studying each item of furniture. 'Did your young man's parents help you buy these things?' There was only the old settee, table and chairs so far.

'No, though they supplied the money. Sam did all that when he was here on business. I'm very grateful to him.'

She gave me a curious look. 'Put the kettle on, there's something I want to talk to you about.' When we were settled and Michael lay asleep in his cot, she continued her questions. 'Did you say Peter's leaving the army soon?'

'With any luck.' I reached for the biscuit tin, thinking how I might change the subject. 'Would you like one to dunk in your tea?'

She shook her head in a decided manner making me dread what might come next. She said it quickly and it was like icy water down my back.

'Jessie, there's not really a Peter from Parbold, is there?'

I sank further down in my seat wishing I could disappear. I couldn't tell her the truth but she might believe half a lie. 'No. Making up a fiancé seemed the best way around it.'

'Is Michael's father married?'

I had to steer her away from that line of thinking. 'No, no...' I grasped the first thing that entered my head. 'He was a member of my chapel for a while and we walked out together a few times but he left without warning. I know I shouldn't have gone with him, but I was weak.'

'Did he know you were expecting? Is that why he left?'

'He didn't know. I thought saying I had a fiancé would sound better. It does a bit, doesn't it?' I said in a small voice.

'Oh, Jessie!'

I thought only people in books wrung their hands. My aunt clasped hers and walked back and forth while I desperately wanted to hide. She stopped and looked at me. 'That's not true either, is it?' Her face was mottled, dragged down.

'I had to make up something!'

'A disappeared chapel man? Then who is paying the rent for this house? Who's keeping you? It's someone we know, isn't it?'

My hands flew up to my face to ward off more questions and I pressed them against my eyes. 'I can't say,' I whispered.

She sat beside me and grasped my hand, not gently but not roughly. It steadied me. 'Look at me, Jessie. I will say a name, and all you have to do is nod. I won't give your secret away because I don't want to make the situation worse than it is.'

She paused a moment. She must have been so disappointed in both of us.

'It's Sam, isn't it?'

I nodded and wanted to explain, but how could I describe the inevitability of loving him? Or him me? Something we couldn't prevent. Starting from the day he saved my life.

'I suppose you'll want to know how I guessed.' She didn't wait for my answer. 'It was the way he looked at you once — when he brought some baby clothes. From then on, I watched him. He was ahead of every step you were going to take: moving to Warrington, finding this house. You and he organised it as a couple. Then Violet told me about the note you asked her to take to Mesnes Street last week. Don't worry, Agnes knows nothing, and it will remain that way. It doesn't help that she's under the weather.'

I managed to murmur my thanks for keeping our secret then the tears started. She didn't mop my face as she had when I was fourteen, running to her with tales of Clodagh's slaps. This was something I'd brought upon myself and I must stand alone.

She left soon after but told me to write if I was in trouble or needed anything. She did not say how she would deal with her feelings. I imagined she thought of us like you do spies: but betraying your family rather than your country, and just as wicked.

I abandoned all attempts to sort out the house after she left and spent much of the day holding Michael close to me, needing the warmth of his body for comfort. I wished with all my heart I hadn't lied to someone so good. Margaret knew, but others were bound to ask about *Peter* when he didn't show up. I supposed I'd have to invent his desertion of me and say his parents continued to send money. Sam once suggested that in a few months, I could put it about that *Peter* had died in South Africa. But I'd seen memorials in the newspaper to local lads who'd perished abroad. Surely there'd be one for *Peter* from Parbold?

The made-up fiancé had been part of my life for nine

months so much so that I sometimes thought he actually existed and was fighting in South Africa. But what if I had met a *Peter*, or a *John*, rather than Sam? Would I have been in this position, loving a man who could never give me a full family life? What might it have been like with someone else? I let the thought linger a moment and imagined sitting with a man who was free to live with me day in and day out, whose name would be on Michael's birth certificate.

I looked at my baby, asleep in my arms, and my heart filled with love. Gingerly, I stood and put him in his cot then came back to the couch where I sat bolt upright. I stared at the window but saw nothing outside. Sam and I loved each other deeply. He said he'd never felt that way about Agnes. Resentment started me on a path with no end: why couldn't he set up here with me? Lease a different shop in Warrington; start another business? He'd make sure Agnes and the girls wouldn't suffer financially, and maybe she'd be happier if they did live apart. Anger fuelled me into action and I found my limbs tingling with a brittle energy. I examined each room for the first time and concluded it was a poor, scruffy sort of house. Scuff marks on the skirting, stains on the woodwork. I scratched an itch on my wrist and went into the kitchen and found what I needed: brushes, *Sunlight* soap, washing crystals, cloths, and an aluminium bucket.

I poured myself into the work and by the time the furniture, floors and woodwork were sparkling, I was exhausted. I lay on the couch, aware that Michael would wake soon and want a feed. But first I had to reconcile the things I couldn't change. I resented my situation: but how was that going to help? It would push Sam away from me like Agnes had when he'd left the pit. My hands were raw and red from scrubbing. Perhaps I'd cleaned away my punishing thoughts. After all, the only person I was hurting was myself.

That evening I wrote to Sam at his rented Post Office box to tell him what had happened with Margaret but said nothing else about my first day in the house. I didn't want to imagine the next meeting he had with her.

JESSIE

Dickenson Street, Warrington: May 1902

or the first time since leaving Mr Urmston's flat, I was living on my own again. Yet not entirely: I had Michael to care for, but no one to ask advice from, or talk to about my worries when he refused to feed or cried in the night. That first month in Dickenson Street was both agonising and wonderful, but from hour to hour, I never knew which it would be. I left the house which sometimes felt dismal as much as possible when all my indoor jobs were finished, and the weather was fine.

One Tuesday, feeling more tired than usual, I pushed Michael's pram only as far as St Elphin's where a flapping paper on the church notice board caught my eye. From the weekly meetings listed there I gathered it was a busy place. A local woman I'd seen going in and out of the corner shop came over to me from the church porch. I smiled at her. Tall, about forty-five, with a long thin nose and greying fair hair, she gave me an assessing look then introduced herself as Mrs Joan Gladwell.

'I'm one of the Mother's Union members here. You moved

into Dickenson Street recently, didn't you? The postman told me. I live at forty-eight. You'd be very welcome to join the M.U. meetings. There's usually a speaker, a few hymns and refreshments. We're looking for new members. Numbers are low at the moment with four older ones passing away this year.'

Her speech was clipped and business-like. She seemed to expect an immediate answer. I'd scarcely spoken to another adult since I'd moved to Warrington, apart from two brief visits from Sam. A rush of panic filled me. I took a few deep breaths, wondering what to say. I hadn't attended chapel regularly since my pregnancy but Michael had been baptised. It took place on a weekday so Sam could be there, with one guest, my father. I'd been full of nerves as I carried our son to the font, and what should have been a happy day was tarnished because we'd had to lie to the minister: the godparents lived too far away to attend.

'I'm not Church of England, Mrs Gladwell,' I said. 'Does that matter? I… we don't know anyone yet who could look after Michael if I was out of the house.'

With no friends, the only people I spoke to were the postman and shopkeepers. Perhaps this could be the start of making a life for myself. I looked down at my son as he slept, and as happened many times a day, my heart, my whole being, overflowed with love.

Mrs Gladwell pursed her lips. 'Well, you'd be an Associate Member if you're not confirmed in the *C of E*, but we have a few of those. I suppose it's difficult with your husband at work. What's he do for a living if you don't mind me asking?'

I'd had the story ready for weeks and told her he was a commercial traveller for drapery businesses. 'Goes all over Lancashire and further off. Means he's away a lot, more's the pity.'

'Is he?'

Mrs Gladwell sounded suspicious but maybe that was my

wavering conscience. She said it was a shame, but her niece, Charity, who lived next door might look after my baby if I could give her a penny for her time. 'It'd only be for an hour or two.'

The band of pain across my forehead which had been there since rising eased a little, and I felt tears prick my eyes. It was so long since I'd gone anywhere other than the shops, and I was still in low spirits after Aunt Margaret's revelation.

'Thank you! I'd love to when Michael's a little older.' I felt myself gushing and we parted with a fervent promise from me, to get in touch.

SAM VISITED for a few hours on Friday of the same week. We hugged and kissed and after a while, I murmured in his ear that I wanted him to stay the night. He stroked my hair but detached himself.

'I wish I could but it's impossible. We've got a dinner invitation this evening. And it's better if we don't start again too soon. Let your body recover. I don't know how we'd cope if you got pregnant again.'

He stood and lifted Michael who had just woken, from his cot, and talked to him in a light and easy manner. I saw how natural and unforced he was. Better than me at times. He'd brought a baby's wooden rattle with him which made a pleasant shushing sound when Michael grabbed it. It was probably one of the girls' old toys though I didn't ask. It was sensible, what he said, about letting my body become stronger, but it only deepened my sorrow that I'd always be a part-time lover.

I told him about Mrs Gladwell's offer. 'What do you think about paying a babysitter?'

Sam put Michael over his shoulder and walked around the room, frowning a little.

'I'm not saying don't go to future Mothers' Union meetings,

but you don't know anything about the girl who'd be looking after Michael. You'd better find out what she's like first.'

'I'll ask them round for a brew and cake so I can get to know them.'

I'd put off asking him about Margaret but I needed to know before he left how things were between them. Time was always at our heels: the mantel clock ticking away the precious minutes and hours.

'So Margaret hasn't told anyone?'

'No, and I don't believe she will,' Sam said. 'But it's put a strain between us. She finds excuses not to invite us round and hasn't accepted our invitations, though nothing stops Agnes from going out if she knows there's a family get-together in the offing. Not even the absence of an invite.'

I admitted to a grudging admiration for my aunt. Victoria was still only two years old. How did Agnes manage all that gadding about? I got weary after a trip to the shops, but of course, she had a full-time nursemaid these days.

'It's made all the difference,' Sam acknowledged. 'I wouldn't be able to come over here so much if Dora wasn't on hand.'

We said no more about Margaret because it was too dispiriting to discuss. After he left I became tearful and flat, and I let Michael lie in my arms sucking his thumb. I loved him more than life itself but part of me longed for the time when I could take him to a park or a library. Or when he could talk to me about the sparrows in the yard. These streets, the same vistas day after day, people I nodded to but failed to fall into conversation with, were a fraction of the life I'd had when I was earning a living. And now there was the worry about Sam and Margaret.

THE NEXT DAY I dragged myself through the daily tasks: sweeping, cleaning, changing Michael. I wasn't ill, but I felt as if

I had a hidden injury resulting in a deep, biting pain. Or was it just loneliness?

The last post arrived with a letter from Emilie and I snatched it up. Curiously, she'd addressed it to *Miss Jessie Gorman*, and the scrawly handwriting looked as if it was written in haste. Had she forgotten I was calling myself Towneley? She wrote that Jean-Luc had visited her in Wigan, and related an amusing tale of his attempt to eat our English food: *huge helpings of greasy meat and vegetables without sauce*, was his assessment. I'd never met the man she loved and wondered if I ever would. It was a side of her life I knew little about. At that moment, Emilie, like Margaret, felt as distant as Africa.

The next week, with Sam's suggestion in mind, I called on Mrs Gladwell to invite her and her niece to tea. It would be good to have someone to chat to. A young girl opened the door of number forty-eight with questions in her eyes. She was better dressed than I'd been at her age: a full skirt down to her calves and tied with a satin sash around her waist. Her long, loose hair was caught up at the back with a bow.

'Are you Charity?' I asked. She nodded and gave me a lopsided grin. I liked her immediately and explained who I was. She was about to invite me inside when Mrs Gladwell appeared behind her.

'It's not convenient, Mrs Towneley.' She edged Charity out of the way, took possession of the door and moved it a fraction towards me. 'I'm baking for my brother and Charity has her jobs to do.' There was no mention of the Mothers' Union meeting.

'I'm sorry for interrupting,' I smiled. 'Perhaps you'll be able to take tea with me on another day?'

She nodded, but her face told a different story. I bid her *good day* and walked the few yards home. After her show of friendliness outside the Parish Church, I found her manner odd and hurtful.

With Michael still in the perambulator where I could see him, I cleaned the outside windows and as the dirty water sloshed down the panes I pondered on what had just happened. Mrs Gladwell must have guessed my real reason for inviting them round - to check on her niece's suitability to look after Michael. She saw through me and was annoyed. But there was another solution. When the time came that Michael could be left, I would put cards in local shop windows enquiring about baby minders.

As I polished the panes, I saw the usual postman coming up the street, stopping at almost every door. He had an unmistakeable gait; a sort of roll from side to side like a comical sailor. I'd scarcely met a cheerier man. He talked to dawdlers on the pavement and grinned whatever the weather. I smiled and said *good morning*, as I had when I worked in the shop, rather than the *how do* of the street. He thrust two letters into my hand. 'For you, *Mrs Towneley*.' He spoke with peculiar emphasis, followed by a snubbing kind of sniff. I watched him roll on; spending time chatting with a bent old woman in black; his smile as wide as a bucket.

It only took a second to figure out why I'd been snubbed. All my letters were kept in a small holder on the mantlepiece, next to the framed photograph Miss Wragg took of me and Michael. The postman had worked it out: seen I was both a *Mrs* and a *Miss*, with two different surnames. How unlucky to have a gossip delivering on this street. His mischief must have infected Mrs Gladwell who was too small-minded to rise above it; and likely everyone else he'd told. No point thinking about future Mothers' Union meetings now. They'd never accept an unmarried mother. I tipped the dirty water down the drain then took the perambulator around the back and into the yard.

In the living room, with Michael settled in his cot, I remembered a leaflet Mrs Gladwell had fetched me from the church porch. I'd stuffed it into a drawer, too busy to read it at the time.

MOTHERS' UNION MEMBERS MAKE A PERSONAL COMMITMENT TO
LIVE OUT THEIR PLEDGE TO STRENGTHEN MARRIAGE AND FAMILY
LIFE...

I threw the leaflet in the dustbin. There was more than one
way to commit yourself to family life. I took the letters from my
pocket and tore them open. Pa wrote to say that all was well and
James was getting on at Rylance's warehouse. The other was
from Sam who always wrote at length which made feel close to
him. He hadn't forgotten our conversation about Charity. *How
have you got on with Mrs Gladwell's niece? Would you say she's a
sensible girl with experience of babies?*

I finished reading his letter, took up my pen and wrote: *Mrs
Gladwell's offer is no longer open to me, so I won't be going to the
meetings until I can find someone I can trust.*

I would have to find other ways to fill the hours and stop the
tide of loneliness that half drowned me. With nothing better to
do, I took up the *Warrington Guardian* where my eye fell upon
the small advertisements. An idea began to form and I put on
my spectacles, running a finger down the columns until I saw
what I was looking for: *A second-hand knitting machine for sale.
Ten pounds.* If I was extra careful for a few weeks and paid in
instalments, I could afford it. I wouldn't ask Sam for the money;
it would be something I did for myself.

JESSIE

Dickenson Street: Warrington, June 1902

... I will visit you on Saturday morning and stay one night.
Send me a telegram if it's not convenient. Emilie Chambres.

*I*f I hadn't been holding Michael, I would have skipped for joy. 'No inconvenience at all,' I sang and turned Michael around to face me. 'Your Aunt Emilie is coming soon, and so is the knitting machine, but not together, of course.' As if he understood, he joined in with smiles and gurgles. Someone else had bought the machine advertised in May, and I'd waited until another at the right price turned up.

Miss Normandy, the seller, was arranging for a carter to deliver it. Throughout visiting her to pay my instalments, she told me that arthritis in her hands had forced her to give up knitting work. Even while drinking tea and eating cake she wore fine white gloves and confessed she hated the sight of her lumpy fingers. The stocking knitting was her only income and there were no relatives to depend on.

'I've applied for Outdoor Relief which won't amount to

much,' she said the last time I saw her. I mentioned the Warrington Benevolent Society which she knew about. 'I will go there despite their attitude,' and she grimaced. 'They label some folk as the *undeserving poor* then send them away. It's in my favour that I can prove I've always worked so should receive cheap coal and money for clothes, but it sticks in my throat to go begging to folk who have three square meals a day and want for nothing.'

I agreed, but I didn't reveal my own situation. She took me for a married woman, but without Sam, and in a similar position, I would not be as eligible as Miss Normandy for any kind of relief. Before I left, she kindly wrote out a list of shops in town where she used to sell her goods.

'Don't let those men fob you off with some paltry payment,' she advised, 'Because they'll try to.'

AFTER THE KNITTING machine was delivered and lifted by the carrier into a cupboard, I tidied the house in readiness for Emilie's visit. At eleven o'clock prompt, she was on the doorstep with her overnight bag, looking stylish for Warrington in a well-cut two-piece. She stroked the light green material of her skirt and twirled around on one foot. Her black hair was done up in an elaborate bun.

'S-bend corset,' we said and burst out laughing.

'It doesn't make my shape too much like those fat birds in the park, does it?'

'Wood pigeons? No, it's very becoming,' I assured her. She kissed me on both cheeks and gave my arm a little squeeze. When we were seated with cups of tea in our hands, I teased her that she couldn't have found her outfit in Wigan. 'Not even at Dunbar's'.

'You are right. I had it made for me in Manchester.' When she saw my astonishment, she leant forward and touched my hand. 'I have come into some money. It is sad for me but at the same time good. It opens my future. Great Aunt Adeline *est mort*. I should wear black but not today. Not while I visit you.'

I frowned, not understanding.

'Aunt Adeline died from heart failure three weeks ago. I did not have time to write to you, or Sam. I am sorry. There is so much to do. Going to St Anne's, to her house, rendezvous with the solicitor and other pompous men who think I am a simpleton. But I understand money and what it can do. My great aunt has left me everything. I have been meeting people who want to buy her home.'

'I am very sorry to hear about your aunt. How did it happen?'

Though her green outfit wasn't the least bit gaudy, Emilie was defying convention in wearing it. What must the solicitor have thought?

'Her housekeeper found her in bed. The doctor said she died in her sleep. A peaceful way to go. Will you tell Sam, please?'

I assured her I would. 'He will be sorry to hear it. He admired your aunt. Said he'd learned a lot about business from her. If she hadn't given him a chance, he wouldn't be where he is now.'

She looked at me consideringly and tapped her fingers against the cup. 'Sam is an unusual man,' she said her lips twisting a little. 'I hated him for a short time many years ago when I thought he'd ruined my life, then that same evening he changed things for me because he was generous with his money.'

'He's never told me anything about that.'

'No, he wouldn't, because it was my secret. He has more sides to him than most men and he slips from one to the other without much trouble. Some would call him *trompeur*, deceitful, but we are alike, he and I. We snatch at life and we get more out of it than most.'

She clenched her fist and flung it open as if to demonstrate her nature, but her laughter softened any toughness I might have imagined. I wondered why Sam was never attracted to her in the past; if he had been, he'd kept quiet about it. The one lover I knew of, Lydia Holdsworth, I imagined, was like Emilie, bold and independent. Yet he fell in love with me. I didn't count myself a beauty, like them, but after well over a year together, I didn't question it. It worried me at first after Michael was born that his love would diminish as it had with Agnes. But I was wrong to doubt him. If possible, he was even more ardent.

'You are not like us, Jessie,' Emilie continued, 'Yet you've found yourself in a deceiving situation. I am sorry for it, and that people like us make it hard for people like you.'

A rush of blood heated my face. Once again I saw how clever she was. I'd never be that intelligent, but I understood perfectly. What she said might be true, but…

'I don't regret what's happened, especially not when there's Michael,' I told her.

'No, I see that. Maybe one day Jean-Luc and I…?'

'You'd like to?' Somehow, I couldn't see her as a mother, but I could have said the same about myself and now look at me.

'Sometimes, when I watch you with your child I think, perhaps, but that may be more about missing Jean-Luc than anything. I don't know. *Pouf…*' She clicked her fingers and her lips formed a pout. 'You have a wan look about you, Jessie. What has been going on?'

I told her that Margaret knew our secret, resulting in a distance between us and awkward family times for Sam.

'I suppose I'm lonely too. Sam can't visit every week and Pa and James only turn up now and then. And my grandparents don't visit either. They realise there's no fiancé and disapprove of what I've done.' No one had seen my grandma's letter, full of Biblical quotes about the evils of fornication. I was too ashamed to show it even to Sam.

Emilie looked uncomfortable and changed the subject by asking if there were pleasant places nearby. 'You can walk to the River Mersey, yes?'

'No, it's too far.' I pulled a face. 'It's wharves, warehouses, factory chimneys, cranes and boats being loaded. Women don't venture into that area on their own. Anyway, I won't have time to be lonely because I'll be working soon.' She looked astonished and turned her head towards Michael in his crib. 'It's something I can do here,' I told her. 'What do you think about me earning money as a stocking knitter for shops? Sam is generous but I don't like taking from him all the time.'

'A stocking machine? Are they not very expensive?'

'Yes, but I found a second-hand one. It arrived this morning, see,' and I threw open the cupboard door to show her. 'I saved up for it.'

Emilie got up to look and touched the metal levers. 'It is impressive, Jessie, and your work is very good. If you need written recommendations, I will do that for you.'

She never learned to knit herself but knew its value to someone like me. 'And you?' I asked. 'What will you do with all this money?'

She turned her head away so I couldn't see her face but I heard the catch in her voice.

'I will use it to return to France to live. I can even pay for Jean-Luc's divorce. We will marry, be respectable.' She stopped and put a hand to her mouth as if to stuff the words back in. 'I'm sorry. I was not thinking.'

I tried to smile. 'I'm used to my arrangement.' I was, but only occasionally. 'Of course, I would marry Sam if I could. But I would never wish for Agnes's death.'

She looked at me and there were unshed tears in her eyes. It had been hard for her to tell me she was leaving England.

'No. You are good like that. I have not always been so pleasant in my thinking about my lover's wife.'

But I wasn't good. And not as honest as Emilie. I said I didn't want to profit from my aunt's death, but if she took the notion to leave Sam and emigrate, I would rejoice with my conscience salved.

THE NEXT DAY, we pushed Michael in the perambulator to Orford Park. Four female figures with cast iron wings stood at the top of the gates. 'Park Guardians?' I hazarded.

Emilie laughed but disagreed. 'I think they are spies. Judging everyone who comes in and out.'

'Then they'd have a lot to write about us,' I said, and she took my hand and squeezed it.

Orford had its flower beds, ponds and shrubberies and was pleasant enough, but I'd never made memories there; unlike in Mesnes Park. And there was no view across it to where *Dunbar's* shop stood. After we'd walked enough, she bought me dinner in a chop house near the station. We even went into a few shops to look at trinkets, admire new ranges of coats and try on hats.

She caught her train and I returned home thinking about the hole she would leave in my life when she left Wigan, my one friend besides Aunt Margaret. Her last letter had said simply that she was under the weather and not yet fit to visit. I'd put the note in a drawer, believing it an excuse not to see me. I couldn't blame her.

55

SAM

Wigan: October 1902

Summer had passed too quickly, like my visits to Warrington, though during the warmer months I'd invented frequent reasons to be there. Time spent with Jessie and Michael was precious and we'd made memories in the house, hanging up pictures, buying new cushions, playing with Michael and his toys. We'd also ventured out, taking trips on the tram into the countryside, teaching Michael the names of the animals he saw.

Come Autumn, events had overtaken me which I would convey before day turned to night. I signed my letter then blotted the list of reasons why I hadn't been to see her recently: sales goods to get ready, Sunday School concerts for the girls, meetings with suppliers in Yorkshire. I'd taken my time over the letter and dismissed phrases that sounded too formal. I wasn't a lecturer, but because of all the studying I'd done, I thought it made me sound cold on the page. How different it would be if I could see her. No stumbling for words then! Jessie knew I found factual books satisfying, that I loved knowing things. But she saw their limitations and once wrote: *Those sorts of books don't tell you how someone's feeling. Only in novels are people scornful, liars, indifferent, or full of love.*

I could never write like a novelist, though Jessie disagreed, saying my letters were full of meaning. I put the pen down and went to the window. Dark and light filtered in through the street. Women clutched shawls as they hurried home. More men out at night than women — always the way — their wives, mothers and sisters enclosed by brick walls and roofs. A kind of prison I supposed. Jessie said that sometimes she felt hemmed in, on Dickenson Street. I'd written back — *a bit like the womb until the little prisoner bursts free*. Not my own invention but a line copied from a book after her letter arrived. I'd wanted to acknowledge the truth of what she'd said, even if it was in another's words.

Our last child, Keziah, was one month old. Not a name I would have chosen but I didn't argue against it. Agnes successfully concealed her disappointment, enough to fool the rest of the family, that she hadn't birthed a boy. To do her justice, she was as attentive as she'd been with the others, though we both had good reason to be. Keziah was a sickly infant. I hadn't mentioned it in my letter so far, but her health was the main reason why I kept breaking my promise to visit.

The truth was Keziah was struggling to live, and I prayed she was too young to be frightened. Her eyes would flicker when we stood over her, so I knew she was aware of us, following the sound of Agnes's voice when having Camphor Oil rubbed into her chest. The sight of those fragile ribs, her deathly white skin, unmanned me. I could hardly bear to be in the room. Caring for Keziah meant we scarcely left the flat or the shop, apart from essential meetings for me. We kept some semblance of normal life going by allowing the older children to attend Harvest Festival. New chapel friends kindly took and brought them home. I tried my best to smile and question them about the games they'd played and songs they'd sung, but it was an effort. I hoped they didn't notice my lack of enthusiasm. Of course, they knew Keziah was ill, just not how seriously. Without the nursemaid, we would have been lost. Dora spent all day and some nights with us, allowing Agnes to recover from her tiredness.

Another reason I hadn't visited Jessie was that I was scared. That if I spent the night away from home, our baby might die in my absence. Sometimes, when the pressure became too great, I would leave the flat telling Agnes I needed fresh air, what little there was of it in Wigan. She would look at me askance when I put my coat on. Conversations were few and strained and always about medicines or what the doctor said. We often quarrelled over how to treat our little girl.

'Surely I know what's best for our child?' she'd once said, her voice harsh with pain, irritated by my suggestions. Agnes was both powerful and weak. I saw it often. She, like I, was wounded and we were too raw to try or want to heal the other.

Wearily, I went back to my desk and screwed up the first letter. I would write to Jessie as if we were face to face. Tell her everything; she was the only person I could be honest with.

> *Dearest,*
>
> *Forgive me for not writing sooner or coming to see you. I miss you both so much but we have been in great fear for Keziah who has this week contracted pneumonia. Doctor Thornton has attended her every day, sometimes twice. She has a fever, a cough and has trouble breathing. Her little chest pumps up and down and I can't bear to hear her wheezing. Agnes can't get her to feed easily, either. All the other girls latched onto the breast, thrived and didn't need substitutes. I worry that the bottled milk isn't nourishing enough. You know the stories going about town that it's adulterated? It frustrates me that Doctor Thornton is of no help about the milk. I might as well go to Reverend Browning for*

medical advice. When Keziah first became ill she was given every kind of preparation and cordial. Many swear by Atkinson and Barker's Preservative and Fenning's Children's Powders but I am not convinced. At one time we wouldn't have been able to afford these medicines. Now we can, Agnes insists we try them, but I have seen no improvement. I delayed writing to you as putting it down seems to set it in stone.

I've turned to the Bible for comfort but even the Good Book is of little help. Agnes and I pass silently through the rooms. She suffers greatly, and then bursts into angry talk against the world. Nothing I say calms her, perhaps irks her even more. I fear the worst, and we must face it together, but I feel so alone. I wish I could come to you, my darling.

Yours always,

Sam.

MY SCRIBBLED feelings brought images of Michael to mind. I did not even carry a photograph of him in my wallet in case Agnes saw it. There was so much I'd missed already: his first steps, hearing him call me *daddy*, watching him develop into a toddling child. It grieved me to be apart from them, but what else could I do? More time spent with them meant more rows with Agnes. No excuses, however plausible, would be tolerated.

56

JESSIE

Dickenson Street, Warrington: October 1902.

 took up my pen, my farewell present from Emilie, to write to her. Pa and James used pencil but school-teachers taught it was bad manners to write in anything other than blue or black ink. I didn't suppose it would matter if it were green, or even red. It might make her smile. No one else would see inside the envelope. I was expert at keeping things hidden, as with everything else in my life. I quickly covered several sheets. As she was living in France it was wasteful to write only on one side. I looked forward to her letters, particularly when needing a sympathetic ear. A dose of her common sense often pulled me through difficult times. Apart from Sam, she wrote to me more regularly than anyone in the family. Pa's letters never said much, and James who could express himself well when he tried, wrote even less. I said I was missing Sam, that he'd only spent a few nights with us since late August. I questioned if it was the end, confessed that the longer it went on, the more I doubted myself, and him...

He constantly tells me he is truly saddened he can't visit frequently but Keziah's health causes much concern. Agnes too complains of stomach pains though Dr Thornton says it is the effects of the pregnancy.

I wonder if Michael, even though he is so young, misses Sam. Sometimes he cries when I put him down. Two nights ago I was at the end of my tether and the woman from next door banged on her side of the wall. I got the message. 'Keep yer blasted child quiet!' I gave him some Pepper's Tonic which sent him off to sleep. The next night I sang to him for ages but he was still listless. I hope he's not ailing.

I crossed out *ailing* and replaced it with *ill* in case it was a word she didn't know. I would send her a new photograph of Michael and searched for it in the box I kept in a drawer. On the top of the pile was the one Sam gave me, taken by Miss Wragg all that time ago. How embarrassed I'd been when she mistook me for his wife. Was there something in our bearing or faces even that early that prompted her error? I owned one of him, sneaked out of a family album: framed and standing on the sideboard. I touched it often. As for mine, was I ever that young or innocent? If only Emilie were here to laugh away my nonsense.

5 7

SAM

Wigan: December 1902 to February 1903

Storm clouds filled the sky on the day of the burial; common enough weather for December but it was a sky unlike any I'd walked under. When I closed the shop door and stepped into the street, I experienced a tilting sensation and stumbled for no reason I could fathom. Agnes looked at me sharply before we and the children crowded into a cab.

'Charles Street, please,' I directed the driver.

The children would spend the afternoon with Rachel and Graham, without us. They knew what death meant and that Keziah was in heaven. We pulled up outside the house and climbed out.

'Be good and play quietly while we're away,' Agnes said.

Helena jumped up and down and Amy copied her, excited by the visit. Rachel was a particular favourite with them now they no longer saw Jessie. I didn't have the heart to remind them why they were visiting their aunt and uncle without us.

'Girls!'

Agnes was on the point of scolding them. I shook my head and assisted her back into the cab before shepherding the children into their aunt's house. Flying off the handle for forgetting Keziah would only make them feel guilty. The cab jolted us away and Agnes took out a black-laced handkerchief and dabbed her eyes.

'I can't hold it in, the grief, and it falls on them instead.'

'They aren't uncaring,' I said gently. 'Just too young to understand. Helena and Grace burst into tears over their meal the day you were at your mother's and Amy sobbed her heart out though I don't think she knew why she did it.'

'We protected them, didn't we?' Agnes sighed, 'All through her illness. Mother thought we shouldn't have shielded them so. That it would have taught them about death.'

'No, it was best they didn't see Keziah suffer.' We'd discussed how often the children should see their sister and concluded we'd allow them short visits at times when she could catch her breath. 'So they won't forget her,' I'd whispered to Agnes as they stood over her cot.

I looked out of the window and saw that we weren't far from the graveyard. A few specks of snow now clung to the cab window.

'They've got a strong bond, Grace, Helena and Amy,' Agnes said, staring out at her side. Talking was stopping her tears. 'They were very well-behaved about having a quiet Christmas. No fuss over the tree and only one present.'

'That sort of friendship will stand them in good stead in the years ahead,' I said. 'You know it yourself with Rachel.'

'More than with Margaret for some reason. It's a pity your Frank and Josiah decided on the paths they did.'

'At least Jos comes home on leave after fighting for King and Country.'

'And your William's not as bad as he was. Doesn't spout doctrine like he did before he got married.' We tried to raise a smile about my once over-righteous brother, and failing, I squeezed her arm. It was the closest we'd been in years.

Leaving the cab, we walked up to the iron gates which led to the cemetery. The cold air gripped my wrists in the gap between my gloves and cuffs. Already, soft flakes of snow were falling. Just beyond, the funeral directors were taking a tiny coffin off a cart. A spray of white flowers lay on top. My heart thumped as if it might burst out of my chest, and I clung to the gate until it lessened. The graveyard, Keziah's coffin. We'd done all we could, but God had taken her. A wave of misery ran through me, and I thought of my other child in another town. I was failing Michael by my absence.

The last time I saw him he tripped over a log in the park, trying to clamber over it without my help. I examined his limbs, back and head. No lumps, only a bruise on his arm.

'Not hurt, Daddy,' he'd said, though his lip quivered.

And he wasn't. But what if something more serious happened when I wasn't there? He seemed unreachable. How would Jessie get hold of me in an emergency? I hoped she'd telephone the shop despite the need for secrecy. A pain stabbed my chest when I thought of them on their own in their little house.

A sombre-looking undertaker with a smattering of white flakes on his shoulders approached me when we were almost at the plot. 'Is everyone present, Sir?'

As if through a wall of shadows I saw my parents, William, Margaret, and the Towneleys, standing across from me. Was there anyone else yet to arrive? I couldn't remember.

'Everyone's here,' I said, then straightened my shoulders and took off my hat.

Reverend Browning was hardly audible above the sound of the wind in the trees, but I was grateful not to hear too much. When it was over we turned away, not wanting to see the spades shovelling soil over our little girl. Family came up and pressed our hands. Margaret hugged Agnes and gave her another handkerchief then we said our farewells. We'd decided against a wake. What was there to say about a four-month-old child who'd lived as she'd died? As we walked along the flag-stoned path back to the gates, I slipped my hand into the crook of Agnes's elbow, but she shrugged it away. The path was already slippery and I didn't want her to stumble.

DESPITE THE MIDNIGHT bells ringing in the New Year, I was unable to move into January.

At home, my thoughts didn't leave the crib in our bedroom. There was no suggestion we move it. I think both Agnes and I wanted to keep Keziah's tiny presence in the house a little longer, though I'd been unable to bear seeing her chest heave and her gasps for breath. *Streptococcus Pneumoniae* was written on the death certificate. A lengthy illness and an unpronounceable name had claimed her. I closed the shop for a week. Black blinds at the window, crêpe tied on the outside door handle. Without daily work routines to occupy me, I was haunted by memories.

Despite the custom that the bereaved stay at home, for three days I travelled to Parbold and let the elements deal with my grief and the things I could not control. Upon the Hill, the wind howled like a banshee. So strong was it that I snatched off my cap for fear of losing it. Conditions worsened and I was glad. After two hours' steady walking, I wound my way back to the station to take the train home. I sank into my seat, soaked and shivering and repeated the journey the following day. I walked as I hadn't done for years, retracing the field paths in Parbold which I'd first discovered with Lydia Holdsworth and later, the lanes with Jessie. Twice in my life I felt I'd owned the world, and knew I was luckier than most men in that respect.

I came home to find the children restless: flitting back and forth between me and Agnes, seeking our attention. We gave it

to them separately. She in the living room to show them a knitting or crochet stitch while I read to them in the parlour from
The Animal Story Book, and *The Wonderful Wizard of Oz.* That
moment in the cab when I thought we might rekindle a
semblance of friendship, never reappeared.

I caught a chill at the end of the week.

'Utter foolishness,' Agnes scolded, as if I were as old as Grace
or Helena. 'What on earth possessed you to go out in a storm?'

I couldn't explain and was barely able to stand, I took to my
bed for three days, something I hadn't done in years. How could
I tell Agnes, whom I barely communicated with, that I'd hoped
walking like a madman might get me beyond December 28th. It
hadn't.

JESSIE'S LETTERS were a life raft during those first weeks of
January. I collected them from my PO box as soon as I felt well
enough to go outdoors. She told me to look after myself, and
spend time outdoors but avoid the rain.

> *Lose yourself in books and study. Write down your thoughts...*
> *Michael and I long to see you again...*

I took her advice to escape the morbid feelings which
possessed me: economic theory, letter writing to the editor of
the local paper. But they were temporary diversions. Poor
substitutes for the ache of missing her and my son with no
chance of slipping over to Warrington. Confined for a week in
the shop while the assistant took her holiday, I grew feverish
with a different desire: to build up the business as a legacy for
the girls.

Agnes seemed to be of the same mind. She suggested
buying in embellishments such as Irish crochet, rhinestones
and lace.

'It's all the rage. Customers decorating their day dresses and turning them into evening wear.'

She looked around the shop, saw faults and nagged me to rearrange the displays. Sometimes her comments were helpful and I re-wrote our advertisements for the newspaper and thanked her for the ideas. It established a dry way of working, pulling us through the barren months ahead.

At the same time, plans for acquiring the flat next door were on-going with renovations starting in early summer. We discussed them over evening meals: a distraction from our loss, our stale marriage and arguments about doctors. Agnes's pains were no better, but she refused to see Dr Griffiths, who I trusted.

I made an appointment for myself and was open with him about the loss of Keziah and the unbalanced feelings I was still experiencing. He recommended a change of scene when I saw him again in February. By now, I knew the room well. A landscape hung on a wall behind his head, perhaps of Snowdonia. It portrayed a range of inhospitable peaks.

'Any possibility you can get away from Wigan for a while?' he asked. 'A change of scenery would help put things into perspective.'

He knew I had a brother in America. 'Unlikely I can spare the time,' I said, 'but perhaps one day.' Talking to Frank, even sharing my love for Jessie with him might help.

Agnes poured scorn on the America idea with no inclination for such a visit and I dropped the subject.

'What about a few days in Cumberland when the weather improves?'

I did not want her company but it was wise to ask. She pulled a face, and said there were fewer shops in the Lake District, unlike in the seaside resorts.

We shared a home, a bed, but were a couple for form's sake. I hoped the girls were too young to notice our lack of affection for each other. But if Agnes and I each supplied enough love towards them, then perhaps it wouldn't matter.

From that time on I planned my visits to Warrington with the flair of an architect. I said I had much business there, including evening meetings, so Agnes never asked why I sometimes required an overnight stay. She had Dora, the nursemaid, who was a lot more capable than myself.

JESSIE

Warrington: April 1903

ames!' My brother shifted from one foot to the other on the doorstep, a newspaper tucked under his arm. 'Come in out of the wind,' I told him, forgetting my manners at the shock of his visit. His face was as pale as his collarless shirt and I steeled myself for whatever news he'd brought. It couldn't be good, not from his expression. He pulled out a chair and spread his paper across the table.

'Where's Michael?' He looked around the room.

'Sitting in his toddler pram in the back yard, why?' I'd sold the hefty one for a lighter, smaller version which he loved sitting in.

'Only it's better if he's not here.'

When he looked down his fringe fell into his eyes. 'You could do with a haircut!' I said. 'No wife to take a pair of scissors to you.' I picked up a shilling lying on the table. 'Use this for the barber. You should look smart in your job.'

He blinked rapidly. 'Shut up about my hair, Jessie! I'm here because Pa attempted suicide'.

His voice jagged on each word. I stared at him across the table and watched his face crumple. He stood up, as if coming to give me hug, then faltered.

'No! You're playing a horrible joke.'

'It's not a joke but it wasn't too serious. He didn't need the hospital.'

My throat seized up and I dashed into the kitchen for water, my heart thumping like a mad thing as I filled a glass. James stood behind me and I felt the warmth of his hand on the back of my neck. I turned around and clutched him, unable to stop my tears. We hadn't clung together since… when? The day Ma died. I reached into my pocket for a handkerchief and dabbed at my face. The back door, which mustn't have been fully closed, flew open in the wind and I heard Michael cry out.

'I can't go to him in this state!' I grabbed a tin of biscuits and whispered to James to give him one. When James returned we both dried our tears and went into the front room. In fits and starts he told me what had happened.

'I wasn't there when he tried it, but I spoke to a constable who was called in.'

'How?' I could hardly get the word out.

'He made a small nick in his throat and because of that he was arrested.'

I remained silent, trying to imagine the scene. Could it have been a mistake? Was Pa only shaving? 'That seems like nothing,' I said eventually. 'Do you think it was an accident that he cut himself?'

'I can't say, but the policeman told me he'd threatened to end the job later. And he was completely sober at the time. Pa's not said anything to me yet, but the constable said it was done to frighten his wife.'

We looked at each other and I couldn't begin to untangle the roiling mass of feelings I had about Clodagh.

'I didn't tell you,' James said, 'but recently things have got a lot worse between them.' He pointed at the newspaper. 'It's written here. Do you remember Mr Anders from when we lived in Sarginson Street, the man who became a Police Court Missionary? He was in the temperance organisation.'

My mind was in a fog. James seemed to be jumping from one thing to another. 'Who?' I tried to place the name. 'Mr Anders? Yes, I think I remember him.' The image of a big man with a kind face swam before me.

'He spoke for Pa and gave the reason for the problem to be *immoderate drinking by the prisoner and his wife.* His testimony persuaded the magistrate to let Pa off. It's all here, written down.'

I cleared my throat. If I'd been that sort of woman, I'd have spit my hatred of Clodagh into the fireplace. James picked up the paper and found the page.

'The chief constable says that if everything Pa told the police is true then the prisoner is more sinned against than sinning.' He lowered the sheet and I noticed for the first time that at just twenty-one he already had lines under his eyes.

'Pa doesn't have a vicious bone in his body,' he said.

He was right, but our father was as weak as water where Clodagh and alcohol were concerned. But James hadn't finished. He told me he'd moved back to Teck Street into my old room, temporarily, which made me want to hug him.

'Mr Anders has called round loads of times since it happened. He says they've sworn to give up the drink and live peaceably, that's why Pa was released. If anyone can persuade Pa, it's him.'

'Do you think they will? Stop drinking, I mean?' I sent up a silent prayer for Mr Anders. What a job, getting people as difficult as Pa and Clodagh to see they were ruining their lives. 'That man's a saint,' I said. 'Pemberton folk trust him because he's distant enough from the police for them to take heed. Pa must have been in low spirits to dream of doing something as

347

terrible as that, even if it was to scare Clodagh. Was *she* affected by it?'

'A bit. The lodger, a new man called Garstang found Pa and went for a doctor, sent word to me, then to Clodagh at work. But she's not slept in the house since Mr Anders spoke to them both.'

Before James left, I wrote a letter to Aunt Margaret saying I'd visit Pa in two days' time, in the afternoon, and that I'd like to see her. James promised to deliver it and after playing with Michael for a while, he left. It was the closest we'd been for a long time but it had taken misfortune to change things.

59

JESSIE

Wigan: a few days later

*L*eaving the station and entering the town, I thought Wigan busier than I remembered it. But perhaps that was only the contrast between how I lived now and my previous, active life. I peered through shop windows, hoping to see familiar faces but was often disappointed. Strangers now served behind many of the counters. From then on, I looked only ahead as I pushed Michael's toddler pram down Wallgate. But the visit to my father which lay ahead… The thought of finding him in a bad way unnerved me. I'd only had brief notes back from Margaret and James, but I was glad she'd be at Teck Street to greet me. Sadly, I knew it would be easier if it wasn't just me and Pa.

Between two streets, navvies were digging up the road, sweat glistening on their muscly arms. The hole they'd dug was deep enough for a man to stand in upright with walls of yellow clay, greasy as mutton fat. Workers in caps shouted instructions to a driver who'd arrived with a wagon full of bricks. I felt sorry for the Shire horse standing patiently by, but Michael's only interest was the crane which swung around at an alarming angle.

'More!' He cried. He could say a few words. *No* was also a favourite.

'We have to go now,' I told him, 'Grandpa's waiting.' I promised him a currant bun when we got there, crossing my fingers it wouldn't be a lie. The clang of spades and drills still rang in my head as I pushed on through the streets. The tram stop for Pemberton lay just a few yards ahead and we made our way towards it. Then I noticed a woman on the pavement, staring at me. Even without my spectacles, I recognised the broad hips, the thatch of hair. An image of Pa in his weakened state flashed across my mind and without hesitating, I marched up to Clodagh Boyle, my hands gripping the pram handle.

'If you ever set foot in Teck Street again I will make sure you are driven out of Pemberton for good,' I told her. 'My father still has plenty of friends who want the best for him and would act on it if I give them the word.' I didn't know if this was true, but it was a threat I would make happen if I had to. Clodagh stepped away, but I was close enough to gauge that I'd shocked her. It felt good, giving her a taste of her own medicine. Her laugh was shrill and uncertain and she avoided looking me in the eye.

She tried to retaliate. 'Found yer claws, have yer? Well, you're welcome to him. Patrick Gorman and I have parted ways. I'm off to live with my brothers in Yorkshire. Wigan's a filthy hole, anyway.'

There was no substance to her words, only false bravado, and she knew it. She dropped her gaze to Michael, and a look of pain flitted across her face before she shuffled around and walked away. She was drunk. Tipsy at best. I could tell by the way she kept one hand grazing the wall as she made her way down the street, afraid she'd keel over. I spent no more than a few seconds watching her before we boarded a tram. With the pram folded up in the luggage rack and Michael on my knee, I experienced a queer mix of elation, anger, and distress.

Five minutes later, we alighted in a familiar street; one I'd run down on my way to the mill. The cobblestones under my feet felt like old friends. If there were any changes to the area they were ones of decay, not progress. The houses were shoddier than when I was last here. Paint flakes clung to doors and windows, ingrained smoke blackened crumbling walls, and yet the women who lived behind them were still chatting in doorways and whitening steps with donkey stones. I got one or two curious glances: I was far better dressed than in previous days.

Margaret opened the door and ushered us inside with a quick hug for me and a pat on the head for Michael. 'Come in. Patrick's looking forward to seeing you.'

I couldn't tell from her expression whether there'd be good news or bad. 'I promised *him* a bun,' I said in a low voice. 'Is there anything he can nibble on?'

She grinned. 'You know me too well. I brought some baking from home. I hoped it would tempt your father... still, there's time enough for him to take a bite.' She led the way inside. 'Michael? There's a paper and crayon on the table. Would you like to draw while I talk to your mother?' He gave her a gummy grin and allowed himself to be seated on a chair. He grasped the crayon in his fist and started to scrawl with it.

'Is Pa upstairs?' I asked, looking around.

'Yes. I'll let him know you're here.'

But before she got to the landing door she looked at me warily. My heart beat faster. I was terrified that Pa was worse and she hadn't had time to write and tell me. Heavy footsteps trod the stairs and when the door creaked open, I forgot to breathe.

He'd lost weight, looked older, and his hair had grown long and straggly. Four paces across and I was with him. He seemed bewildered. I took his hand and led him to his chair which he sank into, resting his head on one side. I cleared my throat and tried for lightness but my voice wobbled all the same.

'What's all this then? Not eating? It's not like you.'

He half shook his head as if to say he was being foolish.

'Good of you to come over, Jessie. Has James made you some tea?' His voice cracked as if he hadn't spoken in a while.

'James is still out,' Margaret said softly. 'I'll brew a pot.'

I was so glad she was there. Pa's greeting nearly undid me. I went over to the window and stood there awhile until I could speak again.

'Pa, Michael's here. I've brought him to see you.'

His eyes brightened and with an effort he raised himself in his seat. 'Michael?'

I gently lifted him off the chair and held his hand as he toddled towards Pa. I whispered in his ear that he should take his grandpa's hand and say hello.

'Rock, rock,' he said.

'It is that, lad. I made it many years ago when I first came over from Ireland. Your grandmother used to like to sit in it.'

Michael flopped onto a rug on the floor, mesmerised by the sound of Pa's voice. I blessed them both and left them to it.

In the kitchen, Margaret and I stood by the sink in silence, listening. This was how it should be. The two of them getting to know each other. Pa's deep voice spinning a tale. I looked out at the yard which seemed full of broken things. If only I could watch the two of them kicking a football in a park or have Pa show Michael how to make a wood carving; not have them separated by illness and distance. Margaret bent to take a tin from a cupboard. She prised off the lid and lifted out a currant cake. With a broad smile for me, she cut four slices.

But what if things were different? Living in the same place, together in one house. Not Warrington, a town where I'd been unable to find friends. Somewhere new where Pa could have a garden to potter around in. A town with jobs that wouldn't compel him to live his days underground. Could it be done?

We chatted quietly for an hour and Pa ate some cake. Mainly, it was my aunt giving us news about her children and their doings.

Before we left, I took Pa's hand, squeezed it and whispered in his ear, 'I want you to come and live with me and Michael. I've money saved, and we'll leave Warrington to do it. What do you think?'

His mouth twitched in the old way and his eyes brightened. 'I'd like that but don't go to any trouble over me. I don't want to be a nuisance.'

'You aren't! And don't talk like an eighty-year-old,' I scolded. His eyes crinkled in return but he hung onto me.

'There's something I have to say that's long overdue. I'm sorry, love, about Clodagh. What I should have done years ago while you were still living here — told her to go.'

I kissed his cheek and tears rolled down mine. 'You've done it now, Pa, and that's all that matters, that and giving up the drink.'

He nodded. 'With God's help and that Mr Anders, I will.'

THE THREE OF us took a tram into town and we all squeezed together on one seat.

'I didn't want to say anything in front of Patrick,' Margaret said, 'But according to James, Clodagh Boyle went into a right spin when she heard what happened and saw your father. She was shrieking it wasn't her fault.'

Margaret didn't mention the knife he used or the wound, and I couldn't bring myself to ask, especially not with Michael on my knee. Pa had been wearing a white muffler around his neck, but that was how he always dressed.

'I saw Clodagh earlier in town before we boarded the tram, tipsy at least.'

Margaret looked at me, astonished, and waited for me to continue.

'She said she was leaving for Yorkshire. I actually threatened her if she showed her face in Teck Street again. I can hardly believe I did that!'

My aunt laughed, an exultant sound. 'Good for you! Didn't she always land on those poor Yorkshire blighters whenever there was trouble brewing at home?' She cleared her throat. 'Good riddance is all I can say. And I think it's a fine plan to have Patrick live with you.'

Our tram was nearing the station so we gathered up the bags lying on the floor. She thanked me for telling her about Clodagh.

'It was weighing heavy on my mind that she might come back even after Patrick gave her the push.' She gave me one of those appraising looks I knew so well. 'I hope you find the money for the move, Jessie.'

'I think I can. I've got some savings.'

She turned to look out of the window, hiding her face. 'You might not have heard the latest. Agnes is still feeling poorly and Sam's still suffering with his nerves because of Keziah passing away. Agnes said his doctor says he's run down, and needs a change of scenery. Suggested visiting their Frank in Wyoming. Had you heard? I don't suppose you've seen him in a while.'

The tram stopped with a clang of the bell and a shudder on the rails and I was saved from answering.

'Don't move, Michael,' I said as we stood up. 'I'll carry you down the steps; they're too steep for your legs.' On the pavement, people strode past, intent on catching their train. There'd be one taking us back to Warrington very soon, and I knew I couldn't get on it. Margaret hovered, waiting for me to answer.

'No, I didn't know,' I said. 'Have you seen him...them?' I

watched a horse bus coming down the road. It faltered in front of a wagon that was crossing its path. *America?* Why hadn't he mentioned it in his letters? How could he think of going away when we saw so little of him?

'I haven't seen them for two weeks or so,' she said. 'Been busy. I'll pay a visit then let you know.'

Her words came out in a rush and I wondered if it was Pa who was taking up her time. Guilt flooded me. She didn't have to concern herself in our affairs, none of Ma's other sisters did. Margaret had always taken a different attitude and somehow she'd cleared her conscience over the path I'd taken.

I swallowed and bid her goodbye. 'Thanks for everything you've done for Pa. It's my turn now to look after him.' I put a hand on her arm and gave her a quick kiss on the cheek. 'I'll write soon.'

'Good luck!' she called as we headed towards the station forecourt. I turned to wave and watched her walk out of sight.

'Trains? Michael asked, putting his hand in mine.

'Not yet, love. There's one more errand I have to do before we go home.'

60

JESSIE

Dunbar's Drapery shop: the same day

*M*id-afternoon is usually a busy time for the shop, but it couldn't be helped. After trouncing Clodagh, I felt braver than I had in a long while. I stood on the edge of the pavement and looked up at the top window in the faint hope that Sam would be standing in front of it. One glance would tell me if he was recovered or still unwell. The glass remained dark; the curtains hung heavily. Nothing for it but to push the door open and step inside.

In the old days, if he were out somewhere and I heard the bell tinkle, my eyes would fasten greedily on the door, hoping it was him. If not, I'd produce a smile for whichever customer was entering and ask how I could assist. If they needed help choosing material it made up for the disappointment of not seeing Sam. Work satisfied and sustained me. Gave me confidence. If only it could have been for longer.

Inside, I dashed a hand across my face to blot the tears. The shop was empty. Michael twisted his head this way and that, mesmerised by the array of goods and colours around him and

356

looked up at the rows of wooden shelves high above his head. I unbuckled the pram strap, lifted him and set him down on a customer chair before folding the pram.

'Mummy used to work here,' I told him.

There were memories everywhere: the yard measure propped against a chair, the window display of summer goods, a scattering of pearl buttons left out on the counter. I stopped myself from running over to tidy them away. Then the door to the back room opened and Aunt Agnes appeared, rubbing her hands. Why was she downstairs? And where was the assistant? I hadn't seen Agnes since I lived in Lorne Street and saw changes. She'd lost weight and looked older than her thirty-seven years. She was also better dressed than I'd ever be. Her eyes widened as she went behind the counter: a barrier for both of us.

'Well, Jessie, this is a surprise. Are you visiting your father?'

'I've just come from there with Aunt Margaret. She said I should call in. Told me...' I swallowed and changed my question. 'How are the children... the business?'

'They're well.' She pressed her lips together in the way I remembered. She was wondering why I'd come. I had to say something but the words refused to co-operate. She jumped in ahead.

'How is Patrick? I heard what happened. A bad business, knife and all.' She shuddered though I doubted it was concern for Pa. More likely disgust. Her attitude blew me off balance. But one thing was clear — the sooner Pa left Wigan the better. I didn't want him distressed by opinions of that kind. I decided I'd tell part of the truth.

'He isn't well in his mind at the moment, Aunt, but I think he'll recover. I want him to move away from Wigan and live with me. It'll be a new start for him.' I let her believe it would be Warrington, best for everyone.

Michael tugged on my arm. He was restless and I didn't blame him but we'd be going soon... once I had news of Sam.

'Drink?' he said.

'When we get to the station.' He'd been so good, hardly any complaints and it was a long day not yet over. For the first time, Agnes turned her attention on him.

'Your son?'

I nodded. Surely that question didn't need to be answered.

'So your long-lost fellow never showed up?'

'I think you know he didn't. It was some time ago. We do very well on our own.' It was hard to keep my voice level.

'Yes, Margaret informs me if I ask.' She waved a hand at the shelves, the glass-fronted drawers full of gloves and stockings, even at the cash register. 'You wanted to know about the shop? As you can see, we're prospering.'

'And the girls?'

'The older children are at school, of course, doing very well. Helena's arithmetic…'

I interrupted before she could quote their school reports at me. 'Margaret said Sam had been ill. I came to see…to ask how he is. Ask after everyone's health.'

'Ma?' Michael pulled on my hand again.

Agnes stared down at him and he buried his head in my skirt. 'If the boy's thirsty then I'll fetch him a glass,' and she went into the back room. I heard the tap running and took a deep breath, trying to stop my mind from leaping from one bleak scene to another. Sam was so ill she couldn't talk about it. He was in bed, feverish…He will go to America to recover…

The door to the storeroom opened and a pretty, fair-haired woman of about twenty-five angled her way through it, carrying five or six narrow rolls of cloth. She looked at me over the top of them. Even without reading the labels I recognised taffeta, crepe and muslin. My replacement in the shop was pink-faced from running up the stairs, but before she could enquire if I needed help, Agnes appeared with the water. She placed the glass on the counter rather than handing it over, forcing me to step across the floor.

I took it and put it in Michael's hand and told him to say *thank you*. He whispered a few words that I doubted Agnes heard, before taking some sips. There'd be no reason to linger once he'd finished drinking and I was still none the wiser about Sam.

Don't finish it too quickly, I told him silently. The assistant chattered away to my aunt about the materials she'd brought up, listing the names of women who'd enquired about them. The way she spoke was friendly, intimate. She'd probably taken over my child-minding role, too.

I watched the water in Michael's glass slowly disappear. Agnes had her back to me. Duty done, she was waiting for us to leave. Bored perhaps, Michael swivelled around on his chair and slid off and planted his feet on the floor. He grasped the edge of the window ledge and the light from the afternoon sun shone on his dark hair and deepened the blue of his eyes. It was only when I heard a soft thud and turned around that I realised the assistant had ceased her chatter. The rolls of material lay on the counter. She stared at Michael then darted over to the window and peered at him.

'How like Victoria this little boy is!'

Her expression showed she enjoyed recognising such things. My heart beat wildly and in the long, desperate moment that followed, I worked out what to say.

'They're second cousins.' It came out louder than I intended. Surely that would be an end to it?

'Only cousins? In God's name, they could be brother and sister.'

How close to blasphemy that sounded to my Methodist ears. I clenched my fingers. *Please, Lord, make her shut up. Don't let Agnes work it out.*

Across the room, I saw a slowness in my aunt. When I first

saw her she was all jerky movements and clipped speech. Now she moved as if wading through water. She put a hand to her back, tried to straighten, frowned, and bit her lip. She glared at him as if he were a puzzle she couldn't resolve.

'Bridget, could you check on Victoria? I left her sleeping. I have some business with my niece to attend to.'

Bridget nodded and smiled, and in the silence that followed Agnes sucked in her cheeks and pursed her mouth, waiting to hear the upstairs door close. If Sam were in bed or lying on a couch in the parlour, I hoped Bridget wouldn't disturb him.

My aunt fiddled with the rolls of cloth on the counter, running them back and forth under her hand until the material rucked up. I was on the point of crying *give over* when she answered my question.

'Sam hasn't been well, but he's recovered. Fit enough anyway to take a trip to Birmingham for two days. The doctor's recommended a change of scenery, and a holiday. I'll tell him you enquired when he returns.'

Her voice beat a rhythm in my ears like a child's tin drum. I looked down, anywhere but at her.

'That's good.' But I was talking nonsense. How could anything be *good* when I had no idea what state he was in? Michael was tracing a finger across the nearest window, leaving smears on the glass. Agnes was watching him too, probably itching to slap his hand away. I could have been mistaken but her eyes seemed to have a yellowish tinge, like a tiger's. She turned away before I was sure. I was about to tell Michael to stop when his elbow knocked against two hand moulds on the window sill, displaying lace and leather gloves, toppling them over.

'Help me pick these up, Michael,' I said, and together we put them back. 'No harm done,' I told Agnes. Her cheeks were a blotchy red and I knew we were in for trouble.

'Perhaps you should think twice, Jessie, before bringing your son into shops.'

Michael wouldn't understand what she was saying. Even so, he knew he was being told off and tears welled in his eyes. I put my hand on his shoulder and gave it a squeeze.

'You've done nothing wrong,' I whispered. Her rudeness astounded me.

'I'm sorry he knocked over your display, but it was an accident. The gloves aren't even dusty. He's tired out. It's been a long day for him.'

She put a hand to her hair and tweaked a curl. 'Perhaps that was something you should have foreseen. Fancy dragging him over to your father's and exposing the boy to the state *he's* in. Everyone's read about the wicked thing he tried to do. And as for your mother, she'll be turning in her grave. Not that Mary had any sense when it came to men. Seems like you've followed in her footsteps with your fly-by-night soldier and the grand plan you had for getting married. Was that even true?'

An intense pain shot across my forehead and I put a hand to my eyes. For over two years I'd lived with the notion that I was beneath respectable people's opinion. That everyone I passed in the street or stood next to in a shop, had somehow guessed my secret. Agnes was very near the truth and I had to move her away from it. But what she'd said about Ma and Pa couldn't be forgiven.

'Mother was…!' My voice croaked but a burst of anger came to my aid. 'How can you talk about your own sister like that! She loved Pa as I love my boy's father.'

'Love isn't the word I'd use, not with a bastard child on your coattails.'

Her dislike crushed me, on top of the weight of everything I'd carried for so long. I dragged my gaze to the door, readying myself to leave.

Suddenly, Bridget burst into the shop, pink-faced. She

darted in front of the counter and waggled a small framed photograph, in front of us.

'Look at the likeness!' She said, giggling.

Why ever did I think her pretty?

My aunt shrunk away from her; her mouth widening in recognition and she clutched her stomach. Agnes glared at Michael and grabbed the photograph out of Bridget's hand.

The girl's face was crimson. 'Sweet Jesus, what have I done? Mrs Dunbar, Agnes? What is it? I didn't mean any harm.' Tears sprang to her eyes and she fled back upstairs.

Agnes understood. How could she not? I trembled, taking hold of Michael and I kicked the toddler pram open.

'It's not true!' She hissed. 'You're no better than a whore, Jessie Gorman. Sam wouldn't...' Her voice was harsh, like a razor scratching paper.

I strapped Michael into his seat then went over and took up the photograph and stroked the smooth wooden frame: Victoria, at about the age Michael was now. Same wide brow, straight nose, dark wavy hair. An Irish look. What was the use in pretending?

'He's half-brother to the girls, not just cousin.'

Agnes clung to the counter, the high colour draining from her face. 'Get out! You'll rot in hell for what you've done.'

'Then Sam will too,' I said quietly. The great heaviness I'd carried for years fell from me. I found the courage to look her in the face, but she couldn't bear it and shielded her eyes with her arm.

MICHAEL CHATTERED to himself all the way to the station, and before we reached the entrance he said, 'No good... no good. Mummy?'

'That was my aunt. We had a disagreement. But we'll never have to see her again.'

'Daddy!'

The word jolted me. Surely a coincidence. How would a toddler know the two were connected? One day I'd have to explain. I wondered what he'd think of me... of us? 'Daddy will see us very soon, I'm sure. But we must be patient a little longer.' I spoke calmly, though my hands trembled as I searched for our tickets in my handbag.

One thought only spun around my head. America. I wouldn't see him for weeks if he decided to go. He wouldn't just be leaving Agnes but me as well. Did he want to be done with both of us? I dropped my bag and scrabbled for it on the floor. On the platform, our train was approaching, wreathed in smoke. I ran with the toddler pram towards it.

'I don't know which carriage it is,' I said out loud. A porter overheard me and pointed to *Third Class* at the other end. Michael whimpered with tiredness. It was impossible to make out faces, or shapes of bodies what with the smoke and my short-sightedness. All I saw were blurry outlines.

I laughed, though I had no intention of doing so. It must have sounded peculiar because a passing elderly gentleman gave me an odd look.

But you've got to laugh, haven't you? The engine smoke didn't make me any more insubstantial than I already was: like a piece of gauze on Agnes's shop counter, scissored into strips.

PART VI

6 1

SAM

Dunbar's Drapery shop: The next day.

I peeled the coins from my sweating palm, passed them up to the cab driver and after a brief exchange of thanks, the carriage lurched off. I watched it till it disappeared around a corner and the clip-clop of hooves faded. After strolling around Birmingham, Wigan seemed to have shrunk. How cramped the shops were, their goods spilling out onto the pavements on both sides of the streets. On the train home, I thought of little else except this homecoming. Children's sense of time was very different from adults'. For the girls, having me away even for three days would have felt an age. As each station whipped by on the journey North, my excitement grew at seeing them again.

My overnight case still stood on the pavement. Why hadn't I picked it up, gone indoors? I turned to the shop and for the first time saw the *Closed* sign and the lowered blinds. It was Saturday, the busiest day of the week. I checked my pocket watch. Fifteen minutes past five, so why close so early? I prayed none of them was ill. But surely Agnes would have sent a telegram to the boarding house if something serious had occurred.

I unlocked the door, knowing the tinkle of the shop bell would alert the family to my arrival. Almost at once, I heard feet clattering on the stairs and felt relieved. The door burst open, and their dear faces, red with excitement, looked up at me. I dropped my bags, knelt, and gathered my girls into my arms.

In the parlour, I was treated like a favoured guest with offers of tea and cake and choruses of, 'Rest your feet on this stool, Daddy', as if I'd walked from Birmingham rather than sat in a second-class carriage. Agnes told me to mind Victoria who was toddling about on the rug in front of the fireplace while she excused herself to prepare the evening meal. The three older ones ran back and forth bringing me drawings and writings they'd done, between describing shocked tales of their friends' misdemeanours.

Their next question was inevitable. 'Where are our presents, Daddy?' with the answers producing much excitement.

Agnes, though, barely looked at the ivory-backed hairbrush I gave her. And there'd been no greeting for me from the top of the stairs. I didn't expect hugs, but a smile would have sufficed, and still no explanation for closing early. She could hardly be aggrieved about my lone trip, having shown no enthusiasm for coming with me when I'd suggested it. And I'd paid for extra help with the girls as well as in the shop. Whatever was irking her would have to wait until the children were asleep.

Over the meal I supplied them with descriptions of Birmingham's streets, the motor cars I'd seen, the museums and shops I'd entered. It carried us through the evening until we retired to bed.

In silence, I lay with my head on the pillow and my arms outside the eiderdown and sniffed. The bed sheets smelt musty. Had Agnes cut down on the laundry arrangements? I touched her arm, signalling a peace offering after the cold evening we'd just spent but she turned her back on me. It was beyond belief this lack of interest in my time away. There had been periods of affection during our marriage, especially in the early days, and she'd accommodated my needs because she wanted a large family.

The last time, when Keziah was conceived, had been perfunctory. Executed to fulfil her desire for a male child. I closed my eyes and imagined how different it would be when I next saw Jessie. I could almost feel the warmth of her welcome.

The last two days had been a novelty: a freedom of sorts, walking alone in a strange city. Going anywhere I wanted. There was no reason why I shouldn't do it again. See a new place once a year: York, Liverpool, even London, then come back to home life. I'd met a single, commercial traveller in my Birmingham boarding house, a man called Philip Craig who I'd talked to at breakfast. He described his peripatetic existence.

'It's free but frustrating.' He spoke of a world where friendships with women led nowhere because of his need to earn and keep moving on.

I turned onto my back, desperate for sleep. I wasn't made for solitariness even as I considered it. I couldn't live Philip Craig's life, not with needing my children and Jessie so much. But my marriage was neither freeing nor fulfilling.

Three days away and my reception tonight only intensified that knowledge. As I had many times, I wondered about separation or divorce. Wouldn't we both be happier apart? I touched Agnes's shoulder to see if she were asleep. If I put this off until morning I might never say anything.

It was too dark to see her expression but her laugh when she turned over, like a sharp bark, made me shudder. I felt her breath on my face. She sat up suddenly, a bulky white nightgown encasing her arms and chest. Her voice was low and full of venom, mistaking why I'd touched her.

'Don't you dare approach me! You'll have nothing from me

in that direction ever again. You've made an idiot of me, Samuel Dunbar, and now you have the gall to want the same thing that you ask of her!'

No light seeped in through the heavy jacquard curtains, but I imagined the beetroot face, the apoplectic eyes. What shame she must feel — my lawful wife. I had wronged her and I was sorry for being the cause of her pain, but I'd known this moment would come and in my mind had planned for it.

'How…?'

'She was in Wigan on Thursday to see her father then visited the shop when she learned from my sister you were ill. Pretended she was enquiring after me and the children.'

The words were bitter, garbled, as if she couldn't wait to get them off her tongue.

She took a deep breath. 'She had your son with her… and if you're wondering why I closed the shop, that's the reason.' She gave the harsh laugh again. 'Five girls and then…'

'How did you guess Michael was mine?'

'It was Bridget. She spotted a likeness, took it upon herself to shove a photograph of Victoria under my nose. Your bastard son was sitting three feet away. As like as two peas.'

'Agnes! I…'

She flopped down onto the mattress and stared up at the ceiling. 'Don't *Agnes* me in that soft voice of yours after all the lies you've spun. Shutting me out with your educated talk, but I wasn't totally blind. Years ago I saw you were fond of her, but I put it down to sentimentality over my sister. I was even glad when you found a room for her in that solicitor fellow's house. Never thought you and she would…'

'It didn't start out like that! She was in danger and frightened. It was the only way she could get out of Clodagh Boyle's reach.'

'Such a soft heart! But you don't deny the affair?'

'Agnes, I kept it secret because I didn't want to hurt you.'

'Well, you have, and as your wife, I think I have rights. I insist you give her and the boy up.'

We'd come to that point where the past was behind us and the future unknown. I switched on the light, saw her blink, and turn her head away.

'I'm sorry, but I won't do that. I can't abandon them. I think we should separate, divorce. You won't be worse off and I'm sure you'll be a whole lot happier without me.'

She laughed again, a bitter sound. 'Happy? How like a man to say that and how little you know.'

'What don't I know? Tell me.'

She said nothing for a while then in a quieter voice began, 'I'll never give you a divorce and I demand that you stay in this flat, continuing the business for the girls' sake, even when I'm not here.'

'What do you mean? Where are you going?'

She didn't answer, then... 'I saw Dr Thornton while you were gone. The man couldn't meet my eyes. Shilly-shallied about what was wrong. Didn't know why I'd lost weight or how to explain the stomach pains.'

She fell silent and I lay rigid beside her, waiting for more. What wasn't she telling me? My mind leapt back ten years to the wife of a mate at Pemberton pit. Hadn't she been in similar distress? I remembered the lass didn't make it to the other side of Winter.

'You must see Dr Griffiths straightaway,' I insisted. I offered her platitudes: there'd be a simple explanation; had she thought it might be a hernia?

She shook her head. 'No one's said but I think it's cancer.'

It was as if a tonne of weight fell upon me. Her tiredness, the complaints of indigestion... she'd brushed them away. My face ached and I found it hard to swallow.

'How long have you thought that?'

'About a week.'

'And you never said anything! Oh, Agnes.' I stretched out my arm to put it around her shoulders but she slithered away.

'That's why there'll be no divorce or separation,' she continued in a voice of suppressed emotion. 'And when I'm gone, you must promise never to put our children's inheritance in jeopardy. The business, the flat, the savings, must all go to them when you die. Without that promise, I will broadcast what you are and what you've done, to everyone we know.'

It was cold and clinical but perhaps it was the only way she could deal with what was happening. My voice shook as I fumbled for a reply. Never in all our marriage had I ever wished for something like this. Poor Agnes! I would have comforted her if she'd let me...

'Of course! Did you think I wouldn't? The will is already made entirely in your and their favour.'

It would only wound her further if I told her about the money set aside for Jessie. She knew the business was my Achilles' heel...that if she spread it abroad I was an adulterer, then customers, friends, chapel folk, would go elsewhere and there'd be no inheritance to pass on. I'd always known our girls must come first and she'd demanded something I had no quibble with. I would not mention divorce again.

She made a sucking noise between her teeth. 'We will fool our families and friends into thinking we are still a happy couple at home and in business. Pay her rent if you have to, but we come first. These are the conditions for my silence.'

There was no avoiding what I'd done, wronged and lied to her and now she was...

'You've a right to know everything and I'll tell you if you want me to.' I switched off the light and we fell into a dark silence.

'Save your breath. I have enough imagination for that.'

. . .

I WOKE in the middle of the night in a state of shock. Beside me lay the hunched figure of my wife hidden beneath the bedclothes. I hadn't thought Agnes would have the capacity to surprise me, but she had. I'd longed for divorce, even separation. But if what she believed was true, how were we to live through the next few months, or years? Were bitter silences and acrimonious arguments to be our bed-fellows? I felt wretched at the thought, but there was no alternative; I had to stay. I couldn't leave the girls when their mother was ill.

Then other thoughts seized me, random and crowded like the contents of a junk shop selling outdated notions and broken beliefs. Men were expected to have knowledge about many things: giving advice, leading the family, knowing how to behave. How would I move forward from the explosion I'd caused?

WHEN I ROSE, I went downstairs, and even though it was a Sunday, I spent a few minutes in the stockroom straightening rolls of cloth, and jotting notes where supplies were low. Up and down the rows I walked, breathing in the smell of clean stone. It brought me back to myself a little. I went into the back room, closed the door and at the desk scribbled down everything that had taken place. I was nothing but a man who had sailed his ship onto the rocks and needed rescuing.

A WEEK later I heard the letter box snap shut. Agnes was in bed, resting. Breakfast was a subdued affair these days. The girls knew their mother was ill and had been to the hospital, but not why. I could hardly bear to look at their bewildered faces. Making an excuse about collecting the post, I rushed downstairs. Jessie's letter lay on the mat. I tore it open and leaned against the shop counter.

Take comfort from knowing your children love you. They will need your presence more than ever now you have the truth. I will find a way to move back to Wigan with my father, but not to Pemberton. I will send you the name of the landlord, and our new address when I have it. Pa and I will pay half of whatever the rent is if you can do the rest. Agnes and the girls are your priority now.

Your loving Jessie.

SAM

Wigan: June 1903

The hospital tower clock loomed in the distance and as on previous visits, I slowed my pace. Margaret noticed the change and fell into step at my side. I'd last entered that world of organised frenzy six weeks ago, the place where Agnes had died and I was dreading returning to it. Depressive thoughts had overtaken me during the walk from Lorne Street where I'd left the girls.

During her illness, my evening hospital visits had been dutiful but despairing. I thought it the longest fortnight of my life. I could still conjure up the squeak of the nurses' shoes and the clatter of trolleys in corridors. The smells of bleach and antiseptic did not mask the end of a life.

At the porter's lodge beyond the archway, Margaret and I were directed to an administrative wing where we sat on hard chairs in a waiting room. Apart from notices, the only things to look at were dull engravings of unknown buildings from an earlier age. We stared ahead of us, not speaking much.

Margaret's face was tired and sad. She asked quietly how I was faring with her parents. I said there was no change.

'They still refuse to speak to me and I can't blame them.'

The secret that Jessie and I had kept from our families for so long was out in the open: the Towneleys and Rachel knew that Michael was my son. And once they knew, I'd confessed to my parents who hadn't been very surprised.

'It was clear to your father and me that your marriage wasn't happy,' Ma had said. 'And we saw your partiality for Jessie.'

Agnes had remained silent during her short illness, but a few days before she died, she told her parents and sisters. I wondered if it had eased her passing and hoped so. A sort of Methodist confession, though she had nothing to feel guilty about. Margaret spoke of her parents' silence throughout the short telling, holding back tears, containing their rage until they were beyond the hospital gates.

And now? The girls' grandparents left me standing outside their house when I took the children over and they slipped inside.

'Helena and Grace have noticed and want to know why I'm not invited in,' I told Margaret. 'I say that their grandparents are still very upset. They don't want adult company just now, only you children.'

That first time, Mrs Towneley had stood on the doorstep and barred my way. The girls were already inside. 'You betrayed everyone! Not only Agnes.' Her eyes seemed dragged down and her face more furrowed with lines.

What could I say? Except I was *sorry*. But that made things worse. I'd wounded them deeply and didn't know if I'd ever be forgiven.

At the funeral, they stood as far away from me as possible and did not come to the flat for the wake.

And there'd been another fracture which I prayed might heal sooner: between Margaret and Rachel.

'Our parents are still speaking to me,' Margaret told me before the funeral, 'but Rachel is distant because I didn't pretend to be ignorant of your secret. She asked how I could have covered up for the both of you.'

A tall, bespectacled man in a navy suit interrupted our talk by calling us into his office. He ran the hospital charity fund and thanked us for the cheques we handed him. Being the chief mourner, he pinned his gaze on me, but it was Margaret who told him the donations were in memory of her sister, and my wife. That we'd seen how well the nurses had cared for Agnes at the end, how they'd spoken of her uncomplaining bravery.

The administrator smiled sadly, and after shaking our hands, we left. A donation was the least I could do. Agnes had tolerated my visits, wanting to keep up the pretence almost to the end, but we'd barely spoken during them. If I found her asleep, I was thankful and left the ward heart-torn, wishing I were a drinking man. Perhaps telling her parents was her way of saying goodbye to pretence.

Six weeks after the funeral my life was in chaos. If it hadn't been for Margaret...

She took my arm on the walk back to Lorne Street, and I determined to respond to the children in as positive manner as I could muster. At the house, we found Daisy and Violet, who were now twelve and ten, supervising the girls. They skipped and threw tennis balls against a wall in the long backyard while Victoria toddled around, getting in their way. Absorbed by their play, Margaret and I had time to talk, and my anxiety lifted a little. It was easier here than at Mesnes Street, where Agnes's presence was in every room.

'This is the rota for next week,' I said, passing her the list of dates and times when the girls needed minding, or an overnight stay. I still employed a nursemaid but without living in; she couldn't be there every hour of the day.

'Thanks for being the go-between. It can't be easy for you. I won't ask what they're saying about me.'

'Honestly, not as much as that first outburst. Mother's thirst for gossip has dried up now the subject is her own family.'

'Do they blame me for Agnes's death?'

'No, they've never said that. Rachel and I sensed for a long time that something wasn't right with Agnes, but if we mentioned her lack of appetite, she sent us away with a flea in our ear.' Margaret pulled a face. 'If I'm honest, that was typical. My sister could be too proud and stubborn for her own good. If only she'd questioned that quack Thornton's diagnosis...'

I agreed. Dr Griffiths, younger, with more advanced views, had arranged an X-ray appointment at the Christie hospital in Manchester which revealed the seriousness of Agnes's illness. He said it would be best to prepare our daughters. I asked later if pancreatic cancer could be caused by an emotional disturbance such as unhappiness or grief. He thought I meant the loss of Keziah. But there was also the state of our marriage to contend with.

'There is no medical evidence to suggest such a thing, Mr Dunbar, but tougher, more positive patients with the disease do seem to survive for longer.'

Remembering those words often brought tears and I struggled to contain them. I would dab at my eyes with a handkerchief and blow my nose. Had Agnes been as tough and unaware as she'd acted? Or had she hidden her loneliness and frustration behind a brittle front?

Margaret and I stopped at the top of Lorne Street. I had more to say before collecting the girls. 'It was a relief to learn that being married to me hadn't caused her illness. Does that sound selfish?' I asked.

'No. Just human.' Margaret seemed sunk in her thoughts but after a while, she asked how Jessie was doing.

'We haven't met yet though she telephones me once a week

from a call box. After the funeral, we decided it was best to keep apart for a while. You know she promised Patrick they'd all live together? It's hanging over her: whether to stay in Warrington or move back here because of Patrick's job. She says she has to remain in the shadows; none of the family would want to see her face. She's postponed the move until she can see a way forward.'

Margaret clenched her fists. 'It's like a storm's raging above us. Sweeping away all we knew, or thought we knew. Tearing up certainties.'

'And I caused them,' I said.

'But Agnes would have become ill whatever you'd done.'

'Jessie and I know we acted selfishly but we couldn't have stopped loving each other. Now, I don't know how to help anyone, or make things even a bit better.'

Margaret tried to smile. 'One day the storm will blow itself out, Sam. There'll be calm and you'll both be able to see your way. I'll do what I can for Jessie. I think she should come back here. Patrick's still not in a good way. It would improve his spirits if she was with him.'

Since she'd found out about us, Margaret had managed to balance her fondness for Jessie against doing right by Agnes. I couldn't expect the rest of her family to be so broad-minded. We concluded the arrangements for the girls' week and before I left, Margaret gave me some good news.

'Rachel is joining us in looking after the children. She said she's missed seeing them.'

I told her to pass on my thanks. I was glad for the children's sake but it might be years before Rachel forgave me and Jessie, if ever.

63

JESSIE

Wigan: A year later, June 1904

I stood at the window to wave goodbye, smiling when Pa saluted. He spun round then set off holding Michael's hand. After six months of taking him out for walks, he was a dab hand at negotiating cobbles, swerving around holes and making sure they both avoided horse dung in the road. He would never fully be the happy, expressive man he'd been when we were children but James and I observed positive improvements in our father's moods. Now, I needed an hour alone with Sam who was expected shortly, and always willing to help, Pa had offered to take Michael to a work friend's house, to show him off; every inch the proud grandfather. But Sam was late. Nearly mid-day and the appointment at the solicitor's office to discuss his will, and other things, had been arranged for ten o'clock. Perhaps it wasn't as straightforward as I'd imagined. My unease grew as the minutes ticked by. I twisted the fake wedding ring around my finger, wondering when I'd get to wear a real one. The refrain, *one day*, sang loud for us both.

Thirteen months since Agnes had died. Not long in some

people's eyes, but Sam and I were ready to be known as a couple. Seeing a solicitor was the first step. He'd left efficient Miss Grey with over twenty years' drapery experience in charge of the shop. I often thought of her predecessor, Bridget, whose impulsive gesture with the photograph had brought to light our lies and the truth. *If only*, had rung in my ears for weeks afterwards. If I hadn't taken Michael into the shop that day, not stood up to Agnes as I had, avoided being proud and resentful when she was carrying the burden of her illness. Bridget's eyes had seen what many had missed.

Then came Sam's letter, and my guilt and shame redoubled over the news of Agnes's diagnosis. Margaret's letters spoke of her sister bearing her pain with fortitude. I tried to do the same but often failed. It was a black period for us all, lightened only by exchanging letters and a weekly conversation in a musty telephone box. Sam and I did not meet for many months. Not even when I moved back to Wigan.

Pa's increasing gloom had propelled the change. Whenever I saw him he said Teck Street was cursed. His low spirits threw me into a dilemma: my grandparents didn't want me anywhere near them but it was James, during a trip to see me, that forced me to decide.

'Pa has too many unhappy memories in that house. I do my best but it's you he wants.'

I couldn't bear to think of our father fretting or trying to harm himself again. No matter what any of the Towneleys might say if they saw me in the street, I knew the move couldn't wait. I paid the rent for the week on the house in Dickensen Street, organised our belongings to be carried to Wigan and the furniture to be stored.

Once back, I trailed around the cheaper areas where I was ushered into houses riddled with damp and infested with fleas by landlords impatient with me for asking if they had anything better.

'Not at the price you can afford,' they sneered.

I grew despondent. Back in Teck Street, listening to Pa reminiscing about my old place in Wisley gave me the idea of contacting Mr Urmston. Being a solicitor he would know the right sort of people to speak to. When we met he greeted me with his former friendliness and complimented me on my appearance. He looked a little older and thinner but had lost none of his exuberance. He ushered me inside an office in King Street that dealt with properties and introduced me to his friend who managed the business.

'Mrs Towneley is looking for a decent house for herself, her father and young son.' Mr Urmston leaned back in his chair, crossed his legs and beamed at me.

A week later, we signed the lease on a house in Wisley and were given the keys. Best of all, it had a garden.

'That Mr Urmston is a magician,' Pa said as we opened our front door for the first time. 'I look forward to meeting him.' Only fifteen minutes out of the Teck Street house and he already he looked brighter.

River Street wasn't as grand as where Mr Urmston lived but the air was cleaner than in Pemberton and the people I met there had a sense of purpose about them. And there was space on the pavement to move freely.

WHEN I HEARD a key turn in the lock and the front door open, I shoved the loaf I'd been cutting for sandwiches back into the bread bin. One glance at Sam made my heart thud. A deep frown etched his forehead; he looked as if he hadn't slept for a week. Without taking off his jacket he slumped into a chair and cradled his head in his hands.

'We can't marry. It's forbidden.'

My mind jumped like a flea. 'Why? Who says so?' I went over and put my arm around his shoulders.

'The Church of England which means the Government.' He looked up and squeezed my fingers. 'When I explained I was related to you by marriage Mr Bailey consulted something called a *Table of Kindred Affinity*. It's a set of laws forbidding certain marriages and hasn't changed since 1560. As it stands, a man can't marry his deceased wife's niece.'

He stood and paced the room. Thankfully Michael was still out with Pa. I couldn't have borne him to see his father so upset.

'It's monstrous! That type of prohibition should just be for blood relatives, not in-laws.'

I sat in the chair he'd just risen from, cold and numb. I thought of Emilie in Calais, now wife to Jean-Luc. I knew she would weep for me. Then a spark of hope gripped me. 'Did the solicitor think the law might change soon?' I turned to look at Sam.

'He didn't know.' Sam had taken hold of a newspaper and was screwing its pages into balls as if about to lay a fire. 'He said he'd consult someone who had more up to date information. But it's unlikely. If there were a parliamentary bill coming up, I would probably have read about it... here.' He looked at his hands, realising what he'd been doing, and threw the lot into the fireplace.

We sat mainly in silence until Pa brought Michael back from his outing and occupied him until it was time for his afternoon rest. When his father took him upstairs, I told Pa the news.

'I guessed as much from the look on your faces,' he sighed and patted my shoulder. 'Carry on as you're doing. Him coming and going from here. Folk will get used to it.'

WE RARELY MENTIONED marriage after that day and the idea of living together in a town where no one knew us was abandoned. We both agreed that after losing their mother, the girls needed to grow up amongst their relatives.

I made suggestions to ease Sam's worries. 'Begin renovations on the upstairs flat next door as you're paying for the lease. You'd have more space and the nursemaid could live in, too.'

He said he'd think about it but the task seemed huge. I squeezed his hand and let the idea rest. His uncertainty worried me. He had the same hesitancy about making decisions after Keziah died and I dreaded that illness descending again. As for his diary, it had more entries in it for one week than most people's had in a season. Was parcelling the girls out for meals and overnight stays the right approach? During shop hours, yes, but every evening and Sundays? I told him that after our mother died, when James and I didn't live with our father, it would have been better if we'd seen more of each other.

'It took Pa years to get back to being himself and then Clodagh wormed her way into his affections. Why not have the children live in the flat as often as you can? They should know it's where they belong — at home with you. I'm sure it's what Agnes would have wanted.'

ABOUT A WEEK LATER, he gave me some startling news. On a warm Wednesday night in late June with the bedroom window open, we lay in the bed brought over from Dickenson Street. For most of my time in that house, I'd slept alone, not knowing when I'd next see Sam. In those days I'd been fearful and ignorant of our future. As it turned out, events had fallen on us with a finality that was hard to bear, but there was still hope.

'Grace wants to see you,' he said, stroking my hair. 'She heard me talking to Margaret and your name was mentioned. She realises you've been back in Wigan for some months and is annoyed that no one told her.'

'Does Grace know about us?' I wasn't sure if I dreaded or welcomed the request.

'No one has told her, or the others. I think she has her

reasons for wanting to see you.' I heard a smile in his voice. 'You're someone she can play with who won't tell her to keep her room tidy like the nursemaid does. I hope you'll come. It's time.'

He was right. I would put my fears behind me. 'I will then. Come for my tea one evening.'

OF COURSE, I had the jitters entering Sam's shop, filled as it was with memories of that terrible last time. With one foot on the stairs, I looked up and saw Grace peering down at me from the landing. I reached her quickly and measured her height against mine when her arms encircled my waist. She was nine now, and I guessed would be taller than me in a few years. Smiling, excited, she pulled me into a bedroom and we crouched on the floor with Helena and Amy, all vying for my attention; chattering and showing off their needlework and paintings. At the doorway, Victoria, a pretty dark-eyed child, watched but wouldn't join in when I invited her. Then Sam's housekeeper called to say the food was ready. The girls pulled me up and we proceeded to the table. It was a lively evening ending with the girls begging me to come again.

BUT IT WASN'T all smiles and good nature. Victoria continued to be shy and one time Amy flared up because Grace had borrowed something Agnes had given her. Quarrels often broke out about belongings and recollections of their mother. I suggested the girls look at her jewellery and accessories which Sam had been loathe to give away. They pinned brooches to their pinafores, swapped hats and scarves and admired themselves in a long mirror. I asked them about the occasions Agnes had worn them and found that former arguments turned into shared memories. They'd only visited their mother's grave occasionally and I suggested they go again, lay flowers, even sing Agnes's favourite songs.

'It's what my Pa does when he visits my mother,' I told them. I'd always taken it for granted that this was a ritual my father carried out on his own. But describing it to the girls changed my thinking. Why shouldn't James and I go with him next time, rather than make our solitary visits?

James and I were closer since he'd visited me in Warrington with the awful news. We both kept an eye on Pa and James took Michael out for jaunts when I had stocking machine work to complete. We did not speak much of Clodagh and the past, it being a painful subject, but when we did we only had to exchange a glance to know how the other felt.

As for Sam's girls, Grace and Helena accepted me early on, and where they led Amy followed. Only Victoria was wary. Too young to remember me, her aunts and grandparents made her their darling. It would take time to understand that I was part of her father's life. And we hadn't yet told them that Michael was their half-brother, a conversation I was dreading.

Often, I took the girls and Michael into Mesnes Park and let them run around as long as they kept within my sight. One day, Grace didn't immediately follow her sisters. She stood opposite me when I'd seated myself on a bench, looking serious; though it was not an unfriendly expression.

'Are you and Daddy going to get married, Cousin Jessie? After all, Michael's his son, isn't he?'

I shouldn't have been surprised; the likeness to Vicky was still there. Grace was proving to be a straightforward talker, like her mother. Such a question deserved the truth.

I swallowed before replying. 'Yes, he is, Grace, and we'd like to marry. But that won't be for a very long time.'

She nodded, 'I'd like that.'

It was a start, a door opening a crack to a wider view.

JESSIE

Wigan: Later that month, June 1904

A tentative rap sounded on the front door. I looked up from the knitting machine, irritated by the interruption. I'd just lined up the yarn on the claws, ready to begin work. It would be a neighbour no doubt, come to borrow sugar or flour. This was a friendly street and Michael had some little playmates a few doors down. Behind the door stood no everyday face but neither was she a stranger. For long seconds I couldn't speak.

'Aunt Rachel! Please, come inside.'

In the midst of fussing about taking her coat and seating her, a dozen thoughts spun through my mind. Why had she called after all this time? Was it to berate me?

'Hello, Jessie. I hope I'm not disturbing you.' Her voice was low and she glanced uncertainly at the knitting machine. I felt relieved at the mildness of her tone but perhaps she was working herself up to a tirade. Her hair was styled differently from when I'd last seen her, after Michael was born and she'd paid Margaret a visit. Now it was coiled up on both sides and parted across her forehead; it suited her.

'The knitting isn't urgent,' I said, waving a hand at the machine. 'A neighbour's minding Michael for the morning while I work and Pa's on an early shift.'

She looked around at the room and I was thankful I'd tidied it early, then she placed her gloves on the table.

'I won't stop for a cuppa. It's a nice place you've found and a bit of a garden, too, I see.'

We looked towards the back window with a view of the vegetable plot. It seemed easier than facing each other.

'Yes, Pa looks after it. He even grows potatoes.' My father's eyes had shone when he saw it. 'We were lucky to find somewhere in Wisley. My old landlord, Mr Urmston, found it for us. Didn't think I could afford this district.'

I was talking for the sake of it whilst wondering how much Rachel knew of our lives. She looked at me directly and her voice grew stronger.

'You must be wondering why I'm here, Jessie.'

She was nearly five years married. Grown into herself; a person to be reckoned with. My heart thumped and I gripped the edge of my chair so I wouldn't flee whatever was coming next.'

'I've known about you and Sam since Agnes confided in us during her last days. It was a shock, but not a great one. It was almost as bad learning that Margaret had kept it secret from me.'

My insides squirmed while she waited for a reply. 'I have no defence for what we did and we felt awful at putting Margaret in that position. Even so, I don't know what I would have done without her. She's been a good friend to us.'

'But not a good sister to Agnes, perhaps?'

Margaret didn't deserve that. 'I wouldn't have blamed her if she had told you! She guessed early on because I was living with her. She saw things others didn't. She kept our secret because it would have wounded Agnes.'

'But you did, in the end, didn't you? Hurt Agnes, the both of you.'

'I'm so sorry,' I whispered. I felt numb. It was all true.

'It was difficult at first, knowing about you and Sam. I couldn't bring myself to call when I knew you were back. Then I tried to put myself in your shoes.' She gave me a tired smile and then lowered her head. 'You and he had a bond. Since you were a child. I don't want to drag up the past... but your life at home. That awful woman...! I saw how you needed him.'

I let go of the chair. There was a red ridge on my palms where the wood had dug into them.

'I know we hurt Agnes and I felt guilty all the time. He didn't want to be in the marriage but it was the girls he couldn't leave. We had to keep it secret, there was no other way, not after Michael was born.' There was more I could have said. How desire and the need to be loved had made us selfish. But it was too soon for that.

Rachel nodded and wiped a hand across her mouth. 'I will have a cup of tea if you don't mind.'

I got up to make it. She followed me and leant against the kitchen door frame.

'His girls accept you, don't they? Grace told me that you go to the flat every week, have a meal and play with them. She chattered on about what you'd all been doing. It made me think — if Agnes's daughters can do it...'

I looked at the blue gas flame and heard the kettle rattle on the stove.

'It's taken me a long time but I'm here now. I haven't told Mother but I will.' Rachel sighed. 'I'll say no more. My sister's dead and what's done is done.'

I brought the pot and cups in on a tray and saw a printed card on the table.

'This is for you. Graham and I would like you to come to our Gregory's christening next Sunday. I'll break the news to Mother and Father that you'll be there. Don't worry; they won't walk out of the service! I've missed you, Jessie. I wish I'd been braver and visited you in Warrington. Defied my parents.'

I went to her and kissed her cheek and smelt lavender on her collar. 'Thank you!'

ON THE DAY of the service, I checked myself in the mirror, fastened my mother's cannel lily brooch more securely and straightened my hat. I'd chosen my outfit carefully: a blue blouse with full sleeves and high collar, and in contrast, a fine, lined, dark red skirt. Nothing flash, but a smart enough outfit for a Towneley gathering.

Before leaving, I dropped a kiss on Michael's forehead and on Pa's cheek. Newspaper, glue, pencils, and paper were spread out on the table. Michael was concentrating on copying a dog from a children's picture book, his tongue poking out slightly.

'Dogs, cows, lions!' He crowed proudly, while Pa waited to cut out and stick the animals onto brown paper.

I stopped myself from saying, *don't make too much clutter.* What did mess matter if they were enjoying themselves?

Fifteen minutes later, I saw Sam waiting for me outside the church porch. He linked my arm despite the curious stares that came our way.

'No more hiding, Jessie. We will face everyone together. Judgements can't harm us now. We've been through too much to let that happen.'

We walked down the aisle aware of the surprised looks from both sides, seeking only somewhere to sit. The opening chords from the organ drowned the tittle-tattle and the first hymn began.

After the sermon, the minister invited Rachel, Graham and

the three Godparents to rise and walk to the font. As she passed, Rachel shot me a dazzling smile which brought a lump to my throat. She was as pretty now as on her wedding day. I thought back to an even earlier occasion when I was growing into a young woman. She'd swapped her birthday cake token with me: her lucky horseshoe for my so-called spinster's thimble. She'd wanted me to have a chance at finding a husband. I'd kept the token. It nestled in a box under Sam's letters.

Even if I owned a thousand horseshoes...

We were adjusting to the notion that marriage was impossible; we were happier than many who could wave a legal certificate in our faces.

The christening party said their vows and the minister sprinkled water over baby Gregory. Under the noise of people shuffling to their feet for a hymn, Sam nudged me and for the first time in months, his eyes shone with mischief and certainty.

'Your grandparents saw Rachel smiling at you. She'll be a welcome supporter when we need her.'

I nodded, and we pressed against each other, not caring who saw and what they thought. We might not be able to have a public service like this one for the child we were expecting next year, but we would stand side by side, when we walked up to the font.

BEFORE YOU GO

I hope you enjoyed reading *Kept* as much as I enjoyed writing it. As you know, it can take years to write a book. They exist through dedication, passion and love. Reviews help persuade potential readers to buy a copy for themselves. In reviewing *Kept* you are helping others to discover and support new writing. It will only take a minute, and can be just a line to say what you liked or thought. Please leave a review wherever you bought this book. A big thank you from me.

Yvonne Lyon

AUTHOR'S NOTE

Kept is a story loosely inspired by my maternal grandparents' lives. But the how and the why will always be like looking at objects in a mist. I had no letters or photographs of their early years to guide me, no relatives left to talk to. And despite extensive research, finding amazing snippets of information through British newspapers online, I knew I'd never have all the pieces of the jigsaw. I decided to try through fiction to understand why they chose the path they did. I changed their names so they became characters, not relatives. I condensed the timeline, erased a couple of real people and invented some who were necessary for the plot. *Kept* is a story of love and betrayal. The truth will be different, but how far away it is from this work of fiction, we'll never know.

ABOUT THE AUTHOR

Yvonne Lyon was born in Bolton but moved to Oxford in her mid-twenties where she gained a degree in English Literature and History of Art at the former Oxford Polytechnic. She self-published a YA novel in 2009 and has had short stories and poetry published in several anthologies and was a finalist in a BBC Get Writing competition. After studying for an MA in Creative Writing at Oxford Brookes University, she was a runner-up in a Historical Novel competition and was published in their Anthology, *Distant Voices*. Her short story, *Day of Silence*, set in Bali, was published in Asian Anthology New Writing Vol. 1 in 2022. *Kept* was completed in 2024 after she returned to live in Lancashire in January 2023, and is loosely based on her family history research.

ACKNOWLEDGMENTS

I would like to thank Lisa M Nathan, Helen Matthews and Annie Murray for their lovely reviews of *Kept*. Thanks also to the other members of the Oxford Narrative Group for continued support and critical advice as the novel progressed.

My cousin, Mary Chapman, for hospitality and driving me to various locations around Wigan. Vera Dudley, for information on local places and Lancashire dialect words. Archives: Wigan & Leigh, for assisting me in genealogy research. Isobelle Lans of *Inspired Creative Co* for her helpful structural edit. Clitheroe Writers' Group for welcoming me into your midst.

Thanks also to my sister Margaret for continued support for this particular book. And last, but not least, Ivy Ngeow, friend, supporter and publisher. Thanks for your brilliant cover design and dedicating your time to this project.

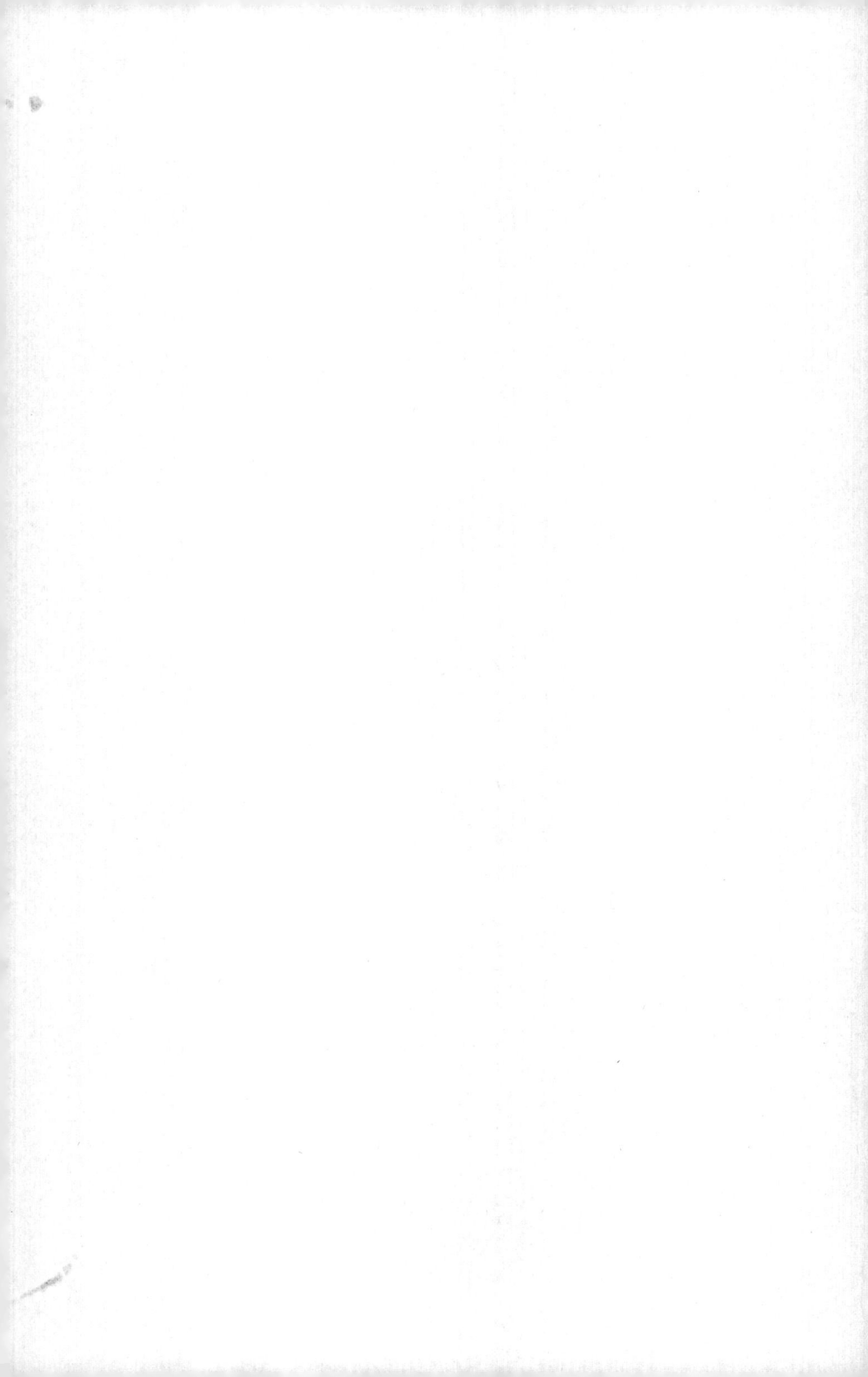

Printed in Great Britain
by Amazon